ZELDA'S CUT

Philippa Gregory is an established writer and
broadcaster for radio and television. She holds a
PhD in eighteenth-century literature from the
University of Edinburgh. She has been widely
praised for her historical novels, including *Earthly
Joys*, *Virgin Earth* and *A Respectable Trade* (which
she adapted for BBC television) as well as her
works of contemporary suspense. Philippa Gregory
lives in the North of England with her family.

PHILIPPA GREGORY

ZELDA'S CUT

HarperCollins*Publishers*

HarperCollins*Publishers*
77–85 Fulham Palace Road,
Hammersmith, London W6 8JB

The Harpercollins website address is
www.**fire**and**water**.com

This paperback edition 2001

1 3 5 7 9 8 6 4 2

First published in Great Britain by
HarperCollins*Publishers* 2000

ISBN 0 00 651177 5

Set in Aldus

Printed and bound in Great Britain by
Omnia Books Limited, Glasgow

for Anthony

One

The question between them, being unresolvable,
remained unresolved. Their irresolution: his and hers,
and the intrinsic insolubility of their relationship
stood between them like a wall . . . like a rock . . . like
a . . .

Isobel broke off from typing and consulted the thesaurus
beside her on the desk.

Like a barrier, bastion, bulwark, dyke, rampart . . . Like
an impenetrable bulwark, like an impenetrable bastion,
like a bastion, like a rampart . . .

She hesitated. Her husband put his fair head around the
door of her study.

'Can't you take a break for lunch now?' he asked plaintively.
She glanced at her watch. It was not yet one o'clock but
Philip's condition meant that he needed regular small meals,
and if Isobel failed to provide these, he became hungry and
irritable.

'What has Mrs M. left for us?' she asked, getting up from
her desk and glancing back at the screen, thinking distractedly
about soup and barrier, bastion, rampart and bulwark.

'Soup and bread rolls again,' he said. 'But I got her to buy
a piece of steak for supper.'

'Oh good,' she said, not hearing him.
The kitchen was a pretty room with sprigged curtains and

wooden units. The view from the window over the sink looked up the hill at the back of the house, the green shoulder of the Weald of Kent, bright now with springtime growth. Beside the Aga stood a saucepan filled with home-made soup. Philip watched as she put it on the hot plate and took the rolls from the bread bin.

'I'll lay the table,' he volunteered.

When Isobel brought the bowls to the table she found that he had forgotten a knife to cut the cheese, and there was no salt. She fetched them without irritation, her mind still on bastion, rampart or bulwark.

'You had two phone calls while you were working,' Philip said. 'Someone from your publishers, I wrote down the name. And Troy.'

'What did Troy want?'

'It's such a ridiculous name,' he remarked. 'D'you think his parents really christened him Troy? Or was he called Trevor and has been trying to live it down ever since?'

'I like it,' she said. 'It suits him.'

'Never having had the honour, I couldn't say. But it is a ridiculous name.'

'Anyway,' Isobel said patiently. 'What did he want?'

'You don't imagine he'd tell me, do you?' he demanded. 'I'm just the messenger boy, the telephone operator. The receptionist at Hotel Literature.'

'Hotel des Lettres,' she suggested and was rewarded by the gleam of his smile.

'Très belle.'

There was a brief silence, he reached across the table and squeezed her hand. 'Sorry,' he said briefly.

'Aches and pains?' she asked.

'A bit.'

'Why not have a lie down?'

'I have all the rest of my life to lie down,' he snapped. 'That's one of the things I have to look forward to. Progressive disability, or as you would say: a nice lie down. I don't especially want to rush towards it.'

2

She bowed her head over the bowl of soup. 'Of course not,' she said quietly. 'I'm sorry.'

Philip put his spoon in his empty bowl and finished his bread. 'I think I'll go for my walk,' he said. 'Stretch out a bit.'

She glanced outside at the clear skies. Their house was in a fold of the Weald, he had the choice of walking upwards to the crest or downwards to the village.

'You could walk to the pub and I could drive down to meet you there later,' she suggested.

'You mean so I don't face the challenge of an uphill?'

Isobel was silent.

'That would be good,' he said reluctantly. 'Thank you. In about an hour?'

She nodded.

He got up from his place at the table and sighed with weariness at the effort of having to move. He went to the housekeeping jar which she kept filled with money, and helped himself to a ten-pound note. She watched the money that she had earned slide into the pocket of his slacks.

'See you later, about two thirty,' he said, and went out.

Isobel got to her feet and cleared the plates into the dishwasher. For a moment she looked at her face reflected in the window above the sink. She hardly recognised herself. The features were as they had always been, strong bones, large grey eyes, but the skin around her eyes and mouth was crumpled with sadness and disappointment. She paused in her work for a moment, looking at the lines around her eyes and the groove which marked either side of her mouth. She might call them laughter lines; but there had been little laughter in the last three years. In her head she heard Philip say, so sharply: 'Progressive disability, or as you would say, a nice lie down.'

'God, what a stupid thing to say.' She shook her head. 'What a fool I am.'

She bent and closed the dishwasher door. When she straightened up and saw her mirrored face again she gave the

3

pale reflection a tight, determined smile. 'I'll have to try harder,' she said to her image. 'I'll just go on trying.'

Troy on the telephone was always at his best. Isobel was glad to be talking to him without the silent presence of Philip, brooding in the kitchen or walking slowly in the garden.

He answered on the third ring. 'Troy Cartwright,' he said warmly.

'It's Isobel,' she said and heard her voice lighten.

'My star writer!' he exclaimed. 'Thanks for calling back. How are you?'

'I'm well.'

'And Philip?'

'He's fine,' she said cheerfully.

'You sound wonderful. How's the book going?'

'It's finished,' she said. 'Actually, all except one word.'

'One?'

'Yes.'

Troy briefly considered asking her which word, but thought that lay within the area of the writer's particular talents and outside the remit of her agent.

'Come out to lunch to celebrate!' he commanded. 'I need to be seen out with a beautiful woman.'

Isobel smiled at the thought of Troy Cartwright, slim, mid-thirties, urbane, and living at the heart of fashionable London, needing to be seen lunching with her. 'Oh, ridiculous.'

'Not at all. I was looking through my client list for someone who combined brains and beauty and there was no contest.'

Absurdly, she heard herself giggle, an unusual sound in the quiet house. 'I could deliver the manuscript, I suppose.'

'Oh please! I so want to see it.'

'Tomorrow?'

'Great. I'll book a table somewhere expensive.'

She hesitated. 'It's not necessary –'

'If I am taking Isobel Latimer out to lunch I want the world to know it.' His voice dropped to a warm caress. 'So you make sure that you wear something beautiful.'

4

'All right,' she said, surrendering to the pleasure of flattery. 'I'll come to your office at one.'

'I'll vacuum the red carpet myself,' he promised.

Philip had walked himself into good humour. He sat in the garden of the pub with a whisky and ice in a glass before him. He waved as Isobel drew up in the Volvo and watched her park and get out of the car. He thought that she looked older than her fifty-two years as she walked across the car park towards him. She was as slim as she had always been, and her glossy chestnut hair had only faded slightly to pale brown. At first glance she could still be the young academic who had sat opposite him at a conference on ethics in the pharmaceutical industry, and argued her case with such precocious confidence and serenity that she had made him laugh and want to flirt with her. He had thought then that a highly intelligent academic wife might be a great asset to a man in his position. He had thought then that he could afford such a wife. He could earn the money, doing work which she considered morally suspect, he could bring home the tainted profits of capitalism, and she could study philosophy. She could be his luxury, a wife infinitely more prestigious and interesting than the flashy blondes of his colleagues. His earning power could buy her a good lifestyle where she could read and think and write. And in return: he could enjoy her.

It all changed the moment he became ill. He knew now that he could have died without her steady strength of mind, her determination that he should survive. But as he watched her walk towards him and saw the droop of her shoulders and the weariness in her very footsteps, he did not feel gratitude, nor even tenderness. He felt irritated. She was always tired these days. She always looked so miserable. Anyone would think that it was her who was ill.

'Come and have a drink,' he called. 'We don't have to rush off, do we?'

She hesitated. 'I was going to work this afternoon.'

Philip tutted. Isobel's problem was that she worked too

hard, he thought. Her agent Troy, her publishers, her publicity people – they all thought they had equal right to her time, and she was too polite to say no. People pushed her around, and she was foolish enough to try to please everyone.

'Take a break,' he ordered. 'You need a break.'

'All right,' she said, thinking that the bastion, rampart, bulwark or dyke question could be resolved tomorrow morning before she took the train to London.

He limped into the pub and brought her back a glass of white wine, and they sat in the sun together. Isobel tipped her head back to the warmth.

'This is idyllic,' she said. 'I love the month of May.'

'Best time of year,' he agreed. 'The field that Rigby left fallow last year is just filled with cowslips.'

'We are so lucky to live here,' she said. 'I couldn't bear to live in London.'

'It was a good choice,' he said. 'I just wish I knew how long we'll be able to stay in that house.'

Covertly, she glanced over at him, nursing his drink. 'Surely we've got a good few years yet.'

'It's the stairs that'll be the first difficulty,' he said.

'We can get one of those stairlifts.'

Philip made a face. 'I'd rather move our bedroom downstairs. We could use your office and you could write upstairs. It wouldn't make any difference to you.'

She thought for a brief moment of regret that she would lose the view from her study window which she loved, and the bookshelves that she had designed. 'Of course. That'd be fine.'

'Provided Mrs M. is prepared to keep coming, and maybe do a little more. We'd need to get someone to do the garden.'

'It's so terribly expensive,' Isobel remarked. 'Other people's wages cost so much. It's paying their tax which is so awful.'

'It's our lifestyle,' he reminded her. 'It makes sense to spend money on our comforts.'

'As long as we have the money coming in.'

He smiled. 'Why shouldn't it come in? You've never written

6

a book yet which didn't win one prize or another. All we need is for someone to buy the option for a film and we can rebuild the barn and put in a swimming pool and a gym.'

She hesitated, wondering if she should state the obvious: that a film was not likely, and that literary prizes and literary acclaim were not guarantees of good royalties from publishers. She stopped herself. She had promised herself that she would never worry him with money troubles. She had taken it on herself to earn the money and to free him from fear of debt when he was facing so many other, greater fears.

'That barn would be perfect for a swimming pool,' Philip repeated. 'I read a paper the other day. Swimming is the best exercise someone with my condition can take. Much better than walking. And if we put it in the barn it would be useful all the year round. It's hard to get the exercise in winter.'

'I don't know that we could afford it,' Isobel said cautiously.

He shook his head at her reluctance. 'What are we saving our money for?' he demanded. 'You talk like we're going to live forever. Well I'm certainly not. We know that well enough. I don't see why we have to be so cautious.'

Isobel made herself smile and raise her glass to him. 'You're right, I know. Here's to the Hollywood option and us as millionaires with a swimming pool in the barn and a yacht in the Med!'

'I might look into the price of pools,' he said.

'Yes, do,' she said. 'Why not?'

Troy's office was in Islington, in a converted Victorian terrace house. He lived in a flat upstairs and the ground floor was occupied by two other literary agents, a beautiful girl behind the reception desk, and one overworked assistant who was required to do the administration for all of them.

Isobel perched on a chair surrounded by manuscripts while Troy slipped on his Armani jacket, set it straight across his shoulders, and smoothed his silk tie. It was a dark navy suit and a dark navy tie. Against the severe colour Troy's light brown hair and clear skin looked boyishly handsome.

'You look gorgeous,' he remarked, patting his pockets to check that he was carrying his credit cards. He picked up his mobile phone to carry in his hand, he would never have destroyed the line of the jacket by putting it in his pocket.

Isobel glowed at his praise. She was wearing a summer shift dress in pale blue with blue court shoes, her soft brown hair was enfolded into a bun on the nape of her neck. She gave the overall impression of being a rather elegant headmistress at a select girls' school. She was not a woman that any man had ever called gorgeous.

'Absolutely edible,' Troy asserted, and Isobel giggled.

'Hardly. Where are we going for lunch?'

'Number Fifty-two – it's a new restaurant. Very hot. I had to almost beg for a table.'

'There was no need –'

'There was every need. Aren't we celebrating the birth of a new manuscript? And besides, I want to talk to you about things.'

Isobel followed Troy down the steps to the street and waited while he hailed a cab with a commanding wave of his hand. But it was not until they were seated in the restaurant – dark-tinted mirrors, real wood floors, marble-top tables, astoundingly uncomfortable chairs but beautiful flowers on every available surface – that he leaned forward and said: 'I think we may have a bit of a problem.'

She waited.

'It's Penshurst Press,' he said. 'They're not offering so much for this book as they did for the last.'

'How much?' she asked bluntly.

The waiter came to take their order and Troy shook his head. 'In a minute.' He turned back to Isobel. 'A lot less. They're offering £20,000.'

For a moment she thought she had misheard him. In the rattle of utensils and the hum of conversation she thought that he must have said something quite different.

'I beg your pardon. What did you say?'

'I said £20,000,' he repeated. He saw that she had paled with shock. He poured a glass of water and held it out to her. 'I'm sorry. I know it's less than half what we were expecting, but they won't shift. I'm sorry.'

Isobel said nothing, she looked stunned. Troy glanced uneasily around the restaurant, hating the discomfort. The waiter returned and Troy ordered for them both, and waited in silence until Isobel had taken a sip from her glass of wine, raised her neat head and spoke:

'This is nearly two years' work,' she said. 'Two years' work for £20,000?'

'I know. There would be foreign sales on top of that, of course, and a book club deal perhaps, and the usual extras . . .'

She shook her head. 'They don't add up to much these days.'

'No,' he said quietly.

The waiter brought them two little plates of appetisers. Isobel looked down at the exquisite parcels of filo pastry, her expression completely blank.

'Why have they offered so little?'

Troy swallowed one of the parcels in a single gulp. 'The signs were there. They've paid slightly less for every book that you've written over the last ten years. They look at the balance sheet, and they can see that your sales are going down. The fact is, Isobel, that although you win the literary prizes and there is no doubt of the merit of your writing, no question of that – the fact remains that you don't sell many books. You're too good for the market, really. And they don't want to pay out in royalties when they're not earning good money in sales.'

She took another sip of wine. 'Should I go to another publisher?'

He decided to risk complete honesty. 'I've asked around already, very discreetly. I'm afraid they all say the same sort of thing. No-one can see how to sell more than Penshurst are doing already. Nobody would pay you any more.'

'Two years' work for £20,000,' she repeated. She took

another sip of wine, and then another. The waiter refilled her glass and she took a gulp.

'What you must remember is that no-one is denying that you are one of the foremost literary writers in England today.'

The look she turned on him was not one he had expected; he thought she would be offended but instead she looked terrified.

'But what am I going to do?' she cried. 'I have to earn enough to keep us, I have to earn enough for me and Philip. I can't go back to teaching at a university, I can't be out of the house all day, he needs me at home now. If I can't earn money from my writing, how are we going to live?'

He did not understand what she meant. 'Live?'

'All the money that comes into our house is earned by me,' Isobel said fiercely. 'Philip doesn't have a penny.'

Troy looked stunned. 'I thought he'd have a disability pension, or something.'

She shook her head. 'It's gone. All gone. I cashed it in to buy the house outright. I told him not to worry. I told him that it had paid off the mortgage and we had bought savings policies. But we hadn't. It just paid off the mortgage. I thought I could keep him for the rest of his life.'

She looked away. 'I thought he was going to die. I thought I'd have to keep him for a couple of years, keep him in real comfort and security. But now he's in remission. I don't know what will happen next. And you tell me that I can't earn the money I need for him.'

Troy took a gulp of his own wine. 'Could you do some more reviewing?'

'It doesn't pay, does it?' she said bitterly. 'Not like the novels ought to pay. And now you're telling me that my novels don't sell. To sell you have to be someone like Suzie Wade or Chet Drake. No-one admires their work; but everyone reads them.'

He nodded.

'And how much do they get for that . . . that drivel?'

He shrugged. 'I don't know. Perhaps about £200,000 for a

book? Maybe more. And then there are film rights or television mini series. They're both millionaires from their writing.'

'But I could do that!' she exclaimed bitterly. 'I could write a book like that in a year! In half a year!'

The waiter appeared and put their first course before them. Troy picked up his fork but Isobel did not eat.

'It's harder than it looks,' he reminded her gently. 'You of all people know that. Even these commercial novels require skill. They're not complicated stories or beautifully written; but they have a real talent for catching the public imagination, they command a readership.'

She shook her head and took another gulp of wine. The waiter refilled her glass. Troy saw with some concern that the level in the bottle had dropped quite dramatically.

'I could write like that!' she exclaimed. 'Any fool could.'

He shook his head. 'You have to really be in touch with the readers' dreams,' he said. 'That's what they're so good at. It's all emotions, it's all gut consciousness. It's not the sort of thing you do. You write from the intellect, Isobel.'

'I could do it,' she persisted. 'I could tell you the sort of story right now.'

He smiled at her, welcoming any change in tone which would move her away from the horror of the initial shock. 'What would you call it?'

'*Devil's Disciple,*' she said promptly. '*Son of Satan.* Something with the devil in it, that's what they all want, don't they? To believe that there are Satanists and that sort of nonsense?'

'That's true,' he conceded.

'It would be the story of a young woman who has to earn money, a huge sum of money, to pay for her sister's operation. Something, oh, complicated. But something that we've all heard about.' She snapped her fingers. 'Bone marrow transplant. The sister is near to death and only this experimental operation would save her.'

He nodded, smiling.

'They're twin sisters,' Isobel said, improvising rapidly. A lock of hair had become detached from the neat bun, her cheeks had flushed. The waiter poured more wine. 'They're twin sisters and the younger sister discovers that a Satanic cult will pay exactly the sum of money they need for a girl who can prove she is a virgin, who will allow anything to be done to her – for one night.'

The waiter hovered, bottle in hand, openly listening.

'Go on.' Troy was intrigued.

'She is examined by a doctor, she is indeed a virgin, and then she walks towards the large house in the country for the cult to use her as they wish for twenty-four hours.'

Troy leaned forward to listen. The woman on the next table leaned too.

'They use her sexually, they tie her up, they cut her with their silver knives so that her body is tattooed with occult signs, then they lie her on the altar and she thinks they are going to slit her throat at dawn. Scented smoke wreathes around her, they give her a strange-tasting drink, a man, a dark and handsome man, comes slowly towards her with his silver knife held before him . . .'

Troy hardly dared to speak. The waiter poured more wine for Isobel, like a fee for the storyteller.

'She wakes. It is broad daylight. She can remember only the faces of the thirteen people of the coven. But in her hand is a cheque for her sister's treatment.'

'Oh, yes,' Troy whispered. The woman on the next table and the waiter were rapt.

'She walks from the house, she goes to bank the cheque.' Isobel paused for dramatic emphasis. 'The cheque is no good. There is no such name, no such account. She has no money. Her sister dies in her arms.'

'Oh, my God!' exclaimed the waiter involuntarily.

'She swears complete revenge against the thirteen members of the coven.'

'Too many, too many,' Troy whispered.

'Against the five members of the coven,' Isobel corrected

12

herself, hardly breaking her pace. 'She goes to the police but no-one believes her. She decides to hunt each one down individually.'

'Very Jeffrey Archer,' Troy muttered to himself.

'There are two women and three men. Each one she tracks down and then ruins. Social shame, bankruptcy, death in a car crash, their house burned down, and then she comes to the last man, the leader of the cult whose cheque was no good.'

The waiter removed their plates as an excuse to linger at their table.

'He has reformed,' Isobel said. 'He is a changed man, the leader of a charismatic Christian church.'

'Television,' Troy whispered.

'He's a television evangelist.' She improved at once on his hint. 'He does not recognise her, he welcomes her to join his flock. She has the decision: should she believe in his genuine reform and help him with the wonderful work he is doing with the –'

'Homeless children,' Troy suggested.

'Homeless abused children,' Isobel supplemented. 'Or should she pursue her revenge against him? Is he, in fact, still an evil man, who has just seized power over these helpless children in order to abuse them further? She joins the cult to discover the best way to destroy him, but then she finds that she has fallen completely in love with him. What will she do?'

'What *does* she do?' the waiter demanded. 'Oh, excuse me!'

Isobel came to herself, tucked back the stray hair, drank a sip of water. 'Oh, I don't know. I always have difficulties with the endings,' she said.

'My God.' Troy leaned back in his chair. 'Isobel, that was fantastic. That is a fantastic story.'

She looked primly pleased. 'I told you I could do it,' she said. 'It is a matter of choice for me – I choose to write well rather than to churn out dross. I have pride in my work. I like to do the very best that there is, not thick books of nonsense.'

The waiter stepped back from the table, the woman at the next table gave Troy a little smile, mouthed the word 'Fantastic', and returned her attention to her lunch. Isobel took a sip of wine.

'But if fine writing doesn't pay the bills?' Troy suggested.

There was a long pause. He watched her brightness drain away. She twisted the stem of the wineglass, her face suddenly tired and heavy.

'I have to consider Philip,' she said. 'It's not just me. If it were just me I could sell the house and reduce my expenses. I would never compromise with my art.'

Troy nodded, concealing a rising sense of excitement. 'I know that . . .'

'But Philip may never get any better, and he may live for many years. I have to provide for him. He was talking only yesterday about converting the house in case he can't get upstairs.'

The waiter brought their main course and set the plate before Isobel with ostentatious respect. Troy waited until he had reluctantly stepped out of earshot.

'I thought you said he was fine.'

She smiled, a sad little smile. 'I always say he's fine, hadn't you noticed that? There's no point in complaining all the time, is there? But it's not true. He's ill and he'll never get any better, and he may get very much worse. I have to provide for him, I have to think about the future. If I were to die before him – who would look after him? How would he manage if I left him with nothing but debts?'

Troy nodded. 'A big commercial book could earn you – I don't know – a quarter of a million pounds? Perhaps half a million with foreign sales too.'

'That much?'

'Certainly £200,000.'

'Would it be possible for me to write such a book, a commercial book, and no-one know that it was me?'

'Of course,' Troy assured her. 'A nom de plume. Lots of writers use them.'

Isobel shook her head. 'I don't mean a nom de plume. I mean a complete concealment. No-one is ever to know that Isobel Latimer has ever written anything but the finest of writing. I couldn't bear people to think I would write something so . . .' She hesitated and then chose a word which was almost a challenge: 'So *vulgar*.'

Troy thought for a moment. 'We'd have to create a false client account at the agency. A bank account in another name, in the name of the nom de plume. I could be the main signatory, and draw the funds for you.'

She nodded. 'I'd have to sign the contracts in the false name?'

'I think you could,' he said. 'I'd have to check with the lawyers, but I think you could. It's the ownership of the manuscript that matters, it's not as if it's not your work.'

She gave him a wonderful secretive smile. 'And I could write an absolutely torrid shocker.'

'Would you want to do that?'

'For two hundred thousand pounds I'd do almost anything.'

'But *could* you do it? Could you work on it for day after day? The story's fantastic. But you'd have to write and write. These books are huge, you know, Isobel. They're not a hundred pages or so like your usual work, they go to seven hundred, a thousand pages. Two hundred thousand words at the very least. You'd have to write in a way you've never written before and it would take you at least six months. It's a long project.'

The look she shot across the table was one of bright determination. He thought he had never seen her so sharp and so focused before. 'I'm in real trouble,' she said bluntly. 'All we own is the house, all that's coming in is my advances. I was counting on a good sum from Penshurst Press and now you tell me all they want to pay is £20,000. It's a hard world we live in, isn't it? If they won't pay me to write good books, then I'll just have to write bad.'

'Can you bear to do it?' he asked quietly.

Isobel gave him a glance and he realised, for the first time in their long association, that this was a passionate woman. Her frumpy clothes and her faded prettiness had hidden from him that this was a woman capable of deep feelings. She was a woman who had dedicated her life to being in love with her husband. 'I'd do anything for him,' she said simply. 'Writing a bad book is the least of it.'

Isobel was silent on her return from London. When Philip asked if she was well she said that she was a little tired, that she had a headache.

'Were you drinking at lunchtime?' he asked disapprovingly.

'Only a glass of wine.'

He raised an eyebrow. 'That Troy always tires you out,' he said. 'Why didn't you just post the manuscript to him? What d'you have to see him for?'

'He's amusing,' she said. 'I like him.'

'I suppose he's a change from me.'

'It's not that, darling. I just like to deliver the finished manuscript. It's a bit of a lift, that's all.'

'I'd have thought you had enough to do without becoming a courier service as well,' he said grudgingly.

'I do have,' she said. 'I'm going to start a new novel at once. I got the idea over lunch.'

'What will it be about?'

'Something about the notion of personal responsibility and whether people can genuinely reform,' she said vaguely.

He gave her an encouraging smile. 'That sounds a bit like *The Dream and the Doing*,' he said, citing one of her earlier books. 'I always liked that one. I liked the way the heroine had to make a choice not between which man she married, but actually between two contrasting moral systems. It was a very thoughtful book.'

'Yes, I think it'll be very like that,' she said. 'Are you coming up to bed?'

'I'll have a nightcap before I come up.'

Isobel paused. 'Oh, come up before I fall asleep.'

He smiled. 'Of course,' he said evasively.

Since his illness, his desire for Isobel had almost completely disappeared. He refused absolutely to discuss this either with Isobel or with his doctor, and if Isobel insisted that they go to bed at the same time, or if she tried to kiss and caress him in the morning, he would gently but firmly push her away. It seemed to be another of the many things that had melted away from Isobel's life, like her looks, her youth, her sense of joy, and now – her ability to make money from her fine writing. She did not complain. When Philip had first become ill she had gone down on her knees to pray. She had made an agonised bargain with the god of her imagination, that if He would spare Philip's life she would never ask for anything ever again.

When they were finally told, after years of tests, that Philip would become progressively weaker for the rest of his life, but would not die in the near future, she thought that God had taken advantage of her trust. God had cheated on the deal. Philip would not die, but the man she had loved and married was gone forever.

Isobel felt that it was not in her power to withdraw her offer to God. She had promised that if Philip lived then she would never ask for anything again and she intended to keep that promise. She would never make any demands of Philip, she would never ask God for extravagant luck or wonderful opportunities. She thought that what lay before her was a life of duty which would be illuminated with the joy of self-sacrifice. Isobel thought that she might create a life which was itself a thing of beauty – a life in which a talented and devoted couple turned their energies and abilities into making some happiness together despite illness, despite fear of death. She thought that she and Philip might be somehow ennobled by the terrible bad luck that they had suffered. She had thought that she might show him how much she loved him in constant, loving, willing self-sacrifice.

Instead, what she actually experienced was a slog. But she knew that lots of women were forced to slog. Some had disagreeable husbands, or arduous jobs, or difficult children.

Isobel's witty, charming husband had become a self-pitying invalid. Isobel's love for him had been transformed from the erotic to the maternal. Isobel's sense of herself as an attractive woman had been destroyed by night after night of the most tactful but unrelenting sexual rejection.

She thought that it should make no difference. She was still determined to keep her side of the bargain with God. She had promised never to ask for anything ever again, and she was holding to her side of the deal.

'All right,' she said, smiling, making it clear that she would embarrass neither of them by making a sexual advance to him. 'You come to bed when you like, darling. Anyway, I expect I'll be asleep.'

She did indeed fall asleep almost at once but she woke in the light of the summer morning at five. Outside the window she could hear the birds starting to sing and the insistent coo of the wood pigeon, nesting in the oak tree beside the house. For a moment she lay beside Philip, enjoying the warmth of the bed and the gleam of the early-morning sunlight on the ceiling. She turned and looked at him. Peacefully asleep, he looked younger and happier. His blond forelock fell attractively across his regular features, his dark eyelashes were as innocent as a sleeping child's on the smooth skin of his cheeks. Isobel was filled with a sense of tenderness for him. More than anything else in the world she wanted to provide for him, to care for him as if he were her child. She wanted to earn enough money so that he could always go to the housekeeping jar to take whatever cash he wanted, without asking, without having to give thanks. She wanted to provide for him abundantly, generously, as if her love and wealth could compensate for the awful unjust bad luck of his illness.

Isobel crept out from the warmth of the bed and put her dressing gown around her shoulders, and slid her feet into her sensible fleecy slippers. She left the bedroom quietly, went downstairs to the kitchen and made herself a pot of strong

Darjeeling tea and then carried her china cup through to her study.

The word processor came alive with a deep, reassuring chime. She watched the screen gleam into life, and then created a new document. The blank page was before her, the little line of the cursor waiting to move, to tick its way into life. She laid her fingers on the keyboard, like a pianist waiting for the signal to play, for the indrawn breath, for that powerful moment of initiation.

'*Devil's Disciple*,' she typed. 'Chapter One.'

Two

Isobel wrote for three hours until she heard Philip stirring in the bedroom above her study. She shut down the file on the word processor and paused for a moment. Philip very rarely came into her study and read her work in progress, but he might do so, there had never been any suggestion that Isobel's work was private. Now, for the first time in her life, she did not want him to read what she had written. She had a very strong sense that she did not want him to know that she was writing a form of literature that they both despised. Also, she did not want him to know that she was spending hours every day letting her imagination roam over erotic and perverse possibilities. Philip would find the scenes of the heroine tied on the altar immensely offensive. Their love-making had always been gentle, respectful of each other, sometimes even spiritual. The notion of his wife writing soft pornography would have disgusted Philip. Isobel did not want him to know that she could even think of such things.

She closed the file and considered what name she should give it to ensure that Philip would not read it. She leaned forward and typed in the name: 'letters to the bank'. Philip never concerned himself with money now. Since he had taken early retirement from Paxon Pharmaceuticals he had handed over to her all the control of their finances. They held a joint bank account into which Isobel's royalty cheques and advances were paid, and it was her task to draw out what was needed and to make sure that the housekeeping money jar on the kitchen worktop was filled once a week with whatever cash he might want. When they went out together, Philip paid with his credit card; he liked to be seen paying in a restaurant. If he wanted new clothes or magazines, books, or CDs, he used his credit card and then Isobel paid the bills when the monthly statement arrived. If he wanted a tenner in his pocket when he walked down to the pub, he simply took it.

It seemed to Isobel absolutely fair that she should support him so completely. When he had been well he had bought the house she had liked, he had paid for the food and wine that they ate and drank. Now that she was earning and he was not, she saw no reason why they still should not equally share. Her only difficulty arose when she realised that she was failing to earn the money they needed.

Philip was not an extravagant man. He seldom went out without her, he preferred to wear old clothes. The greatest expense in his life was his occasional visits to exotic and overpriced alternative therapists in case one of them might, one day, have some kind of cure. Isobel learned to dread those visits because they were so costly both in money and in emotion when Philip soared into hope and then dropped into despair.

'I wouldn't mind them being so pricey if they worked,' she had said to him once as she wrote a cheque for £800 for an Amazonian rainforest herb.

'They have to be expensive,' he had replied, with a flash of his old worldliness, taking the cheque she held out to him. 'That's what makes you trust them, of course.'

She heard him coming slowly down the stairs. She could tell by the heaviness of his pace that today was a bad day. She went swiftly into the kitchen to put the kettle on to boil and the bread in the toaster so that he should be greeted with breakfast.

'Good morning,' she said brightly as he came into the room.

'Good morning,' he said quietly, and sat at the table and waited for her to serve him.

She put toast in the rack, and the butter and marmalade

before him, and then the small box which contained the dietary supplements for breakfast – an array of vitamins, minerals and oils. He started taking the pills with dour determination and Isobel felt the usual pang of tenderness.

'Bad night?' she asked.

He made a grimace. 'Nothing special.'

She poured the tea and sat beside him with her cup.

'And what are you going to do today?' she asked encouragingly.

Philip gave her a look which warned her that he was not in the mood to be jollied out of his unhappiness. 'I'll do my exercises, and then I'll read the newspaper, and then I'll start the crossword, and then I'll have lunch, and then I'll go for my walk, and then I'll have tea, and then I'll have a rest, and then I'll watch the news, and then I'll have dinner, and then I'll watch television, and then I'll go to bed,' he said in a rapid drone. 'Amazing programme, isn't it?'

'We could go to the cinema,' she suggested. 'Or the theatre. Why don't you ring up and see what's on? Wasn't there something you liked the sound of the other day?'

He brightened. 'I suppose we could. If we went to a matinée we could go on for dinner after.'

Isobel mentally lost another afternoon's writing. 'Lovely,' she said. 'Could we go to that Italian restaurant that was so nice?'

'Italian!' he exclaimed. 'We're going to the White Lodge if we can get in.'

Isobel dismissed the little pang of dread as she mentally doubled the likely bill for the cost of the whole evening. 'Lovely,' she said enthusiastically.

The house at the end of the drive loomed up as Charity walked nervously towards it. Her little heels tapped on the paving slabs as she walked up to the imposing door. There was a thick, rusting bell pull to the right of the massive wooden doors. Charity leaned forward and gave it a gentle tug.

Isobel hesitated. It seemed to her that there was a good deal too much landscape and furniture in this paragraph. Her usual novels concerned themselves with the inner psychology of her characters and she generally had only the mistiest idea of the rooms they inhabited or the clothes they wore. Her usual style was too sparse to allow much room for description of material things. Besides, Isobel was not interested in material things. She was far more interested in what people thought than the chairs they were sitting on as they thought.

There was a ring at the front door bell. Isobel pressed 'save' on the computer and waited, listening, to see if someone answered the door. From the kitchen she could hear Mrs M. chatting with Philip as she cleared the table. There was another ring at the door bell. It was clear that although there were three people in the house, and two of them were doing virtually nothing, no-one was going to answer the door. Isobel sighed and went to see who it was.

There was courier with a large box. 'Sign here,' he said.

Isobel signed where he indicated and took the box into her study. The sender was Troy Cartwright. Isobel took a pair of scissors and cut the plastic tape. Inside the box were half a dozen violent-coloured novels. They had titles like *Crazed*, *The Man Eater*, *Stormy Weather* and *Diamonds*. Isobel unpacked them and laid them in a circle around her as she kneeled on the floor. The note from Troy read:

> *Just a little light reading to give you a sense of the genre. Can't wait to see what you'll do. Hope it's going well. Do call me if you want some moral support. You're such a star – Troy.*

A footstep in the hall made Isobel jump and gather the books into a pile. She threw the note over the topmost one, which showed a garish photograph of a woman embracing a python, as Philip put his head around the door.

'I thought I heard the bell.'

'It was a delivery. Some books for me. For review.'

He hardly glanced at the pile. 'Can we have an early lunch?'

'Yes,' she said. 'And have you rung the cinema?'

'Give me a chance,' he said. 'I'm going to do it now.'

'All right,' she said and smiled at him until the door closed.

As soon as he was gone Isobel took the glossy dust jackets off the books and crammed them in the wastepaper bin. Underneath the garish pictures the books looked perfectly respectable, though overweight compared with Isobel's library of slim volumes. She scattered them round the bookshelves and wrapped one – *The Man Eater* – in the dust jacket of *The Country Diary of an Edwardian Lady*, and left it beside her desk to read later.

She turned back to the screen.

The door swung open, on the threshold was a man. He had a dark mop of long black hair, dark eyes set deep under heavy eyebrows, a strong characterful face, a firm chin marked with a dimple. Charity stepped back for only a moment, fearful and yet attracted at the same time.

Isobel paused, she found she was grinning in simple delight at the unfolding of the story.

He took her cheap raincoat from her thin shoulders

Isobel hesitated. 'Cheap' as well as 'thin'? She shrugged. She had a reckless sense of pleasure that she had never felt when writing before. 'What does it matter? If it's got to be two hundred thousand words it could be a cheap, light raincoat. No-one is going to care one way or another . . .

'No-one is going to care about the writing one way or another,' she repeated.

She flung back her head and laughed. It was as if the great taboo of her life had suddenly been rendered harmless.

'How's it going?' Troy telephoned Isobel after six weeks of silence. He had been careful not to ask before, frankly doubting that she could manage such a revolution in style.

'It's fantastic,' she said.

Troy blinked. In all their long relationship she had never before described a book as 'fantastic'. 'Really?'

'It's such a complete holiday from how I usually work,' she said. He could hear something in her voice which was different, something playful, lighter, younger. 'It's as if nothing matters. Not the grammar, not the choice of words, not the style. Nothing matters but the narrative, the flow of the narrative. And that's the easiest thing to do.'

'That's your talent,' he said loyally.

'Well, I do think I might be rather good at it,' she said. 'And I've been thinking about who I am.'

'Who you are?'

'My persona.'

'Oh yes. So who are you?'

'I think I'm Genevieve de Vere.'

'My God.'

'D'you like it?'

He giggled. 'I adore it. The only thing is, that it sounds like a pen name. If we want no-one to know that it is a pen name we need something a little more ordinary.'

'Griselda de Vere?'

'Griselda Vere?'

'Oh, all right. But it seems a bit prosaic. Tell you what, let's call her Zelda, like Scott Fitzgerald's wife.'

'Fantastic,' he said. 'Not too romantic. Leave the romance for the novel.'

'I do. It is romantic,' she said enthusiastically. 'The hero has a dimple in his chin.'

Troy let out a squawk of laughter. 'I bet he hasn't even got an MA!'

'I don't mention his academic qualifications,' Isobel said with dignity. 'But he does have something extraordinary in the sex department.'

'What?' Troy asked, utterly fascinated.

'That's the difficulty,' she said, lowering her voice to a whisper and glancing at the closed study door. 'I'm not entirely sure. I want him to have something remarkable about his genitalia.'

Troy had a sense of an Isobel Latimer that no-one had ever seen before. He kept his voice very level, he did not want to frighten away this new side of her. He thought she might prove to be delightful. 'Oh, any reason why?'

'It's clearly a feature of the genre. In those books you sent me, a number of the heroes have – remarkable attributes. They're generally very well endowed, but they also have some kind of gimmick.'

'What about a couple of rings?' Troy asked. 'Like an earring, a hooped earring. Only inserted . . .' He broke off. 'Inserted not in the ear.'

'In the genitalia?' she demanded.

'In the foreskin, I believe.'

There was a stunned silence.

'So I'm told,' Troy added hastily.

'And who does this? Do you do it to yourself?'

'Oh no! You go to a body-piercing studio.'

'A studio?'

'Not like an artist's studio. Like a beauty salon.'

'And why would a man do this?'

Troy hesitated. He had known Isobel for six years but he had never had a conversation like this with her before. He had a sense of exquisite discomfort. 'Partly it's fashion,' he said cautiously. 'And some people take pleasure from the experience of inserting the ring. I'm told that it enhances sexual pleasure once it is, er, fully operational.'

He was afraid that he had shocked her, perhaps even offended her.

'D'you know anyone who has done this? Would he show me?'

Troy could not repress the giggle. 'I know one guy who's very proud of it. He would probably show you. But –'

'I'll come up tomorrow,' she said. 'Let's have lunch. I'll buy him lunch. Tell him that Zelda Vere would like to meet him.'

*   *   *

26

Zelda Vere turned out to look and dress exactly like Isobel Latimer, except that she wore her hair down around her shoulders and had dark glasses hiding her eyes.

'Would you have recognised me?' she asked Troy hopefully.

'Instantly,' he said. 'As would all of literary London. You're going to have to transform if we're really going to do this.'

'I thought wearing my hair down –'

'Zelda Vere would have big hair,' he said certainly. 'I mean huge bouffant blonde hair. And loads of makeup, and ostentatious jewellery, and a suit in acid green with enormous gold buttons.'

Isobel blinked. 'I don't know if I can do it,' she said. 'And I don't have anything at all like that in my wardrobe.'

'We'll start with the suit,' he said. 'Come with me.' He strode out of the office, calling to the assistant: 'Cancel Freddie for lunch, would you, darling? Say I'll catch him later.' And then ran down the steps and summoned a cab.

'Are we serious about this?' he asked her as they slammed the cab door. 'The book's going to be finished? You really intend to be Zelda Vere?'

'Are you sure Zelda Vere can earn a quarter of a million?' she countered.

He thought for a moment. 'Yes. If the book's as good as you say.'

She nodded. 'I'm sure it's that good.'

'And you're sure you want to do it? It's going to cost us some serious money to get you dressed. Worse than that, it will have to be *my* serious money. And it's my reputation on the line when we start approaching publishers. You really want to go through with this?'

'I have to,' she said flatly. 'I can't provide for Philip any other way.'

He leaned forward. 'Harrods,' he said shortly to the driver.

Isobel touched his arm. 'Did you say *your* money?'

He gleamed at her. 'I'm trying to think of it as venture capital.'

'You are lending me money?'

Troy nodded briskly. 'Have to,' he said. 'You have to be styled and buffed and polished and that's going to cost serious money. You haven't got it – not till we sell the book. So I'll lend it to you.'

She hesitated. 'What if nobody wants the novel? Or what if they don't pay that much for it?'

He laughed shortly. 'Then I shall share your disappointment.'

Isobel didn't speak for a moment and he saw she was trying to control a rush of tears.

'You are putting your own money in to help me?' she confirmed.

He nodded.

To his surprise she gently touched the back of his hand with her fingertip, a gesture as soft as a kiss. 'Thank you,' she said quietly. 'That means a lot to me.'

'Why?'

'Because no-one has helped me with anything since Philip became ill. I've been completely alone. You make me feel as if this is a shared project.'

Troy nodded. 'We're in it together,' he promised her.

They did not trouble themselves to look for the clothes they needed. Troy said a few words to the chief sales assistant on the designer floor and they were ushered into a room which looked like an ornate sitting room in a private house.

'A glass of champagne, madam, sir?' a sales assistant offered.

'Yes please,' Troy said calmly, and nodded to Isobel to conceal her awe.

The mirrored doors opened and another assistant came in, pushing a rack of hanging outfits.

'We'll also need an appointment for makeup, and hairdressing,' Troy murmured.

'Of course, sir,' she whispered back. 'And first, the outfits.'

One suit after another was whipped off the rack, stripped

from its protective plastic coating and swung like a matador's cloak before Isobel's gaze.

'Try the pink,' Troy advised. 'And also the yellow.'

Isobel flinched back from the garish colours. 'What about the grey?' she asked.

'Will madam be colouring her hair?' the sales assistant asked.

Isobel glanced at Troy.

'Bright blonde,' he confirmed.

'Then the pink will be wonderful,' she said. 'A pity not to maintain a high presence. The pink and the yellow both have a very high presence.'

They hung the suit inside the curtained changing room. Isobel went reluctantly inside and the curtain was dropped behind her. A pair of high-heeled gold sandals and a pair of high-heeled pink mules were inserted discretely underneath the curtain. Isobel regarded them with suspicion.

She took off her cream linen dress and flinched slightly at the sight of herself in the mirror. She was wearing a bra and a pair of pants which had been machine-washed so often that they were a creased grey, and a thread of elastic was fraying from the seam. Her hips were rounded, her thighs a little slack, her belly was podgy. Under the uncompromising lights of the fitting room there was no concealing the fact that she was a middle-aged woman who had not taken care of herself.

She shrugged and slipped on the pink jacket. It fitted perfectly. At once the upper half of her body looked tailored, constructed, somehow ordered. The skirt glided up over her hips and she fastened the zip at the waist without difficulty. It looked startlingly slim but it was generously cut. The hem of the skirt skimmed her knee. Isobel had not worn anything shorter than mid-calf length for the last ten years. She stepped into the pink mules. At once her legs looked longer. The pink of the jacket gave a brightness and a colour to her face. She tossed back her hair and tried to imagine herself blonde.

'Come out,' Troy begged. 'Let's see.'

Cautiously she drew the curtain to one side, almost

apologetically she stepped out. Troy, glass of champagne in hand, regarded her with sudden, flattering attention.

'Good God, Isobel,' he said. 'You are a knockout.'

She flushed, and teetered slightly on the high heels. 'It's so unlike what I usually . . .'

'It's very easy to get set in our ways . . .' the sales assistant remarked gently. 'Very hard to keep up. And it is difficult if madam lives in the country . . .'

The junior assistant stepped forward with a large tray of earrings and matching necklaces. Isobel was gently guided towards the mirror and the sales assistant scooped up the mass of light brown hair and piled it on Isobel's head with two deft pins.

'Just to give you an idea,' she whispered.

Isobel's ears were not pierced, but the sales staff put a Perspex band over her head and hung the earrings at ear level. They chose massive chunks of glass which looked like diamonds, and big, bright enameled flowers. They draped the matching necklaces around her neck.

'Madam has such a long neck, she could wear almost any-thing,' the sales lady said, as if genuinely delighted with the discovery. 'I'm surprised you have not had your ears pierced.'

'It's just not my sort of style,' Isobel said weakly.

'A shame not to make the most of that lovely neck,' the sales lady remarked.

Isobel found she was dropping her shoulders and raising her chin to her own reflection. She had never before considered the length of her neck, but with her hair swept up and the pink shedding a rosy radiance on her skin she did indeed think that she was blessed with a rather special feature which she should exhibit more often.

'I want to see you in the yellow too,' Troy said. 'And perhaps a cocktail dress? Something for parties?'

Isobel disappeared back behind the curtain and tried on the yellow suit. She wore it with a sparkling golden scarf at her neck and looked years younger. The golden sandals were sur-prisingly comfortable. While she was changing they brought in a rack of cocktail dresses and Isobel swept through a range of blue lamé, pink tulle, black velvet and midnight blue, finally settling on a radiant Lacroix and a modest navy blue Dior which was to be worn with a silver jacket.

'For added presence,' the sales assistant advised.

'And stockings and underwear and shoes,' Troy commanded. He was on his third glass of champagne and they had brought him some sandwiches to eat while he waited. 'Just some nice stuff. Two of everything.'

'A fitting for the underwear?' the sales assistant whispered.

'Oh yes,' Troy said.

They waited only a few moments and then a woman came into the room pushing a trolley of the most exquisite underwear Isobel had ever seen. Everything was embroidered or lace or silky with the sheen of high-tensile satin. There were bodies and teddies and bras and basques and French knickers and thongs and pants.

'I've never seen . . .' Isobel gasped.

Troy regarded the trolley with a certain amount of awe. 'Whatever would suit madam best,' he said, recovering rapidly.

Isobel vanished behind the curtain with the assistant. Shyly, she took off her bra, miserably conscious of the overstretched elastic and the garment's air of dingy age. The assistant made no remark but merely whispered: 'Lean forward please, madam.'

Blushing miserably, Isobel leaned forward and the assistant flung around her a smooth, cool band of silk, fastened it in a moment, and then with deft fingers tightened the straps and tucked Isobel's breasts this way and that until the bra fitted her like a pair of perfect palms lovingly cupped and holding her firmly.

'Oh,' Isobel breathed. 'So comfortable!'

'And so flattering,' the assistant pointed out. Isobel looked in the mirror. Her breasts were inches higher than their usual position, it made her waist, her whole body, look longer, slimmer. The profile flattened her waist, made her hips smoother. The assistant smiled. 'It makes such a difference,' she said with simple pride. 'Now put the jacket back on.'

It fitted a little snugger than before, it looked even better. Isobel drew back the curtain and went out to Troy.

'Oh yes,' he said as he saw her. 'Surprising. It makes a real difference. We'll take half a dozen of everything,' he told the assistant.

She smiled. 'I'll have them wrapped.'

The sales assistant opened the door for the underwear assistant and remarked, 'The makeup artiste is ready.'

'Oh, let her come in,' Troy said cheerfully.

They ushered Isobel to the mirror and swathed her in a pale pink towel. The makeup girl cleaned her face with a sweet-smelling gritty cream and then wiped it all off with a scented water. 'Your toner,' she whispered reverently. 'And now your moisturiser. You *do* cleanse, tone and moisturise every day, don't you, madam?'

'Some days,' Isobel said through closed lips. 'It depends.' She did not want to admit that her beauty regime consisted of washing her face with soap and water, slapping on a bit of face cream and then lipstick.

The makeup artiste prepared Isobel's face as if she were sizing a canvas, and then made the equipment ready: first laying out the range of brushes which would be needed and then spreading the palette of colours.

'Are we wanting a natural look?' she asked.

'Yes,' Isobel replied.

'No,' Troy said.

'High presence,' the sales assistant explained. 'Madam requires a high-presence appearance.'

'Of course,' the girl said. 'For a special event?'

Troy scowled at her. 'Highly confidential,' he said firmly.

'Ah, of course,' she said, and smeared peach foundation all over Isobel's cheekbones.

Isobel closed her eyes at the caress of the two organic sponges and gave herself up to the sensation of being stroked all over her face with tiny feather-like touches. It felt like being kissed, very gently and tenderly, and she found she was slipping off into a daydream of Darkling Manor where the hero with the dimple in his chin laid poor Charity on the altar and unzipped his trousers to reveal . . . She was quite sorry when the process stopped and the makeup girl said: 'There, madam. How do you like it?'

Isobel opened her eyes and stared at the stranger in the mirror.

Her eyes were wider and larger, a deep mysterious grey where before they had seemed pale. Her face was slimmer, her cheekbones enhanced making her look mid-European and glamorous as opposed to fading English rose and ordinary. Her eyelashes were dark and thick, her eyebrows stylish and arched. Her lips were an uncompromising cherry, a bright smile in a beautiful face. She looked like a stylised, enhanced painting of herself.

'I'm . . . I'm . . .'

Troy rose from the sofa and came to stand behind her, his hands reverently on her towelled shoulders, looking at her in the mirror, meeting her reflected eyes and not her real ones.

'You're beautiful,' he said quietly. 'We're not just making money here, we're making a person. Zelda Vere is going to be beautiful.'

'Hairdresser?' the sales assistant inquired. 'A colourist and a stylist?'

'No!' Isobel exclaimed with sudden determination. She turned to Troy. 'I can wash this off in the train on the way home,' she whispered. 'And I can hide the clothes. But I can't go home blonde. It'd be too awful.'

He recoiled as he realised what she was saying. 'You're never thinking of keeping this a secret from Philip?'

Isobel glanced around. The sales assistant withdrew to a discreet distance and the makeup artiste was absorbed in packing her brushes.

'I have to,' she said. 'If he knew I was writing a book like this at all he'd be heartbroken. If he knew I was doing it for him then he'd feel completely ashamed, it would be unbearable to him. He hates books like that, and he hates authors like this. It's got to be a complete secret. To the whole world and to him too. He would be completely mortified if he knew. He . . .'

'He what?' Troy demanded.

'He thinks my books are still doing well. I haven't told him that we've been in trouble for years. I can't tell him now. And I won't tell him about the new book.'

Troy whistled a silent arpeggio. 'He thought you were doing well? He didn't know?'

Isobel's desperate eyes looked out of the serene, beautiful mask. 'Yes,' she said. 'Worry is really bad for him, I couldn't risk him worrying. When he first became ill he handed over everything to me to look after. I just cashed in all our savings, and told him that it was all right. I didn't know what else to do.'

'So everything hangs on this?' Troy queried.

Isobel nodded. 'But I can't change how I look permanently,' she warned him. 'So I can't go blonde.'

'Well, OK by me,' Troy said with a sense of the stakes in this gamble growing greater by the minute. 'OK by me, if you think you can get away with it. The bank account was going to be secret anyway so it makes no difference to me. As long as you think you can keep it up at home.'

'But I can't have my hair dyed.'

'No,' he said. 'What about a wig?' He turned to the sales assistant. 'Wigs,' he said firmly. 'Blonde wigs.'

'Of course if madam does not wish to alter her own style, that is an ideal solution,' the sales assistant said smoothly. She nodded at her deputy and the woman slipped from the room. 'Perhaps just a little trim, just to enhance the profile, would be a good idea?'

'I'll have a trim,' Isobel said. 'But I won't colour it.'

The sales assistant nodded and stood aside as the rack of wigs came in with the fitter behind them.

'Another glass of champagne Sir?' she asked Troy, who settled down on the sofa once more as the hairdresser came in and started to trim Isobel's hair into a neater shape.

'Yes please,' he said.

Isobel faced the mirror, ready to be fitted with her wig. First they crammed her own hair into a flesh-coloured skullcap as tight and uncomfortable as the bathing hats she used to wear for swimming at school, and then they forced the huge mane of hair on top. Isobel felt so mauled by the struggle to get them on that she was scowling when she looked at the mirror to see the effect.

She saw a petulant beauty, a spoiled, glossy, golden woman who could be almost any age from mid-twenties to forty. The brightness of the hair enhanced the perfect colour of her skin, made her eyes darker, made her eyelashes dramatically thick and black. The wide bouffant style made her face look slim and elegant. She had the look of all the women who gaze from the pages of the society magazines, the women who feign unawareness of the photographers, who share a joke laughing but never screw up their eyes when the flashbulbs pop, who are always there at the parties, at the awards nights, who ski in winter and sail in summer, who know New York and go to the Paris fashion shows, who call each other 'darling' and kiss without lips touching cheek. They are the women who once married rich men and are still managing to hold on to them. They are the women who organise the charity balls, who launch fragrances, who own racehorses, who put their names to bestselling autobiographies created by ghost writers about imaginary events.

'Bingo,' Troy said from the sofa. 'Cinderella.'

'A very high presence,' the saleswoman said approvingly. 'Delightful.'

Troy rose up. 'We'll take it all,' he said. 'We'll take it all now.'

'Madam should really take two of the wigs,' the hairdresser advised. 'When one is being washed and set she can use the other.'

'Oh I suppose so,' Troy said.

'And of course we can deliver,' the saleswoman offered.

He shook his head. 'We have a car outside.' He turned to Isobel. 'D'you want to keep it all on? We could invite Freddie over here for tea. Try it out on him?'

The wealthy woman in the mirror smiled with perfect confidence. 'Why not?' she asked her reflection.

Freddie, pouring tea for the three of them on the terrace, was delighted to meet Zelda Vere.

'An author of mine.' Troy introduced her. 'A new author, and a very exciting new book to be finished . . .'

'Within the year,' Isobel promised.

'Whenever,' Troy said. 'Freddie is an interior designer, and man about town.'

Freddie grinned. 'D'you take milk? Really? How can you, Troy?' When Isobel accepted milk and sugar he looked stunned. 'I'm so lactose intolerant you wouldn't believe.'

'Zelda has a professional interest in body piercing,' Troy said quietly, with a discreet glance at the nearby tables. 'I was attempting to describe to her a Prince Albert.'

Freddie's bright gaze met Isobel's. 'You really need to see one,' he said.

'I was hoping that I might,' she replied, and then realised that her voice, her hesitant politeness, was all wrong with the acid pink suit and the brassy blonde hair. She tossed her head and tried again: 'I promised myself a look at yours.'

Freddie let out a small scream of laughter. 'Here?' he asked.

The new brassy-headed Isobel did not flinch. 'If you like.'

'Now, now, children,' Troy interrupted. 'We'll go back to my flat for the Doctors and Nurses experience.'

'But why d'you want to know?' Freddie asked, pouring hot water into the tea pot.

'For my novel,' Isobel said. 'My hero is a dark, brooding Satanist and I wanted to give him something of a . . . a gimmick.'

Freddie looked slightly offended. 'A Prince Albert isn't a gimmick,' he said firmly. 'It's a statement.'

'About what?'

He hesitated for a moment, and then decided to tell her. 'You can either be the person that you were born to be: nicely brought up, good parents, nice job, reasonable income, polite children, agreeable home – right?'

Isobel nodded, feeling the weight of her hair give her nod an extra emphasis.

'Or you can redefine yourself. You get to an age when you've done all that was expected of you. You've got the education that gets you the job that gets you the pension and then you look around and say – so have I lived all my life and worked all my life just so that I can have a pension when I'm old? That's what happened to me. I was an accountant, I spent years and years getting my exams, getting my partnership, working for my clients, and suddenly I woke up one morning and thought I am so damn bored of this I can hardly get out of bed. It's my life, and it bores me to tears.'

Isobel waited. She had an odd sense that she was hearing something of immense importance, that this man whom she had taken at first to be something of a fool was telling her something that she should hear.

'Well, I cut loose,' Freddie said quietly. 'I came out. I told my mother and father that I was gay. I chucked in my job, I trained as an interior designer, and I studded my penis with jewellery.'

Isobel blinked and felt her mascara cling to her eyelashes like tears.

'It's my way of saying that I don't have to sit in a pigeon-hole. I don't have to be what people think of me. I can find my own way, I can be someone else. I don't have to have the identity my parents chose for me. I don't even have to stay with my first choice of identity. I can set myself free.'

Isobel nodded. 'I do know what you mean,' she said. 'Though it's not true for everybody. Some people have to stay inside their boundaries. Some people take a choice, which isn't perhaps the easiest choice, but it's the right thing to do. Some people want to do the right thing more than they want to do anything else. Some people see the rules and stay inside them. Some people have to.'

Freddie shook his head. 'No-one has to.'

Three

Back at his flat Troy poured pink champagne. Freddie raised an eyebrow at him and said: 'I have some stuff on me, if you'd like it?'

Troy glanced at Isobel, who was pretending to examine an antique mirror over the mantelpiece but really admiring in wonder the sheen on her hair and the glow of her skin.

'Excuse us for just a moment,' he said to her.

Freddie looked surprised. 'Wouldn't Zelda like . . . ?'

'No,' Troy said briefly. 'Allergic.'

Freddie was astounded. 'Allergic to cocaine? But how dreadful! You poor dear! How d'you ever manage? I would just die . . .'

'What?' Isobel asked, suddenly realising what he was saying.

Troy shook his head warningly at Freddie, but it was too late.

'D'you take cocaine?' Isobel demanded, deeply shocked.

'He doesn't, I do,' Freddie said, desperately lying. 'I'm always trying to persuade Troy to try it, but he won't.'

'I should think not,' Isobel said staunchly. 'It's terribly addictive, isn't it? And bad for you?'

Troy looked meaningfully at Isobel. 'You surprise me,' he said carefully. 'I'd always thought of you as a woman of great sophistication. Everyone says to me that Zelda Vere is very much a woman of the world.'

39

Isobel checked herself for a moment and then wiped her look of indignation from her face. 'Oh, of course,' she said, recovering. 'I've just seen so many people have so much trouble with it.'

Troy nodded. 'Let's just stick with champagne, shall we?'

'Sure,' Freddie said, agreeably.

Troy poured them all another glass and the two men started to exchange anecdotes, for Isobel's amusement. Isobel kicked off the pink mules and curled her long legs underneath her, and felt young and bohemian and daring. They laughed together as the level in the bottle fell lower and lower.

'Now then,' Troy said as the conversation paused. 'Let's see the family jewels, Freddie.'

Isobel followed the two men to the spare bedroom. Troy closed the door behind him and there was a sudden moment of delicious, clandestine intimacy. Isobel, dizzy from the champagne and aroused: by her own new beauty, by the company of two handsome men, by the whole extraordinary circumstances, leaned back against the door and absorbed the fact that she was in a bedroom, rather drunk and quite alone with two attractive young men.

'I feel quite shy,' Freddie said.

'*Do* show,' Isobel encouraged him. 'I really *do* need to know.'

Freddie unzipped his trousers, let them fall to his knees and then slid his black silk boxer shorts downwards to show her his gently rising penis. 'Excuse us,' he said charmingly. 'It's just all the attention.'

She regarded it with fascination. This was only the second penis she had ever seen in her life. Philip had been her first and only lover and she had not seen him naked and aroused for more than three years. 'Why, it's lovely,' she breathed.

He had ringed the foreskin with delicate studs of silver and the very peak boasted a delicate silver sleeper. The three of them gazed at it, quietly impressed.

'Will it be of any help?' Freddie asked.

The question was too much for Troy. He exploded into

raucous mirth. 'I should think it would be of tremendous help!'

Isobel hesitated, trying to keep a straight face, and then was caught by the wave of laughter, howling with merriment until the tears came into her eyes and smudged her mascara.

Troy bundled Freddie out of the house at ten and then turned to Isobel. 'C'mon, Cinderella,' he said. 'We've got to get you back into rags to catch the train.'

They were like actors in a play, intent on the work they had to do. He helped her take off the pink jacket and hang it on the hanger, he put shoe trees in the mules. The wardrobe in his spare bedroom was now dedicated to Zelda Vere's shrouded clothes. There were two stands for the wigs. Zelda Vere's expensive cosmetics were in the dressing-table drawer. Isobel let Troy draw the plastic covers over the jacket and skirt while she pulled on her linen dress. She realised for the first time that it did not exactly fit. It gaped slightly at the armholes, you could glimpse her old ill-fitting bra from the side, the waist was too long; the fall of the skirt to mid-calf with the flat shoes made her legs look short and fat.

'I could take one of the suits home,' she said wistfully.

'Not one of them,' Troy ruled. 'If you overlap your identities at all, someone will see you and make the connection. You've got to be like a spy. You've got to have waterproof compartments. Zelda waits for you here – in the drawers and in the wardrobe. Isobel is catching the train home tonight and you'd better have some idea where she's been all evening, if you're hoping to keep this deception up.'

'He already knows I'll be late,' Isobel said reluctantly. 'I rang him from Harrods to tell him I was having dinner with my publishers. He isn't expecting me home.'

'Just get your story perfect,' Troy urged her, putting her jacket round her shoulders and opening the front door. 'Where did you have dinner? What did you eat? That sort of thing. If this deception is to work it has to be totally, totally convincing.'

She hesitated on the doorstep, reluctant to leave him. 'Thank you for today,' she said. 'We've never spent so much time together before and you've been my agent for – what? – six years.'

In an odd courtly gesture he took her hand and kissed it. 'It was my pleasure,' he said. 'We did great shopping. And I loved sitting on the sofa like a sultan and seeing you modelling things.'

The thought of him enjoying her gave her pause. 'You liked seeing me?'

He made a little deprecatory gesture. 'Of course. You were transforming from one sort of woman to another. One would have to have a heart of stone not to be fascinated.'

Her face warmed at the thought of being fascinating. 'Oh Troy! I always thought that you . . .' She hesitated to choose her words carefully. 'I always thought that you were not very interested in women.'

He laughed. 'I'm interested in *people*,' he said. 'I love Freddie because he's bold and risk-taking and exciting. And I like you because you're determined and courageous and suddenly you have embarked on some kind of new path here that could take you anywhere – and that's fascinating for me.'

'But your preference?' she asked delicately.

He stepped forward and hailed a cab. The car swung in and Troy opened the door for her. 'Neither here nor there. Don't forget to construct your alibi on the way home.'

'You were late last night,' Philip said at breakfast. 'I didn't hear you come in.'

'I know,' Isobel said. 'It went on and on.'

'You should have told them you had a train to catch,' he said with disapproval. 'You must have got the last one home.'

'I didn't want to make a fuss.'

'You should make a fuss,' he corrected her. 'They may be the publishers but you're the author. Where do they get their living from, that's what I'd like to know?'

'They look after me very well,' she said. She put his toast

down before him and poured his tea. She wondered at the readiness of the lies that were sliding from her mouth.

'I sat next to James Ware,' she told Philip. 'Of the *Sunday Times.*'

'Did you tell him what I said about that last review of your book?' Philip asked.

'No,' she said. 'We talked about Spender.'

'Fat lot he'd know,' Philip said crossly, and opened the newspaper. 'You should have told him what I said. If I'd been there I'd have made sure that he knew he had completely the wrong end of the stick.'

She hesitated. 'What are you going to do today?'

He looked around the paper. 'Nothing,' he said. 'My exercises, the crossword, lunch, walk, tea. What are you doing today? Writing?'

Isobel looked at her navy calf-length skirt with mild dissatisfaction. 'I thought I might go to Tonbridge and look at some clothes. I'm so bored of all my clothes.'

'Why bother?' he asked. 'You hardly go anywhere. What d'you want a smart dress for?'

'I don't know,' she said wearily. 'I just thought in London yesterday that the cream shift is awfully – ordinary.'

He smiled his charming smile at her. 'We're ordinary people,' he said. 'That's our strength. We don't need the gloss. We have genuine substance.'

'I suppose one could have both,' she said. 'Gloss on the outside and substance underneath. We don't have to be wholly solid and worthy and always wearing flat shoes.'

Philip looked puzzled at her disagreement. 'Of course you can't have both,' he said. 'You're either a trivial person or a deep one. You either care about the things that matter or you run continually after fashion. We know who we are. How we appear doesn't matter.'

'Yes,' she said reluctantly. 'Yes, I suppose so.'

'So no point wasting your time and our money on shopping.'

'No,' Isobel conceded. 'I'd better get to work.'

*   *   *

She closed the study door behind her and pulled out her chair. She switched on the computer and watched the screen come to life. She thought that she had been doing these actions, like a line worker in a factory, every morning at this time for the last six years. It seemed very odd to her that this was perhaps the first morning ever that she had resented it.

It had been the conversation at breakfast. Philip's certainty in her seriousness, in her moral values, should have been a matter of joy to her. That her husband thought well of her should please any woman. But because she was held so high in his esteem she was never given new clothes. Because he admired her intellect and her seriousness, she was never given treats. He discouraged her from taking an interest in fashion, or from changing her appearance in any way. Isobel had worn flat shoes, calf-length skirts and her hair tied back at their first meeting when she had been a scholarly postgraduate; and nothing had ever changed. Isobel thought that she was fifty-two and she had not known till yesterday that she had a beautiful neck. Perhaps fifty-two was rather late to discover such an asset. Who would admire it, other than well-trained shop assistants selling earrings? Who would notice if she had her ears pierced? Who would run a finger from ear lobe to collarbone? Would anyone ever sweep up her hair and kiss the nape of her neck and graze the skin with his teeth?

Isobel clicked on the file marked 'Letters to the Bank' and put the vision of a man caressing her neck out of her mind. She had made a commitment to Philip and a promise to herself, never to look back, never to wonder how their marriage might have been if he had not been ill. She believed that she should be grateful only that he had lived. That was the most important thing. Shopping, and a man with a liking for long necks, and vanity were supremely irrelevant. She opened chapter one and started to format and print it.

Isobel carried the first ten chapters of her novel into the village post office and put it on the scales. It weighed as much as a complete manuscript of one of her usual books. She paid for it to be sent recorded delivery to Troy's office, and then stepped back from the counter. Isobel normally never ate sweets of any kind. She had been forbidden them as a child, except for one chocolate egg at Easter, and had never acquired the taste. But she felt that the posting of the first instalment of the Zelda Vere novel deserved some reward. And she was certain that Zelda Vere ate chocolate.

She looked at the confectionery counter. There were few things she remembered from her childhood. Then she saw a large box of chocolate brazils. She smiled. Of course Zelda Vere would eat chocolate brazils, probably while drinking crème de menthe. 'I'll have them,' she said, pointing.

'For a present?' the woman asked, reaching for the large box.

'Yes,' Isobel said.

'Lucky lady,' the woman said.

'Yes,' Isobel agreed. 'She is terribly lucky.'

She parked on the side of the road on the way back to her house and ate a dozen of them, one after another, with intense relish, filling her mouth with the sharp taste and then savouring the warm nuttiness of the centre. When she had eaten so many that she felt slightly, guiltily queasy, she hid the rest of the box under a scarf on the back seat. She was just about to start the car when she remembered Troy's warning that the compartments between Isobel Latimer and Zelda Vere must be watertight. She must be like a spy. Reluctantly she got from the car and looked at the land falling away from the road – a patchwork of fields intersected by half-hidden lanes, a farmhouse down to her left, her own house hidden by the fold of the hill. With a powerful overarm throw she flung the box high into the air. It went up in a grand arc into the blue sky and then turned over in the air and scattered chocolate brazils like a rain storm of incredible richness. Isobel clapped her hands together in delight and watched the expensive chocolates tumble recklessly down on Kent.

'That was pure Zelda Vere,' she whispered to herself and wiped the chocolate from her lips, pulled up the sagging waistband of her navy skirt, got back into the car and drove home.

'Did you get some whisky?' Philip asked her. 'We're nearly out.'

'Didn't you put it on the list for Mrs M? It's her day to shop tomorrow.'

'I don't like her buying my whisky,' Philip complained.

'I don't see why not.'

They were at lunch together. Isobel, a little sick from too many chocolate brazils, was eating very little. Philip had a green salad before him and a slice of cheese on toast.

'Doesn't seem right,' he said.

Isobel raised her eyebrows. She knew that she was being unusually impatient with Philip. Something of the spirit of Zelda Vere had entered her with the chocolate brazils.

'Well, I wasn't planning to go down to the village again,' she said shortly. 'I want to work this afternoon.'

'I suppose I'll have to go then,' he said. There was a pause while he waited for her to say that she would drive down rather than make him go. Isobel said nothing.

'I could walk down and you could pick me up,' he said. 'It could be my afternoon walk.'

Isobel hesitated for only one moment and then she experienced the familiar rush of guilt at the thought that she was being selfish and ungracious to Philip. 'Of course,' she said. 'Shall I pick you up from the pub at two thirty?'

He smiled, pleased that he had got his own way. 'Call it three and that'll give you time to pop into the off licence and buy the whisky on your way,' he said. 'I'd rather not trek down the High Street. I'll wait for you in the pub.'

'All right,' Isobel said again. 'At three.'

'There's a problem with the manuscript,' Troy said on the telephone.

Isobel felt the falling sensation of fear. 'What?' she asked quickly.

46

'I don't think you completely understand the genre,' he said.

'What d'you mean?' Isobel demanded. She looked at the screen before her where Charity was about to confront the businesswoman who had left the coven and founded an international cosmetics business. Charity was posing as a model, the face of the spring collection. At any moment she would tie the woman up and scar her face forever. The woman would never be seen in public again. Isobel was as certain as she could be that the scene was a perfect example of the genre.

'It's these semi-colons,' Troy said, the glee at last revealed in his voice.

'What?'

'Nobody in popular fiction uses semi-colons. They wouldn't know what to do with them.'

'What do they use?'

'Commas. They use nothing but commas.'

'But what about subjunctive clauses?'

'Commas again.'

'Lists?'

'Still commas.'

'Do they use full colons?'

'Never!' Troy exclaimed gleefully. 'You're still too erudite, Isobel. It's a dead giveaway. You'll have to re-format these chapters before I can send them out. They have to have nothing but commas and full stops. Nothing else.'

Isobel could hear the laughter in her own voice. 'But the story?'

'Perfect,' Troy said. 'Perfect in every way. It's a hit, Isobel. Or rather, I should say, Zelda. We've hit the jackpot. You're going to make a lot of money with this one. I promise.'

She closed her eyes for a moment and felt the sense of relief wash through her, unknot the tightness in her shoulders and the strain around her eyes. 'A lot of money,' she repeated softly. She visualised the swimming pool they would build in the barn so that Philip could exercise his muscles daily. The gymnasium they would put next to it. And she would buy some clothes – not in the Zelda Vere league of course, but some well-cut, elegant clothes. And she might get her hair tinted, just to give herself a little more – 'Presence,' she whispered. She would get her ears pierced and wear earrings which would show off the length of her neck. And Philip, fitter from swimming, might yet admire her looks.

'Replace all the semi-colons with commas or full stops. And rough up the text a bit,' Troy commanded. 'Your imagery is still too precise, think cliché, darling, not original imagery. More cliché and not so many long words. And then send it to me again and I'll send it out to all the publishers.'

'All the publishers?' she queried. 'Not just Penshurst?'

'Absolutely not!' he declared. 'We're going to be fighting them off for this manuscript. They'll all want to buy it. We'll have to hold an auction.'

Philip put his head around the study door. 'Isn't it time for lunch?' he asked.

Isobel flinched and moved her head so that she blocked his view of the screen.

Philip saw that she was on the telephone. 'Who is it?'

She put her hand over the mouthpiece and whispered: 'Troy, I'll only be a moment.'

'Can't he phone back?'

Isobel nodded. 'Just one minute more.'

Philip waited for a moment, and when she did not put down the telephone he made a little irritable tutting noise, pointed to his wrist watch, and went out of the room, closing the door briskly behind him.

'An auction?' Isobel whispered into the phone.

'Is it safe to talk?'

'Yes, if I'm quick.'

Troy, miles away in London, lowered his voice as if to keep the secret safe. 'I'll send the three chapters and a synopsis out to all the big London publishers. They'll read it, and then they'll bid. We'll give them a starting price and we'll take bids over the telephone. We'll let it go on for a day – not longer. At the end of the day the highest bid gets the book.'

'But how will they know what price to pay? How will they know what it's worth?'

'That's the joy of it! They won't know. Because nobody knows Zelda Vere so they can't set a price based on her previous sales. She's a dark horse. They have to gamble. But when they know that all the others are in and making bids they'll all make bids too. It's my job to get the buzz going, to get the excitement up.'

Isobel closed her eyes again and saw once more the warm waters of the heated pool and the clean white tiles. 'And my job to write the novel.'

'And lose those semi-colons,' Troy advised. 'How long before you are finished?'

Isobel looked at the screen. This was only Charity's second victim, she had to seek revenge on two others and then meet and fall in love with the leader. 'It's got to be two months,' she said. 'I can't see how to do it quicker.'

'Perfect,' Troy said. 'I'll get the buzz going at once.'

Four

Rhett crushed her in his strong grip, his powerful member pressing against her thighs in a forceful reminder of their pleasure of the night before when she had lain whimpering with ecstasy beneath the pounding rush of his thrusts.

'Do you swear that you love me more than you have ever loved anyone?' Charity demanded.

'I swear it,' he said hoarsely. She could feel him pressing against her more urgently. In a moment, she knew she would succumb –

'No, melt.'

– melt into his arms

'No, beneath . . .'

beneath his desire and her resolve would be lost.

'I love you more than anyone,' he promised. 'If I lost you my life would not be worth living.'

They were the words she had been waiting for.

'I will be your wife,' she said. 'Love me.'

'Mmm,' Isobel muttered critically. She sat back for a moment and then typed a new version.

They were the words she had been waiting for. She drew back from him, quickly before the seduction of his body should entrap her.

'You will never see me again,' she said icily. 'You will spend the rest of your life longing for me, longing for another night like last night, aching for my body, crying for my smile. This is the great revenge I have played out upon you. You will never be happy again.'

He would have snatched her to his mouth for a rain of hungry kisses but he was too late. Charity had slipped out of his embrace and was gone.

The last thing she heard was the cry of a man completely destroyed.

'The end,' Isobel wrote in quiet triumph. 'The end.' She hesitated, looking at the screen. 'But which end?'

She turned to the bookshelves and pulled out the hidden commercial novels and flicked through to the last pages. They all ended happily. Isobel paused. 'I can't do it,' she said with sudden resolution. 'Even to work inside the genre, I can't do it. This is a story about a woman who takes revenge, about a woman taking a decision about the sort of life she wants to live. I won't have her melting at the last moment. I want her to be free, I want her to leave the man and go.'

She pushed her chair back from the desk and unconsciously unravelled the knot of her hair, ran her fingers through the thick softness of it and then tied it back up. 'I can't bear to have her just collapse under a man, after all she's been through,' Isobel whispered. 'This isn't a story about wanting a man. This is a story about a woman making her own choices. About a woman who has the guts to say that love is not the important thing: the important thing is autonomy.'

She stabbed a grip firmly into the re-made bun, pulled her chair closer to the desk, and with one sweep of the computer mouse, highlighted the tender reconciliation scene and cut it. It disappeared from the screen leaving Charity's curse on the man she had loved and her disappearance from his life.

'Quite right too,' Isobel said with satisfaction. 'Why should a woman be stuck with a man?' She paused for a moment, savouring the sense of completion. Then she picked up the telephone.

'It's finished,' she announced to Troy. 'I've done it.'

'Zelda Vere – well done!' he said in a whisper. 'And something's come up here.'

'What?'

'You know the auction date is next Tuesday?'

'Of course,' she said. 'I wanted it finished by then so you could tell them you had the whole book, as soon as it is bought.'

'One of them wants to meet you.'

'What?'

'It's not unreasonable. They're talking about investing a lot of money. But it does leave us with a bit of a problem. D'you think you could come up and be Zelda Vere for a day? Say on the Monday?'

'For how many people?' Isobel spoke cautiously but she had a great sense of excitement and anticipation at the thought of putting on Zelda Vere's beautiful clothes and her golden head of hair and that wonderful makeup.

'I don't know how many would want to come. You'd have to be prepared for half a dozen. And you'll have to have a back-story. You'll have to think who Zelda is, where she comes from. Where she got the ideas for this novel. Why don't you come and stay the night before, Sunday night, and we'll spend some time and get our act together?'

Isobel thought quickly. Mrs M. usually came in to sleep if Isobel was away at literary conferences or at book festivals. She generally brought a videotape and she and Philip would settle down for the evening and watch something trivial. He would complain for days after that her company rotted his brain; but his relish for the light thrillers which she chose was undeniable.

'If I can, I will,' Isobel said. 'I'll have to sort out things here.'

'I think we need to spend some time on this,' Troy said. Unusually for him, he sounded anxious. 'I didn't look ahead to this. I thought they'd just snap at the book. I didn't think they'd want to meet you before the auction.'

'It's all right.' Isobel heard herself sounding calm and reassuring. She realised that she was looking forward to being Zelda Vere. She wanted to wear that lovely suit, to be a blonde beautiful woman. She wanted to see her long legs in the gold strappy sandals and to wear the expensive underwear against her skin. She even wanted the firm sensation of the underwired bra pressing against the bones of her chest. She wanted to be that other woman, far away from the tedium and the responsibility of her normal life.

'I'll be there,' she promised. 'We can do it.'

'It's a reading,' she told Philip. 'First thing at Goldsmiths College and a discussion about the novel. Apparently someone dropped out at the last minute and they asked me to step in.'

'Should have thought of you in the first place,' Philip said. 'You shouldn't let people treat you like second best. You shouldn't be the one they fall back on, Isobel, you should be their first choice.'

'Well, they've chosen me now. The only thing is, I'd like to stay Sunday night, so that I don't have to rush on Monday morning. I hate that commuter train going into London in the morning.'

'Away all night?' he asked.

'Mrs M. could come in. I'll ask her.'

'I suppose she'll bring one of those ridiculous films and insist on watching it.'

Isobel smiled. 'I expect she will. She always does.'

'When would you be back?'

'After lunch sometime, Monday afternoon,' Isobel said. 'It's an all-day conference. I might stay and listen to the other papers if that's all right with you.'

'Makes no difference to me,' he said ungraciously. 'I'm not going out dancing after all. I can do the crossword and my exercises whether you're here or not. What did you think you might be missing? Riding on the motorbike? Cross-country skiing?'

'No,' Isobel said quietly.

There was a brief silence. Isobel kept her eyes on the table-top and thought that Philip's bad temper was as much a symptom of his illness as his wasted legs. She should embrace them both with equal tenderness. She kept looking down until she could meet his eyes and smile at him with real affection.

He was not looking at her, he was reading a brightly coloured leaflet. He nodded at the information and then pushed it across the lunch table towards her. 'Here, I sent off for this. I thought it would give us a general idea.'

It was a glossy brochure from a swimming-pool company. It showed a seductive picture of a beautiful indoor swimming pool, the lights glistening on the blue water, a bikini-clad girl poised on the diving board.

'Does it say how much?' Isobel asked.

Philip laughed shortly. 'I think if you have to ask the price you can't afford it. And anyway, it varies in terms of the volume of the pool and whether you have an electric pump and heater or a gas one.'

Isobel felt a familiar sense of dread. 'I can see you've gone into it,' she said lightly.

'I just like to know things,' he said with dignity. 'I measured up the barn the other day. We could easily fit it in there and even a small sauna.'

'A sauna!' she exclaimed. 'Very grand.'

'I think it would help my condition,' he said. 'The heat. And of course the exercise. I could do my exercises in the water, it would take the strain off the joints, and I would swim. It'd do you good too. You never take any exercise. You drive everywhere. At least I walk once a day, but you only drive to the village. You'll get overweight, Isobel, flabby. Women always run to flab. We're neither of us spring chickens any more.'

'I know.' Isobel nodded, swallowing the retort that she drove to the village to collect him, to spare him the return walk home; that before his illness she had walked every day. Now she never had the time.

'There you are then.'

'So how much do they cost? Swimming pools? About?'

'We'd get a nice one in the barn and the barn converted with sliding picture windows for under £50,000,' he said judicially. 'We could do it a lot cheaper, of course, but I think it'd be a false economy.'

Isobel blinked. 'We simply haven't got that sort of money darling.'

'Not now we haven't, I know. But when they bid for your new book we'll have a lump sum come in.'

Isobel recoiled, thinking for one extraordinary moment that he knew all about *Devil's Disciple*. Then she realised that he was talking about the literary novel that Penshurst Press had bought for only £20,000.

'Yes,' she said, rapidly improvising. 'I have great hopes for it.'

'Troy not told you yet?'

'Not yet.'

'He's so slow, that man, anyone would think he was doing you a favour.'

'He's discussing with the editors.'

'Lunching out at your expense, more like,' Philip grumbled. 'You ought to tell him, remind him who it is that earns the money.'

'I know I should,' she said mildly. 'I'll talk to him next week.'

'I'll see what sort of planning permission we need,' Philip said. 'I'll phone the town hall. Do us no harm to get planning permission and some drawings done.'

'Perhaps we should wait till we know how much I'm going to earn . . .'

'It'd be an interest for me,' he pointed out.

'Oh of course then, yes. Let's get some drawings done.' She hesitated. 'They won't be very expensive, will they?'

'For God's sake!' he exploded. 'You're so mean these days, Isobel! We have to spend some money if we want to go ahead with this. If you're so anxious about it then I'll pay for the drawings myself. All right? I'll cash in some shares, I'll use my own money. Will that satisfy you?' He stamped to the back door and threw it open. 'I'm going for my walk,' he said irritably.

'I'll pick you up from the pub,' she said quickly to the closing door.

'You don't need to,' he said crossly. 'I'm going up the hill. I don't know how long I'll be.'

Isobel let him go. There was no point in running after him. She went to the kitchen window and watched his endearing limping stride carry him slowly to the end of the garden and then out through the wrought-iron gate to the track that wound steeply up the side of the Weald. He would never manage to walk to the crest of the hill, she knew. He would be too breathless and his weakened legs could not carry him up that hard gradient. She watched him with a pity which was so intense that it felt like passion. She wanted to go after him, she wanted him to lean on her, she wanted to support him.

Philip would be back by teatime, she reassured herself. He would be tired out within half an hour and sit down to rest, too proud to come home straight away. As long as he did not take a chill he would come to no harm, stubbornly sitting out the afternoon, wanting to worry her, insisting on his independence. By four he would limp homeward, wanting his tea. He would hate it if she ran after him, he would hate it if she showed how easily she could catch him up, even if she were following him for love. He would even hate knowing that she had watched him go. He did not want pity, he wanted them both to behave as if nothing was wrong. The best thing that she could do for him was to earn the money to buy the things he wanted, and to maintain the life that they had chosen.

Isobel turned back to the study. She could get the full text of *Devil's Disciple* formatted and printed out and ready to take to London when she went on Sunday night. She felt that the most loving thing she could do for him was to sell the Zelda Vere novel and earn him the money he needed now.

*   *   *

Troy opened the front door of his London flat almost as soon as she rang the bell. 'This is getting a bit tense,' he said, leading the way from the little hall up the carpeted stairs. Isobel followed, carrying her overnight bag. 'I told one of the publishers they could meet you and now they all want to come. I said they could come here, each of them, at hourly intervals. Half an hour quick chat and then go. So I've kept it as short as I can.'

Isobel heard herself give a nervous little laugh. 'Well, the worst that can happen is they don't bid for the book, isn't it? It's not as if we're impersonating a policeman or anything. We're not doing anything criminal.'

'No,' he said, slightly cheered. 'I thought we'd have a practice tonight, a dress rehearsal.'

'Of course.'

Troy threw open the door to the spare bedroom and Isobel went inside. The wardrobe doors were open, the plastic covers were off the suits. The makeup was laid out on the dressing table, eyeshadows and liner and mascara to the left, lipsticks to the right, foundation powders and blushers in the centre. The shoes, free of their shoe trees, were standing side by side at the foot of the bed.

'You got it all ready!'

'It just seemed the right thing to do – preparing the star's dressing room.'

Impulsively, Isobel turned around and kissed him. He held her lightly for a moment and she had a sudden surprising sense of his nearness, of the intimacy of his touch.

'Now get out of that dreadful skirt and into Zelda's lovely clothes and we'll get started,' he said briskly.

She hesitated for a moment, waiting for him to leave, but he had turned aside to the wardrobe to slip the suit off the hanger. He was so matter-of-fact, so uninterested that she felt that it was all right to undress before him. It was as he said, like being an actress, like being a star. He was her dresser; he was not a lover watching her strip.

'It's your fault it's an awful skirt,' she said stoutly, pushing the elasticated waistband down over her hips. 'I wanted to take the suits home.'

'Zelda stays here. I take care of her clothes. You can go and buy yourself some new things if you need them. But not too glamorous. You two have to stay separate.'

Isobel stepped into the pink skirt and carefully pulled it up, zipped it up, and settled it on her hips with her hands in the odd coquettish gesture that all women in snug skirts naturally adopt.

'Nice,' Troy said. 'And the jacket?'

'I need the new bra,' Isobel said. 'It won't fit right without it.'

'Oh, of course,' he said. 'Top drawer on the right.'

Isobel opened the drawer. He had unpacked all the underwear and folded it meticulously on scented liners. There was also a new silk nightdress.

'What's this?' Isobel asked.

'I couldn't see Zelda sleeping in a pair of cotton pyjamas, so I bought her something a bit silky.'

'Thank you,' Isobel said. 'You've been to a lot of trouble.'

'I enjoyed it,' he said simply. 'I liked getting the things just right, and I loved the makeup. All those little bottles, it's just like the little pots of model paints I had when I was a kid.'

Isobel hesitated, wanting to take off her bra but feeling shy.

'I'll get us a couple of glasses of champagne,' Troy said. 'Help the alibi along. Zelda always drinks Roederer, I think. I got some in.'

Isobel dressed swiftly while he was gone and when he came back she was seated before the mirror pulling the skullcap over her hair.

'It would be miles easier if I did go blonde,' she said.

Troy put the cold glass of champagne on the dressing table beside her. 'Absolutely not. You'd be too alike, and anyway, I like having her hair waiting here, along with her clothes. I looked in last night and she was like a ghost waiting to be raised.'

Isobel sipped her glass, and then ducked her head and pulled the wig on.

'Careful!' Troy snapped. 'You'll tear it! Here! Let me.'

'It's so tight!' she complained.

'Hold it at the front while I pull it down at the back.'

Isobel held the fringe as firmly as she dared while Troy heaved from behind. Slowly the skin stretched and then encased her head. She pushed the hair back from her face and looked into the mirror. A face halfway between Isobel and Zelda looked back at her, with Isobel's tired skin and dark-shadowed eyes and pale lips, but Zelda's glorious mane of barmaid blonde.

'Put some makeup on quick,' Troy urged her. 'Shall I do it? I was watching what she did.'

'Oh yes please.' Isobel tipped her head back, closed her eyes and gave herself up to the pleasure of his touch. He cleansed her skin with the same gritty, sweet-smelling cream, and then wiped it clean, patted it with toner and then moisturiser and then stroked on the foundation cream with tiny sensual sponging gestures, intruding like a lapping kitten into the corners of her eyes, sweeping like the wing of a bird across her cheeks.

'Don't open your eyes,' he whispered, his lips very close to her ear. 'I want to do the lot.'

She stayed completely still, as he commanded, her eyes closed, the sensitive skin of her cheeks, her temples, recognising the warm breath of the powder, the soft brush of the blusher. Her eyelids were soothed by the soft stipple of the eyeshadow, pressed by the application of false eyelashes, and then slicked by the wet line of the eyeliner.

The touch of the lipstick brush on her lips was like a hundred small, slow kisses. She felt her soft lips dragged gently one way and then another in a slow, tantalising, dabbing gesture.

Then the soft tissue was laid over all her face and patted gently down.

'*Et voilà!*' Troy said, his voice husky. 'And Zelda is with us.'

Almost unwillingly Isobel came out of the darkness which

had been filled with such passive sensuality, and found herself looking into the radiant face of Zelda Vere.

'You are beautiful,' Troy said. His face was beside hers, looking over her shoulder into the mirror.

'She is,' Isobel reminded him.

'Well, you are her now. So *you* are,' he said. 'I feel like a magician. I made you. I painted you like a doll and here you are. Coppelia.'

The two of them gazed and gazed at the image they had made for long moments.

'Now,' said Troy. 'To work. We'll go into the sitting room.'

Isobel reached for her glass and got to her feet.

'No! No!' Troy exclaimed. 'Don't rush. And Zelda never picks up her own glass. Someone will carry that for you. You move slowly, and elegantly, as if you were paid by the minute.'

Isobel walked slowly to the door.

'More hips,' Troy said.

'I'd look ridiculous,' Isobel argued, pausing at the door.

'Of course. All rich women look ridiculous. But who would ever dare to tell them? Sway your hips. Think Marilyn Monroe.'

Isobel set off down the corridor towards the sitting room, conscientiously swaying her hips. Her high heels snagged slightly in the thick pile carpet. She did not feel glamorous any more, she felt incompetent. She turned at the doorway and met Troy's encouraging smile.

'Nearly,' he said. 'Look. Watch me.' With both glasses held steadily in each hand he walked towards her, his weight well forward, his hips tilted, each step a little dance movement as he flicked his hips to one side and then the other. 'The hips go sideways, the legs go straight on,' he said, announcing a discovery. 'And it's a narrow path, the feet go along a line. Try again.'

Isobel walked back to the bedroom.

'Brilliant. Once more for luck?'

She walked the length of the corridor and then returned, moving like a model on a catwalk before his judging eyes.

'Perfect,' he concluded. 'Now. Go in and sit down.'

Isobel was gaining confidence, she swayed across the sitting-room floor, chose to sit on the sofa and spread herself along it, long legs outstretched, leaning diagonally back against the cushions. She crossed her legs at the knee, stroking the pink skirt downwards. She allowed one mule to drop slightly, showing the arch of her foot.

'That is *very* sexy,' Troy said with deep approval. 'I knew you had it buried in you, Isobel. God help us all when it comes seething out.'

She giggled. 'I don't seethe.'

He clapped his hand over his mouth. 'My fault. I shouldn't have said Isobel. *Zelda*, I should have said – Zelda, you look wonderful. You are a woman full of seething sensuality. Here's your champagne.'

'Thank you,' Isobel drawled. She put her hand out but did not stretch towards him. She made him walk to her and give her the glass.

'Good,' he said. 'Now tell me about your early life.'

'I was brought up in France,' Isobel started, telling the story she had devised on the train. 'My mother was a cook to a family of ex-pats in the South of France. I don't want to release their name. I was educated at home, so there's no record of me at any French school. At eighteen I became a secretary in the family's wine business. At twenty-four I made a brief, unhappy marriage to a Frenchman and when I left my husband I did a number of jobs, all of them clerical, temporary. I've always written, I've always kept a diary and written short stories but this is the first novel I have ever completed. It took me ten months to write. I got the idea from a newspaper cutting, I can't remember quite where, and from the stories that the French maids used to tell me about strange goings-on in the neighbouring chateaux.'

'Excellent,' Troy said, pouring them both some more champagne. 'And your parents?'

'Both died in a car crash twelve years ago, leaving me very well off. With my inheritance I have travelled all round the world.'

61

'Any other family?'

'I was an only child. Books were my only friends,' Isobel added. A wink from Troy commended the addition.

'And where d'you live now?'

'I was travelling. But now I am going to buy myself a flat beside the Thames in London. I have a great affinity for ports, being such a traveller.'

'Romantic interest?'

'I feel I must preserve my privacy.'

'But your passionate love scenes, are they all imaginary?'

'I have known deep desire. I am a woman of passion.'

'Age?'

'Forty-six?' Isobel hazarded.

'Go for forty-two,' Troy commended. 'D'you drink or do drugs at all?'

She shook her head. 'I have a horror of drugs, but I drink champagne and mineral water. Never coffee, only herbal tea.'

'Beauty routine? Writing routine? Lifestyle?'

'Cleanse, tone, moisturise,' Isobel recited. 'I write every day in a fountain pen in special French exercise books. I read in the afternoon in either French or English. I am very disciplined. I prefer to travel by train so that I can comfortably work and watch the scenery.'

'Lonely?' Troy asked.

For a moment, surprised by the question, her face came up and she met his eyes. 'Oh yes,' she said, in her real voice. 'Oh yes.'

Troy flicked his gaze away, determined not to hear the note of true desolation. Isobel looked away as well. She had not meant him to know. She had not meant ever to know it herself.

'I mean, despite all this foreign travelling, d'you have no friends?'

Isobel slid back behind the mask of Zelda Vere. 'I meet people and talk to them, perhaps intimately. But then they go on their journey and I go on mine. From now on I shall live for my writing.'

'Do you think you are a good writer?'

Zelda Vere leaned forward. 'What the world needs is storytellers,' she breathed. 'People make so much fuss about these so-called literary novels which are read by maybe one or two thousand people. My stories will reach millions of people. People need stories and magic and hope in their dreary day-to-day lives. I happen to have the wonderful talent of being a great storyteller. I may not know about semi-colons, but I do know about life.'

'Brava!' Troy cried, applauding. 'Brava.'

They practised a few more questions and answers before Troy ruled that they should eat before they were drunk on champagne. He would not allow Isobel to keep on the wig or the clothes while they ate. 'What if you dropped food on her skirt?' he asked. 'I want her to wear the pink tomorrow.'

Isobel went and stripped off Zelda Vere's clothes, and wiped Zelda Vere's makeup from her face. She came into the kitchen-diner wearing the despised skirt and a baggy jumper, her face plain and slightly shiny from the makeup remover.

'Hello, Isobel,' Troy said encouragingly. 'Here, have a nibble.' He pushed a dish of olives and nuts towards her and peered under the grill where two dishes in silver foil were starting to bubble.

'Are you cooking?' Isobel asked in surprise.

'I sent out. I'm just warming it up,' he said. 'Chicken breasts in pesto and beetroot, with wild rice. Hope you like it.'

'Sounds lovely,' Isobel replied, thinking of her usual supper at home: plain dishes like cottage pie or grilled trout, lamb cutlets or steak. Philip preferred simple food and only had a little appetite. At the end of a day of writing, she had no energy for shopping, preparing, and cooking.

They ate companionably either side of the worktop, perched on kitchen stools. 'I turned the dining room into my study,' Troy said. 'I so seldom eat at home, it seemed stupid having a room standing empty.'

'Where do you eat?' Isobel asked.

'Oh, restaurants with people, or quite often at parties,' he said vaguely. 'Or dinner parties, you know.'

Isobel nodded but she did not know. She was invited regularly to literary parties, but she did not like to go alone, and standing around and talking was obviously unsuitable for Philip's condition. In any case he hated those sorts of social occasions. The few parties they had attended when Isobel's career was starting to take off, before Philip was ill, had been uncomfortable for them both. Philip regarded any other author as a rival to his wife, and any attention paid to any other writer as a snub to his wife. He tried to defend her by loudly decrying everyone else's work. He was shy in a room full of strangers and his shyness took the form of abruptness, almost rudeness. Equally, he felt insulted that people would ask him briefly what he did and yet have no genuine interest in his experiences, in his lifetime's work in the pharmaceutical industry. Their eyes slid past him to Isobel, they expected him to introduce her and then stand back.

What made this even more galling was that Isobel would never have written in the first place without Philip's encouragement. In the early days she used to read to him in the evening and he would often suggest a change or a correction. He thought deeply about the things that she cared about. He had skills of critical reading and self-discipline which he taught her. He bought her a word processor and introduced her to it, helping her to make the transition from her old typewriter. He encouraged her to write every day, whether or not she was in the mood. To find that she was now something of a celebrity and he relegated to the position of driver and handbag carrier was quite unbearable.   His sudden illness put an end to Isobel's social success and his descent into second place, and spared them both the challenge of maintaining a husband's pride when his wife was suddenly regarded as more interesting, more successful and, even worse, a better earner.

Philip's illness kept him at home, protected him from Isobel's fame. It kept her at home, too.

'You could come up to town more than you do,' Troy remarked.

'It's the trains,' Isobel said easily. 'And I don't like to leave Philip too often.'

'Oh yes, how is he?' Troy uncorked a bottle of white wine and poured them both a glass.

'Just the same,' Isobel said. 'If things go well tomorrow then perhaps I'll make enough money to put in a swimming pool. He thinks that would really make a difference. There have been some studies. Heat and exercise in buoyancy can really make a difference, apparently.'

'And what is it that he's got, exactly?' Troy said. 'Sorry, I feel I should know, but I really don't. He's been ill ever since I first knew you. I never really liked to ask.'

He saw how the very question drained her of energy. Her face grew grey with weariness. 'Nobody knows. That's the hardest thing about it. He has some kind of neurological malfunction which is rather rare. Nobody knows quite what causes it, it could be genetic, or it could be a virus, or it could be an allergy. What it means is that the part of the brain which activates the big muscle groups, arms, legs, sort of misfires. The messages don't get through. So the muscles weaken and waste. The real struggle is to keep mobile. Swimming would be ideal, and he does exercises and walks every day. He's very brave.'

'What's the prognosis?'

'That's part of the difficulty. Nobody knows for sure. Some people just get spontaneously better – about a third of people get better. About a third get very bad and then stay there. And the final third get weaker and weaker and then die. We know now that he's not got the worst case, he won't die. But we didn't know that for the first two years.' She made a little grimace of pain. 'That was the worst time, but in a way it was a good time. We were very passionate together, because every day was precious. We really felt that we were on borrowed time. But now . . .' She broke off. 'Now we don't know how he'll be over the next few years.' She made her voice cheerful. 'He could stay the same. Or he could get better, you see. He could get better tomorrow. He won't die. It'll probably be like this forever.'

Troy looked across the worktop at her with compassion. 'But it means that you're only fifty, and married to a man who won't ever take you dancing.'

'Dancing's the least of it,' she said quietly.

There was a brief silence and then Isobel found a smile from somewhere. 'There's no point grieving over it,' she said briskly. 'I made my mind up to it years ago. I was sure he was going to die when he first had it. I promised myself then that if he was spared, if we were spared, that I would be happy. I would make him happy. This is so much better than it might have been.'

'Oh yes,' Troy assented emphatically, privately thinking that it was not.

At eight thirty in the morning Troy called Isobel; but she had been awake for an hour, listening to the unaccustomed noise of the London street, nursing a hangover, and wishing she felt free to go to the kitchen and make herself a cup of tea.

He opened the bedroom door and presented her with a cup of pale green liquid smelling of straw. 'Herbal tea,' he said. 'To get you in the mood.'

'I'm terrified,' Isobel said.

'You'll be wonderful. You were wonderful yesterday and that was only a practice.'

'And there'll be no-one who has ever met me? No-one from Penshurst Press?'

'Penshurst!' He waved them away. 'They don't have the kind of money we're looking for here. They're a small-time literary house. We're playing with the major league here.'

Isobel nodded and leaned back against the pillows.

'You're pale,' he said with sudden concern. 'Feeling all right?'

'I have a hangover,' she confessed. Philip would have been shocked and disapproving.

'Oh yes,' Troy said. 'I'll get you something. We did go it a bit.'

He disappeared from the bedroom and came back with a small effervescing drink. 'Here you are. And I've run you a hot bath. As soon as you've had it we'll have breakfast and then start to get Zelda ready. She needs to be beautiful by ten o'clock. The first editors are here at ten thirty.'

'Isn't that awfully early?' asked Isobel, who had learned over the years that it was impossible to reach the editors at her publishing house much before eleven in the morning.

Troy grinned. 'They're hungry. They'll be here.'

'You make me sound like a picnic,' Isobel remarked.

'Zelda is,' he said, lingering on her name. 'Zelda is a picnic and a dinner and a drink all rolled into one. Zelda is cordon bleu, and everybody wants her.'

Isobel, perfumed, blonde-headed, perfectly made up and dressed in the pink suit with the pink mules, was draped over the sofa at ten fifteen, and at ten thirty the first editors came in. She did not get up from her seat but merely lifted a languid hand to them. The woman shook hands, but the man was so overcome that he kissed the well-manicured fingertips and then sat down opposite her and gazed.

'How much of this is based on real life?' Susan Jarvis, the senior editor, asked.

Zelda Vere smiled. 'It's fiction, of course.'

'But I would guess that you have had some kind of experience with a Satanic cult?' Susan pressed.

Zelda's gesture indicated an invisible wall before her. 'I based the novel on my research and my own intuitive sense,' she said. 'And on my experiences, of course.'

'In this country?' Susan hinted.

'In this country, and abroad.'

'Of course Zelda's great talent is telling a great story,' Troy intervened, speaking to Charles, the junior editor.

'It is a great story,' he concurred. 'May I say, Miss Vere, what a great story it is? And what a great all-round package

– if I can use the word – you are? I think we can do great things with you.'

'What sort of things?' Troy asked encouragingly.

'Oh, we'd be looking at a major advertising campaign in all the media including television. We'd be looking at a major author tour in five, maybe six or seven, cities. We'd be submitting this book for the appropriate prizes, extracts in suitable magazines, a big publicity campaign and a big push in the non-book outlets in particular.'

'Non-book outlets?' Isobel asked, confused.

'Supermakets,' Troy said briefly. 'More than bookshops.'

'You would sell my book in supermarkets? Like cans of beans?'

Troy's eyes snapped a warning at her. 'Miss Vere, Justin and Freeman Press would undertake to place this book where it would sell the most copies. That's what we all want.'

'Of course we'd try for the bookshops,' Charles said feebly. 'But the great strength of this book, as we see it, is the common touch.' He turned back to Zelda Vere. 'You really know how the ordinary woman thinks. It struck a chord with all of us at Justin and Freeman. I gave the manuscript to my secretary and to my wife, and I can tell you, I knew, when those two ordinary women came back to me and said that they saw themselves in this wonderful story, that we had a winner on our hands.'

'Both very normal and at the same time very bizarre,' Susan confirmed. 'That was what attracted me: the bizarre quality of the story. And, more than anything else, fresh; but absolutely central to the genre.'

'And which genre is that?' Troy asked.

Susan looked at him as if there could be no doubt. 'Survivor fiction,' she said bluntly. 'This is a survivor fiction novel. We couldn't make it work any other way. This is Zelda's own story, fictionalised and told in third person – though we may need to see an editorial amendment there – but this is the real-life story of a woman horrifically abused who survives and revenges herself.'

Isobel felt her hand tighten on the stem of the champagne glass. 'But if it were real life, if it were true, then Charity would face dozens of criminal charges.' She stopped herself, realising her snap of irritation was quite unlike Zelda Vere's slow drawl. 'I'm sorry. What I meant to say was – it can't be offered as a true story. Not possibly. Can it? Because Charity kidnaps two children and burns down a house, and bankrupts a business and blackmails a politician, and scars a woman.'

'I assumed there was a fictional element,' Susan said briskly. 'And we'd make that clear. But this is a survivor fiction, isn't it? There is a core of truth, and that a terrible truth.'

'Yes,' said Troy.

'No,' said Isobel.

Troy crossed the room and took her hand and kissed it. Under the warm touch of his lips she felt the warning pinch of his fingers. 'She's such an artist she does not know the truth she has told,' he said firmly. 'She's still in denial.'

Five

There was no time for Troy and Isobel to speak before the
next pair of editors arrived, and then the next. All morning
they trooped in, drank a glass of champagne, praised the novel
to the skies, promised astounding sales, and all of them, every
single one, tried to persuade Isobel to confess that the novel
was autobiographical. When Troy closed the front door on
the last editor he found Isobel in her bedroom, wig on the
stand, precious pink suit discarded on the unmade bed, frantically scrubbing at her red face with tissues.

'What's the matter?' he asked tightly.

She turned to him, her eyes blackly encircled with wet
mascara. 'This is impossible,' she said. 'We invented her, Zelda
Vere, and now they're all at it. They want her to be a Satanic
cult survivor and it's nonsense. I can't stand it. I can't begin
to pretend these things are true. And I can't begin to pretend
to be in denial about it either, so don't try that way out. We'll
have to call it off.'

He was about to snap at her but he held himself back. 'How
much is the swimming pool?'

She paused and turned towards him. 'Fifty thousand pounds
. . . I don't know.'

'And it would help Philip's condition?'

'He thinks so.'

Troy nodded. 'That last editor, from Rootsman, said they
would be starting the bidding for the world rights at £200,000.
That's *starting* the bidding. You could go to half a million.'

Isobel dropped a grubby ball of cotton wool on the dressing-table top and looked at him in silence.

'I'll go and buy some sandwiches,' Troy said. 'I think we could both of us do with some lunch.'

Isobel appeared in the kitchen doorway wearing her country skirt with the baggy waistband, a cotton shirt, and a sweater draped over her shoulders. Her brown hair was tied back in her usual bun, her face was clean and shiny without even a dab of lipstick. She could have wilfully designed her appearance to remind Troy that she was a middle-aged academic, up from the country for a visit and already longing to be home again.

He put the plate of sandwiches before her and poured her a strong black coffee.

'The money is fantastic,' he said after she had eaten.

She nodded.

'And all the work has been done. All they want is a few editorial changes. *I'll* do them if you don't want to. I can set up the bank account tomorrow, they all understand that the money's to be paid into a numbered account overseas. They think it's a tax issue, so that's all right. Then you collect the money and you're free to write whatever you want to write.'

Still Isobel said nothing.

'The rest of your life, you can write exactly what you like. Or take a break,' he said persuasively. 'Go for a cruise. Go somewhere warm with Philip. Take a holiday. It'd do you both good. You can invest this and have an income, or you can buy the things you need. And if it goes to a TV mini series, which is very likely, then you'll be provided for all the rest of your life. You can replace his shares and his savings so he'll never know you raided them. You can take out insurance so that you know that he's safe whatever happens to you. You need never work again, unless you want to.'

'They'll want a sequel,' she said flatly.

He shrugged. 'It's a one-book contract. They can want all they like. You can decide to write another, or we could hire a ghost writer and I could brief her. Or they can do without. It's up to you. You're the star.'

Troy saw the brief gleam of ambition in her eyes before she looked down.

'You're an author who has been immensely influential in the literary world,' he continued. 'But you will never earn the money you need to keep yourself, let alone to support Philip. This one book can redress that injustice and nobody will ever know. This gives you the money you deserve. And if they do alter the book – why should you care? This was a book to make money, why should you mind what they call it: fantasy, gothic, survivor fiction, who cares? As long as it sells?'

She turned on him then. 'Because if it's commercial fiction then it doesn't matter that it is nonsense,' she said fiercely. 'They put a jacket on it which says it is nonsense. It's read as entertaining nonsense. Once we start saying it is based on fact we are telling lies about the nature of the world itself. We are misleading people. We're not producing fiction, we're telling lies. We are doing something morally wrong.'

He nodded, thinking fast. 'People pretend all the time,' he argued. 'In their own lives. They say they are a certain sort of person because it keeps them where they are. You say that you love your husband and that you are a highly moral woman because that keeps you at home when someone with less motivation would have cut and run.' He heard her gasp but he would not be interrupted. 'People's lives are fiction. All autobiographies are fiction. When some supermodel says that what she really wanted to do was to work for charity, when some rich man's wife writes that she married him for love: it's fiction. Sportsmen's autobiographies, ballerinas' own stories: they tell the truth of their lives as they want it to appear, not what it was really like. We all know it. That's what we're selling. Whether the manuscript says "Charity thinks, Charity does" or "I thought, I did" makes no dif-ference.'

Isobel was on to it like a flash. 'It makes a difference to me!

I have to stand by this nonsense and pretend that it is real. I have to say that it was me!'

'*Zelda* says: "it was me", not you. And you were happy to pretend to be her, brought up in France, worked as a secretary, married once, unhappily, parents dead in car crash. Now we pretend as well that she had a sister, that she was entrapped by a cult of Satanists. What difference does it make?'

She hesitated. 'I'll have to think about it,' she said slowly. 'It does make a difference. There is a difference between fiction and telling lies.'

'It's fantasy whichever way you look at it,' he said. He took a breath, forcing himself to stay calm. From this one morning's work he stood to earn £20,000. The prestige from being known as Zelda Vere's agent had already had an impact in the way he was treated by publishers. No-one had ever before returned Troy's calls within the same day. Overnight he had become a major figure in the publishing scene.

'Please, Isobel, think,' he said quietly. 'The auction is tomorrow. I can't be seen to let people down. I can't conduct an auction and then withdraw the book. The auction is a binding agreement. If we're going to cancel then it has to be by nine o'clock tomorrow morning. And then you'll have lost everything. You'll be back where you were when we started. You'll never again earn enough to live on from your writing, Penshurst simply won't pay more. And worse than that: you've just wasted four months on a novel that you won't publish. I'll have wasted a small fortune on Zelda's clothes. You've destroyed my confidence in your work.'

She looked quickly at him and he saw her lower lip quiver. 'You?' she asked. 'I've lost you?'

Troy was relentless. 'I asked you in the cab before we went to Harrods if you were sure. I told you then that it was my reputation as Zelda's agent that was on the line. I bank rolled you. I said we were in it together. If you pull out now it doesn't just hurt you and Philip, it's bad for me too.'

She shook her head as if it were too much for her. He thought for a guilty moment that he was bullying her as

73

persistently as her husband must bully her. Philip must do something like this: intellectual argument and then emotional blackmail. This must be his technique to make her responsible for everything. She was so endearingly vulnerable. She could struggle forever with that sharp, trained intelligence, but she could not tolerate the thought of being abandoned, of losing someone's love.

He saw her shoulders hunch under the burden he had laid on her. 'I'm sorry,' she said. 'Sorry to appear indecisive. I'll ring you tonight. I'll think about it as I go home on the train. I'll decide by six o'clock.'

He nodded. 'I hope you decide to take the plunge,' he said. 'For the swimming pool, for Zelda, for Philip. I hope you decide to take good money for good work. I'd be really disappointed if you failed at this stage.'

Isobel nodded. He noticed that she did not meet his eyes. 'I'd better go,' she said.

There was an odd atmosphere between them as she came from the spare bedroom with her little overnight bag. They were like lovers parting after some mutually unsatisfactory experience. The cramped hall was filled with the atmosphere of mild blame, of dissatisfaction. At the door, on a sudden impulse, Troy put his hand on her waist and at once she turned her face up to his. He leaned forward and kissed her. Extraordinarily, her mouth was warm and inviting under his. She dropped her bag, her hands slid up his arms to his shoulders and then one cool palm pulled his head down to her lips. He kissed her hard, passionately, his irritation dissolving into a surprised desire. She kissed him back and for a moment he did not see her as the tired middle-aged woman, but with his eyes closed in her kiss he imagined that he was touching the golden, languid, arrogant beauty who had sprawled all the morning on his sofa with a high-heeled pink mule swinging, showing the curve of her instep.

Isobel stepped back and they looked at each other, a little breathless. She would have said something but awkwardly, shyly, he opened the front door, and in that moment's dislocation she slipped away. The door closed behind her and Troy froze, listening to her sensible shoes clumping down the stone steps to the street but hearing in his mind the light feminine skitter of high heels.

On the other side of the door, Isobel stepped into the road and raised a hand for a taxi. 'Waterloo,' she said to the driver, her face blank.

She had her hand clamped over her mouth as if to hold the kiss and the power of the kiss inside her. Unprecedentedly, for a woman who was mostly intellect, and often worry, she thought of nothing, nothing at all. She sat back in the seat and stared unseeingly, as the taxi turned in the street and headed south through the early-afternoon traffic. Still she kept her hand over her mouth, still she felt, under the unconscious grip of her fingers, the heat and the power of his kiss.

'Good talk?' Philip asked her when she arrived home.

'Fine,' she said distractedly. The breakfast things had not been washed up, his soup bowl and bread plate from lunchtime were still on the table along with the litter of Philip's morning: orange peel, a couple of pens, a rubber band from the post, some empty envelopes, some flyers which had been shed from the newspaper. Isobel looked at the room and the work that needed to be done without weariness, without irritation. She looked at it all with calm detachment, as if it were the kitchen of another woman. It was clearly not the kitchen of a woman who had, this very morning, been offered more than a quarter of a million pounds for a novel, lounged on a sofa like a beauty queen and been passionately kissed.

'Sorry about the mess,' Philip said, following her gaze. 'Mrs M. thought she might go off early after staying overnight and I said: "Yes". I didn't quite realise . . .'

'That's all right,' Isobel said. 'Won't take a minute.'

She started to clear the table, watching her hands collecting debris, throwing it in the bin, watching herself stacking plates in the dishwasher, adding dishwasher liquid, still feeling on her lips the scorch of Troy's touch.

'Did it go well?' Philip asked again.

'Oh yes,' she said. She heard her voice assemble lies. 'They were very bright, they asked some interesting questions. Then there was a buffet lunch. I saw Norman Villiers. He was doing the afternoon session. He was well, said some interesting things about Larkin. Then I came home.'

'You should do that sort of thing more often,' Philip said generously. 'It's certainly done you good. You look quite radiant.'

'Do I?' she asked, her interest suddenly sharpened.

'Yes,' he said. 'Glowing.'

Isobel's hand stole to her mouth, her fingers covered her lips as if their bruised pinkness would betray her. 'Well, I did enjoy it,' she said, her voice very level. 'There was some talk of a series of lectures. Replacing someone on maternity leave. I didn't say yes or no, but I would like to think about it.'

'Surely you don't want a regular commitment,' he protested.

'Just a short series. In a few months' time,' she said. 'I might go up and stay overnight and then come back in the afternoon, like today, once a week.'

He rose from the table and stretched. 'As you like,' he said. 'Makes no difference to me. There were a couple of phone calls. The ansaphone took them. I was outside in the barn. I've been measuring up. I marked it out with spray paint so you can see the size the pool would be on the ground. And I've got on with the drawings.'

'You have been busy,' she praised him as she moved towards the door, wondering if it was Troy who had called.

'I told you it would be an interest for me,' he said. 'And I found a swimming pool company who will do it at a discount if we order within four months.'

'Even so,' she said, '£50,000 . . .'

'I'll show you the figures when you've finished work,' he said, wanting to detain her. 'But I think you'll see that if we do it now we can get real value for money. We could always borrow the money, the house could be security for the loan.'

Isobel nodded and went into her study, closing the door behind her. The ansaphone showed two calls. One had left no message, the other was an invitation to judge a minor literary prize. She noted for a moment the disproportionate sense of disappointment that swept her at the realisation that neither call was from Troy.

She rested her head in her hands and looked at the telephone, willing it to ring. One part of her was fully conscious of the absurdity that she was a woman in her fifties, sitting by a telephone like a girl of thirteen waiting for a call from a boy. Another part of her mind revelled in the fact that she was treasuring a kiss, like a girl of thirteen, that the thought of him ringing her made her heart pound, that even Philip, who rarely noticed anything about her, had called her radiant.

She realised that she could ring him. There was no convention that said that she could not initiate a call. She picked up the telephone and dialled the number of Troy's office. They put her through to him straight away.

'Isobel,' he said. She listened intently for an undercurrent of extra warmth in his voice, and found she could not be sure. The uncertainty was as thrilling as if he had told her he loved her. 'I've been waiting and waiting for you to call.'

'I only just got in,' she said breathlessly. 'And then I had to talk to Philip.'

'Sure. So. What do you think?'

'Think?'

For a moment she believed he was asking her about the kiss.

'About the auction, about the book, about letting them sell it as survivor fiction?'

'I don't know,' she said. 'I can't seem to decide. What do you think?'

Troy felt the tense muscles of his shoulder blades suddenly blissfully uncurl. All afternoon he had been afraid that Isobel would stand on her principles, or stand on her pride and refuse to go ahead. Now, at the role of doubt in her voice, he warmed to her.

'Oh, I think you would regret it all your life if you didn't take this opportunity,' he said. 'It's just a question of some minor editorial changes and a bit of extra acting. And we saw today how wonderful you are when you are Zelda Vere. It's just all of that, only a little more.'

'I don't know that I can do it,' she said.

'I so want you to find the courage to do it,' he said. 'I feel like the whole idea is our creation, I feel so proud of you. Writing the book like that, and then creating Zelda Vere. And I do love the deception, it's probably some terrible psychological flaw in me, but I just love it. I love that we have created her. I loved having her in my house. When you left today I felt quite . . .'

She waited. 'What?' she whispered.

'Bereft.'

She drew in a sharp breath.

He could sense her concentration on his words, the bright spotlight of her undivided intelligent attention. 'I would be so disappointed if we didn't go ahead,' he said, dropping his voice to a low, seductive whisper. 'I've enjoyed it so much this far. The shopping, and the dressing, and the . . .'

'The?'

'Warmth.'

Her hand was at her mouth again, touching her lips. 'All right,' she said softly. 'I'll do it. But you must promise to be with me. I can't do it on my own.'

'I'll be with you,' he swore. 'Every single step. I'll be there. Every step of the way.'

Troy heard her whispered 'goodbye' and put the telephone down. He was conscious that in that one telephone call he had earned £20,000 and who knew how much more? But he knew himself well enough to recognise that he was feeling more than an entrepreneur's enthusiasm for a good deal. There was something about Zelda Vere and about Isobel's transformation into Zelda which was pulling at him: some deep, genuine attraction.

'She is sexy,' he said softly to himself, thinking of Isobel in the blonde wig and the pink mules. 'Who would have believed it? Who would have dreamed she could have walked like that and sat like that?' He looked over at the silent phone. 'Who would have believed she could kiss like that?'

Troy took the opening call from the first publishing house at 9 a.m. prompt. They bid £200,000 as they had promised they would. Troy made a note of their bid and kept his voice calm and impersonal. When the second publishing house telephoned he told them the bid already made, and they went to £205,000. The third publishing house dropped out straight away but the fourth bidder went up another five thousand. The calls came in throughout the day but by two o'clock there were only two major publishers left in the bidding and the price was £335,000.

'I tell you what I'll do,' said Susan Jarvis of Justin and Freeman. 'I'll offer £350,000 and you tell me yes or no. I can't go higher than that.'

'I'll tell you "Yes" now,' Troy said quickly, knowing that the rival publishers would not go over that. 'Miss Vere liked you so much, I know that you would be her preferred publishers.'

'It's a deal then,' Susan said with quiet pleasure. 'Would you tell Miss Vere that we're very happy. Can I telephone her?'

'I'll ask her to phone you,' Troy said. 'She's very protective of her privacy, as you can understand.'

'Oh yes,' Susan said. 'After all that she's been through. I understand perfectly.'

'Yes.' Troy grasped at the straw. 'She won't take phone calls unless they're cleared, and she won't release her address, of course.'

'So how are we going to do publicity?' Susan queried. 'We'll need a big publicity tour.'

'Get her a hotel room as her base,' Troy said. 'She can do everything from a hotel, and when you take her on tour she'll need me to go with her. She needs support. She's still quite fragile.'

'She's wonderful,' Susan Jarvis said. 'And how much of her story is actually true, d'you know?'

'Certainly the Satanism, and the sex,' Troy said happily. 'And at least one of the revenge episodes. I know, because I saw the newspaper cutting. Someone else was prosecuted for it so there's no danger of a police investigation. She got clean away with it.'

'It's remarkable. To endure all that and write so well. Is she working on a sequel?'

'We'll discuss it,' Troy said. 'What d'you think is going to be the next big genre?'

'High living,' the editor said without a second's doubt. 'We've had a whole load of novels about the dangers of sex and the misery of promiscuity. We've had a lot about simple joys. Now people want a bit of lightness in their lives again. Sex and shopping, but up the social scale. High living, fast cars. Think *Hello* magazine crossed with *Playboy* from the old days. And health too. Health stays big.'

'Zelda could do that,' Troy said delightedly. 'That's perfect for her.'

'Just what I thought,' Susan declared. 'This is more than a one-book deal, this is the creation of a new star.'

'We've done it,' Troy whispered on the telephone to Isobel. 'It's £350,000.'

There was a stunned silence.

'How much do I get straight away?' she asked.

'Best part of £150,000,' he said. 'You can order that swimming pool today.'

He heard her sigh, but she said nothing more.

'You must be pleased?'

'I am,' she said. 'I'm just – incredulous, I suppose.'

'You earned it,' he said loyally. 'It's what the market pays. There's nothing to be incredulous about.'

'I feel like I want to rush out and tell Philip that he can have the swimming pool and that we've made our fortune,' she said. 'It's so odd that I can't tell him. I feel like I've got no-one to celebrate with. I shall have to act as if nothing has happened.'

'You can tell him you did well on your literary novel,' Troy offered. 'Tell him that it's the royalties for that which are paying for the pool. Crack open a bottle of champagne for that. It's a good book.'

'Yes, but only you and I know what's really happening,' she said. 'No-one knows, but you and me.'

'Come up for lunch,' he said, hearing the appeal in her voice. 'Come up to the flat and change and you can go out as Zelda Vere. I'll take you somewhere wonderful and everyone can come and congratulate you.'

Isobel gave a little gasp. 'I don't know if I dare!'

'Got to start somewhere,' he said. 'Then we'll go and buy some more clothes. You're going to need them.'

'Tomorrow?' she whispered.

'Tomorrow,' he replied.

Six

When Susan Jarvis heard that her new author was coming into town for a celebration lunch she insisted that it should be at her expense and that Zelda should also meet the other people in the team who would work on her book. Troy, conscious of the mounting expense of entertaining Zelda, was relieved to hand over the cost to Justin and Freeman Press. Six people would sit down to lunch with Zelda Vere: the publisher David Quarles, the two editors Susan Jarvis and Charles Franks, the publicist, the marketing man, and the head of the sales team. They booked the large window table at the Savoy River Room, and the publicist notified the gossip columnists that the newest, hottest, and most expensive novelist of the year would be at lunch.

Troy laid out Zelda Vere's clothes with loving attention. This time she should wear the yellow suit, he thought. He unwrapped it from its cover and put the skirt on one hanger and the jacket on another to air. There was a neat satin bustier to wear beneath it, the lace could just be glimpsed at the neck of the jacket. He spread it out on the bed and felt his own response to the silk under his fingers. He put out the sandals, the thin-heeled gold sandals, and a pair of absurdly silky fine tights. 'She'll have to wear gloves to put them on,' he said thoughtfully.

He laid out the makeup on the dressing table: the foundation cream in its gold-topped bottle, the dusting powder, the blusher, the concealer pen, and then the jewel colours of eyeliner, eyeshadow, mascara, and lipsticks. He looked at them with a pang of conscious envy. It was so unfair that women should be able to change themselves so completely. Even on a bad day they could, with the skill and the equipment, make themselves look years younger, ten times happier. Artifice was part of their nature, their accepted social nature; whereas for a man to attempt to deceive was regarded as morally wrong.

Troy seated himself at the table and looked at his own neat face over the gold tops of the bottles. His hair was golden brown, his skin very smooth and fair, no shadow of stubble, no darkness at the sideboards. Acting on impulse he reached forward and swept the wig on to his head, like a little boy playing at dressing up in his mother's room. He held the front of the wig and pulled it down at the back as he had helped Isobel to do, and then he looked at himself in the mirror.

He had expected to laugh at the reflection, he had expected to see a man absurdly dressed in drag, he had expected a pantomime dame. Instead he saw his twin, his sister, his anima. It was a pretty woman who looked back at him. A blonde woman with bouffant, wide hair but a narrow, interesting face. A strong chin set off a sensual mouth, narrow nose, wide blue eyes, high cheekbones. A beautiful woman, a woman like him, recognisably like him, but undeniably a woman.

'Good God,' he whispered. 'I could be Zelda Vere.'

The illusion of Zelda that he had created with Isobel was so much of a type that almost anyone could be her. She was characterised by the big blonde hair, by the good bones. The details of eye colour and expression were almost lost under the impact of the overall appearance.

Thoughtfully he took up the lipstick brush and painted on the cherry-red lips, dusted his whole face with powder. He looked at his reflection again. He expected to see a gro-tesquerie. But it was not so. A woman looked back at him with a bright, confident smile, a shock of blonde hair, eyes which were more sparkling and bluer than before, enhanced by the even skin tone and the vivid lips.

The door bell rang, Troy jumped; as guilty as if he had been caught stealing. He pulled the wig from his head and smeared the lipstick from his mouth. He was still rubbing at his face with a big tissue as he ran down the stairs to his front door. He whisked it out of sight and opened the door to Isobel.

She was looking excited and fresh. Her mouse-brown hair was swept back off her face and held with two slides, not confined in a bun. She was wearing navy-blue slacks, a white shirt and a navy-blue blazer. She had been thinking ahead to this moment all the way up on the train. She had put her writer's imagination to how she would look, how she would feel; how he would look and feel. She had even heard in her head the things that they might say to each other.

But Troy just took her in, in one long, comprehensive gaze, and she looked back at him, her chin raised, her eyes unwavering. It was the one thing she had not predicted, that long, devouring look. As soon as she met his eyes she had the shock of encountering something she had not predicted, a man she had not imagined.

'Come in,' he said, stepping back into the hall.

Isobel followed him in. He noticed a hint of perfume, the sweet smell of Chanel No. 5. She saw the tissue in his hand.

'You'll laugh,' he said uncertainly. 'I tried on the wig, Zelda's wig. And then I put on some lipstick.'

She did not laugh. 'How did you look?'

'I looked like her, I looked like . . . you, when you were her,' he said. 'It was extraordinary.'

'Will you show me?'

Troy opened the door to the spare bedroom, Zelda's bedroom.

'I don't know if we have time . . .'

'I should so like to see . . .'

Troy tried to laugh away his embarrassment; but Isobel's gaze was steady and unsmiling. He realised that her naivety protected them both from the farcical nature of this scene. Isobel would not laugh because she was genuinely engaged by the question of what he would look like, dressed as Zelda.

She had no knowledge of the shady absurdities of trans-vestism, of cross-dressing, of transsexualism, of drag queens and pantomime dames. She was completely innocent of any speculation about that world and so she brought no preconceived ideas or prejudices to this experience. It was as pure for her as a first love, untainted by knowledge.

And she was right. It was a different thing from anything anyone had ever done before. Their creation, Zelda, was not born out of a forbidden lust, or some private, secret perversion. She had come upon them quite innocently, quite unexpectedly. She transcended the boundaries of gender. She had been made by them both, both of them had an equal claim to her. Troy had coached Isobel in Zelda's walk, he had painted Zelda's makeup on Isobel's face. Now it seemed perfectly natural and right that Isobel wanted to see Zelda as manifested by Troy.

He paused for only a moment. 'I must make it clear that I'm not into dressing in women's clothes,' he said, laying down a boundary as if he thought it would somehow keep them safe.

'Of course not,' she said simply. 'This is not anything to do with that. This is about being Zelda.'

He turned and pulled on the blonde wig, clumsy in his embarrassment. Without meeting his own eyes he looked into the mirror and painted a little dab of scarlet on his lips, which were still slightly stained from before. He turned to her judging look. He shrugged his shoulders, trying to hide his sense of shy embarrassment. 'Ridiculous,' he remarked.

Slowly Isobel shook her head. 'You look beautiful,' she said. 'A beautiful woman in a man's beautiful suit. You look wonderfully –' she searched for the word '– ambiguous.'

'You put on the other wig,' he suggested.

They stood side by side before the dressing table, like a pair of girls sharing the mirror in the Ladies cloakroom. Isobel pulled on the blonde wig and fluffed out the bouffant hair. With her eyes on Troy's reflection she reached forward and painted her own lips to match his scarlet. They stood in silence: twin girls, twin women.

Watching himself, watching the movement in the mirror, Troy slid his arm around her waist. Isobel, watching them both, turned inside his arm and the mirror saw his beautiful face full-on under a cascade of blonde hair, and her absorbed profile. Troy watched from the corner of his eye as his blonde hair fell forward when he turned a little and bent to kiss her. He felt the warm taste of the lipstick as they kissed gently, and then deeply, taking in the heat of each other's mouths, the touch of the tongue, the smooth glide of the waxy coloured lips.

Troy released Isobel and she stepped back a little, her grey eyes very dark with desire.

'This is extraordinary,' he said, a slight quaver in his voice.

She nodded, she did not trust herself to speak.

They stood in silence for a moment.

'You'd better start to get ready,' Troy said, clearing his throat. 'We have to be at the Savoy at one.'

He turned back to the mirror and pulled the wig from his head, placed it gently on the stand, wiped the scarlet from his mouth. He saw her looking at him in the mirror, he saw the naked desire in her eyes.

'I'll make us a nice cup of tea,' he said.

When Troy came back into the bedroom, carrying the tray, he recoiled at the sight of her. Isobel was gone, completely gone. In her place was Zelda Vere. Zelda was seated before the dressing table naked but for the silky bustier and a tiny pair of high-cut satin pants. Her breasts were tightly encased in the lace, her hips moulded by the stretchy satin. Her arms were raised above her head, teasing further height out of her mane of blonde hair. Her eyes, dark-lidded, freighted with the weight of the false eyelashes, shadow, eyeliner, mascara, looked back at themselves in silent adoration from the mirror. Her skin, Isobel's smooth, always-concealed skin, gleamed like white marble in the shadowy room. Her long, pale, bare legs were flexed to hold her feet on demi-point on the floor. The slack of her thighs, Isobel's office-chair thighs, was concealed

86

by the tense pose, perched on the dressing-room chair like a piece of fifties pornography, modest by today's standards, but gleaming with the gloss of glamour.

For Troy, who had first seen a half-naked woman on the paperback books in the carousel at the corner shop, and glimpsed calendar girls at the back of the petrol station, she was an echo of adolescent desire, resonant with meaning. She was an icon, gilded with the longing of a boy's half-recognised guilty desire.

Isobel heard the chink of the tea pot against the cups as Troy trembled at the sight of her, and she turned and put down the comb with unshakable serenity. 'Come in,' she said silkily to Troy in her Zelda voice. 'I'm dying for a cup of tea.'

'Perhaps you'd like champagne?' Troy stammered, trying to keep pace with this transition.

'D'you have some chilled Roederer?'

Troy nodded.

'Perhaps later,' she said.

He poured the tea and put a cup at her right hand on the dressing table. She leaned forward and added another flicker of blusher with the thick sable brush, then she leaned back.

'How do I look?'

'Beautiful,' Troy said.

She turned from the reflection and looked at him. 'You want me,' she stated.

Troy cleared his throat. 'I don't know what I want,' he said honestly. 'I can't answer you. I don't even know who you are. I don't know who I am, nor what I want. I thought we were doing a brilliant scam here, to get Isobel Latimer a proper deal for once in her career; but we seem to have unleashed something else. Something much more powerful.' He paused. He drew a shaky breath. 'Please, it's my job to make sure that we get the contract signed. Let's concentrate on that first, and talk about the rest later?'

She thought for a moment, and then to his relief and to his disappointment, he saw the sultry, sexual look pass from her face. She nodded, as Isobel would have nodded at an appeal to her common sense.

'Of course,' she said briskly. 'You're right. I apologise.'

'Isobel?' he asked tentatively, as if there could be some doubt.

She nodded. 'I'm sorry,' she said. 'It's very – er – taking – being her.'

'I know,' he said. He drank his own tea. 'You can be her all lunchtime, and then we'll go and buy her some more clothes.'

'All right,' she said. 'And then we'll come back here and talk?'

Troy felt himself shrink from the suggestion that any of this heated ambiguity could be pinned down in Isobel's matter-of-fact words.

'All right,' he agreed.

Zelda Vere was seated between the publisher David Quarles and her editor Susan Jarvis at lunch and they plied her equally with champagne and promises. She smiled and accepted both. Troy watched with what he recognised as absurd concern as Zelda drank three glasses of champagne and let them pour a fourth. When they had finished eating and coffee was served, a photographer appeared and Zelda was photographed, listening attentively to Susan Jarvis and laughing merrily at a joke from someone else. The whole restaurant, alerted to the fact that a celebrity was lunching, took care not to look in their direction, while managing to scan them and speculate about the event.

When the coffee had been poured the publicist, quietly delighted that she had managed to get a photographer to come to the hotel, and that he had established so effectively the importance of the new author, laid before Zelda the plans for the publicity tour they would want her to embark on in January.

Zelda glanced at the first page and looked in horror towards Troy.

'We have to preserve Zelda's privacy at all costs,' he said quickly, reading over her shoulder.

'Of course.' They all nodded.

'Daytime television,' Zelda quietly pointed out.

'Yes,' the publicist said. 'We were especially lucky to get that. They're doing a special feature on lucky breaks the week after next. I hoped you would talk about a rags to riches story. How your talent has brought you an amazing advance.'

'It's just so . . .' Zelda broke off.

Troy, separated from her by the table, could only look at her inquiringly.

'So . . . public,' she said. She scowled at Troy but could find no way to warn him that Philip watched daytime television while Mrs M. was clearing up the breakfast things, and then generally left it on while he was doing his crossword and drinking his coffee. He affected to despise it, but the truth was that he seldom missed a programme, and often talked at lunch about the immense folly and waste of time of the whole premise and how amazing it was that anyone watched such drivel.

Troy grasped at once what she was saying. 'No-one from your childhood would recognise you now,' he said quickly. 'It's OK, Zelda, I promise you.'

'And it is a wonderful opportunity,' the publicist added. She was a young woman, a little flustered that Zelda was not thrilled at the opportunity of appearing on television. 'I thought you'd be pleased.'

'I am pleased,' Zelda said. 'It's just I didn't expect it all to happen so soon.'

'We have the contract ready to go,' David Quarles said. 'We're working on the artwork for the jacket already, we'll have something to show you within a month. We're hoping to publish in the winter season. No point wasting time or good publicity opportunities.'

Zelda looked towards Troy. He nodded firmly. She pinned her cherry smile on her painted face. 'Of course.'

*   *   *

They had ordered a limousine to take her home from the Savoy. Zelda stepped into it and arranged her long legs. Troy got in the other side. 'Harrods,' he said to the driver. 'And then wait.'

He pressed the button and the glass screen slid up between the passenger seats and the front seat.

'Don't worry,' he said.

Isobel's apprehensive expression gleamed through the confident mask of Zelda. 'It's Philip,' she said. 'He never misses a programme.'

'He'd never, never recognise you in a million years,' Troy assured her. 'Honestly. No-one would. And you've not said a word, have you? Not one word?'

'No,' she said.

'And we've kept all of Zelda's stuff at my house so he won't even recognise the clothes. You underestimate how little attention men pay. Really. He'll have the television on in the background and he'll look up and glance at the screen and see a woman who looks like all the others. Zelda is part of a look. She's a genre. He wouldn't even be able to tell her apart from the others. They all look the same.'

'But I'll have to be away that night.'

'Can't you lie to him? Make up a literary conference or something?'

'I said I might do a series of lectures at Goldsmiths,' she confessed. 'I was sort of preparing.'

'Very sensible,' Troy commended. 'Tell him that you're doing them and that they're on different days. We'll always have plenty of notice of these things. Look, this is a fortnight ahead. Come and stay with me the night before, I'll help you with your makeup. I'll come to the television studios with you. I'll be there every step of the way. We'll do it together.'

She nodded, but she still looked doubtful.

'Let me show you something,' Troy said. He drew an envelope out of his pocket and spread the thick document out on his dark-suited knee. 'This is your contract. D'you see what it says here? It says £350,000. D'you know how many Isobel

Latimer novels you would have to write to earn that?'

Isobel shook her head. 'I hadn't thought of it that way.'

'Seventeen. D'you know how many years you would have to work?'

'Thirty-four years,' she said precisely. 'Longer, if I got stuck.'

'It's a lifetime's pay,' Troy said. 'For one book. And all you have to do now to earn it is to wear some beautiful clothes and go on television and be polite to some idiot of half your intelligence before a daytime audience that is barely watching.'

'If Philip recognises me . . .' she began quietly.

'If he recognises you he can lump it,' Troy said brutally. 'He wanted a swimming pool, didn't he? He wanted the lovely house, didn't he? He left you to earn it, didn't he?'

'He can't earn,' she said indignantly. 'You know how ill he is. That's terribly unfair.'

'But he does spend,' Troy said, going to the very heart of the burden on Isobel. 'He wanted something that you would never ever be able to provide unless you wrote this sort of novel. So you did it. And you did it for him. And you even lied to protect him from the hurt of knowing about it. If he ever finds out he should go down on his knees and kiss your feet.'

He was afraid that he had gone too far. She turned her blonde head away from him and looked out of the window at the slowly moving traffic.

'You don't understand,' she said in a small voice.

Troy could have let it go. He could have agreed that he did not understand. But some strand of mischief in him led him on to nurture her doubts. 'I think I understand very well,' he said flatly. 'And I know that if the worst comes to the worst and he recognises you as Zelda, then he will take Zelda's money just as he has taken Isobel's money and he'll find one way or another to make himself feel all right about it. Because he doesn't mind leaving you to carry the can. He doesn't care what you've got to do as long as he has he gets what he wants.'

The car drew up outside Harrods and she forgot to wait for the driver to open the door. She got out of the car with Isobel's hurried graceless speed. Troy jumped out too, strode after her and caught her as she pushed her way through the doors into the store. He touched her arm and she turned to him.

'Calm down,' he said. 'We both had a bit to drink. This is a big deal for both of us. Let's go and get a cup of tea and then look at some clothes for Zelda.'

'You didn't mean what you said about him?' she demanded.

Troy shrugged. Words cannot be unsaid, their effect lasts even when they have been denied. 'Of course not,' he said. 'Who knows him better than you do? I was just worried about you.'

She nodded. He opened the door for her and stepped back as she went through with Zelda's swaying stride.

Seven

This time they were more confident of Zelda's taste. They chose her clothes themselves, wandering in great sweeps of the designer-clothes floors, selecting and rejecting. They agreed that Zelda did not need another suit but that she should have a couple of dresses, one with a matching coat for the cold days of spring when she would be on tour, and another evening dress. Isobel especially wanted to buy some silk pyjamas and a matching silk gown. 'For lounging around in,' she said.

Troy made no comment, it was obvious to them both that any lounging around that Zelda might do would take place at his flat with him.

They found one beautifully cut simple shift dress which Isobel would have bought. Troy shook his head. 'Too tasteful,' he said. 'Isobel Latimer would wear it. Zelda is much more barmaidy.'

'She needs a winter coat,' Isobel said.

'A fur,' Troy ruled.

'Surely not!' Isobel was shocked. 'Nobody wears fur.'

'Nobody used to wear fur,' Troy corrected her. 'That was the immensely tedious political correctness of the eighties. People wear fur now. Rich women wear fur.'

Isobel was about to argue. 'Let's go and look,' Troy said persuasively. 'See if there's anything we think she would like.'

They went outside to the street and strolled down the road into the first fur shop they encountered. When they stepped over the threshold they were both, at once, persuaded. The place was filled with the scent of cool pelts. It was an irresistible perfume of wealth. The coats were chained to the rail with small, light chains as if they were too priceless even to be looked at without permission. The assistants came forward to serve customers with keys at their waists like eighteenth-century chatelaines. A man sat at a desk by the door and served no-one at all but bowed his head and smiled as they came in as if it were his own exclusive private club.

One of the saleswomen accompanied by an assistant came forward and as Troy pointed to one fur coat and then another, they unlocked them in a reverent ritual and then slipped them off the hanger and slid them over Isobel's shoulders. They draped her in dark mink, in pale ocelot, they contrasted her blonde hair with the dark velvet gleam of sealskin. Then they found a coat with two colours, a coat beautifully made from soft short pelts, a coat of unmistakable expense.

'That's the one,' Troy sighed.

It was a pale honey-coloured mink, with a wide collar in contrasting dark mink which could be folded up to make a warm ruff around the neck. Isobel looked at the vision of her blonde hair cascading over the dark collar and the matching honey fur in the mirror.

'How much is it?' she asked.

The assistant glanced at Troy before answering. Troy inclined his head towards her ear. Isobel caught a whisper. It sounded very much like £40,000.

'Doesn't matter,' Troy said grandly. 'Working capital. We'll have it.' He gave his gold credit card to the assistant and they left her wrapping it while they went back to Harrods.

'How are you paying for this?' Isobel asked anxiously.

'Credit,' Troy said grandly. 'I'm making you an advance on your earnings.'

'Advance from where?' Isobel asked. 'Who's paying? The publishers?'

'My bank manager,' Troy said with a grimace. 'What can we do? You have to have the clothes.'

'I don't have to have a forty-thousand-pound coat,' Isobel said, as they strolled back to Harrods and went up in the lift to the designer dress department.

'Yes, you do,' Troy said. 'Come on.'

They walked into the room as if it were their own. One of the assistants recognised them and came forward with a smile.

'A few more dresses,' Troy said grandly. 'Winter cocktail dresses, and some kind of matching jacket or stole thing.'

They agreed on a shift dress in electric blue with a matching boxy jacket, a white and gold cocktail dress with matching coat, and a beaded blue evening dress. Then they went to the shoe department and chose shoes to match, then to the lingerie department and bought several sets of new underwear.

'This is gorgeous, gorgeous stuff,' Troy said, looking at the detailed embroidery on the lingerie. 'It feels like silk, it feels better than silk, it feels like water. God, if I was a woman I'd never spend money on anything but underwear. This is so lovely.'

Isobel leaned over to look at it with him and her blonde hair brushed against his cheek.

'What would be better?' she asked very low. 'To see it worn, or to wear it oneself?'

He was silent, the challenge went so close to his desire that he could not answer her. She turned without saying more, and headed back to the dress floor. Troy followed.

'You want more?' he asked.

The look she turned on him gave him a jolt of sexuality, as powerfully as if he had touched a live wire.

'What is it?' he asked.

'They had that blue dress with the jacket in a 16,' she said. 'So?'

She met his eyes shamelessly. He recognised at once Zelda's greed for sensual experience and Isobel's practical determination. It was a powerful combination of the two women.

'I want us to buy it for you,' she said.

He stood stock-still, the bags in his hands creating an

obstacle for other shoppers to push around. He did not even know they were there.

'You want to buy a dress for me?'

She turned and confronted him. 'I want us to match,' she said. 'Like we did this morning. You liked that, didn't you?'

The swimming in his head was the lunchtime champagne, but also the dizzy sense that Isobel Latimer, the dull, worthy, academic, middle-aged woman from the country had somehow penetrated to secrets that he did not know he had. She had cut with a stiletto to the very core of him.

'Yes,' he whispered. 'I did like it.'

'Well, why not?' she demanded fiercely. 'Why not, Troy? In for a penny? We're doing everything else, aren't we? We're lying to the publishers and lying to my husband and pretty soon I'm going to go on television and on the radio and in the newspapers and lie and lie to the whole nation. Why shouldn't we be truthful amongst ourselves? Why should we pretend to each other? Why shouldn't we see how we feel? Dress how we want? See who we are when we are not stuck with being Troy Cartwright and Isobel Latimer? We've done something here, haven't we? We didn't mean to do it, it wasn't our intention, but something has happened. We're set free. We've got some choices. I want to take them.'

Troy closed his eyes briefly as if he would hide from her the sudden snap in his mind as she named his desire and gave him permission. 'All right,' he said. 'Let's buy it.'

'And everything else,' she said with fierce greed. 'The underwear, the tights, the shoes, everything. We're going to be rich, aren't we? We can have everything?'

They said nothing in the limousine on the drive back to Troy's flat. The driver helped them carry the shopping bags up the steps and left them inside the hall. Troy gave him a tip and closed the door. They were alone in the silent building.

'I should pop down to the office and check for messages,' Troy said.

'Don't,' she said simply.

He glanced at her, but said nothing. He picked up the shopping and followed her up the stairs, along the corridor into the spare bedroom. She tossed her bags on to the bed and pulled his blue dress out of the tissue paper. 'Do,' she said, her voice gentle. 'Do try it, Troy.'

He held it at arm's length as if he had never seen a dress before. He felt the lightness of the fabric, saw the fine working of the seams.

'It won't fit,' he said. 'I've got no bust. Even if it goes up over the shoulders.'

'Take your suit off,' she whispered. 'We can make it fit. We can pad it out a bit or something. Come on, try it.'

He slipped his jacket from his shoulders and pulled his shirt from the waistband of his trousers. He was conscious of her gaze, taking in his nakedness. He heeled off his shoes and peeled off his socks and dropped his trousers.

'Go on,' she said gently. 'You've seen me all but naked.'

He pulled down his silk boxer shorts and stood before her. Isobel gave a little sigh, a little breath of a sigh.

'These,' she said monosyllabically, and pulled the tissue-wrapped underwear and a pair of hold-up stockings in palest coffee from the distinctive bag.

Troy smoothed on the stockings, feeling the strange adhesion of the hold-ups on his naked thighs. Then he pulled on the French knickers, felt the whisper of silk around his penis, the stroke of the slight seam against his deepest crotch, the weight of the embroidery, pale blue silk on pale blue silk.

'I want the wig on before the dress,' he said. 'I'll feel a fool wearing a dress without her hair and face.'

Isobel brought the wig from the stand and held it for him as he pulled it on. 'Let me do your makeup,' she begged. 'You did mine.'

Troy sat, half-naked as he was, on the dressing-table stool and felt the cool silk of the French knickers against his buttocks, the erotic silkiness of the stockings on his legs. Isobel stood behind him and pattered his face with her fingers, cleansing with the perfumed cleanser, dabbing him clean with the toner, and then sweeping over his skin with the moisturiser. Then he felt the sensual strokes of the foundation, the slick line of the eyeliner, the feathery dabs of eyeshadow, and the butterfly kiss of the mascara wand.

'Keep your eyes shut,' Isobel breathed. When she leaned over him he could feel her blonde hair tickle his bare shoulders and mingle with his own, he could feel her thighs and her belly pressed against his bare back. He felt himself becoming aroused by her touch, but he kept his eyes shut and his face serene.

The lipstick brush against his lips was like a thousand small kisses, tiny provocative nibblings, like a sexual teasing. When it ceased, the sweep of the big powder brush across his face was like a release.

'Keep your eyes shut and stand up,' Isobel commanded.

Troy stood and moved as she told him, stepping into the dress, feeling her pull it up over his shoulders, zip the back, feeling the sensuality of the silk against his bare body, the way it warmed to his skin, the way the dress fell so easily against him, unlike a suit, unlike trousers, the way it fitted and yet did not constrain.

He stretched out his arms behind him and she slid the little jacket on.

'Now wait a minute, wait for me,' she said urgently.

He stood, his eyes still closed, hearing the fall of her clothes as she undressed, and the rustle of the tissue paper as she took the new dress from the bag. In a few moments she said: 'Turn around,' and he knew that she had placed them side by side before the mirror. Then she said: 'Open your eyes.'

Before him were two beautiful women, in identical blue dresses. It looked like an illusion, a magic illusion, created by mirrors in which one woman was reflected back to look as if there were two. But then his gaze picked up the differences. Isobel's face beneath the blonde wig was rounder than his, her eyes grey while his were blue. His shift dress hung from his shoulders, while hers fitted snugly over her breasts. But the illusion was what drew him, the two women, side by side, as alike as twins.

Isobel turned to him. 'We're both Zelda,' she whispered. 'We've made two of her.'

This time he did not kiss her. He looked from her beautiful painted face to the reflection of his own, and then back again. 'We are both Zelda,' he said and saw his crimson lips move as he spoke. At once he felt an extraordinary rush of desire – for the creature in the mirror, for both creatures in the mirror. He wanted to possess them both, he wanted to be them both, and he wanted to be possessed by them. He wanted to lose Troy Cartwright with his work and his worries and his day-to-day consciousness. He wanted to be Zelda, he wanted to be her lover. He wanted her to love him.

The beautiful doppelgängers stood for long moments regarding their reflections. There were four silent Zeldas absorbed in the moment of their own creation. Absorbed in the desire to be; absorbed in the desire to possess. Then Isobel stepped forward and reached towards the other beautiful image. Gently, she touched Troy's painted lips with her own cherry-red mouth. He took her hand and held it.

'I want to make love,' she whispered.

He shook his head. 'It's too soon.'

She closed her eyes, her hazy dark-lined eyes. 'I'm longing.'

'Not yet. Not when we have just started this. And not when you have to go home in a couple of hours.'

She opened her eyes abruptly, looked at him as if she were completely confused. She had the startled look of the woken sleepwalker. 'Oh, my God, I had forgotten,' she whispered. 'I was so much Zelda. I had quite forgotten that I would have to go.'

'It's another life. As we said. Another life which you can come to. I'll keep her here.'

'Are you gay?' she demanded. 'Is that why you don't want to make love? Why you want the dress? Do you want to be a woman?'

He recoiled from her bluntness and felt suddenly ashamed.

'I can't talk like this. I can't speak of it in – I don't know – such categories. It's not that simple as being one thing or another.'

She knew she had said the wrong thing and flushed for her clumsiness. 'I'm sorry,' she said quickly. 'I know. You're right. This isn't a condition. It's an experience. This is Zelda. We've raised her, and now she's possessing us both.'

He put his hand up to his own head and felt the silky richness of Zelda's hair at the nape of his neck. 'That's what I want,' he said. 'What I have always wanted. To be possessed so completely that I lose all sense of myself.'

Isobel, travelling home alone on the train in her blue trouser suit, gazed unseeing out of the window as the familiar shabby landscape of south London and then the suburbs went by. All she could see, against terrace gardens, industrial estates, and parking lots, was Troy's entranced look when he touched his thick blonde hair and spoke of being possessed.

She felt as if they had entered some extraordinary pact, some deep magic that could take them onward to some deeper place of being, and instead of being shocked or afraid at what they were doing she felt a wild, anarchic desire to plunge deeper, to go farther. She felt reckless, she felt as if she did not care what they did together, what it might be called or how it might seem to others. Inside the privacy of Troy's flat, with the spare bedroom door closed behind them, Isobel had felt free in a way she had never been free before.

She recognised her station with a jolt of surprise, the journey had passed so quickly. She walked to her car, listening to her footsteps on the tarmac and watching her shadow on the car-park wall as if she were not sure that she was completely substantial. Then she drove up the lanes towards her home.

There was a light in the hall and at the kitchen window. She parked the car and went into the kitchen. The television was on and Philip was watching it as he ate his supper. When she came in he got up from his chair and turned it off.

'I saved you some, I didn't know how late you'd be,' he said. 'Good lunch?'

'Yes,' Isobel said. 'And good news. They're going to pay £60,000 for the new novel. Isn't that excellent?'

'I say, that's good,' he said. 'Better than ever. Good old Penshurst Press. I was afraid they were cutting back. There were a couple of reviews of your last book that had me a bit worried.'

'It is good,' she agreed. 'They've been very generous.'

She fetched a knife and fork and water glass and watched him cut a slice of the chicken and ham pie for her.

'Does that mean we can go ahead with the swimming pool?' he asked eagerly.

She smiled, he seemed a long way away. 'I don't see why not,' she said.

'I'll tell them tomorrow,' he said. 'I am pleased, Isobel. About time that Troy did something for his ten per cent.'

'He's very good.' Isobel defended him. 'I think he's very good.'

'He's a hanger-on,' Philip said precisely. 'He's got no talent or initiative of his own. He lives off you. He makes his money off your sales, and I don't even think he handles the sales very well.'

'Oh, for heaven's sake!' Isobel exclaimed in sudden irritation. 'He's a wonderful agent, he just got me £60,000 for a novel when I didn't think he'd get half that. He's brilliant! Why d'you always have to be so critical and carping? I've written a good novel and he's got a good price for it. He's a good agent. What else is there to say?'

Philip gave her a hard, unfriendly look and said nothing. In the offended silence Isobel picked up her fork and started to eat again. She felt noisy and clumsy; and she felt that she was gross to be greedily eating when he was so clearly distressed.

The silence dragged on. She glanced sideways to see if Philip was going into one of his deep sulks. When Philip was angry with her he could maintain complete silence for days at a time in which Isobel could rage or weep or reason without response. She always had to apologise first. She always had to apologise deeply and in detail for offending him. But tonight, for the first time in their long marriage, she did not look at him and dread his displeasure. She looked at him and wished that he would keep his bad temper to himself. She knew that he would not. And she thought with irritation that she had better apologise now and get it over and done with.

But Philip was not sulking. He was looking thoughtful. 'I tell you what it is,' he said mildly. 'I don't trust him. That Troy. I couldn't tell you why. Just a hunch. I don't think he's got your true interests at heart. You're just one of a dozen to him, nothing special.'

She picked up her plate, took it to the bin and scraped it clean. 'I am special to him,' she said firmly. 'I am.'

He could have left it alone, but he did not. 'He's not serious though, is he?'

She hesitated, unsure of his meaning.

'He's not a young man who has suffered in any way,' Philip said acutely. 'Anything that has ever gone wrong in his life has been his own choice, perhaps his own misjudgment. But he's never been in real hardship, never been in danger. He's not like someone of our parents' generation who was brought up and went through the war, brought up by the generation before them who suffered the First World War. He's not even like us who were brought up in the fifties and knew that things were hard. He's a child of the sixties, the seventies – everything comes easy to him. He was brought up in a world where people liked to think that everything was easy.'

'You can't say that, you don't even know him,' Isobel protested. 'You've never even met him.'

'I know the type,' Philip said. 'They think nothing matters more than themselves, nothing matters more than their own amusement, or their own ambition or their own career.' He looked at her with warmth. 'They're not like us,' he said. 'Not like you. We're serious people, we know that serious things matter.'

Isobel felt a deep pang of guilt. 'It doesn't have to be either-or,' she said weakly. 'Surely you can be someone who lives life to the full? You can be someone who thinks seriously and yet has a full social life, someone who has fun? Who puts a priority on enjoyment?'

Philip shook his head. 'No,' he said simply. 'Everyone has to choose whether to live their life to benefit themselves or live it to benefit others. Young people like your Troy – they're pure hedonists. But people like you and me, we live the life of the mind. You make people think, you encourage them to use their brains, you give them serious intellectual pleasure. And before I was ill I did things that mattered too. I used to give lectures and write papers which raised important ethical questions, environmental questions. I devoted myself to doing a good job, a serious job. But people like Troy: they're people who won't grow up, they don't want to be serious and think hard. They only want fun. I can't imagine what the world will be like when they come to hand it on to their children.'

Eight

Over the next few days Isobel found that she was learning the heartbreaking skills of adultery. She already had the concealed novel hidden under a false name on her computer, now she also had a false appointments diary filled with untrue entries, in case Philip should glance at it to check her whereabouts. She learned to watch for the postman so that she got to the mail first to make sure that there were no hefty pages of proofs sent from the wrong publisher to alert Philip to Zelda Vere's book. She exploited Philip's routine, which before had seemed so tragically dull and predictable, but now provided a series of safe havens when she knew she could call Troy. Philip's afternoon walk, the half hour when he did his exercises, his late nights in front of the television, his late rising in the morning: these were times when she would not be overheard or disturbed, and instead of watching her husband with love and concern, she watched him with a deceitful care to ensure that he left the house on time and would not return while she whispered on the telephone to Troy.

Isobel watched these changes in herself with a deep grief but found she could do nothing to prevent them. She had not thought when she embarked on writing the novel that it was anything other than the most devoted of wifely sacrifices. Her sole motive for writing *Devil's Disciple* was to provide for Philip; she anticipated no other consequences. Even the initial shopping trip with Troy had left her with nothing more than a sense of mild dissatisfaction with her clothes, with her looks, with the dullness of her life. But somehow, in a moment, in a careless second, she had gone far away from Philip. Without awareness, without foresight, she had taken a definitive step and suddenly Philip no longer seemed the deeply desirable man of her girlhood, and the mentor and lover of her womanhood. Now he seemed like an old man, a sick man, whose companionship was a burden. No longer did she feel deeply bound to him; now she felt tied down.

She could not have said when such a thing happened. It was like magic: a dropping of a veil, the clearing of a vision. Troy's kiss had been a symptom of it, not the cause. She would not have kissed like that if she had not already been moving away from the habitual loneliness of Philip's bed and towards a hot desire. Whether she was ever kissed by Troy again seemed irrelevant. Something had started in Isobel as irresistible as the first lick of flame around a match.

Sometimes she thought with mild distress that a sexual infidelity would hardly matter since the worst betrayal of her marriage had already taken place. Her mind was now hardly ever with her husband, or on the day-to-day detail of married life. Mentally, she was almost always elsewhere. She viewed Philip from a distance, as someone that she should not hurt, someone that she should manage with care and consideration. She no longer saw him as a man that she had chosen in passion and stayed with for love. The long slide of her marriage from one of love between equals to that of a benignly parasitic relationship where the invalid battened on the weary host, was finally completed when she still did everything she had once done for love; but now she did it from a sense of duty, from pity, and from a determination that he should notice no difference. She realised that she was out of love with him, and had probably been out of love for years, when she understood that she could live with him motivated only by courtesy and compassion. She realised also that he was out of love with her when he accepted her work, her care, and, most of all, her money, without even noticing that the love had gone.

Isobel did not feel any real sense of regret about this, and that was a part of the strange coolness which had seeped into her marriage. She did not feel regret, she did not feel guilt. She felt almost nothing at all for Philip, except a determination to keep things as they were, and to make sure that he never knew that emotionally she was gone, long gone. Her protective kindness which had developed during his illness was now all that was left. It was enough to make her as careful of her behaviour in front of him as the most cynical and practised adulterer. Philip must never know that she had lost all trace of her passion for him, because it would distress him and make him ill. Whatever happened next in her life, she would not allow it to impinge upon her care of Philip. She was not going to become demanding. She was not going to ask for her freedom or a separation or a life of her own. She had made an agreement with God that if he would grant Philip's life then she would never ask for anything again. At that moment she had shut down her desires, and thought them gone forever.

But the memory of that burning kiss, of the sight of Troy wonderingly touching his blonde mane of hair, of sliding his hand around her waist, remained with her like the scenery of another planet; one quite outside her universe.

At first Isobel tried very hard never to think of it at all. She busied herself with her work, with the management of the house, replying to letters from readers, from foreign publishers, answering countless requests for information, for signatures, for permission. But since seeing Troy in electric blue, since seeing Zelda-as-Troy before her, everything else had become pale and insubstantial. She saw Troy in her mind's eye all the time. He was her first conscious thought in the morning and her last thought as she slid into sleep at night, to dream of him.

Troy telephoned her several times to check dates for the publicity tour in the New Year and to assure her about the progress of the contract. The sum of money was so very large that he was using a lawyer to confirm the clauses, and there was also the paperwork to create the bank account. They had decided on an account based in Switzerland, and it was to be operated under a number, no name would be used at all. Only Troy would know the number and the details of the bank account, all the paperwork would go to his address.

Isobel, knowing how Philip liked to greet the postman and that he often scanned through the envelopes, was insistent that not even the bank should have her true name and address. Troy had to invent fictional references for the account to preserve Isobel's complete anonymity. 'I should think the Swiss hang you for this sort of thing,' he worried.

There were other matters to agree. The publishers sent a couple of suggestions for book jackets for Isobel to see. They sent them to Troy, everything went through Troy, and he photocopied them and sent them on to Isobel. They featured a doll-faced woman with plump breasts spilling out of a lace-trimmed blouse, behind her a man in a hooded cloak, an inverted cross, and a ruined chateau. Isobel peeped at them, then slipped them back in the envelope in horror. She rang Troy.

'These are really awful,' she said.

'Yes, aren't they fab?'

'No, I mean they're so garish, and they look like a women's magazine: this dreadful picture of Charity. She looks like some kind of goiterish peasant. What *is* she wearing?'

There was a brief pause while Troy pulled out the picture of the book jacket from the Zelda Vere file in his office. 'Kind of peasant blouse thing.'

'Why would she be wearing that?'

'French but innocent.'

Isobel yelped. 'French?'

'I did say that I'd give them permission to do small editorial changes. I didn't think either of us needed to tell them to dot ''I''s and cross ''T''s.'

'Why have they made her French?'

'To match your biography,' Troy said simply. 'And it's all first person now, anyway. It's being sold as your story, a fictional account of your story. She's an English girl growing up with a sister in France.'

'Someone will find out,' Isobel said fearfully. 'They only have to start looking at the passport office or at the birth certificates.'

'We don't say anywhere that it's true,' Troy pointed out. 'That's the joy of it. If anyone asks you directly then you will just say that it is based on your experience and researches in France. That's all you need say, Isobel, I promise. The publishers will do the rest. They'll do the press release and the hype.'

'Why can't they just put the book in the shops?' Isobel demanded. 'Why does everything have to be hyped?'

'Because there are thousands of books in the shops,' he replied. 'That's why your own books never sell more than they do. There are thousands and thousands of books out there, Isobel. You have to do something special to be the one that people remember.'

There was a silence from her end of the telephone.

'She looks ridiculous,' she said stubbornly.

'It's a selling commercial jacket,' he said bluntly. 'I promise you, Isobel. They don't just throw these things together. This is a jacket that the sales reps and the supermarket buyers like.'

'You show books to supermarket buyers?' Isobel asked incredulously. 'Supermarket buyers who usually buy baked beans?'

'Yes,' he said. 'As far as they're concerned a book is a commodity exactly like a can of beans.'

'I have been an author for nearly twenty years,' Isobel said. 'And I have never, never had my book judged by a supermarket buyer.'

Troy sighed. 'You've been a *literary* author. Nobody wanted to sell you in the supermarket. Your publishers wanted to sell your books in small, elegant bookshops, where intellectuals who know what they want go and buy their books. But Zelda Vere is a commercial author. Intellectual bookshops won't even stock her. We don't mind about that. We want to be in Asda. We don't care about Littlehampton Intellectual and Critically Acclaimed Book and Stationary Store, six weeks' delivery on written orders only.'

There was a brief silence from Isobel. He was afraid that he had offended her.

'Please, Isobel, trust me. This is going exactly to plan,' he said gently. 'Jacket and all. Can I tell them you approve the jacket?'

'Would it make any difference if I said no?'

'Of course,' he lied. 'We all want you to be happy. But I'd be really sorry if you held up publication over something as unimportant as this. And it would hold up the payment of the money, you know.'

'All right then,' she said ungraciously.

'I can tell them yes?'

'Yes.'

'Are you still coming up to town on Sunday night before the television show on Monday morning?' he asked.

'Yes,' she said grudgingly.

'And you know that we're doing an interview with the *Express* straight after?'

'Yes,' Isobel said sulkily.

'I'll be with you,' he promised. 'They wanted to send a publicist to escort you but I said I'd do it. That you wanted only me.'

'Yes.'

'It matters to me,' he said, deliberately seductive, lowering his voice so that she leaned forward over her desk to listen, the telephone pressed against her ear. 'I am really, really looking forward to being with you. I'm really looking forward to seeing Zelda out in the world.'

'Yes,' she said. It was the same word but it was a quite different tone of voice.

'See you Sunday night,' he whispered. 'Bye.'

Philip drove her to the station. 'Are you looking forward to it?' he asked.

'I am,' she said. 'And the teaching next term as well.'

'I'd have thought you'd rather stay home and write,' he said.

A school child pressed the pelican crossing button and darted out on the yellow light.

'Look out!' Isobel cried.

'I can see,' Philip said crossly. 'I'm not completely incompetent as yet.'

'Sorry.'

There was a brief, offended silence.

'I do want to get on with my writing but I haven't taught for so long I thought it was a good opportunity. And with this tutor taking maternity leave, I thought it was rather nice of them to ask me to step in. A lecture now, and next term a course of lectures.'

'You'll be up and down to town every day,' he grumbled.

Isobel hesitated and then started the preparation for the lies which must follow over the next few months. 'I could come home if you needed me, of course, but I thought I'd go into the Frobisher Hotel, somewhere like that, and not do the journey every day.'

'I could come with you,' he said, brightening. 'A week in London at a nice hotel in the New Year. I could manage that!'

Isobel felt her heart miss a beat in alarm. 'That would be nice,' she said steadily. 'But I'd be out teaching all day. Don't you think you'd get bored?'

'I could potter round,' he said. 'Go to the museum or something.'

'Yes,' she said. 'Not every day, surely. And weren't you going to get on with our swimming pool?'

He turned the car into the station car park. 'I thought you'd want me to wait until the payment from Penshurst came in,' he said. 'I didn't want to rush you.'

'Oh no, we can manage,' she said reassuringly. 'Why don't you get on with it? Since we know the money is coming in, you could start. The contract with Penshurst is signed. There's no problem. The money will arrive any day now. And it'd give you something to do while I'm away. Then it would be ready for spring.'

Philip took the bait, pleased at the permission. 'Thank you,' he said with rare gratitude. 'I would love to do that. And I'll plan it really nicely for you, good design, a bit of thought to it. It'll be a real asset for us. A real asset if we ever sell the house. The man from the pool people was very sure that you can really add value to the house with a pool. Everyone wants them. And an inside pool is even better.'

She leaned over and kissed his cheek, taking in the familiar, beloved smell of him, the lemony tang of aftershave, the scent of clean cotton shirt, the shampoo he had used for the thirty years of their marriage.

'I wish I wasn't going,' she said with sudden sorrow. 'I wish I had never agreed to it.'

'Cancel then,' he said cheerfully. 'Why not? It's not as if it pays much, is it?'

She tried to smile cheerfully at him. 'Oh, I couldn't let them down. Not now I've promised.'

She opened the car door, got out and reached for her over-night bag from the back seat. 'I'll phone,' she said weakly to the back of his head. 'When I get into Frobishers.'

'Don't leave it too late,' he said. 'I thought I'd have an early night unless Mrs M. brings one of her dreadful films up to watch.'

Isobel smiled. 'I'm sure she will,' she said. 'I'll phone about ten. Goodbye, darling.'

She would have watched him drive off, she wanted to see his familiar profile go past her and away; but it would have irritated him if he had thought she was doubting his ability to handle the car, so she went instead into the little station, bought a return ticket to London and went out on to the cold platform where the lines curved south to the sea and north to London to wait for the train that would take her to Zelda Vere, Troy, and the whole alternative life.

*　　*　　*

Troy was in exuberant mood, he had a bottle of champagne already opened and he greeted her at the door with a glass in his hand. He kissed her cheek, not actually making contact of lip to skin, and Isobel felt a pang at the theatricality of the gesture.

'Here's Freddie,' he said happily. 'He's just going, *aren't* you, Freddie?'

Freddie appeared in the small hall behind Troy and smiled over his shoulder at Isobel. 'How d'you do,' he said politely.

Isobel realised that the last time they had met she had been Zelda Vere, and so he did not know her.

'How d'you do,' she said awkwardly. 'I am Isobel Latimer.'

'Freddie has to leave,' Troy announced. It was obviously an established joke.

'I rather thought I'd come out for dinner with you two,' Freddie smiled.

'We don't want you!' Troy exclaimed. 'Do we, Isobel?'

She hesitated, not knowing what was the right thing to say.

'*Do* say that I can come,' Freddie pleaded with her. 'I can be awfully entertaining.'

'I'm sure you can,' Isobel said stiffly. 'It's just that . . .' She looked down at her skirt and white cotton shirt. 'I don't have anything to go out in, really. I just came up to town to give a lecture tomorrow.'

'So go,' Troy commanded. 'Isobel and I are going to have a quiet night in, you're missing nothing. Go and party with someone else.'

He thrust Freddie's cream suede jacket at him, and Freddie squeezed past Isobel towards the front door. 'It was a great pleasure to meet you,' he said politely. 'I do admire your work so much.'

'Thank you,' Isobel replied coolly. After many years she could distinguish at once between someone who had read her novels, and someone who wanted to give the impression that they had done so. Freddie was definitely a reader of reviews and a producer of re-hashed opinion.

'And thank you for your – er – generous hospitality,'

Freddie said to Troy, with a quaver of laughter in his voice. 'I had a lovely time. Thank you for having me.'

Troy giggled and pushed him towards the front door. Isobel was reminded of over-excited children at the end of a birthday party. She picked up her bag and went up the stairs to Troy's flat, so that she could avoid watching Freddie leave. She felt that he would only behave badly if given more attention.

She went into the spare room and closed the door behind her. At once it was like entering another world. She paused and inhaled the scent of the room. It smelled very lightly and elegantly of Zelda: a combination of her perfume and the smell of her cosmetics. Troy had stripped the clothes of their plastic covers and they were lined up on their padded hangers in the wardrobe like the shed skins of a jewel-coloured snake, waiting to slither on, waiting to take the shape of Zelda's body. On either side of the mirror were the two matching blonde wigs on their stands. One looked absurd, exotic as a Tudor headdress with fat, symetrically placed rollers. The other was a mane of blonde, absurdly glamorous, beautiful even on the blank face of the polystyrene stand. Between the two was the array of makeup: the exquisite little bottles holding colour, texture, and tone, the specialist brushes, each designed for its own exclusive task.

On the floor of the wardrobe were Zelda's shoes, each one still plugged with a shoe tree, each peep-toe sandal showing red velvet like a carmined toe.

Isobel opened a drawer. There were Zelda's bras: satin, lace, wire and padding, perfect in design, in finish, and perfectly untouched. There were her pants: two tight-fitting, so they would glide on without wrinkles, two pairs of French knickers which would fall to Zelda's thighs like a little slip, and leave no line on a sleek skirt. In the next drawer down was her nightwear: the silk negligee which Troy had bought her, and the silk pyjama lounging suit that they had bought together in Harrods.

She heard the front door slam and Troy come up the stairs, humming a song under his breath. She heard him fall silent as he saw that she was not in the living room, she heard him hesitate outside on the landing, and then she heard him tap gently on the bedroom door.

She opened it and stepped to one side so that he could come in, but he paused on the threshold.

'Would you like dinner out, or to eat at home?' he asked.

Something in his voice alerted her to his awkwardness. 'Whichever you prefer,' she said coolly. 'We need to be up quite early tomorrow morning, don't we?'

'They want us there at eight,' he said. 'They'll send a car at seven fifteen. There's a little Italian place round the corner which is quite pleasant.'

She glanced at the open wardrobe. 'Should I change?'

He looked at her suitcase. Isobel was acutely aware that everything that was said and done now carried a multiple set of meanings. She did not mean should she change her dress for dinner, she meant should she change and become a different woman altogether. For a moment she longed for the quiet certainty of home and the comfort of Philip, who knew her so well and who expected nothing of her but a high standard of nursing care.

'Oh, it's not at all smart,' Troy said. 'No need to change. We'll go as we are. Shall we have a glass of champagne before we leave? I'll phone and make sure they have a table.'

Isobel felt suddenly so powerfully disappointed that she thought she might cry. She swallowed and felt the prickle of tears behind her eyes. She had waited for long days to spend a night with Troy, she had tried not to speculate as to what they might do, and how they might be together. But in the careful walling-off of her imagination she had always assumed that there would be some sort of hidden secret. Now there was nothing. A middle-aged woman going out for supper with a young man, her colleague. Conversation about their business, about mutual acquaintances. The most exciting prospect: zabaglione. The greatest temptation: a brandy after dinner.

'I don't want a glass of champagne,' she said pettishly. 'Not if we're going straight out.'

'All right,' Troy said, deliberately unruffled. 'D'you want to unpack? Wash your hands? No? Then we'll go now.'

Nine

They walked briskly to the restaurant. Christmas trees glowed in some windows, the curtains drawn to show the lights to the street. Isobel walked with her head down, hating the smell of the streets, the pungent exhaust fumes, the thickness of the fog. She thought that she could be at home now, with a programme about tropical travel on the television and Philip mildly complaining that none of it ever looked real and that the issues of the impact of tourism on the environment were always ignored.

'Here we are,' Troy said, determinedly cheerful, and opened a door for her.

Inside it was noisy and bright, decorated with red and white tablecloths. Chianti bottles hung in clusters from the ceiling and served as table lamps. Unframed posters of Amalfi and Capri were stuck with drawing pins on the terracotta-colour walls. Isobel looked around her in amazement as Troy took her coat and hooked it on the stand by the door. It was identical to the restaurant where she had gone on her first date. She remembered even now the sense of delight at the warmth and the bright colours of the place, her teenage excitement when the waiter gave them their empty bottle of Chianti as a souvenir of the evening. She had taken it home and then gone to an electrical shop for a special bulb unit which had been made just to fit the neck of a wine bottle, so that she then had her own bedside light made from her own Chianti bottle. She had kept it safely for years.

'Isn't it wonderful?' Troy asked. 'So ironic! A wonderful pastiche, don't you think? A sort of tribute to all those awful old bistro places.'

Isobel compressed her lips but said nothing. She thought that if you had dined in a place like this and seriously enjoyed it, then perhaps the joke was ineffective when the style was parodied only thirty years later.

Troy slid into a chair. 'Isn't it a hoot?' he asked.

'A hoot,' Isobel repeated coolly, taking the chair opposite him.

A waiter came and offered them a gigantic laminated menu. Isobel lifted hers up like a barrier and hid behind it while Troy ordered mineral water and wine for them both. She emerged to order spaghetti and a green salad.

'What's the matter?' Troy asked, surrendering at last.

Isobel hesitated. 'Nothing, really. I just thought everything would be different.'

The waiter came and filled their glasses.

'After last time,' Isobel added.

Troy tasted the wine, looked thoughtful, tasted it again.

'I thought that something extraordinary was taking place between us,' Isobel persisted. 'I have thought of nothing else since I went home. I thought that was where everything was going. And now we seem to be back where we started. Actually, further back,' she said pointedly.

Troy sighed. 'Yes. All right.' He took a large swig of wine. 'I was very tense about you coming,' he said. 'Because of last time. I had lunch with Freddie, which was a distraction. Probably not a very good distraction to choose. The whole thing went on rather too long, and was rather too distracting. So I was a bit, a bit high when you came. I'm sorry. And I don't want to start anything really difficult, especially when you're on television tomorrow. I think we should really focus on the work for the moment. We should leave everything to one side but the task of getting Zelda launched on the publication trail. There's a steady two-month build to publication day, we want Zelda everywhere. We have to concentrate on her more than anything else.'

'But what about me?' Isobel said.

The waiter, putting the salads on the table, heard the neediness in her voice and could not help but glance at Troy to see how the handsome younger man was reacting to this. Troy looked painfully embarrassed.

'What about you?'

'I'm stuck . . .' Isobel said, much more quietly. 'I'm stuck in the countryside with a husband who is a good man, but . . . so very ill. And Zelda was like a glimpse for me of how another life could be. I thought I was going to enter that life.'

'You are.'

'I thought *we* were going to enter it. I thought everything would be different for us both, if we went into that life. Like going through the looking glass, a world in which nothing is quite as it seems. Nothing is how it seems.'

'You have Zelda,' he reminded her.

She met his gaze openly, with the confidence of her years. 'I thought I would have you, too.'

The waiter bringing the spaghetti was a relief to Troy, an escape from Isobel's forthright intensity. Isobel waited, unsmiling, while the waiter offered dressing for her salad, black pepper, more water, and when he had gone she said to Troy, 'I was hoping for another world, as well as the one that I live in. Something more.'

'As well as the one that you live in?' he asked cautiously.

'I can't leave,' she said simply. 'There is no possibility of me leaving home. I am tied to Philip forever. Till death. But now I've been Zelda, just a little, such a little, it's like I've seen a vision of something else, something more. And I feel like I can't live without it.'

He nodded. 'Like Freddie said, that day we had tea at Harrods. Living life to the full.'

'Exactly. You know, my life is nothing but the pursuit of excellence. That's what I was taught to do: at school, at university, in my work, in my marriage. A self-conscious, self-determined attempt to do the right thing, to do the very best I could. Carefully and consistently to do well.' She looked impatiently around the restaurant. 'Not to imitate, not to plagiarise. Always to make the attempt to do something new, sincere, rigorous.'

Troy nodded. 'And you do. That's what the reviews always say. You can always recognise an Isobel Latimer novel because of the seriousness of the moral perspective. You do that.'

'I know I do!' Isobel exclaimed impatiently. 'What I am saying is that living like that, working like that, isn't enough!'

Troy looked shocked. 'The pursuit of excellence isn't enough?'

She shook her head. 'I want to pursue something else. Something more . . .' She hesitated. 'More visceral.'

'Like what?' he whispered, fearing her answer.

She said nothing. Her dark steady gaze was answer enough.

There was a brief silence. Troy crumbled bread in nervous fingers. Isobel, watching his hands, thought that the bread would be quite wasted. No-one of her generation ever played with their food.

'I want to be free of being me,' she said eventually. 'That's what Zelda is for me. The chance to be free of being me. Dutiful, half-dead me.'

Isobel slept that night in her own cotton nightdress and woke in a tangle of duvet, sweating and hot. Troy's central heating stayed on all night, the orange street lights penetrated the curtains creating a permanent uneasy daylight at three in the morning. Isobel lay in the unnatural glow, uncomfortable in the unnatural heat, and longed with all her heart to be in her own bed in her own bedroom with the window ajar so the cold air of Kent could breathe into the room and frost the window with ice.

She heard Troy's radio alarm go off at quarter to six in the morning and then he tapped on her door at six.

'Come in!' Isobel called, sitting up in bed and instinctively holding the sheet to her chin.

He brought a tea cup and put it on her bedside table. 'How's the star?' he asked pleasantly.

They scrutinised each other. Already, they were learning to read each other's moods. Troy was excited, nervous. Isobel was reluctant, filled with a sick dread.

'They have hairdresser and makeup at the studio but I thought you'd feel better if you did everything here first. That's why I called you so early, so we've got plenty of time,' Troy said, speaking rapidly. 'I'll run a bath for you and then you had better eat some breakfast. I got some cereal in, or you could have an egg and toast.'

'Just toast,' Isobel said.

'Don't worry, everything will be fine,' Troy assured her. 'I'll run your bath now.'

'What shall I wear?' Isobel asked as he went to the door.

'The pink suit is perfect for morning television,' he decided. 'Go and have your bath and come to breakfast, and then I'll help you make up and dress. And I had a thought. If you like, I'll phone your home, when you're actually on television, that way we know he isn't watching it intently. And it's good covering our tracks. If I'm ringing asking for you then he knows you're not with me.'

Isobel hesitated. 'I suppose so.'

'I don't have to.'

'No, it's a good idea. It just seems so . . .'

Troy waited.

'So clinical. Planning to deceive him like that.'

'We're not deceiving him for any bad thing,' Troy pointed out. 'We're just completing the task we set ourselves. Covering you completely.'

She nodded. 'It makes me feel as if I am betraying his trust,' she said quietly. 'Agreeing with you to lie to him. Conspiring.'

'It's for his swimming pool,' he observed. 'It's for his keep. He benefits from it. You're not ashamed of Zelda on your own account, are you?'

'Oh no!'

'Then we're keeping it from him for his benefit, not for yours. And certainly not for mine. We're doing it for him, not for us.'

Isobel nodded and reached for her tea.

'Bath in five minutes,' Troy said and gave her a quick, encouraging smile.

When he had left the room she dropped the concealment of the sheet and slid from the bed. She went to the window and looked out. It was too dark to see what sort of day it would be. The orange sodium lights obscured any dawn. Isobel drew the curtain, feeling sick with apprehension, pulled on her woollen dressing gown and went obediently to the bathroom.

She felt more cheerful after breakfast. Troy was already dressed in a dark silk shirt and matching tie and the trousers of a dark suit. He was at his most unctuously supportive. When she returned to her bedroom the bed was already made and her clothes were laid out on the cover: the silky underwear, the pink suit with the close-fitting jacket, the sheer peachy tights, the pink mules. Thrown with deliberate extravagant casualness on the bed was the new fur coat.

'Wig and then make up first,' Troy ruled.

Isobel sat on the dressing-table stool and took hold of the rich head of hair from the stand. She held the front as Troy forced the body of the wig over her head. 'Ouch,' she said.

'Il faut souffrir . . .' Troy warned her. 'Now close your eyes.'

Isobel shut her eyes and felt the gentle pattering of the moisturiser on her face, Troy's fingertips fluttering at her cheeks, her eyelids, her forehead. Under his touch she felt the habitual thoughtful scowl of Isobel Latimer melt away, she felt the radiant blankness of Zelda take over.

'Heaven,' she said through closed lips.

'Hush,' Troy whispered. 'It's magic.'

With small dabs of the sponge he covered her face with foundation. Isobel felt the cream going on as if she were being repainted into a new and better version of herself, felt the lines of her forehead melt away under the sweet smelling slickness. Then she felt the gentle, loving dabs of eye shadow, the lick of eyeliner, and the stroke of the mascara wand.

'Nearly ready,' Troy promised her.

The powder brush freighted with peach powder swept over her face, penetrating every line, every pore, and then the blusher brush loaded with coral colour circled her cheek bones. Finally the lipstick pencil outlined her lips, drew her smile as one might draw a face on a blank screen. Then Troy brushed at her lips with tiny kisses of colour. The sweep of powder, the tissue to blot, the colour applied again and then:

'Perfect,' Troy breathed.

As Zelda, she opened her eyes and saw herself. As Zelda, she took in her own beauty and saw the carmine lips curve up in a quiet smile of complete satisfaction. As Zelda, she rose from the stool and hardly looked at him. She went towards the bed and sat on the edge, on the very edge so her thighs were taut and beautiful, and she slid on her stockings while he watched, watched her as if she were on a film screen, not a real woman at all. As Zelda, she slithered her skirt up over her hips, then turned her back to him, let him hold out her jacket and lift it on to her shoulders. As Zelda she fastened the large gilt buttons of the jacket, and then leaned towards the mirror to clip on the big gold earrings, paused, and took in the whole effect.

'I'm ready,' she said simply.

'You are wonderful,' he said, gazing at her. 'You are a wonderful, wonderful . . .' He paused, looking for the right word. 'Specimen.'

It would have made Isobel Latimer giggle, but Zelda looked at him under her darkened lashes as if he were rendering to her no more than her due. 'I know.'

The car was waiting outside for them when they came down the steps, Zelda tapping daintily on the cold paving stones in her high-heeled mules. The driver held open the door and she sailed past him as if he were no more to her than the lamppost. She sat on the side of the car nearest the pavement, it did not occur to her to move over. Troy had to walk round the back and take the offside seat. Zelda lowered her head so her nose brushed the soft collar. She looked like a woman in an exotic purdah of fur, he could not see the crimson lips at all, nothing but the grey eyes that glowed at him in the darkness of the car.

They drove in silence without speaking. The driver paused at the security barrier at the television studios and then swept up to the glass doors of reception. A researcher was waiting to greet them, she stepped forward politely and then her surprised face registered the impact of the floor-length blonde fur, of the pink mules, of Zelda's lowered face.

'This way, Mademoiselle Vere,' she whispered and led the way through the double doors and down the corridor.

'Would Mademoiselle Vere like to go to her dressing room, or to the green room?' she asked Troy, glancing back to where Zelda strolled down the corridor behind them, looking incuriously at the publicity pictures of old film stars on the walls.

'Her dressing room,' Troy decided. 'She'll need Darjeeling tea and mineral water.'

'Of course, of course,' the young woman said. 'The director will want a quick word with her, but you've already seen the list of questions?'

Troy nodded.

The researcher, with a deferential bob which was almost a curtsey, turned a corner and held open a door for Zelda. 'Your dressing room, Mademoiselle Vere,' she whispered.

'*Merci*,' Zelda replied and sailed past her to sit on the chair before the brightly lit mirror.

The door closed behind them.

'"*Merci*" is very nice,' Troy commended.

She turned quickly to speak to him but he held up an admonitory finger. 'Be Zelda,' he urged. 'Don't stop being her until you're home again. This has to be seamless.'

She drew a breath, nodded and leaned back in the chair. 'I do feel rather wretched,' she said in Zelda's drawl. She extended her hand and he saw her fingers tremble. 'I am such an intensely private person.'

'Tea,' he recommended. 'I'll make it.'

Beside the star's dressing table there was a little fridge and on top of it a kettle, a tea pot, some loose Darjeeling, and cups and saucers. Troy disappeared into the adjoining shower room, filled the kettle and came back and put it on. He peeped in the fridge.

'Milk,' he said. 'And – hello!'

'What?'

'A nice half bottle of champagne. A very good idea.'

'I'd rather have tea.'

'Have both,' Troy ruled. 'That should help with the confidence. And something else . . .'

Zelda raised a perfectly groomed eyebrow. Troy went quietly to the door and dropped the latch. He opened his wallet and took out a small sachet of white powder. As Zelda watched he took a magazine from the coffee table and tipped a little of the white powder on it. He sliced it up with the edge of his credit card and arranged it into two little windrows of snow.

'It's cocaine,' Zelda said wonderingly. She recognised the ritual of preparation, though she had not recognised the drug. She had seen people take cocaine in films. This was the first time she had seen it in reality.

'Very good for confidence,' Troy asserted. 'Surely, you've had some before?'

Zelda shook her head but it was Isobel's bright eager curiosity which looked out from the beautiful face. 'Never. No. Never. Philip and I used to smoke cannabis when we were younger but that was a long time ago – I've never even seen this.'

'You do it like this.' Troy rolled up a twenty-pound note and showed her. He put it in one nostril and closed the other nostril with his finger. He sniffed gently, following the tube down the line of cocaine. He tapped the tube gently and licked his finger, dabbed at the invisible remainder of dust and then handed the tube to Zelda.

'I don't think . . .'

'Zelda does,' he said definitely. 'And I know it will help.'

Without another word of protest she took the bank note from him, and bent over the magazine. She observed with dispassionate interest that there was an odd pleasure at seeing the white dust disappear, which seemed to be quite unrelated to the dizziness that she felt seconds after.

'Don't forget to taste,' Troy reminded her.

Hazily, Isobel licked her finger, dabbed it in the remains of the dust and rubbed it against her gums. At once her tongue felt gross and swollen.

'Just check your face,' Troy warned her, looking at his own reflection, his face tipped up to the mirror so he could see the underside of his nostril. He gleamed at her, revitalised. 'Perfect.'

He turned as the kettle boiled and set to work daintily making tea.

'What am I supposed to feel?' Isobel asked.

'Uplifted, confident, a little buzz,' Troy said, pouring tea and stirring in milk. 'I only gave you a little taste. Just enough to cheer you up.'

He handed her the cup and turned to unlock the door. Almost at once there was a knock. Troy shot Isobel a quick, smiling, conspiratorial glance. 'Go for it, girl,' he said and opened the door.

It was the producer. 'Just dropped in to say welcome,' he said. 'We've done a run-through and we're all ready to go. The audience is just coming in now. Fifteen minutes before you're on, we'll have someone come and fetch you and show you where to go. You walk down five steps and sit with Raine and Stephen on the sofa. You'll see where.' He stepped forward and switched on the television which was suspended over the dressing table. It showed the studio before transmission, with young men and women moving cameras around, checking the shots, hiding cables.

'There are the steps,' the producer said, pointing to a shallow flight. 'And you sit there. On that cushion.'

'Certainly,' Zelda said, her tongue felt awkwardly big in her mouth. She hoped that she was speaking clearly.

'If you'd pop in to makeup and have your hair checked in ten minutes that'd be great.' He paused and looked at her.

'Though I think you're perfect as you are. Perhaps just check if they want to put on more powder. The lights, you know.'

Zelda smiled. 'Thank you.'

'D'you have everything you need?'

'Oh yes,' Troy said cheerfully. 'We have everything we need.'

The producer looked at Zelda, she had the back of her hand to her nose and she was delicately sniffing. 'Are you all right, Mademoiselle Vere?'

She gave him a radiant, confident smile. 'I'm very very well,' she said.

They took her to makeup where they told her she looked beautiful and needed nothing but a touch more colour, and brushed powder on her forehead and blusher on her cheeks. The hairdresser came in and made a few passes with her hairbrush at the thick bouffant gold cloud which was Zelda's hair. They unwrapped her from the gown and gently brushed her suit down, admiring the cut and the seams and the brightness of the large gold buttons. Then a skinny girl, little more than a child, put her dark-eyed face around the door and said: 'Mademoiselle Vere, please.'

'Good luck,' Troy whispered.

For a moment she stumbled. 'Won't you be with me?'

'I'll be with the producer, in the viewing gallery. You won't be able to see me but I'll be there. I'll be watching every single thing. I'll be there for you. Give me a smile so I know you're happy.'

She gave him a thin, nervous smile. 'Zelda!' he implored her. 'Zelda, you have everything a woman could want!'

At that, her face warmed, she smiled a little wider, and followed the girl from the room.

Troy, feeling a rather urgent need, stepped quickly into the toilet, locked the cubicle door behind him, and laid down a short line of cocaine on the top of the cistern.

By the time he arrived in the viewing gallery they were introducing Zelda. She was part of a theme of the morning:

126

people who had enjoyed extraordinary strokes of good fortune, or were on the rise. They had already spoken to someone who had saved a racing horse from the knackers yard only to see it win against all the odds at York racecourse, and a man who picked up a winning Lottery ticket off the street. They had spoken to a mother who had discovered a miracle cure for her child's asthma, and now they were ready, as the smooth-faced presenter told the camera, to meet a woman whose own talent had made a fairy-story ending of her own life: 'Zelda Vere.'

'Careful!' Troy exclaimed in an agony of anxiety as Zelda entered, paused at the top of the steps as she had been told to do, looked around as if she could not believe her own pleasure at being in a small television studio before an audience of slightly confused pensioners at this time in the morning, and then with a delighted smile ran lightly down the steps to the sofa and sat on the right cushion.

'Bingo,' Troy said to the gallery, feeling the drug and Zelda's entrance fill him with mild elation. 'Good, isn't she?'

His eyes on the screen, he picked up the gallery phone, dialled Isobel Latimer's home number and asked for Isobel, as he had promised he would. Philip, who resented having his breakfast interrupted, was his usual unhelpful self. Troy smiled, apologised, and put down the phone.

'Now, Zelda,' Raine said, leaning forward. 'You are lucky on two counts, one, because you have written a wonderful wonderful novel which has been bought by your publishers for, what was it? More than any sum that has ever been paid for a first novel before?'

'Well, for £350,000,' Zelda said modestly. There was a spontaneous music-hall noise, 'Ooh-er,' from the audience.

'Yes. More than quarter of a million pounds,' Raine confirmed, smiling at the camera. 'But that's only part of the story, because the novel concerns an horrific experience of Satanic abuse happening to a very young girl ... and you were that young girl, weren't you?'

Zelda, high on nerves, champagne and cocaine, looked her

straight in the eye. 'I have to be very discreet,' she said breathily. 'As I am sure you understand.'

Stephen leaned forward. 'Of course we understand, but Raine is right in saying that you have survived an extraordinary ordeal.'

Zelda cast down her eyes. 'Terrible,' she whispered.

'Can you tell us a little about it?'

She looked up and even the old ladies in the back row could see the impact her large grey eyes had on Stephen. 'I was kidnapped,' she said softly. 'And held captive. I swore if I ever got free that the kidnappers would suffer as I had done.' She paused, and then drew from behind her back the much-despised jacket of her book. '*This* is my story,' she said simply.

The producer rounded on Troy. 'She can't do that!' he exclaimed. 'She can't come on here and do a straight plug like that! She's simply not allowed to do it!'

'I'm terribly sorry,' Troy said. 'The publishers must have put her up to it. It's awfully embarrassing. She wouldn't have known that she wasn't allowed. Being French.'

The producer gave him a sharp look. 'French?' he asked sceptically.

'Born in England, brought up in France,' Troy amended. 'I'm so sorry.'

The two men turned their attention back to the screen. Stephen and Raine had a difficult job to do. They had to get the book off Zelda's knee, and out of shot, and they wanted to draw from Zelda the fact that she had been sexually abused and that her book was graphically erotic. But this was daytime television before an audience of pensioners. Everything had to be done with hints.

'And from this painful experience you have made a work of very – er – racy style,' Stephen said, winking at the camera and trying not to leer.

Zelda regarded him glacially. 'I wouldn't call it racy.'

In the viewing gallery Troy found he was gripping the back of the seat. 'Oh no,' he said faintly, recognising the edge of Isobel Latimer's schoolmarmish tone.

'Well, you can't deny it's a sexy book,' Raine interpolated.

Zelda, about to snap into irritation, remembered who she was. 'I would describe it as deeply erotic,' she breathed. 'I would think that it belonged in the category of private reading for women who have known love and life . . . wouldn't you?'

'Some people might find it a little too much,' Raine suggested, unpleasantly.

Zelda leaned back on the sofa and smiled at her. 'Oh, you must not be afraid of desire,' she said warmly. 'So many of us are so afraid of desire. We have to learn to move towards it. We have to learn to seek it. I don't really believe in the concept of a little too much.'

Ten

'How did I do?' Isobel asked him urgently. 'Really?'

'Really, you were magnificent,' Troy told her. He slid an arm along the seat of the limousine and cupped his palm on the nape of her neck. 'Zelda, Zelda, the world is not yet ready for you. You pulled out your book cover on daytime television and they were having a fit in the gallery, and then you looked Raine and Stephen in the eye and told them that they were discussing female soft pornography and that they must not be afraid of desire. It was bliss. They didn't know what hit them. I didn't know what hit me. It was heaven.'

'I suppose I don't understand the mores of this sort of transaction,' Isobel said, frowning under Zelda's brassy, perfect fringe.

'No! Please! No! Don't even think about it,' Troy insisted. 'Zelda, darling, come back to me. I don't want Isobel, right now. Don't think about mores or anything like that. They adored you, all the grandmas in the audience adored you, and all the kids in the gallery thought you were a gay icon. Don't diminish it by worrying about whether you understand daytime television or not. Let *them* understand *you*.'

She was thoughtful for a moment.

'I'll discuss it with Isobel Latimer later,' Troy offered. 'We can talk about it as a social construct or something like that. Something that she knows about and likes to think about. But Zelda would just be having a good time. And now we're going to meet a journalist for an early lunch, so Zelda must be herself, her beautiful, immaculate self.'

'Do I look all right?'

'You look glorious. Would you like a little more coke?'

She glanced at the back of the driver's head. 'Can we?'

'Sure.' Troy raised his voice so the driver could hear. 'Could you put the privacy screen up, please?'

'Yes, sir,' he replied. 'We will be at the hotel in approximately twenty minutes.'

The screen of darkened glass rose silently and then Troy and Zelda were alone in the cocooned privacy of the limousine's back seat. Troy took a magazine and prepared two short lines along it, rolled a bank note and proffered it first to Zelda. She bent down and inhaled it, then she threw her head back and closed her eyes. Troy absorbed the line of her neck, clear and smooth. He snorted his own line of coke and then dabbed the remainder with his finger and licked it clean.

'I've never done such a thing before,' Isobel said wonderingly.

'Zelda Vere has never done drugs?' Troy asked.

She opened her hazy grey eyes. 'Oh, Zelda has,' she said confidently. 'She gave it up for a while but now she does it when the mood is right. In the backs of limousines with handsome men on the way to interviews with journalists, after being on television. She does that sort of thing all the time.'

Troy smiled at her and leaned forward. There was a scent which was Zelda's own, a combination of her perfume, the scent of her makeup, hair spray, and the warm, rich smell of the fur coat. Zelda moved a little closer. Troy savoured the tantalising few inches between them.

'I daren't kiss you,' he said. 'I don't want to smudge your makeup.'

'I could re-do it,' she whispered. 'Or you could.'

'I should so hate to smudge you,' he whispered, their faces so close that his breath moved the light blonde fringe as he spoke.

'I should love you to smudge me,' she replied.

The driver's intercom switched on. 'Excuse me, sir, but we are approaching the hotel entrance.'

'Certainly,' Troy said, leaning back in his seat and straightening his tie.

The car door was opened, the uniformed doorman bowing as he saw Zelda. She unfolded from the car like a lap-dancer coming out of a cake. Troy, getting out of the other side, found himself admiring her as an object, as sleek as the car, as expensive as the coat; and then going forward to offer her his arm to take her into the hotel.

They were meeting Jane Brewster, the journalist, at the lunch table. Zelda left her fur in the cloakroom and entered the dining room teetering on her pink mules, in her pink suit. Heavy-jowled businessmen stared at her as if she were the dessert trolley. Italian waiters beamed as if she were a descending angel. Jane Brewster, a resolutely hatchet-faced woman in a creased navy business suit, rose to her feet and briskly shook hands as if she had never in her life felt a pang of envy at the sight of a wealthier, infinitely more beautiful woman.

Zelda slid on to the velvet banquette and demurely looked around her. Troy held the chair steady for the descending broad bottom of the journalist and then seated himself.

'A glass of champagne?' he murmured to the journalist.

She fixed him with a hard glare. 'I never drink during the day,' she said. 'It spoils my concentration.'

'Oh, neither does Zelda,' Troy said smoothly. 'A bottle of mineral water, please.'

'Do you mind?' the journalist asked Zelda, producing a small cassette player and placing it on the table. 'I find it assists my memory. Just forget that it's there.'

Zelda shot a brief, appalled look at Troy, and then nodded to the journalist with a smile. 'Of course.'

The waiter came back with the mineral water. Jane Brewster waited until the fuss of ordering food was over and then leaned forward. 'What age were you when these events took place?'

Zelda sat back a little in her seat. 'The novel is a work of fiction,' she reminded her gently.

'Your publishers make it very clear that it's based on your own experience.'

'It's not based directly on me,' Zelda said. 'It's based on an incident, a series of incidents. Some of them happened to me, some of them I read about, some of them happened to people I knew. Like all works of fiction it is a weaving of disparate elements.'

'Did you say desperate?' Troy asked.

'Disparate,' Zelda corrected.

'It's not a word I know,' Troy said pointedly.

'Oh . . .' Zelda said. She absorbed the hint and then giggled. 'I got it in a crossword puzzle.'

'You're not a highly educated woman, then,' the journalist remarked, watching this exchange with bright little button eyes.

'No,' Zelda said. 'It's one of my great regrets. But now I read, I constantly read.'

'What are you reading at the moment? What's at your bedside?'

Zelda had a sudden vivid image in her mind of the Kent bedroom, the linen pillows, the bedside table and the books she was reading for pleasure: Simon Schama, *The Embarrassment of Riches*, and Lisa Jardine, *Worldly Goods*.

'Jilly Cooper,' she said quickly. 'Dick Francis.'

'Which one?'

'The one about horses.'

The waiter brought their starter and Troy picked up his fork with a sense of relief at the interruption.

'And what about your personal life?' Jane asked. 'Is there a man in your life?'

Zelda lowered her gaze to the blinis with sour cream and caviar. 'I am seeing someone,' she said very quietly. 'But I have to be discreet. He's rather well known.'

'A movie star?'

'International financier, one of the few household names

of currency trading,' Troy murmured, thinking that would confuse her for a good long time.

'And is it serious?' the journalist asked with the engaging tone of the professional confidante. 'D'you think you'll marry?'

'I'm scarred,' Zelda confessed. 'Not just on my body, I still carry some tattoos, and he has seen them.' She gave an engaging smile. 'He kissed them better. It was so sweet. But also I'm mentally scarred. Spiritually scarred. Some damage goes very deep. I couldn't marry a man while I am still haunted with the fears that I have.'

Troy found that he was gazing at Zelda with total adoration and the waiter, coming to remove the plates, had to serve around Jane Brewster's blind avidity.

'Scarred from your ordeal?' she asked.

'Oh yes.' Zelda lowered her blonde head almost to the other woman's shoulder and whispered in her ear. Jane nodded, nodded again, made a face of complete horror and nodded again. Troy leaned back in his chair and summoned the wine waiter with a smile. 'I think we'll have a bottle of Roederer,' he said. 'I think we'll all enjoy it now.'

Jane Brewster did not leave till four, flushed and tipsy. While she was in the Ladies, Troy took the simple precaution of taking her tape recorder, erasing the recording at high speed and then putting it back on the table.

Zelda looked at him doubtfully. 'What was the point of that? She knows what I said. She's not that drunk. She'll remember most of it.'

'Deniability,' Troy said cheerfully. 'If we don't like what she reports, we can deny it and she has no record. Neat, eh?'

Zelda looked at him with some admiration. 'That's very unscrupulous.'

Troy smiled. 'Isn't it? Now I'll get your coat. I want her to see you in it.'

When Jane stamped back from the Ladies she found Troy

was paying the bill and Zelda was waiting in the lobby of the hotel, wrapped in honey coloured mink.

'Can we give you a lift anywhere?' Zelda asked. 'We have a car waiting.'

'No, no,' Jane said. 'I'll walk. It's been a pleasure to meet you.'

Zelda bestowed a radiant smile on her.

'The photographer should be here any moment, he was due at three,' Jane said, looking irritably around.

A small man unfolded himself from one of the giant cushioned sofas in the lobby.

'Oh, there he is. George, this is Mademoiselle Vere and her agent. I'll leave you to it.' She turned to Troy. 'Of course we'd rather have done it at her home. We could still come to her home, tomorrow, say. Our readers do expect to see her in her home. We like that sort of intimacy for a big piece like this.'

Troy shrugged apologetically. 'Her home is Rome at the moment,' he said. 'Mademoiselle Vere is staying with friends in England and their home cannot be photographed for security reasons.'

Jane brightened at that. Troy leaned forward and Zelda caught only a few whispered words. She was sure that one of them was: 'Sandringham.'

'Oh, really?' Jane said, looking at Zelda with renewed interest. 'And can we expect a public appearance together at any time soon?'

'Next spring,' Troy replied. 'But you will be the first to know, I promise, Jane. It's the least we can do in return for your discretion now, and your understanding.'

Jane grasped Zelda's hand in farewell. Zelda smiled in a way that she hoped combined royal acquaintance with a survivor's courage. Jane went out through the swinging doors.

The photographer stepped forward. 'I thought sitting on the sofa with the bowl of flowers nearby,' he said. 'And then a few more informal shots, perhaps in the restaurant.'

'I'll hold the coat,' Troy said quickly to Zelda.

'Won't I keep it on?'

He shook his head. 'Animal rights people. Anti-fur people. We don't want people getting all agitated and forgetting to buy the book. We want them on message and on retail. Not thinking about anything else when they hear your name.'

Zelda handed over her coat and sat in the chair. George posed her, touched her cheek to turn her head this way and that, darted around her making small encouraging noises. 'Lovely, that's lovely.' Zelda lost any self-consciousness and lolled back in the chair, smiling seductively.

'Perhaps a glass of champagne in her hand?' the photographer murmured to Troy. 'And maybe some carrier bags with store names on them? She's a sex and shopping author, isn't she?'

'Not at all,' Troy said, offended. 'She's an aspirational survivor. Champagne certainly, but no shopping bags.'

'Flowers?'

Troy snapped his fingers at a passing waiter and at once a small table was produced to Zelda's right with a bowl of scented lilies, and another glass of champagne was presented to her on a silver tray.

'Hang on a minute, I'll have that,' the photographer exclaimed. 'Bow a bit more, would you, son? And don't look at me, look at her. And look at her a bit more servile.'

The waiter bowed lower, proffered champagne, smiled at Zelda. She took the glass, let one pink mule swing from her arched foot.

'Lovely,' the photographer said.

They went back to the restaurant and took some photographs with her jacket off. Then they went outside to where the limousine was still waiting and took some pictures of her seated in the back, and emerging from the car. They got the doorman to hold the car door, and the driver to offer his hand. They did everything they could think of doing with a car. 'Might as well use it as a prop,' Troy said. 'It's forty pounds an hour.'

Finally the photographer said: 'That's me finished. Thanks very much.'

'Thank you,' Troy said.

Zelda nodded, her cheeks aching with smiling. Troy draped her coat over her shoulders, she slid into the limousine and the driver shut the door.

'Phew,' Troy said, joining her from the other side. 'That was a bit of an effort. But good photographs, I know. And a good interview. She does have tremendous pull. You did fantastically well. Fantastic.'

Zelda leaned back on the cushioned seat and closed her eyes. 'I am exhausted,' she said. 'It's absurd how tiring this stuff is.'

He took her hand and kissed the perfect false fingernails. 'Poor love. And you've got to go all that way home. D'you have to go?'

She paused for a moment. 'It's so far away,' she said wonderingly. 'You know I can't believe how far away it is. But yes, I do have to go home. I have to find a way to do this and then go home after doing it. It's only part of the job, being Zelda. The other part is being Isobel Latimer. My life now is to learn to be both.'

They went back to Troy's flat so that she could change. He did not offer to help her and she did not want him to watch the transformation from the butterfly back to the dull chrysalis. She hung the suit on the hanger and she left the pink mules by the bed. She was very conscious that Troy would come in later and put things away, as he liked them to be. She knew that he would do that this evening, as his farewell to Zelda, as she was saying goodbye to Zelda now.

Isobel sat before the dressing table and rubbed at her face with cleansing cream. The perfect skin came off on the tissue leaving her face shiny and blotchy. Her eyes stripped of mascara and eyeliner looked small and undistinguished. Isobel scowled at her reflection, brushed on a sweep of powder, slapped on a little lipstick and turned to her clothes. She dressed in her brown skirt, jacket and cream blouse, and turned to look at herself in the mirror. It was a profoundly ordinary reflection of a country matron of fifty. She looked like any one of the women who wait in reliable cars outside private schools at four o'clock, or who shop in Sainsbury's with enormous trolleys crammed with wholesome food on Saturday mornings. She looked a little tired, a little bored, a little dutiful. At a dinner party no-one would hope to sit next to her, at a committee meeting she would be trusted to take the minutes.

Suddenly Isobel stepped towards the mirror and swept her hair off her shoulders and piled it on top of her head. Her smile was radiant, transforming her whole appearance. 'Ah yes,' she said. 'But there is more to me now than that woman. I am still Isobel Latimer. But I am not *only* Isobel Latimer.'

On the train home she sat in a daydream as the train went through the dark countryside. Bright uncurtained windows made pin-pricks of light in the darkness, the stations were little islands of noise and shining lights in the winter gloom. Isobel looked at her reflection in the darkened window as it flickered and jumped as the train moved, and found that she was in absorbed in herself, in her dark reflected eyes, in the rippling pale oval of her face. Then she saw the light industrial warehouse buildings which marred the outskirts of her village and she rose to her feet and buttoned up her coat.

Philip was waiting outside in the car.

'Seven minutes late,' he said, without any other greeting. 'I'm glad I wasn't hanging around waiting for you on the platform.'

'I'm sorry,' she said. 'Did you get cold?'

'I could have done.'

He started the car and they moved into the queue waiting to leave the station.

'Good lecture?' he asked.

'Oh yes,' she said. 'I enjoyed it very much. Bright students, interesting questions.'

138

'There were a couple of phone messages,' he said. 'I wrote them down. Nothing important. Troy rang.'

She nodded.

'The fool didn't seem to know where you were. I said to him, "She's your client, shouldn't you keep track of her?"'

Isobel smiled to herself, thinking of Troy in the viewing gallery watching Zelda and hearing Philip's irascible voice.

'What did he say?'

'He said he thought you wrote at home in the mornings. I said to him that you were in London lecturing. But you'd think he'd keep track of you himself.'

'If it's not work for the publishers, it's not really much to do with him,' Isobel said quietly.

Philip nodded, watching the road. 'Mrs M. put a casserole in. I let her go off early, there didn't seem much point her hanging about, there was nothing for her to do.'

'Did she do the bathroom?' Isobel asked.

'I don't know. I was out in the barn with the pool man. We had a long talk about heating systems. I'm thinking very hard about going for solar power. We could put the panels on the roof of the barn, they'd be quite unobtrusive, and then we'd have free hot water for life. It's a much more economic way to do things, though of course the technology is fairly new.'

'Yes,' Isobel said quietly. Already her day as Zelda seemed very distant. The morning with Troy, the television studio, the line of cocaine, the pink suit, the triumph of the interview with the journalist: it all seemed a long way away.

'He's a very personable young man, a salesman of course with all the usual small-print contracts, but he really knows his stuff. It's so nice to meet someone with a bit of get up and go. We looked at some decorative finishes of pools that he's done. You can have tiled or a kind of aggregate finish, which is cheaper but looked all right. I thought we'd go for tiles. It hardly seems worth penny pinching when it's a once-and-for-all purchase.'

'Yes,' Isobel said.

'He's almost sold me on the idea of putting in a sauna cabin at the far end. We've just got room for one of the smaller models and they are terrifically relaxing. What d'you think? D'you fancy a sauna?'

'How much are they?' Isobel asked.

'Depends on the size, on the finish. All sorts of things. I should think we could get a nice one for around five thousand.'

Isobel blinked. 'It does seem awfully expensive, on top of the price of the pool as well.'

'I don't know,' Philip said. 'Not when you think what you're getting for the money.'

'But we've never wanted a sauna.'

'We've never had a pool before,' he said logically. 'Of course you wouldn't want a sauna without a pool. But if you have a pool, then a sauna is an obvious addition. And if you have a sauna, you can use the surplus heat for a jacuzzi at the end of the pool. And they're practically standard.'

Isobel felt a sense of intense weariness. She assumed it was the descent from the high of the drugs and excitement and attention. But the countryside seemed unbearably dark and forbidding as they drove home. The headlights of the car hardly pierced the winter darkness; all they could illuminate was the hedgerow and verge running alongside the lane, beyond them was nothing but black. A rabbit ran out and hesitated in the road.

'Look out!' Isobel cried.

Philip neither braked nor swerved.

Isobel shut her eyes, and flinched at the little thud as the car struck the animal.

'They're only vermin,' Philip said. Isobel tried not to think that it might not be dead but injured, scrabbling with its back legs on the cold tarmac.

'Natural selection,' Philip said. 'Rabbits will have to learn to dodge traffic.'

'I don't see that cars are a part of natural selection,' Isobel said irritably. 'Rather unnatural, I would have thought.'

'They're the environment now, aren't they?'

'It always makes me feel suspicious whenever a man tells me that something is inevitable, or part of natural forces, or part of the new environment,' Isobel said waspishly. 'I always know then that something peculiarly unpleasant has just been invented and I am supposed to put up with it.'

Philip gave a grudging chuckle. 'Touché. But rabbits are a complete nuisance. And most of these are myxomatosis-immune. So we're just going to have more and more of them. Rigby was telling me that he can't run horses on his pasture because the rabbit holes are so bad this year.'

Isobel nodded, too tired to argue, and leaned her head back and closed her eyes. She knew from the sway of the car that they had turned in the gate and heard the scrunch of the gravel driveway under the wheels of the car.

She got out of the car and went in the back door, into the kitchen. It was untidy, with the remains of Philip's day. There was a plate with orange peel on the table and a couple of mugs in the sink. There were newspapers on two chairs and the morning's post on the worktop. There were plans for the swimming pool spread over the kitchen table. There was a sticky patch on the floor by the Aga where something had been spilled and not wiped up. Isobel felt a sense of immense weariness, as if these few trivial things were a mountain of cleaning which had to be done. She sighed and set to work.

Philip came in behind her and watched her stack the dishwasher and then gather up newspapers and post. He intervened when she was about to fold up the swimming pool plans. 'I left those out for you to see,' he protested. 'We need to decide on the finish of the pool in the next few days.'

She hesitated.

'Here's the technical specification,' he said. 'And here are the artist's impressions of what it would be like finished. And here are the drawings.'

'Can't we look at them after dinner?' Isobel asked.

She went to the Aga. Mrs M.'s casserole was drying rapidly, the gravy had turned to sludge and the vegetables were dissolving into mush.

'Oh all right,' Philip said crossly. 'Though I'd have thought you would have been interested.' He folded up the plans and put them on the sideboard. He laid two plates and two knives and forks on the table and fetched glasses and an open bottle of red wine. Isobel spooned the casserole out and sat down opposite him to eat. Then she got up from the table to fetch salt and pepper, and then bread, and then water glasses and water.

When they had eaten and she was clearing away, Philip spread out the plans again.

'Now,' he said.

She suddenly thought that he was like an insistent child who had to be humoured. She looked at him with love mingled with impatience.

'All right,' she sighed. 'Clearly I'll get no peace until I've seen them. Let's have a look.'

At once he was animated, pointing out the design features, explaining how the system worked. When he got to the third and fourth page of the benefits of solar power over electric or oil heating, Isobel sat back in the chair.

'You really have gone into this,' she congratulated him. 'But it's more than I can take in right now. I want to open my post and then go and have a huge bath and an early night.'

'But we have to decide,' he insisted. 'I said I'd call Murray back and tell him what system we want. I promised to get back to him tomorrow or the next day.'

'Then we can decide tomorrow,' she said.

'You'll want to write tomorrow,' he said. 'You know you will. And I want to get on with this.'

'You decide, then,' she said. 'It's your project. You've gone into it. You've been running it from day one. It can be all yours. You take the decision, that's fine by me.'

Philip looked delighted. 'Well, clearly I do have more interest in it than you.'

'I shall love it when it's finished,' she promised him. 'I'm just not very inspired by drawings. You know that. I don't have that sort of brain.'

'I've always been a design sort of man,' he said. 'I saw it in my mind's eye as soon as we started talking about it. Murray said he'd never had a customer with such clear vision of what he wanted. He said most people just say they think they'd like a swimming pool, sometimes they get him out and they haven't even got room enough for a paddling pool! I said, "No, I measured the whole barn up before I even picked up the phone."'

'I'm sure you've been very clear,' Isobel said. She could feel a headache starting behind her eyes. 'That's why I have so much faith in you taking the decisions.'

Philip folded up the plans and put them away in a special folder marked 'Swimming Pool'. 'Leave it to me, then,' he said with pleasure. 'I'll see to it all.'

In the morning Philip was up before her. He brought her a cup of tea in bed.

'Whatever time is it?' Isobel said, struggling to sit up, looking out of the window at the uninviting winter darkness.

'Seven,' he said brightly.

'Are you all right?' Isobel asked, taking the proffered cup. Philip always slept late, it was one of the effects of his condition. He had not been up before her for years.

'Right as rain,' he said cheerfully. 'But Murray called last night and said he could drop in on his way to another job first thing, so I thought I'd be ready for him. I'm ready to take the decision about the design of the sauna, and I can get a discount if I get the order in before the end of the month.'

'Oh,' Isobel said.

'I'll make him a cup of tea when he comes,' Philip said. 'He's always ready for a cup of tea in the morning. Runs out of his house without breakfast half the time.'

Isobel nodded.

'Get dressed and come down and you can meet him,' Philip said. 'You should meet him really. He's going to be here a lot once the work starts.'

When Isobel entered the kitchen Murray, the swimming pool contractor, was seated at the kitchen table, a plate of buttered toast and a cup of tea before him. As Isobel came in he rose to his feet and gave her a slight, roguish smile. 'This is Murray Blake,' Philip said. 'My wife, the writer.'

'Mrs Latimer,' Murray said, holding out his hand. 'It's such a pleasure to meet you at last.'

'How d'you do,' Isobel said stiffly. She had a moment's foolish regret that she was wearing an old cardigan with rolled-up cuffs and a rather shabby skirt. Murray wore a warm viyella shirt, a leather waistcoat, a pair of dark brown moleskin trousers and big, enormously big boots. His handshake was gentle, his brown eyes smiled down at her. He tossed back a fringe of curly dark hair as if he were shy.

'Please do sit,' Isobel said politely.

'D'you want some toast?' Philip asked. 'Murray couldn't resist it.'

'I'll make my own later,' Isobel said. She found that she did not want to eat breakfast with the pool man.

'Oh, I won't be long, let me get out of your way,' Murray said, instantly understanding the snub.

'Oh! I just meant –' Isobel broke off. Clearly there was nothing she could say to repair the awkwardness of her refusal. 'I needed to look at something first,' she said. 'You two have your breakfast, I'll go and do some work.'

She left the room and heard Philip say with satisfaction, 'Now we can get on,' as he spread the plans on the kitchen table.

Eleven

On Wednesday, Isobel drove down the hill to the newsagents and bought a copy of the newspaper. She did not even look at it until she had driven to the lay-by at the top of the hill where she had parked before to eat chocolate brazils. Then she switched off the engine and unfolded the paper.

At the very top of the front page, above the headlines, was a row of small pictures and one-line quotes from the articles inside. There was a picture of a limousine and a beautiful blonde woman leaning forwards as if to step out. The caption said: 'From Horrors to Hype: Who is the real Zelda Vere?' Isobel turned the pages to the centre spread, the women's pages. There were three pictures of Zelda, used across the two double pages. One was her emerging from the limousine, one was her seated in the restaurant, one was the waiter serving her champagne. Isobel scanned all three with a sort of fascinated horror. The limousine picture was good, the photographer had taken her at an angle so she was smiling up at him and the half-open jacket showed off the tops of her breasts. The restaurant picture was less flattering. It was full face and Isobel noticed the lines around her eyes and the tired skin of her neck. The final picture, with the waiter serving champagne, was so stylised that it could have been almost anyone. It said 'rich spoiled beauty', and the hint of dominance with the man's bow only enhanced that impression.

Isobel nodded soberly, and looked at the text. Jane Brewster did indeed possess a good memory. She told Zelda's story from birth to now with all the embellishments that Isobel and Troy had dreamed up over lunch. She hinted that there was a royal attachment and a private room at Sandringham for the novelist. She made it very clear that the novel was autobiographical with added material. She hinted titillatingly at the background of Satanic abuse – but in such a way as to give no offence to a family newspaper readership.

The overwhelming impression of the article was the extent to which it had been marketed for sale. Everything, even the wildest horrors of Isobel's imagination, would soon be available in hardback. Everything was open, everything was explicable, everything was sanitised, everything was available. The reader could buy the book, read the interview, look at the pictures. The picture credits even named the hotel so that the reader could go and eat at the same restaurant as Zelda, hire a car from the same company, buy clothes from the same shop. Everything was for sale, everything was labelled with its price.

Isobel read the article, checking the journalist's inventions against her own, and was satisfied that there were no discrepancies that she could not tolerate. Some of the exaggerations she rather liked; she committed them to memory. Then she read the article again, thinking a little more carefully about what they were doing. They were conspiring to tell – what? Some hundred thousand people? – a pack of lies. Somehow it did not seem to matter. This was not reality, this was hype. The restaurant had not been as nice as it looked in the picture. The waiter only bowed when he served champagne when the photographer told him to do so. Nobody looked like Zelda when they got out of bed early in the morning. Women could only look like Zelda when they had bought cosmetics, bought clothes, spent hours of time on preparation and dressing. None of this world was real. What did it matter if a story spliced on to this world was also untrue?

Isobel thought for a moment what would have happened if she had told the true story of her life: of her long, loyal love for her husband, of his struggle against his illness, his lapses into bad humour, her gradually being forced into nannying, into mothering him. The denial of her own desires, the slow fading of her hope that he might recover. These were not stories that people wanted to read. People wanted to read about glamour, about luck, about astounding changes and swings of fortune. This was the modern world; it was not interested in years of quiet labour, in thoughtful, careful work. It was not interested in a struggle against heavy odds or sustained difficulty. It wanted quick fixes and dramatic reversals, short stories and twists in the tails. It wanted results at high speed.

Isobel got from the car, scrunched up the newspaper and put it in the litter bin. Zelda was now truly launched, she had been on daytime television and she had been featured on the women's pages of a national newspaper. She was now a real person to millions of people. They might doubt the details of her story, they might dislike her or think she was a liar; but no-one could deny her existence. She was a real person; better, far better than that, she was a celebrity.

Troy rang at midday.

'Have you seen it?'

'Yes.'

'What did you think?'

'I thought that she looked very well. And the story was good.'

'The publishers are thrilled. It's going very well.'

'She's real now, isn't she?'

Troy paused. 'How d'you mean?'

'It's not a private thing between us. It's not even an experiment, an experiment in identity or a literary experiment. It's a real thing now.'

Troy hesitated. 'Are you sorry?'

Isobel shook her head. 'No. It feels immensely frightening and risky and exciting. Like being a spy or something. But seeing her in the paper made her feel very real and at the same time very unlike me. She's a separate person.'

'Are you still OK for her to go on tour in the New Year?'

Troy asked. 'They're putting more dates in her schedule all the time. Everyone in the country wants to meet her.'

Isobel felt a quiver of excitement. 'I'm OK, if you are.'

'I wouldn't miss it for the world,' Troy assured her. 'It's the most fun I've had in years.'

At lunchtime Philip was preoccupied with the swimming-pool plans. Murray was coming in the afternoon and Philip had found a mistake in one of the technical drawings.

'Makes you wonder how competent they are,' he said crossly to Isobel. 'They say they're the country's leading swimming-pool installers and then you see they've got this wrong.'

He showed her the layout of pipework.

'I don't quite see the problem,' she said.

'There!' He pointed the handle of his soup spoon impatiently at an offending pipe. 'I should think it was obvious that the return pipe is wrongly sited.'

'Oh,' Isobel said. 'Better check it with Murray.' She noticed inwardly how the man had become on first-name terms with them both.

'I certainly will.' He looked up at her. 'Sorry. This is of no interest to you, is it?'

She smiled. 'It's not anything I know about, that's all.'

'What have you done today?'

'Writing.'

'How's it going?'

'OK.' Isobel often discussed work in progress with Philip. His comments were helpful, but more than that, it gave them something to talk about. In this case she genuinely had nothing to say. After reading the newspaper and talking to Troy she had sat in her study and stared out of the window for a long time, the computer humming companionably beside her. The new Isobel Latimer novel, *The Choice and the Chosen*, was no further forward at all. The moral world inhabited by Isobel Latimer characters, when they struggled between the rival claims of love or desire and duty, was difficult to imagine.

For some reason their carefully considered morality had become supremely irrelevant. Isobel could not concentrate on high seriousness when Zelda was centre-page spread of a national newspaper and journalists all over the country were calling the publicist to book a slot on the Zelda Vere publicity tour.

'When d'you think it'll be finished?' Philip asked.

'Oh, a couple of years, I suppose.'

'And when will they pay?'

She looked at him in surprise; it was so unlike him to ask about money. 'Why?'

'For the pool. We need to pay a deposit when we make the order. It's a third of the price.'

'How much will it be?' Isobel asked uneasily.

'Well, that depends. I do keep telling you. There are so many options and they all cost. In principle I think we agreed that we should build something attractive and lasting. There's no point in throwing something together that we'll have to renew every five years.'

'No.'

'And no point in not putting in an extra that we really want, and then kicking ourselves a year down the line because we don't have it.'

'No, I suppose not. Like what? What sort of extra?'

'Like the sauna. No point in not building the sauna at the time, so all the pipework is done together. It would be a real waste of money to come back later and have to redo it.'

'I suppose so,' Isobel said unenthusiastically.

'It makes it more expensive now, of course,' Philip said fairly. 'But I think it would be a false economy not to do a proper job if we're going to do it at all.'

Isobel hesitated. 'I'll have the money from the last book by the end of the month. But I was hoping not to offer this one for sale until it's finished. The £60,000 should really last us the two years.'

'We might have to dip into our savings then,' Philip said cheerfully. 'Liquidate a bit of capital. Murray said he can arrange a loan using the house as security. He's got a contact, he can do it with one phone call.'

'The thing is, we don't want to spend a fortune on it,' Isobel said cautiously. 'If it's going to cost the same price as two cruises in the Caribbean, we might as well go to the Caribbean instead.'

'Now that's just extravagance,' Philip said firmly. 'Two tickets to the Caribbean and what have you got? An enjoyable fortnight if you're lucky. And that's all. After it's over, it's all over. But a properly designed and laid-out pool – this is an asset. It'll add value to the house. It's very worthwhile.'

Isobel watched Murray and Philip from her study window. The computer waited on her desk, the black line of the cursor flashing gently, as if waiting for her to stop daydreaming and get on with the job they both did so very well. Isobel, chin in cupped hands, watched Philip striding along beside Murray. When he was happy, as he was now, enthusiastic, gesticulating, talkative, his limp was much less pronounced. She imagined the blood flowing through his veins with more energy, the wasted muscles of his body springing suddenly lithe into action. Philip was bareheaded, he wore a thick, warm jacket, jeans, and walking boots. He was slight beside Murray's solidity, he looked like an actor playing the part of a country gentleman. Murray looked like a working man, a carpenter, a builder. He had a tape-measure clipped to the belt loop of his trousers, he had mud on the thick soles of his big boots.

For some reason they were walking around the outside of the barn, looking up at the roof and pacing out the perimeter. Philip was gesturing urgently as if he would beckon the walls to extend backwards. He paced out the ground and put a marker in the ground. He and Murray unfolded the plans and looked carefully at them. Murray said something which Isobel could not hear through the glass and they both laughed.

There was something immensely touching about seeing Philip in the company of another man. His laziness, his bad temper, had fallen away from him. Perhaps Murray had never even seen the ordinary day-to-day Philip. The man that Murray always met on the swimming-pool visits was this energetic, enthusiastic man with a great love of design and a great openness to excitement. As Isobel watched, Philip paced out the perimeter of the barn once more, with Murray standing on a dry patch of ground and watching him. When he came up to Murray they unfolded the plans again and checked something.

Philip led the way to the house. She heard them come in the back door to the kitchen, Philip commenting on the cold and offering a cup of tea. His voice too had changed. With Isobel and Mrs M. he spoke softly, he was feminised, almost infantilised. With Murray he was authoritative, loud. When he laughed, he laughed the full-bellied laugh of genuine amusement, of a man pleased with life. Isobel, idle in the study, smiled with pleasure to hear her husband laughing with a man.

She started to type, the words coming slowly from the cursor. The beginning of a novel was almost as hard for Isobel as the end. The first paragraph was crucially important. Isobel knew full well that some reviewers would read no more than that. But the first paragraph was also an opportunity to set the tone of the novel. It said everything about what the book would be like. Isobel wrote a sentence and then erased it without regret. This was the process of writing. If she was unlucky then it might be like this for days. If the process was going well she might keep one sentence in six.

She heard the kitchen door bang and then the sound of Murray's car drawing away. Then the door opened and shut again and from the vantage point of her study window she saw Philip go out again to the barn. He had forgotten to put on his jacket, she was about to tap on the window and call to him to wrap up warm, but something in his stride, in the set of his shoulders, stopped her.

He went to the barn smoothly, his limp almost erased by his hurry to get there. He threw open the double doors but he did not go in. He stood back, the doors flung wide, his arms outspread. As if he were dancing he stepped forward, his head up, his arms outstretched. Isobel could not see his face but she knew that he was smiling. He was exalted. In a strange, silent, long-distance pantomime she saw him walk into the barn and then pause, stand very still, both hands by his sides as if he were a swimmer at the brink of the water with the long blue lane stretching ahead of him.

Slowly his arms came above his head in the classically beautiful pose of the dive. He bent his knees, both knees equally strong and then he gave a little leap in the air, a little leap of longing which told Isobel, without any doubt, that if she loved this man at all then she must buy him his swimming pool.

Her eyes still on him, she picked up the telephone and rang Troy.

'When will the money come through?'

'You're eager,' he remarked. 'Got a taste for champagne now?'

'Certainly not,' she said. 'I'll leave that to Zelda. No, it's for something here at home. I need some money fairly soon. I want to get on with the pool.'

'The lawyer's looking at the contracts now. I can hurry him up, I should think we could get the contracts to you within the week. You sign and return them and they should pay within the month.'

'How much is the first lump sum? The payment on signing?' Isobel asked.

Troy laughed. 'You know how much, Isobel. You just want to hear it again.'

She smiled. 'Tell me.'

'OK, it's £150,000 on signing and then £100,000 on hard-back publication. You, or rather Zelda, will make £250,000 in the next twelve months.'

'I'd like it in before Christmas,' she said. 'If they could do that.'

'Oh certainly,' he said. 'I'll make sure they know. They'll pay it into the Swiss account. When you want funds, you tell me and I draw them. They'll come into the agency. To anyone working in the office, or to Philip, it just looks like your usual royalty payment. As long as no-one looks too closely they won't notice that you're getting far more than before, and drawing it down far more often.'

Isobel nodded. 'That's fine,' she said. She was looking out of the window at Philip, who was carefully closing the doors of the barn as if he were locking away something very precious. 'That's fine.'

Twelve

After their usual quiet Christmas and New Year at home, Philip was happy that Isobel should go up to London for a week's teaching. Mrs M. arrived on Sunday afternoon with her suitcase and a carrier bag full of video cassettes. Her husband waited in the car to give Isobel a lift to the station.

'There should be enough food in the freezer, but if he wants something special there's money in the housekeeping jar,' Isobel said to Mrs M. on the doorstep. 'If he's ill at all then phone the doctor, whatever he says. I'll telephone every evening at about six and you can tell me how he is then.'

'Don't you worry,' Mrs M. said comfortably. 'I know what he's like. I'll keep an eye on him.'

'And do encourage him to have his walk every day,' Isobel said.

'Now he's got his interest in the pool he's out there all the time,' Mrs M. said. 'Measuring it up and looking at that barn. He's hardly ever in.'

Philip came down the stairs. 'Hello, Mrs M. You off, darling? Got everything?'

'Everything,' Isobel said. Mrs M. vanished to the kitchen and Isobel stepped towards Philip. He opened his arms to her and she felt his familiar touch, and his kiss on her hair.

'Look after yourself,' she said tenderly.

'Of course,' he said. 'And you. Enjoy yourself. This is a good break for you.'

'I'll ring,' she said. 'Every evening at six.'

'Or I'll phone you,' he said. 'But I don't have the number.'

'I don't have it on me now,' Isobel said quickly. 'I'll ring and tell you it tonight.'

She stepped back and kissed him on the mouth. The taste of him was the one she had loved all her life, the taste of the only lover she had ever known. She had a pang of regret. 'I wish I was staying.'

'Oh, go on with you,' he said, giving her a little push towards the door. 'You'll love it when you get there. Are you out to dinner tonight?'

'Yes, with Carolyn,' she said, naming another writer that she knew he disliked.

'Huh, well, give her my best wishes, and say that her last book was remarkably reminiscent of yours.'

Isobel put her suitcase in the boot of the car without arguing and got into the passenger seat. Philip paused at the open front door and waved goodbye to her as Mr M. drove down the drive and out on to the road.

On Sunday evening, Isobel and Troy ate supper in her hotel room. Troy spent a little time briefing her on how she should behave with the provincial press and what they would expect.

'But surely,' Isobel exclaimed, surrounded by a sea of press cuttings, 'it must be obvious to everyone that this is untrue. They can't seriously believe it.'

'Of course they don't believe it,' Troy said. 'It's not about believing you, believing what you say or believing what they write about you. That's why we're picking your interviews so carefully. Everybody knows it's a fiction. We're avoiding the journalists whose speciality would be to expose it as a lie. We're only using the ones who like lies.'

'Why would anyone like lies?' Isobel wondered.

'Some of them because they're lazy: it's easier to go along with the lies than discover the truth and set the lies right. Some of them because they're clever: the lies sell more news-papers and magazines than mundane truth. Some of them

155

because they really are stupid, they've talked themselves into believing that abusers and survivors and all these dramas happen every day and people rise above them and buy designer clothes and are fresh and untouched a few weeks later.'

Isobel shook her head. 'It feels like a lifetime away from home.'

'You don't watch enough telly,' Troy pointed out. 'If you did you'd know that all the channels, even the respectable terrestrial ones, are full of exaggerations and nonsense. Anything from aliens to spontaneous combustion. Two or three nights a week, perfectly skilled producers and cameramen recreate emergencies where people jump in the river to save drowning dogs, and think that their dead children are warning them not to take the number 22 bus. Police forces release film of people stealing baked beans from supermarket shelves and appeal for help in arresting them, as if anyone cared. People go into hospital for life or death operations and let the camera crew come in with them. Not even your own death is exciting enough any more, unless it gets on the telly. Everyone wants to have a bit of drama in their lives, everyone wants a share in melodrama. Everybody wants their own experiences reflected back at them, enlarged, airbrushed, properly lit. Nobody wants to be ordinary any more.'

'Well, she's certainly not that,' Isobel remarked, pointing to the magazine with Zelda on the cover. Above her highly coiffed head was the title: 'A new Princess of Hearts?'

'I think we went a little far on the royal spin,' Troy said thoughtfully. 'We don't want people to get so excited that Buckingham Palace issues a denial. And if they start staking Zelda out to see if she goes to Sandringham, they'll know she doesn't.'

Isobel shrugged. 'It's only a giveaway supermarket magazine.'

'We'll cool it anyway,' Troy decided. 'Better yet, we'll deny it before anyone else does. Then no-one can accuse us of lying and we'll keep the interest stoked up. You can deny it tomorrow in Newcastle, it'll be a nice scoop for the provincial oiks. They'll feel they're at the hub of things.' He rose to his feet. 'And now, I'd better go. We've got a big day tomorrow. We'll take the early train to Newcastle and you do local media all day and night there. Have you got your schedule?'

'Yes,' Isobel said. 'But won't you stay for coffee tonight?'

He shook his head. 'I have to go to the office. Pick up some calls. Sort some things out before we go away.'

He noticed that she did not rise from the sofa to see him out, but stayed where she was, lying back against the cushions, self-consciously seductive. He realised, with mild irritation, that without the mane of blonde hair and the dramatic eye makeup she was Isobel Latimer to him: an intelligent, interesting, middle-aged writer. Not a woman he would envisage for one moment as a sexual partner. Not a woman who would inspire very much desire in anyone, he thought.

Something of that must have showed in his face because she rose abruptly from the sofa, and moved awkwardly to the door, as if she felt she had been rude in not standing earlier. Troy followed her. He felt he should perhaps apologise for not responding to her discreet invitation. It was clearly in his interests to keep Isobel happy. For if Isobel were not happy then what mood would Zelda be in? She paused with her hand on the door knob.

'Sure?' she asked.

Troy decided. Isobel Latimer was earning a cool £350,000 for her writing and for her part in this charade. For that sort of money she could take responsibility for her own feelings, she could bear a little disappointment. She could handle a little sexual rejection.

'Quite sure,' he said firmly. 'We'll have dinner tomorrow night and all the nights after, when we're on the road. But tonight I have to pack. We have an early start. King's Cross at seven thirty.'

She nodded and stepped to one side. Troy had a feeling of being released, of getting off scot-free.

'About your packing . . .' she said quietly.

Troy stepped out into the hushed, carpeted corridor so that she could not detain him. 'Yes?'

'Bring your Zelda dress and shoes.'

Troy wheeled around. 'What?'

Isobel smiled at his shock and Troy knew that she had caught him, and seen her hold over him. 'Bring your Zelda dress and shoes,' she repeated. 'We can dress up in the evenings.'

He gulped at the thought and looked at her, so coolly composed in her bedroom doorway, the woman who only a second ago he had thought of as middle-aged and undesirable; and then she had got to the very heart of his secrets in a moment.

'What else are we going to do in Newcastle, Manchester Liverpool and Birmingham?' she asked. 'Nobody will know us there. We answer to no-one. We can dress up if we like. We could even go out. Zelda and her sister Isobel could go out for dinner together.'

Troy felt his heart pounding a little faster at the thought of going out in the lovely clothes, of feeling the open air against his smooth-skinned cheek, the night drizzle on his mane of blonde hair, of hearing the tap of his own high heels on the pavement.

'Why not?' Isobel asked.

They met on the platform. Troy had arranged the first-class tickets and their seat reservations. They travelled in silence. Troy had bought a selection of newspapers and magazines in case she wanted to read but she spent the journey looking out of the window.

'What are you thinking about?' Troy ventured at one stage, just north of York.

'I was thinking about the question of free will in a society without God,' she answered simply. 'I don't think anyone has really approached the issue very centrally in a novel. We have all assumed that humanism and a post-Freudian sense of guilt are the new controlling forces. But I was wondering if there is something in the human make up which makes free will a deep taboo. Something we can never really take on.'

'Oh,' Troy said respectfully. 'I won't interrupt you then.'

She gave him a sweet, abstracted smile. 'It's for my novel,' she said. 'The Isobel Latimer novel is all about free will, really.'

At Newcastle station Troy hailed a taxi which took them to the best hotel in the town centre. They had an early lunch date booked with a journalist, and Troy looked critically at Isobel before the taxi drew up under the awning over the hotel steps.

'Go round the block once more,' he said quickly to the driver.

Isobel looked at him in surprise.

'Too much thinking about free will, too much Isobel altogether,' he explained. He snapped open her handbag and took out a small makeup mirror and held it up for her to see. 'Push your hair back, fluff it up.'

Obediently, she did as she was told.

'Now smooth out the skin under your eyes, the makeup's gone into creases. And pinch your cheeks. Have you got any eye drops?'

He rummaged in her bag like a competent theatrical dresser. There was no sense of him intruding into her things. They both felt that Zelda's things belonged to them equally. Zelda's image was their own shared property. He pulled out a small bottle of eye drops.

'I can't do them,' Isobel said. 'I can never get it in the right place.'

'Tip your head back,' he ordered, and squeezed a drop into the corner of each of her eyes. 'Now blink. Now let's see? Good.'

He looked carefully at her. 'Can you pull over?' he asked the taxi driver. He brought out the lipstick brush and touched up her lips to their usual cherry perfection. At the gentle touch of the brush, Isobel closed her eyes and gave herself up to the sensuality of the little dabbing kisses. The frown of

159

concentration dissolved from her forehead, she looked at once serene, self-satisfied.

'That's more like it,' Troy said gently. 'Zelda. Zelda Vere.'

'Yes,' she replied softly. 'I am, now.'

Troy sat back in his seat. 'Hotel Majestic,' he said with a smile. 'The lady is ready.'

From lunch they went straight to the local radio station where Zelda talked about being a survivor and writing a novel, and took a number of telephone calls from people who were either overtly curious about the amount of the money she had made in advances on royalties, or covertly probing whether it was some remarkable scam that the caller could also employ to deceive a publisher. It was a nasty mixture of hope, greed and envy. Zelda fielded it all with consummate ease. Troy thought that nobody could really work a local radio audience like a humanistic philosopher. She started ten miles ahead of everyone else, she could see where they were coming from long before they even arrived.

From the local radio station they went to a television studio where Zelda was to be live on the local evening news in a discussion about censorship.

The studio was tiny, there was only one woman to do hair and makeup, and she took one look at Zelda's immaculate *maquillage* and stepped back. 'More powder?' was all she asked.

'No,' Troy said. 'Madame does it herself.'

He had been afraid that the discussion would lead into deep waters, but it was a vapid and predictable canter through the explosion of pornography in the media and the difficulty of protecting young children. The woman who chaired the debate had been briefed only ten minutes before the programme went out and had only the sketchiest of notions as to who Zelda was, and what the discussion was to be about. Zelda was able to mention the title of her book five times in the fifteen-minute programme, and came out of the studio glowing with triumph.

'Superb,' Troy said, meeting her with her blonde mink at the door. 'Absolutely superb.'

The taxi was waiting to take them back to the hotel. Troy was shepherding her to the open door when a smartly dressed young man came out of another door and said: 'Miss Vere?'

They both turned together, they both said: 'Yes?'

'That was very impressive,' the man said, speaking earnestly past Troy to Zelda. 'I wonder if you would be interested in appearing in a programme I am making for broadcast this week. It's a late-night discussion programme, we aim to take some of the serious issues of the day and examine them in some depth.' A mild sneer on his face indicated that he had not thought much of the depth of the discussion on the early-evening show. 'You'd have the opportunity to develop your ideas. I thought from what you were saying in there that you would have some interesting comments to make.'

'Miss Vere is on a book tour,' Troy interjected. 'She's not really here to do late-night discussion programmes.'

'We could mention the book,' the man persisted, still not looking at Troy. 'I actually thought that one of the points we could touch on would be the overlap of fiction and reality. The whole notion of autobiography, and fictional first person narrative.'

He was not talking to Troy, he was talking past him to Zelda, who was half-frowning with Isobel's thoughtful scowl, as she considered what he was saying. Troy was filled with unease.

'Zelda,' he said quietly.

She was recalled to her false self. At once she turned her radiant smile on him. 'When would we do it?' she asked.

'Wednesday night?' the young man said. 'We go out live. The only thing is, it's a regional programme, we use the Manchester studios.'

'That's no problem,' Zelda said. 'We're in Manchester on Wednesday.'

'You are?' he beamed. 'Well, that's fab. Could you be at the studios for half past ten?'

'She really doesn't . . .' Troy essayed.

Zelda nodded. 'That'll be fine,' she said firmly. 'Come, Troy.' She swept past him and got into the taxi. Troy closed the door gently on her and turned to the young man.

'Don't worry,' he said to Troy with a conspiratorial wink. 'It's a doddle. We call it high intellect, but that's just because everyone goes on and on for a long time. If she can string two words together she'll walk it. And if she gets stuck we'll have someone on with her who can help her out. Someone from Manchester University, someone who knows a bit about books, about the whole philosophical position. Someone with two brains to rub together. Know what I mean?'

'Oh yes,' Troy said bitterly, going round to the other side of the car. 'I know just what you mean.'

They ate dinner in the restaurant. Zelda attracted glances as she entered in her dark navy cocktail dress and high, high heels. She drank champagne as an aperitif and then water with the meal. Troy, relaxing after a day on tenterhooks, found that he was drinking most of the bottle of red wine that he had ordered for them both.

Zelda refused dessert but had a small black coffee. She took one sip and then put it to the side.

'Is it no good?' Troy asked.

'I only ever drink Colombian,' she drawled.

Troy grinned at her, guessing that Isobel Latimer never had anything but instant coffee at home.

'I'll send it back,' he offered.

She shook her head. 'Oh no, don't make a fuss. We'll have a bottle of champagne instead.'

Troy glanced at his watch; it was ten o'clock. 'Shouldn't you have an early night?' he asked.

Zelda sent him a look across the table which made him catch his breath with desire. 'Yes, I think I should,' she said. 'Let's order a bottle of champagne from room service in my room.'

Troy followed her out of the restaurant, catching the looks

of men who gazed after Zelda. When he reached the hotel lobby she had already pressed the button for the lift.

Zelda's suite was the best in the hotel. She waved Troy into a brocade-upholstered armchair and stretched herself out on the sofa like a blonde persian cat. Troy rang for room service as Zelda kicked off her shoes and stretched her arched feet in the sheer tights. 'Not a bad day, anyway,' she said.

'Not bad,' Troy said, sitting in the uncomfortable armchair. They were silent for a little while, waiting. Then there was a knock at the door and Troy opened it to room service with the ice bucket, champagne, and two glasses. Troy uncorked the bottle and poured them both a glass. Zelda shifted her feet from the sofa cushion. 'Why don't you come and sit here?' she said silkily.

Thirteen

Troy crossed the room to the sofa and sat down beside her. Zelda drank some champagne and then turned to him.

'Did you bring Zelda's size 16 dress?' she asked.

'Yes,' Troy said quietly.

'Why don't you go and put it on?'

The alcohol swam in Troy's head. 'I don't know.' He hesitated.

She smiled at him. 'We can wait,' she said fairly. 'We can wait forever. Or we can give up on the whole thing and not bother at all. It doesn't matter. It's only the price of, what? a dress and a pair of shoes. We can just leave the whole thing. Leave it unsaid. Undone.'

At once Troy protested. 'No, I *do* want . . .'

She smiled confidently. 'I know you do. But you're afraid to start. I understand that. It was easier for me to start changing myself because I thought at first that I was just dressing up for the book, for the money. It's only now that I understand that I was changing me. I had to change. I needed to change. I wanted to be someone else,' she corrected herself. 'Someone else as well. I had to have another life. I couldn't bear to just be Isobel Latimer any more.' She broke off for a moment. 'I doubt that you understand that.'

'Why shouldn't I understand it?'

'I doubt that you understand that one can look at one's own life and be filled with such terrible despair,' she said quietly. 'You can look at your life and say, "My God, my God, I am fifty-two, more than half my life has gone and I have only this, I have done only this, and I had such *hopes*."'

'You've written some wonderful books,' Troy suggested.

She gave a short harsh laugh. 'I know. But it's not enough, Troy. I wanted to live, not just to write about living.'

'I don't see how Zelda would solve that,' Troy said slowly.

She smiled. 'No. Odd, isn't it? From the outside one would think that Zelda is just an extraordinary, eccentric piece of behaviour, or a perversion, or an excuse for an affair. But inside it is different, isn't it? We have raised some sort of ghost, we've made some third person, and when I am her I am not Isobel Latimer with her disappointed hopes and her shrinking horizons. When I am Zelda I am another woman with another life ahead of me. And I suppose that when you are Zelda something like that happens for you too.'

Troy cleared his throat. 'Something like that,' he said huskily.

She looked at him thoughtfully. 'Just start, Troy. Just let yourself start.'

He got up, a little drunk, and staggered slightly. His room adjoined hers, they had unlocked the door between the two earlier in the evening. He went through to his room and she heard him opening the wardrobe door and the tiny, half-heard susurration of silk.

'Can I come and help?' she asked.

'No.' His voice was as hushed as that of someone preparing a mystery. 'I want to do this alone.'

'D'you want to use the makeup? And the wig's in here.'

'Yes. Don't look, though. I'm not ready.'

'I'll go into my bedroom,' she offered. 'Everything is in the bathroom, just help yourself.'

Troy heard her take the ice bucket and her glass and go to her bedroom, then he came cautiously through the adjoining door and went to the bathroom. Her paints and powders and blushers were laid out with the careful efficiency of a serious artist. He pulled the blonde wig on before he could face his reflection in the mirror, and then he opened the bottle of foundation cream and sniffed at the sweet, subtle scent. He sponged his face with cream, but left his eyelids bare. He put only a touch of mascara on his eyelashes, and only a little gleam of lipstick at his mouth. At once he looked less like a man impersonating a woman, and more as he felt: some strange, almost genderless, being, halfway between male and female. He felt free from the usual constraints, he felt passionately alive.

Troy opened the door and went into the bedroom. Zelda was already sprawled on the bed, her navy blue dress the match of his, her hair tousled and beautifully blonde like his, her stockings as sheer, her underwear as expensive. The two lovely faces looked at each other. Zelda did not move except to lie back against the thick pillows.

'Come here,' she said silkily.

He moved easily, elegantly, across the carpeted floor between them. He moved as gracefully as a beautiful woman when she knows she has the eyes of the room on her. He walked to the bed and then hitched the skirt provocatively a little higher, so that he could kneel up on one knee and come close to her.

She did not reach out and pull him towards her. She lay back, waiting for him to make the first move. Troy smiled very slightly and saw the answering gleam in her eyes, and then he bent his blonde head and kissed her on the lips.

Her mouth under his was warm and tasted of champagne and lipstick. There was a different feel to the kiss from the usual touch, as one lipsticked mouth met another. The lips were softer, a little slick. Troy pressed forward rather than moving back, wanting the kiss to go on and on, wanting it to be deeper, more intense. Under the pressure of his mouth and his encroaching body Zelda relaxed against the pillows, let her head slip back, let her mouth open longingly. Troy moved forward again, impelled by desire to get deeper and deeper towards her, into her. Zelda's arms came around his shoulders and her hands wonderingly touched the silky back of his dress and the smooth line of the zip.

Troy slid the skirt of the dress up a little higher so that he could press his thigh between hers. At the feeling of the silky stockings on his leg between hers he gave a little involuntary groan of pleasure. Zelda, her eyes shut, drew her hands down to where his dress was pushed up around his waist, put her hands on his buttocks and felt the contradictory sensations of hard muscle and silky hosiery.

'Oh,' she said longingly. 'Oh, Troy.'

He pulled away a little as she said his name and she opened her eyes to see him slightly frowning. 'No,' he said slowly. 'Don't call me that. I'm Zelda.'

'Yes, you are,' she whispered. 'You are her. And I am too.'

Gently he pulled her so that she was sitting on the bed and unzipped the dress. She raised her arms so that he could strip it off her and then she lay back in her beautiful pale blue bra, French knickers, and pale hold-up stockings. Troy peeled the stockings down, admiring their sheer lightness, and dropped them on the floor, then put his hands to the waistband of her knickers. She hesitated for a moment, her eyes questioning him.

'I'm sure,' he said. 'Please.'

She lifted her hips and let him peel them off her. She undid the hooks of her bra and lay back for his caress. She was naked now beneath him and he pulled back from her to kick off his own knickers, but he left his dress and his stockings still on. When he leaned down on top of her again Zelda put her cheek against his warm, male-smelling face, and when she half-opened her eyes she saw his mane of blonde hair, his beautiful makeup. She gazed at him as his body came closer and she felt his erection nudge against her softness. His beautiful navy dress was pulled up over the long lean line of his thighs, his stockings made his legs exquisitely silky. His arms held her hard, like a man holding a woman, but his lipsticked lips kissed her with teasing, feminine gentleness. Zelda's eyes flickered shut and she clasped her hands around the long lean strength of his back, creasing his silk dress as he penetrated her.

* * *

Zelda stirred and opened her eyes. On the pillow beside her was her double, her mirror image. As she watched the mirror eyes opened and smiled at her.

'Are you all right?' Isobel's practical, considerate voice inquired.

Troy nodded. 'Yes.'

The two of them regarded each other steadily for a moment. 'I think I'll go to my room,' Troy said. 'I want to change, and wash, and sleep. We've got a lot to do tomorrow.'

Isobel nodded. 'Goodnight,' she said politely.

'Goodnight,' he said.

They met at breakfast in the dining room without embarrassment, in their daytime personae. Troy was wearing a formal, dark, well-cut suit and Zelda was wearing her yellow skirt and jacket. In the morning Zelda had an interview with a regional magazine and a lunch party with the leading booksellers of Newcastle. After lunch she had to tour as many shops as they could manage and sign stock for them to display in their windows under the banner 'Author signed copy'.

'Sign as many as you possibly can,' Troy urged her in an undertone in the first shop.

'Why?'

'Because then they can't return them, they count as spoiled.'

Isobel hesitated, quite shocked. 'They've been signed by the author and that counts as spoiled stock?'

'To the distributors it does,' Troy said. 'They've been opened, haven't they? And scribbled in?'

'But this is the author signature!' Isobel exclaimed. Someone looked over at the two of them, perched at the display table in the middle of the shop. 'What would they call a signed Shakespeare? Spoiled?'

'Probably,' Troy said cheerfully. 'Anyway, why would you care? You sign them, they have to sell them. And every time you sign you earn one pound and sixty nine pence.'

'It still takes an awful lot of them to make three hundred and fifty thousand,' Isobel remarked.

'So get signing,' he said brutally.

After the booksellers they had tea with a woman's page journalist who wanted to do an in-depth profile of Zelda. She asked exactly the same questions as everyone else had asked and Isobel found that she was responding with exactly the same answers. For one moment she found she could not remember if she had told a small anecdote to this journalist, or to another on a previous day. Examining the glazed look on the journalist's face, she thought it probably didn't matter and told the story anyway.

The women left at six, as her photographer arrived. Zelda stood and walked and turned and smiled for him. She held her book cover as he directed, picture outwards as if to demonstrate to an admiring world the extraordinary fact that someone as blonde and as pretty as she had actually written a hardback novel. Then she held the book open before her as if she were reading her own words with complete fascination. These were the poses which provincial photographers unfailingly chose as the only ones suitable for an author on tour. Zelda had learned to obey, and to smile while doing so.

'Fantastic,' the photographer said with pleasure. 'Just fantastic.'

When he left Zelda dropped into her chair and signalled to a waiter. 'A glass of champagne, please.' She nodded to Troy. 'One for you?'

'Yes,' he said. 'And then a quiet supper I think, don't you?'

She waited until the waiter had brought her glass and set one before Troy. She raised the glass to him in a silent toast. Troy returned the gesture but watched her carefully. He was starting to know her now, he was warned by that dreamy, smiling look.

'I thought we might do something a little different,' Zelda said. 'Since we have the car here, and everything.'

'Such as?'

'I thought Zelda and her friend Isobel might go out for dinner together,' she said. 'We could take the car and find somewhere nice. If it's fine, we could walk home, if it's not too far.'

He was silent for a moment. 'You would come out to dinner as Isobel Latimer?'

She nodded. 'And you as Zelda,' she whispered. 'Why not, Troy? After last night. Don't you want to go a little further?'

He briefly closed his eyes at the thought of it. He knew that he wanted to, very, very much. 'We'd never get away with it,' he said. 'Not with other people. Not in daylight.'

'It's not daylight,' she pointed out. 'It's nighttime. And nobody knows us in this town. And we would get away with it. You're beautiful as her. You know you are.'

Still he hesitated, wanting to be persuaded.

Her voice was as seductive as silk. 'Well, why don't we go upstairs and get her ready?' she asked. 'See how it feels. See how it looks. If you're happy with being her we could go out for dinner. And if you're not we could have room service and stay in. Whatever you prefer.'

He rose to his feet and picked up her glass for her. 'Isobel, you are a very, very surprising woman,' he said feelingly. 'I wish to God I had met you when I was twenty.'

To his surprise she blushed very deeply and her eyes suddenly filled with tears. 'Oh, I wish it too,' she said, heartfelt. 'So much.'

There was a sudden, shocked silence between them, then Isobel deliberately broke the spell, gave him a little smile, and rose to her feet. Troy walked across the lobby floor and pressed the button for the lift. When she joined him she was composed, there was no trace of that brief, betraying moment. The lift doors closed on them, cocooning them in privacy.

Troy thought of asking her why her eyes had filled with tears but he held himself back. He did not want Isobel Latimer's intensity. He wanted Zelda Vere's greedy hedonism.

The lift doors opened and they went to their suite in silence. Troy glanced at her face to see if it was Isobel's frown or Zelda's beautiful blandness. When they reached the door it was Zelda's flirtatious gesture when she felt in Troy's pocket for the room key, fitted it in the lock and let them in. And it was Zelda in his arms when they closed the door behind them.

This time Troy let her help him in the transformation as he shed the business suit and the prosaic black socks and black shoes and exchanged them for Zelda's embroidered silk underwear, sheer hold-up stockings and then the blue cocktail dress. Isobel zipped the zipper for him and felt a moment of intense, almost unbearable desire.

He already had the wig in place and the foundation cream stroked gently all over his smooth-shaven face. Isobel did his eye makeup and painted on his lips.

He sat on the dressing table stool as she worked on him, obediently still, his eyes passively shut.

'How do I look?' he asked, as she dusted powder on his perfect face.

'Beautiful,' she said accurately. 'Wait a moment.'

He sat with his eyes shut and then felt the weight of the blonde fur coat on his shoulders. He felt the warm, silky sensation of the fur nestling at the back of his neck and tickling his ears and his cheekbones as Isobel turned up the collar.

'Now look,' she said softly.

He opened his eyes and saw Zelda, just as she would appear in the newspaper tomorrow, as she had appeared in the magazines and television programmes on the tour. The characteristic Zelda looks: the blonde, thick hair, the wide, glamorous eyes, the brightly coloured lips, were all there. Troy's version of Zelda was a touch harder. The jawline was stronger, the brow a little more defined; but when he smiled, it was Zelda's glamorous, heartless smile.

'You're her,' Isobel said simply.

He heard the desire in her voice and quickly glanced at her. 'Do you want to go out?' he asked.

'Do you?'

He looked back at the flawless reflection. 'We could, couldn't we?'

She nodded. 'Nobody would guess. Truly.'

'It's extraordinary,' he said.

'Because Zelda is a genre, just as much as the book,' Isobel observed. 'What you see when you look at her is the hair and the clothes and the makeup. You hardly see her features at all. There are hundreds of women who have this look. Zelda has it so accurately that almost anyone, from the chambermaid to me, could put on the hair and the clothes and the makeup and look like her.'

'We could go out,' Troy said.

She nodded. 'Yes.'

'What will you wear?'

She smiled. 'I want to wear her clothes, but they'll look different enough on me. Wait a minute in the sitting room and I'll come through.'

Isobel changed quickly, hardly caring what she wore. She cleaned her face of Zelda's bright makeup and put on only a little dab of powder and a pale lipstick. She took off the brassy wig and tied her own brown hair back into a modest pony tail. She chose a black cocktail dress and a sequined jacket. Above the brightness of the jacket her skin looked tired and pale. She added a little foundation around her eyes and a little blusher on her cheeks. Beside Zelda's bright glamour she would be a slightly faded English rose, a little wallflower.

'I'm dull,' she said, coming into the room. Zelda was sprawled, as she always sprawled, on the sofa, her long, lovely legs stretched out, one high-heeled shoe swinging from her arched foot. She rose up when she saw Isobel and came over to her and took her in her arms and kissed her gently, so that their lipstick did not smudge.

'You look endearing,' the beauty said to her more ordinary friend. 'I've ordered the car. We can go.'

Isobel hesitated. 'I have to telephone Philip. You go on down.'

'I'll wait for you,' Zelda said. 'I don't dare go down on my own. I can wait next door.'

Isobel shook her head. 'You can wait here. We never say anything private.'

As she dialled the number Troy thought how revealing of her marriage was that little statement of fact: they never said anything private. Then why be married at all? he thought.

'Hello, darling, it's me,' Isobel said.

Philip had been dozing in his chair, Mrs M. was in the kitchen laying the table for their supper.

'Oh yes,' he said. 'How are you?'

'I'm fine. How are you feeling?'

'Perfectly well,' he said at once. Isobel listened to see if she could hear the strain of pain in his voice. He sounded well.

'You sound sleepy,' she said hopefully.

'Well, I've had a big day out,' he said. She could hear the pleasure in his voice and it made her smile. 'Murray came round and took me on a mini-tour. He wanted me to see the other pools he's put in. I met a couple of rather pleasant people with pools in their garden and it gave me a chance to see the tiles that I was considering for us. I've gone off blue, it's a bit of a cliché, I think – the blue pool. I'm rather thinking about a sort of iridescent green.'

'Iridescent green?'

'Like marble, with a sort of gold thread in it.'

'Golly,' Isobel said.

'Murray was very good. Took me out to lunch at the Blue Boar,' Philip went on. 'We took in a couple of pools in the afternoon. We saw only one indoor one, you know. I would be surprised if there were more than half a dozen in the whole county. And none the size that we are planning.'

'Oh, really? Would ours be so very big?'

'Exactly, that's the great mistake. People build them too small and then of course you can't extend them. It's a completely false economy.'

'We only need room for two,' she observed.

He laughed. 'It's not the space for swimming that counts. It's the aesthetic effect,' he said. 'Murray told me all about it. The last thing you want is to feel that you'll do half a dozen strokes and crash into the far end. It stops you swimming hard. It actually prevents you from getting the most that you can out of the pool. It diminishes your pleasure in the whole thing, so it makes it less worthwhile in the long run.'

'I see.'

'Anyway, what I'm thinking about now is building a little covered walkway from the barn to the house. The last thing we want to do is to come out of the gym or the pool all warmed up and then have to trek back to the house in the rain.'

Isobel said nothing.

'So Murray's going to price one for me and we can put in a supplementary planning permission. I'd like something that looks a bit solid, in the style of the house.'

'I see,' she said.

'I can't wait for you to come home and see the plans,' he said. 'Saturday midday train, is it?'

'Yes. But I'll phone you tomorrow, as usual.'

'Good,' he said happily. 'I might have rough sketches of the walkway by then.'

'That'll be lovely,' she said. 'Goodnight, darling.'

Isobel put down the phone. Troy saw her face, grave and weary as she turned to the door. Then she caught sight of him in his Zelda dress, his lovely hair and his beautiful face with the blonde fur draping from his shoulders to his heels. At once her face changed; she became the entranced lover that she had been the night before.

'Are you ready?' he asked, meaning really: 'Can you put that responsibility and that worry behind you and come and be happy with me?'

And she smiled, a radiant smile, and tucked her arm in the crook of his silky, furry elbow. 'Oh yes,' she said.

Fourteen

The waiters in the restaurant hovered around Zelda as they always did. There was not a question in anyone's mind, there was no scrutiny in any look. The imposture was perfect and as the evening went on Troy as Zelda became more and more confident, more and more comfortable with this new identity. Zelda ordered lasagne and a green salad. Isobel had her usual spaghetti bolognese and watched the way that Zelda could scan the room and still give their conversation her full attention. They drank white wine and sparkling mineral water. Zelda asked for a long glass and drank hers mixed together. Isobel gave her a sceptical look over the top of the glass and Zelda gave her a sexy, smiling wink.

They laughed a lot, as women who enjoy each other's company will always laugh a lot together. They tempted each other to eat puddings, and then to have brandies with their coffee. At the end of the evening they paid the bill and over-tipped. The manager himself held Zelda's fur to slip it over her shoulders and then, as a secondary act of homage, wrapped Isobel in her pashmina. They left the restaurant together, arm in arm, in the car they held hands. When they walked through the lobby of the hotel, men turned their heads to watch Zelda's swaying stride. She was unquestionably a head-turning, beautiful woman. She walked with her head high, all the confidence of beauty in her movement, she swayed her narrow hips, she turned her head slowly from side to side and looked around, an unfeminine gaze, as if she owned the place. She looked back at men boldly, as only a beautiful woman will do. She was not a modest woman, not a lady. She was a proud beauty, and she looked as if any man might have her – if he were brave enough to ask.

In the lift she leaned back against the wall and put her hands to her head. 'I feel dizzy!' she said.

'It can't be the drink,' Isobel said. 'We only had a bottle of wine, and a glass of champagne before we went out.'

'And a brandy,' Zelda reminded her.

'But even so . . .'

'It's not that,' Zelda said. 'It's the attention. It's the way that men look at you as if they had every right to look at you, as if you're an object for their inspection.'

Isobel nodded. 'D'you find it demeaning?'

Zelda laughed, a gurgle of sexy laughter. 'I find it heavenly,' she said. 'I'd wear shorter and shorter skirts all the time just to get that look. It's like you could run the whole world. It's like every man in the world would do anything for you, just for a smile.'

Isobel stepped out of the lift. 'If you'd had it all your life you'd know it doesn't quite work like that,' she said. 'They do look; but they don't make you president of America just because you have nice legs. And sometimes they look as if they owned you, as if they had a right to look, as if you were a meat pie, not a rose. It's a feminist issue: the woman as object.'

'But I *love* that look,' Zelda protested. 'I love that kind of consuming, demanding, superior look. Exactly as you say. As if they had a right to you and didn't even have to ask.'

Isobel laughed and opened the door. 'You want to be seen as a secondary being? As a sexual object?' They stepped through the door and Isobel took Zelda fiercely in her arms. 'Like this?' she whispered into the blonde hair. 'D'you want me to take you without asking? As if I had a right to you, without ever asking?'

Zelda's long eyelashes fluttered and closed. 'Yes,' she whispered. 'Yes.'

*   *   *

176

They spent the night in Isobel's bed, wrapped in each other's bodies, continually drawing closer and drawing apart through the night. Twice they woke and made love in a state of dreamy desire. Isobel slept naked, she wanted the touch of Troy on every inch of her skin. Troy slept in Zelda's beautiful silk nightdress. They felt wildly glamorous and beautiful. The smoked glass mirrors of the big wardrobe reflected two sapphic beauties, wrapped in each other's arms, sometimes a waterfall of blonde hair tumbling from Zelda's outstretched head, sometimes Isobel's brown hair spread across the pillow.

But in the morning Troy found that he had shed the false eyelashes from one eyelid and his stubble was growing back, his scalp itched under the hot wig and he felt sweaty and ridiculous in crumpled silk. He slid from the bed, feeling nothing but dismay and revulsion. He left the negligee on the bathroom floor while he had a scaldingly hot shower.

Isobel, knowing only that everything had changed again, waited for him to finish in the bathroom and then took a bath. Dressed in one of Zelda's suits she went down to breakfast on her own. Troy joined her only when the car was at the door and they had to set off for another full day, travelling to Manchester and then calling at two radio stations and opening a new branch of a national book chain. Troy wore his most sombre dark business suit, a white shirt, and a dark tie, and hardly spoke to Zelda all the morning except to ask her if she would like a drink, or if she had a copy of her schedule and was aware of where they were going next.

Far from feeling embarrassed, or rebuffed, Isobel was relieved that they could separate the pleasures of the night so completely from the work of the day. All day she made no attempt at all to restore any intimacy between them. Anyone watching them would have thought they had a relationship which was highly professional, perhaps even a little chilly. Just before the last interview of the day Troy said that he would see her back at the hotel, he did not even stay to monitor what she would say. Without his watchful presence Isobel found she was giving the same replies but that she was even more superficial than usual. She was impatient to take the car back to the hotel and find him waiting for her with two glasses of champagne in the bar.

They had only time for a snatched supper and for Isobel to have a shower and change before they were due at the television studio.

'I need to phone Philip first,' she said. 'I can't miss a night.'

'Are you sure it won't put you off?' Troy asked nervously. 'It's live television, remember.'

'I'll just be a moment,' she said. 'I always phone him every evening and it'll be too late by the time we come out tonight.'

'OK. I'll wait downstairs with the car,' Troy said. 'Bring the room key.'

She flashed a quick smile at him. She liked him telling her to remember things, it was like a pretence of domestic life. Neither of them had mentioned the night before, it was a secret too deep for speech. Isobel had spent all her life thinking about things, bringing them to the surface of consciousness, putting them into words. Now, paradoxically, she wanted to have an experience for which there were no words. She could not describe what was happening between her and Troy. She had no name, no definition, for the relationship. It was just the three of them: Isobel and Troy . . . and Zelda.

Philip answered on the third ring, which meant that he was sitting by the telephone, in front of the fire in the sitting room.

'It's me,' she said.

'Ah. Late tonight. How are you?'

'I'm fine. How are you?'

'Perfectly well,' he said irritably. 'Why not?'

From that, Isobel knew at once that he was in pain. 'Is it the same old pain?' The thing they both dreaded was change, or deterioration.

'Nothing worse than usual,' he said grudgingly.

'I can come home,' she offered wildly.

'No need unless you want to,' he said shortly. 'How's the teaching going?'

'Wonderful, very worthwhile,' she said. 'I'm enjoying it tremendously.'

'Have you been out on the town this evening?'

'I was at the theatre,' she said. 'With Carla.'

'I hope she paid for her own seat,' he said crossly. 'Last time you went out to dinner with her she forgot her purse.'

Isobel laughed. 'Of course she did.'

'Well, I don't like to see you being cheated,' he said stubbornly. 'When you're a success, people assume you're made of money, and they all want their cut. You have to make sure they don't take advantage.'

'I was friends with Carla when we were all living on students' grants,' she said mildly. 'We shared our only can of baked beans with each other.'

'That was a long, long time ago.'

She sighed. 'Yes, I know it.'

'Murray was here today,' he said more cheerfully. 'He was going to eat his lunch in his car. I said he could come in, join me.'

'How nice for you. And how are the plans for the pool going?'

'We've finalised them at last,' he said. Isobel could hear how his excitement revitalised him. 'Murray took them in to the planners' office this afternoon when he left here. Now we have to wait for permission. But while we're waiting we can crack on with the design of the detail. The style issues as opposed to the broad brush.'

'Style issues?'

'The tiles for the poolside, the finish of the inside of the pool, the position of the diving board, the shape of the jacuzzi, the finish of the jacuzzi, the internal furnishing of the sauna. That sort of thing.'

'Oh,' she said. 'It sounds very . . . glamorous.' She meant expensive, but she feared to damp his enthusiasm.

'It is glamorous,' he confirmed happily. 'I told Murray to start from the assumption that we wanted absolutely top of the range. Nothing but the best. It's much easier to see the very best thing that money can buy and then work down from it, than start rooting around in the economy section and then discover that you simply can't bear it.'

'But this is just a little swimming pool for you and me to enjoy,' she reminded him. 'Not Hollywood.'

He laughed, a thin little laugh because of the pain; but she was glad that he would laugh at all. 'Not so little,' he said gleefully. 'You just wait till you see it.'

She swallowed. 'And Murray must have done a detailed financial estimate by now, if it's so far advanced that he's applied for planning permission.'

'He's got it all in hand,' Philip said cheerfully. 'You can sit down and we'll go through the figures when you come home. I think you'll be pleased.'

'What sort of sum are we talking about?'

'I'll show you when you come home,' he promised. 'It's really good value for money. You'll be impressed.'

'I'm sure I will,' she said feebly. 'Look, darling, I have to go now. I'll call you tomorrow, about the same time?'

'All right,' he said. 'I'll be here. I'm not gadding around London pretending to be working.'

Isobel tried to laugh. 'I'm working very hard. I'll speak to you tomorrow.'

There was no makeup girl or hairdresser for the late-night discussion programme. There was no dressing room either. The four participants gathered in uneasy proximity in the studio green room and were offered a choice of wine, water, tea or coffee by a young girl, while the producer put his head around the door from time to time and said: 'Everyone all right? Not long now.'

The guests were to be the promised university lecturer, Dr Mariel Ford, who was there to provide intellectual weight and keep the discussion going; Zelda Vere, who was to represent — Isobel swiftly guessed — the anti-censorship, commercial marketing argument; a tense-looking man, who would take up a right-wing position on censorship, or indeed on anything else; and an artist in residence from the nearest arts centre, who would argue for artistic freedom.

'This is going to be dreadful,' Isobel murmured to Troy as he poured her a glass of wine.

'I did warn you,' he said. 'Too late to get out of it now.'

She nodded and took her seat on the sofa, stretching out her long legs. Her blue skirt rode up above her knees and the stern university lecturer regarded her with some distaste. Ronald Smart, the right-winger in favour of censorship of sexual material on all the broadcast channels, could hardly take his eyes off her.

'Ready now,' the producer announced breathlessly. 'You can bring your drinks and there's water on the table.'

They all rose to their feet and went into the studio. It was a dark, echoing barn of a place and in the middle, artificially cosy, was a studio designer's idea of a library-cum-gentleman's club, intended to stimulate thoughtful discussion. The walls were lined with artificial books. Isobel took a look at them and was shocked to find that they were real spines of real books which had been cut off from the bindings and stuck on the walls to imitate a hardback library.

'This is the most dreadful vandalism!' she exclaimed.

Troy, who was following her, carrying her glass, said: 'Zelda!'

'Yes?'

'I didn't think that was the sort of thing that *you* would worry about.'

She recoiled slightly. 'Yes. Of course it isn't. Of course I don't. Sorry.'

'Don't forget,' he ordered her in a whisper, handed her the glass and stepped back into the darkness of the studio.

The other guests seated themselves on the leather sofas and tried to look both relaxed and erudite. Zelda, thinking only of how she looked and not at all concerned with seeming clever, leaned back to show her legs to full advantage and listened to the floor manager running through the rules of the discussion: they were not to rise from their places, they were to take it in turns to talk, they could interrupt, they could even raise their voices, but they were not allowed to get up from their seats. They would have alcoholic drinks served to them in the breaks; there would be three breaks in the hour. They could, indeed should, be interesting, provocative and, above all, *lively*.

'Lots of life!' he said despairingly, looking at the four of them and the presenter who came into the studio at a jog, smoothing his tie down and running his hands through his hair. 'I know it's going to be a great programme.'

The presenter dropped into his chair at the head of the table. 'Sorry I'm late,' he said. 'You know how it is.'

Isobel took an instant dislike to him. She longed to say rather sharply to the young man: 'No. I have no idea what you mean by that. How is it, precisely? And what is *it*, precisely?' Consciously repressing Isobel Latimer's waspish pedantry, she made an effort to smile at him and moved a cushion behind her back for greater comfort.

'Coming to you in five,' the studio manager said loudly. 'Five, four . . .' He held up three fingers, two, then one. The red bulb blinked on top of the camera and the presenter beamed at it.

'Good evening,' he said warmly. 'And welcome to "Brain Aerobics", the late-night discussion programme for people whose minds are still awake. I'm your host, Justin Wade. With me tonight is Dr Mariel Ford from Manchester University, an expert on ethics, Zelda Vere, whose raunchy bestseller takes the genre of the confessional autobiography to a new high – or should I say low? Ronald Smart from the "Monitoring Media" group, who would like to see greater control over what vulnerable people can watch, read or see – and that means a loss of freedom for all of us, folks – and artist in residence Matt Fryer, whose work at Newbridge Arts Centre is known to so many of us. Ronald, if we could come to you first, what sort of things are you trying to prevent on our screens?'

The man leaned forward. 'I don't think I need to describe

them,' he said. 'We all know, surely, the tide of filth that has washed over this country, and now that we are entering the digital age and the video age it will be unstoppable unless we put up strong legal blocks now.'

'Is your particular concern violence? Or sex?' the presenter asked.

'Oh, sex,' the man answered. 'The vast majority of offensive material is sexual.'

'You don't find scenes of violence offensive or corrupting?' Isobel asked, raising an eyebrow.

'Let me explain. It's not *corrupting*,' Ronald spoke slowly as if to a dense child. 'By corrupting we mean material which overrides normal decent behaviour. Violence is part of normal, decent behaviour. It can be regulated by ordinary rules as part of our ordinary way of life. But an obsessive interest in sexual material is corrupting. People, especially young people, lose their sense of judgement.'

Isobel looked politely amazed and waited for the presenter to challenge him. But he did not, he turned to the academic. 'Would you support that, Dr Ford?'

'I don't know that logically one can differentiate by the impact of one sort of material or another,' Dr Ford said judicially. 'But I do see the point that Mr Smart is making.'

'Well, I don't,' Isobel said acerbically, irritated at being ignored. 'It seems to me a complete tautology. First he makes a definition of normality which is unquestioned, then he makes a definition of corrupting materials which is unquestioned, then he makes an assertion about the impact of corruption on everyone and especially on young people. This is nothing more than unsupported opinion.'

Troy in the viewing gallery saw that Zelda had disappeared completely from Isobel's consciousness. It was constitutionally impossible for Isobel Latimer to let a sloppy argument go by, whatever she might be wearing, whatever rôle she was playing. She simply could not do it. Troy leaned back in his chair and closed his eyes in horror.

'There is clear evidence . . .' Ronald Smart started, heatedly.

'No, there isn't,' Isobel replied promptly. 'As far as I know there has been only one major study and that suggested that children are far more affected by violence on television than anything else. And a great deal of this violence takes place in programmes which are passed as suitable for children anyway, such as cartoons or light entertainment.'

The producer in the viewing gallery swore loudly and glared at Troy. 'What the hell is she doing?' he demanded in a tone of low fury. 'She's supposed to be the bimbo. What's she talking about?'

Troy shook his head. He alone knew that Isobel had abandoned the persona of Zelda. He alone knew that years of academic training were now locking Isobel's mind on to the argument. Wearing a beautiful suit and a blonde wig would not be enough to silence Isobel. She had forgotten everything but the folly of the opposing argument, destroying the argument would be irresistible. Zelda had gone completely. It was Isobel who leaned forward. It was Isobel's spiky brain and sharp voice. Troy put his hands over his face and racked his brains to think how Zelda could be recalled. 'Tell him to ask her about her work,' he said. 'Get her talking about her novel. Bring her back to herself.'

The producer muttered urgently into the little microphone which spoke to the presenter's earpiece. At once, in the brightly lit little studio below them, Justin turned to Zelda.

'But what about your own novel?' he asked. 'There are scenes both of very graphic sex and violence in your novel. And indeed violence, very graphic violence, to women.'

'Not like that!' Troy shouted in the sound-proofed viewing gallery. 'Not a question like that! Nothing that allows her to think! Ask her about clothes or about writing a bestseller or something. Not a question of ethics!'

Isobel leaned forward still further, every line of her tense body completely unlike the relaxed grace of Zelda. Under the blonde wig she was scowling in concentration.

'What you're suggesting is an inability by the reader to distinguish between fact and fiction,' she said. 'This is a traditional criticism of fiction which goes back to the very dawn of the novel. Critics as early as 1690 were arguing that novels should be banned, or at the very least banned for children and indeed servants, because it was thought that ill-educated people would not be able to make the distinction between reality and pretence. In fact, of course, people are perfectly competent to make such a distinction. Indeed, the ability to pretend, and to learn from the pretended situations, is one of the most powerful learning tools that we have as a species. Probably every human society has had storytellers to preserve and embroider their history. It's a vital part of learning, memory and speech. It's nonsense to suggest that it might be damaging.'

Dr Ford, recognising with surprise an equal intellect under the bimbo suit and the mane of blonde hair, focused on Isobel as a worthy foe. 'You can hardly make a comparison between the great archetypes of pre-literacy storytelling and novels such as your own which are clearly formulaic and commercial and are written, not to preserve a history or to teach a lesson, but merely to sell as successfully as possible to an ill-educated market,' she said roundly.

Zelda would have shrieked in horror, she might even have dabbed at her eyes at the unkindness. Isobel didn't even blink.

'What a ridiculous concept,' she retorted. 'Of course my novel taps into the darkest archetypes. Its subject matter is the oldest story ever told: the battle between good and evil and the concept of revenge. And of course it's told in a medium which is appropriate for the time in which it is written. Would you only accept material which was sung around a camp fire? What about the Greek tragedies? What about the *Oresteia*?'

'*Oresteia*?' the producer howled at Troy. 'What's the silly bitch talking about?' He whirled around and stabbed the talk-back button. 'Cue a break!' he said abruptly. 'Roll VT,' he said to his assistant. He left the desk and dragged Troy up from his chair. 'You get down there,' he hissed. 'You have

185

exactly twenty minutes. That's adverts, plus a filmed insert about that stupid artist's work. You take her out and get her sorted out. I hired her to sit on the sofa and look beautiful and say one or two suggestive things about sex. She's supposed to do sex. She's supposed to *be* sex. I've hired intellect from the university. I've hired argumentative from the Conservatives. I've hired artistic from the Arts Centre. But I hired *her* for sex and decoration. Tell her to shut her mouth up and simper. I don't want another word out of her, I want her to look decorative and shut the fuck up!'

He half-hurled Troy from the viewing gallery and Troy scampered down the stairs to the studio. The little red light on the camera was off, Troy stepped up the half-step to the set floor and peremptorily held out his hand to Zelda. She had disregarded the fact that the cameras were off and was pursuing her argument with the academic.

'Zelda!'

She turned at his voice and looked in his direction, shading her eyes from the bright lights with a frown at the interruption which was pure Isobel Latimer.

'Oh? What is it?' she asked.

'Come,' he said abruptly.

She rose from her seat and he threw her coat around her shoulders and drew her outside into the corridor and swiftly out of the front door.

'What are you doing?'

'You're going back to the hotel.'

'Why?'

'Because anyone who sees you looking like that and talking like that will know that you're Isobel Latimer. Don't you know that you're instantly recognisable? You've not been Zelda for the whole programme.'

'I was!' she protested.

Troy flung her into the waiting car and slammed the door. 'To the hotel,' he snapped. 'And wait.'

Inside the car he put his mouth to her ear and hissed: 'You're going to blow the whole thing, you're going to spoil the whole thing. Why did you start talking like that? Why didn't you just sit there? Why did you have to start thinking and talking and being Isobel?'

'I didn't mean to,' she said, coming rapidly back to earth. 'It was just that they were saying such nonsense. I couldn't sit there and hear it. I didn't know how to answer it with nonsense of my own. I couldn't stop myself thinking, Troy, I'm sorry. Let me go back. I'll try again.'

'Never mind *try*,' he said urgently. 'Can you promise, really promise, to do it? Whatever they say, just sit and smile and keep quiet?'

She thought for a moment. 'It's really hard. It's like asking me not to see. I can't help seeing, can I?'

He nodded. 'That's what I thought. You'd argue, wouldn't you?'

'If they say nothing to me I'll stay silent,' she offered. 'But if they ask me for an opinion, it's really hard not to think. And then I start thinking about not thinking, and of course that's . . .'

'Shut up!' Troy snapped. 'You're doing it now. It's hopeless. We'll have to scratch, say you've been taken ill or something.'

'No.' Isobel pulled at his sleeve. 'We can't do that. It'll just make it worse. I'll go back. I'll really try.'

Troy shook his head. 'Would I pass for her?'

Isobel was stunned into silence for a moment. 'In your dress? With the hair and the makeup?'

'Would I?'

'Yes,' she said. 'You saw the waiters in the restaurant in Newcastle last night. Yes. You'd pass for her.'

'I look enough like you look when you're her?'

She nodded. 'You saw us in the mirror, we said we were twins.'

'Right then,' Troy said determinedly. 'Here's what we're going to do. We're going back to the hotel and you're going upstairs to bed. Don't answer the door and don't answer the phone. OK?'

She nodded, her grey eyes wide.

'I'm getting dressed as Zelda,' he said. 'I'm getting dressed as her and I'm going out to be her. It's the only thing we can do. We have to keep the PR running, we can't have anyone asking who she is and why she's so bright. We can't have someone running a story about her collapsing on tour after arguing on a late-night discussion show and showing the clip of the programme. We can't have anyone looking past the clothes and the hair and seeing you.'

Isobel gasped. 'You can do it?'

'Ten times better than you,' he said savagely. 'I don't have a brain that's bursting to come out. I don't have thoughts that I have to speak.'

She grasped his hands. 'Thank you,' she said fervently. 'I really can't do this. I'm sorry. I can't stop myself somehow. I should never have got us into this.'

'And we're not out of it yet,' he said grimly.

The car drew up to the front steps of the hotel. 'Wait,' Troy ordered the driver. 'Wait right here. Don't let them move you on. Miss Vere is only going to be ten minutes and she'll be going back to the studio on her own. I don't want her to have to walk to the car.

'Of course, sir,' the driver said. 'I'll be right here.'

Troy grabbed Zelda and swept her through the lobby and up to the bedroom. He slammed the door behind him.

'Help me,' he said, undoing his trousers and heeling off his shoes. 'I've got ten minutes to turn into her.'

Fifteen

They flew at the transformation like a pair of professional actors, experienced at quick change. Troy frantically sponged foundation cream over his face and forced his head into the wig, while Isobel laid out Zelda's clothes on the bed. She came into the bathroom in time to do his eye makeup, steadily she pressed the false eyelashes on his lids, painted the thin line of eyeliner, combed his eyebrows into a copy of her own arched style. She pencilled on the lipliner and then plastered on the lipstick. He looked at himself in the brightly lit mirror. He had become yet another being. He was wearing his most conventionally cut, sombre Armani suit but then above it was this bright, glamorous face and this tousled mane of blonde hair. He looked like a woman dressing as a man, he had that cheeky boyish look of a woman wearing a man's suit. But at the same time he looked like a man with a woman's porcelain face. He looked more perverse than ever he had done in Zelda's clothes. He gazed at this new version of himself in wonder.

'We don't have time,' Isobel interrupted, following his entranced eyes to the reflection in the mirror. 'We'll do this again tomorrow night. But you have to go now.'

'Of course!' Troy was recalled to the urgency of the moment, and went swiftly to the bedroom.

He stripped off his suit and pulled on his Zelda underwear, taking care with the silky stockings. He stood still while Isobel fastened the bra across his broad back and adjusted the silicone pads inside the cups. Then he threw the navy-blue cocktail dress over his head and stepped into the shoes as Isobel zipped up the back.

He took one careful glance at the mirror as Isobel fetched the mink coat from where she had dropped it on the sofa in the middle room.

'Am I OK?' he asked, his voice tight with nerves.

'You're perfect,' she said. 'You were perfect last night, remember the manager at the restaurant? He was all over you. You'll be perfect again. Go.'

She held out the mink coat for him, as a lady's maid serves a proud society beauty. It was the cue for him. He raised his chin and gave a smile to the mirror which was pure Zelda. A smile which was at once mocking and arrogant, inviting and rejecting. Then he turned from the flawless reflection, slipped on the coat and went to the door.

'Don't answer the phone,' Zelda said in her commanding voice.

'No, Zelda,' Isobel said obediently.

Zelda's blue eyes gleamed. 'And wait up for me,' she said huskily. 'I shall want you when I come home.'

Isobel's grey eyes met hers. 'I'll be in bed,' she said quietly. 'I'll be naked. I shall want you, too.'

Zelda flicked around, opened the door, and was gone.

The driver took her to the front door of the television studio where a nervous researcher was hovering outside. 'We're cutting it very fine,' she said.

Zelda strode out along the silent corridors of the studios.

'In here,' the girl said. 'I'm afraid you have to go straight to the set. There's a glass of water for you on the table. They're just coming out of the break.'

Zelda nodded and dropped her fur off her shoulders as she went up the two shallow steps to the set. The researcher caught it and fled out of the way of the camera as the producer's hand counted down the seconds and the host turned once again to Camera One with his practised smile.

'Zelda Vere, before that interesting filmed contribution you were making rather strong claims for your novel as part of the storytelling tradition?'

Zelda turned her lovely head to him so that Camera One could get her classical profile. 'Oh, I'm just a storyteller,' she said sweetly. 'People want stories. It's what we all want, don't we? Something to take us out of our humdrum lives?'

'But your story describes a life which was far from humdrum, and you have chosen to write it as if it were real, and so you take the reader into some pretty unpleasant scenes: sexual assault, rape, Satanic abuse, and that's just the first few chapters.'

Zelda turned to the camera, her eyes inviting sympathy. 'The experience on which I based my book was a very dreadful one which I survived only by a miracle,' she said throatily. 'I would not have been true to myself or true to the people who have also been through such trauma if I pretended that it was not dreadful. Dreadful and yes, at one level, deeply erotic.'

'But this is just what I object to!' Ronald Smart interrupted. 'You've just confessed to doing it deliberately. Taking something which is hardly suitable for light reading, and deliberately making it appealing. It's just disgusting!'

Zelda turned her dark blue gaze on him. 'I don't make it appealing,' she said flatly. 'It simply is. The line between pleasure and pain is a very narrow one. The line between fear and desire is very fine. I survived a traumatic experience where the line for me was crossed and crossed again. But I cannot deny . . .' there was a small potent silence '. . . that such experiences are at their core *both* deeply pleasurable . . . and very dreadful.'

Ronald Smart blushed suddenly, a deep surprising scarlet. 'But hardly the stuff for a ladies' novel,' he said in a choked voice.

Zelda gave him her most seductive smile. 'You would be surprised what you would find in ladies' novels,' she said sweetly 'I would think that you would be surprised at what you might find in ladies' imaginations.'

Dr Mariel Ford, still smarting from her earlier exchange, leaned forward. 'So by your own admission, your novel is closely related to pornography.'

Zelda gave one of her most feminine shrugs. 'Oh, I don't know,' she said carelessly. 'I've never read pornography. I've never had the need to draw on someone else's imagination. In my own mind I have pictures enough, I have desires enough. Haven't you?'

Dr Ford looked rather taken aback, as if it had been some years since anyone asked her about the detail of her erotic fantasies. 'I don't claim to be a pornography expert,' she said shortly.

Justin, feeling the evening was rather getting away from him, gestured to Matt Fryer, the artist. 'Matt, what are your thoughts on this?'

Matt was aroused from a dreamy contemplation of Zelda's long, strong legs, provocatively and surprisingly hairy under the smooth stockings. 'I think there is an obligation on the artist to be responsible,' he said. 'In my own work I try to create things which will move people to a sense of beauty. But even then, I think you have to recognise that what one person will see as beautiful another person might see as offensive.'

'Exactly!' Zelda turned to him with delight, as one artist greeting another. 'You can be responsible for your own vision, but not how someone reads it or sees it.'

The floor manager made winding up gestures to Justin who ran a hand through his hair to indicate his natural informality and smiled at the camera dollying in towards him. 'And there we have to leave it for tonight. This was "Brain Aerobics" with me, Justin Wade, and my guests. Same time next week, when we will be discussing cigarettes: a personal right or a social menace? Goodnight.'

They remained as frozen as a set of waxworks as the camera pulled back for a long view of them all, and then the red light on the top of it went out, the red light at the back of the studio winked and went out, and the floor manager said wearily: 'Thank you very much, everybody, that was excellent.'

Zelda stood up and looked around for her coat. 'You were marvellous,' Justin Wade said to her. 'Especially in the second half, you were very challenging, very provocative.'

'Thank you,' Zelda said without interest.

The researcher came up and held out the coat, expecting Zelda to take it from her. Zelda turned round and presented her back so the girl had no choice but to slip it over her shoulders. 'Thank you,' Zelda said, stroking the pelt. The girl nodded sulkily, and went off. Zelda smiled.

Justin Wade turned to say goodbye to his other guests, and then turned back quickly to Zelda who was heading for the door. 'Miss Vere?'

'Yes?' she hesitated.

'Would you like a drink? Can I offer you a glass of champagne, perhaps? There's quite a pleasant little club over the road.'

Zelda thought of Isobel waiting for her, naked in bed. She smiled. 'That would be lovely,' she said.

Troy, adjusting his makeup in the privacy of a locked cubicle in the ladies' powder room of the bar, had a sense of delicious infidelity, of savouring complicated and forbidden fruits. Isobel would be waiting for him with increasing anxiety. Justin thought he was dating a glamorous and successful woman. Troy, inside these interconnecting disloyalties and deceits, felt himself to be at last most truly himself, defined by the things that he was not, defined by the masks that he could take off one at a time, or equally put on and overlay.

He retouched his lipstick, he fluffed up the blonde hair. Then he flushed the toilet and came out of the cubicle, washed his hands by turning on the tap and putting the very tips of his fingers under the water, and emerged into the restaurant. Justin Wade had ordered a bottle of champagne and was pouring the second glass as Troy returned to the table.

'Zelda!' he said, he rose slightly in his chair to acknowledge her return. Zelda smiled as a woman accepting her normal homage, smoothed her skirt down over her thighs, sat on the chair and crossed her legs.

'You are a natural for television,' Justin assured her. 'Has anyone else told you that?'

'A production company approached me in London,' she said modestly. 'Before I came away on tour. I promised them I would think it over.'

'For what sort of thing?' he asked.

'A chat show, about surviving difficulties, with real-life stories and people talking about their own troubles,' Zelda said.

At once he shook his head. 'You have to be terribly careful with these fly-by-night production companies. Some of them are little more than a freelance on spec with a telephone. You need someone to advise you, really.'

'Oh, I do, I know I do.' Zelda leaned forward.

'Do you have an agent?'

'I have a literary agent,' Zelda said provocatively. 'Troy Cartwright. You met him earlier. He had to go back to the hotel to make some calls. He does my publishing deals, I don't know if he could advise me about television.'

Justin Wade emphatically shook his head. 'Not at all, it's a completely different world,' he said. 'And a tough world. You need the advice of someone who is completely at home in the world of television, someone who's been there, done it all, and got the T-shirt. Your literary agent might know his way around the publishing houses but put him in the world of film and television and he would be an innocent abroad.'

Zelda fixed her blue eyes on his face and nodded trustingly.

'I tell you what I would do if I were you,' Justin said thoughtfully. 'I'd set up my own production company and offer the idea of a talk show to the TV companies on my own account. Why give away your control? Why let someone else employ you?'

'But I wouldn't begin to know how to do it!' Zelda protested. 'I wouldn't know where to start.'

He waved a dismissive hand. 'That's no problem,' he said. 'You could take advice. But – if you will excuse me talking about you as if you were a can of baked beans for a moment – you're a very marketable product. For instance, I could place you in half a dozen slots.'

Behind Zelda's rapt, admiring expression, Troy understood for the first time the difficulty that Isobel experienced in staying in character. Justin Wade might be looking at her adoringly, but he was playing Zelda as if she were a fool. Troy had to fight to hide his irritation and keep his face serene.

'I don't know if I like being baked beans,' Zelda remarked flirtatiously. 'You speak of me as if I were a thing.'

Justin dropped his hand on hers as it lay on the table. 'Jar of caviar,' he amended. 'Whatever. And in a sense, as far as the market goes, you are a thing: a deliciously new, unexpected thing, the very thing that everyone wants at the moment. A very marketable thing.'

'Not a person,' Zelda confirmed.

'You are your own asset,' Justin said. 'You have to sell yourself. You could have a very substantial career in television.'

'I don't know that I would be able . . .'

'Trust me. You are a natural. You were wonderful tonight.'

'I would love to do it, of course. But where to start?'

'I can tell you that. What you need is a first-class television producer. Someone who really knows their way around, someone you can trust to guard your interests.'

Troy had a weary sense of bringing a glaringly obvious game into check. 'Oh, but where would I find the right person?'

'Oh, anyone could do it. Why – I could do it!'

They both affected amazement that the conversation had brought them to this point. 'Oh, but how could you?' Zelda asked. 'With your own career so busy?'

Justin shrugged. 'I can do a programme like "Brain Aerobics" in my sleep.'

Troy had the discretion not to agree.

'I've been looking for my chance to get into production. I have the skills and the contacts and the knowledge. I was waiting for a project that I would find interesting. I'm not a man who can commit to something that doesn't really fascinate me. I'd need to be really fascinated.' He paused. 'You really fascinate me,' he added softly. 'I'd like to be the one that takes you up where you belong. You could go so far . . .'

Zelda's fingers stirred under his touch. 'I really don't know,' she said helplessly. 'How would we go about it?'

'Well, we'd have to set up a production company in both of our names, we'd be joint shareholders. We'd have to take a London office and employ a couple of staff, absolutely minimal, a researcher and a receptionist, say. And then we'd put a proposal or a couple of proposals together and take them to the television companies. When they say "Yes" we go into production, take on more staff, and make the programmes. We sell the programmes to them and take the profit. Very nice too.'

'How much would it cost to set up?' Zelda asked cautiously.

Justin thought for a moment. 'Off the top of my head I'd say – oh – about £200,000. Maybe that sounds a lot to you but we'd pay ourselves a salary of course, and we'd have to pay rent.' He hesitated. 'That's the difficulty for me. My capital is tied up in a house I've just bought. I could put the house in as my share if you could match it with cash.'

Zelda looked thoughtful.

'If you have that sort of cash,' he said. 'Forgive me asking. I thought you might have, after the book deal.'

'I do have it,' she said with quiet pride. 'I think it's generally known what my advances were. So would I put in a hundred thousand?'

'Two,' he said. 'My house would have to be our security against our further borrowing. It's worth about two hundred thousand, so we'd be square.'

Troy thought savagely that they would not be in the least square with a property undoubtedly carrying a heavy mortgage contributed by one side, and £200,000 cool, hard cash on the other; but Zelda's lovely face was eager.

'And we'd be partners?'

Justin squeezed her hand a little. 'I hope we'd be more than that,' he said. 'It's a tough world, you need a friend. They take new talent and slice it into ribbons out there. But I've read your book, I understand that you've been through a terrible time. I'd like to make it up to you. I'd protect you.'

Zelda nodded. 'You're very kind,' she said softly.

'The moment I saw you I wanted to know who you were,' Justin said urgently. 'I saw you on the television monitor in the studio and I ran round to intercept you before you got in your car. That's not a thing I've ever done before.'

Zelda smiled, and looked down.

'Another glass of champagne?' he offered. 'Shall we drink to a deal?'

'No, I really must go,' she said. 'I'm working tomorrow.'

'But we have a deal?' he asked with studied casualness.

She smiled. 'Oh yes. This is really exciting.'

'So give me your phone number and I'll get a contract drawn up. It should be ready for signing by the end of the week.'

'No, you give me your number,' Zelda said. 'I'm on tour till Friday and I don't know the number of the mobile. You'll want to speak to me before I get home, won't you?'

'I'll want to speak to you tomorrow,' he said, his voice a little deeper with studied sincerity. 'And the next day. I'll bring the contract to you wherever you are on Friday. Where will that be?'

'Birmingham,' Zelda said mendaciously.

'Birmingham it is,' he gleamed. 'Oh! And what shall we call ourselves? Vere and Wade?'

'Or Wade and Vere?' she offered.

He took up her hand and kissed it. 'You come first,' he said. 'Now and always. We'll be Vere and Wade.'

*　　*　　*

Zelda put her key in the suite door and opened it. Isobel was very far from being naked and aroused in the double bed in her bedroom. She was seated on the sofa in the sitting room, wrapped in a frumpy, quilted dressing gown. When the door opened she leaped to her feet.

'Where have you been? I've been going out of my mind!'

Troy's mischievous smile gleamed at her through Zelda's face.

'The programme ended nearly two hours ago!'

'I know. Justin Wade took me out to a club.'

Isobel recoiled from him, in shock. 'You've been out? Like that?'

Troy nodded. 'Why not?' he asked in Zelda's cruel, light voice, and went into the bathroom, closing the door.

Isobel stayed where he had left her, standing alone in the middle of the room in her dressing gown. She found she was stunned with shock at the thought of Zelda going out without her, of Zelda taking on this separate identity and life. Zelda had been out and talked to someone else, perhaps flirted with someone else. Other people had seen them together. Zelda had said words which had neither been spoken nor heard by Isobel.

It was as if a child had grown up and left home – except so much, so very grossly worse. It was as if a husband had been unfaithful. It was as if a friend had been deceitful. It was as if she herself had somehow been sleepwalking and had gone out in the night and behaved in quite uncharacteristic ways and then come home again and been forced to face the fact that her life was not her own.

Isobel stood very still and heard the sounds of Troy shedding Zelda's skin in the bathroom. She heard him moving around, washing her makeup from his face, the sound of the running water of the shower, the tap being turned off, then the door opened and he came back into the room, fresh and clean in the hotel's white towelling robe, looking years younger than his true age, unquestionably masculine, clean and sexy and young. Beside him Isobel felt old and uncertain, worn and wary.

'I don't like the thought of you going out as Zelda without me,' she said hesitantly.

He went over to the minibar and opened it, surveyed the little bottles with pleasure. 'Drink? No?' He selected a brandy and poured it into a glass. He dropped into the armchair opposite, raised the glass to her and then took a sip.

'Oh, why not? What harm does it do?'

'It's risky,' she said feebly.

'This whole venture is risky,' he said. 'Did you watch the programme?'

'Yes,' she admitted unwillingly. 'You were wonderful. She was wonderful.'

'Would it have crossed your mind for a moment that it was me being her?'

She shook her head.

'That's what I thought,' he said. 'I was just testing her out in the club. I wanted to see how she played with a complete stranger. It was good. There's no harm done.'

'But what did he want?' she asked, for all the world like a fretting mother with an errant daughter. 'Why did he suddenly ask you out like that?'

Zelda gave Isobel a long, knowing look. Isobel put her hands to her temples where her pulse was throbbing. 'Are you saying he was making a pass?'

'He wanted to make money out of Zelda,' Troy said indignantly, abruptly abandoning his provocative pose. 'Imagine the cheek of the man. Some two-bit provincial presenter thought he was going to talk Zelda Vere out of a cool quarter of a million to set him up in a production company and then she'd have to do all the work.'

'Never!' said Isobel, temporarily diverted.

'Yes he did. He thought we were going to call ourselves Vere and Wade.'

'But I never would!'

'Neither would I. And Zelda would eat him up for breakfast.'

Troy giggled. 'He told me he wants to make it up to her for her scarring experiences. He can't have done more than look at the jacket of the book. If he'd read any more he'd have realised that she took her own revenge. I wouldn't go into business with Zelda Vere planning to take advantage of her.'

'But this is really awful,' Isobel said. 'He must be completely unprincipled.'

Troy smiled at her over the top of the glass. 'Honey, this is an unprincipled world. If you have the sort of money that Zelda talks about in public, *in public*, remember, if you are rich like Zelda and richness is your motif, then all sorts of worms are going to come crawling out of the woodwork to take it off you. Everyone, but everyone, is going to want their cut.'

She shook her head. 'I always thought of Zelda living in a world where there are other rich and beautiful people,' she said. 'I never thought that people would try to exploit her.'

He smiled. 'She's the talent, isn't she?' he said. 'You don't realise how rare that is. For every one person who can generate original ideas, there are something like half a dozen people who benefit. The trick is finding the one person. When you find that one person, you put a little fence around him or her so that it is clear that you own them, and then you put them to work. You work them and work them and work them and you find all sorts of ways to draw advantages from them.'

'But it wasn't like this for Isobel Latimer,' Isobel said.

Troy shook his head. 'Wrong sort of talent. I never made much money out of Isobel Latimer and neither did you. But since it became known that I was Zelda's agent, d'you know how much my business has increased?'

She shook her head.

'More than double,' he said. 'Party invitations? Three times as many. Dinner invitations? Doubled. Lunch invitations? I can't eat enough lunches to accommodate the people who want to take me out and feed me because they think I have the ability to spot up-and-coming talent and I might direct a little profit their way. It's not just the royalties, you know. It's a lot more than that.'

She shook her head. She looked troubled. 'You speak as if you are eating her up, cutting her up amongst you and eating her up.'

Troy's smile was wolfish. 'We both are, aren't we? She's our goose that has laid one golden egg. The trick is to exploit her without destroying her. We want to take everything we can while the going's good without spoiling any more that might come after.'

'But it's more than that between us, isn't it? It's more than just exploitation of a talent?'

Her worried voice recalled him to his job of reassuring her, of concealing from her the commercial reality which she only sometimes glimpsed. He put down his glass, crossed the room and kissed her gently on the cheek, as he would kiss his mother. 'Of course it is. It's much more than a slice of the profits between us. And now you must excuse me, I have to go to bed. We've got a big day tomorrow and you must look your best. We take the train to Liverpool at ten past nine. Car at eight thirty.'

Isobel would have held him but he slipped from her grasp and headed towards his bedroom door.

'Troy!' she said. He hesitated, his hand on the door knob.

'I thought we might . . .' She could not complete the sentence, she did not know how to invite him.

He pretended not to know what she meant. 'Tell me tomorrow.' He smiled at her. 'I'm dead beat tonight. Tell me what you thought tomorrow.'

Sixteen

Isobel, dressed as Zelda, was silent on the train journey to Liverpool with Troy, silent as they checked into the hotel.

'I'd like to get a chance to look at the museum and gallery,' she said in the foyer.

Troy gave her a hard look. 'I wouldn't have thought you'd have had much interest,' he said pointedly. 'It's only full of old stuff.'

For a moment he thought she would argue but then she nodded her blonde head as if she lacked the energy to insist on her own identity, took her key in silence and followed the porter up to her room. She checked her makeup and her hair and was down within half an hour for the first of the interviews of the day with a woman from the local paper who wanted to do an in-depth piece on Zelda's transformation from the victim of abuse to a bestselling author. Troy sat back in his seat and watched Zelda parry the usual questions and retell the familiar anecdotes. When she had finished and the woman had gone he smiled his most charming smile at her.

'Lunch?'

She shook her head in a gesture very unlike Zelda's idle grace. 'I want to phone Philip.'

He noted that it was not her usual time of day to call; and he opposed her. 'Zelda doesn't have a Philip.'

She glared at him, an expression at odds with the smooth face. 'Well, I do,' she said stubbornly.

He hesitated for a moment. 'Shall I get them to send lunch

up to your room?' he asked. 'You could take a break for a couple of hours. Nip out to the museum if you liked?'

'I'd like that,' she said sulkily.

'You go on then,' he said pleasantly. 'Just make sure no-one sees you. I'll amuse myself here till our next interview. Three o'clock at the radio studios, remember. Car here at two forty-five.'

Isobel rose to her feet and then hesitated. 'You won't call that man when I'm not here?' she said, fearful of making a demand on him, but more fearful of what he might do next.

Troy rose too and kissed her gently on the cheek. 'No,' he said quietly. 'I promise. Last night was a one-off. I only became her because I had to, and then I got over-confident and probably took it too far. We'll talk about it tonight, over dinner. You go and have a rest from her and don't worry about it now. She's not going to go wandering off without you. And I called Justin Wade this morning as myself, I told him to get lost.'

Isobel nodded and went to her room and felt a sense of relief and comfort in dialling her home number to get in touch with the certainties of her life.

Philip took a long time to come to the phone and then he was breathless.

'Murray and I were out in the barn,' he said. 'Choosing the lighting. He has some lights that we can rig up and some samples of wall finishes so I can see how the light will fall. He says it's one of the most important decisions you can make.'

'Oh, good,' Isobel said. Home seemed a long, long way away. She desperately wanted Philip to speak to her in a tone of some intimacy, say something to recall her to her marriage and her long, faithful love for him, remind her that she was doing this for him.

'We're going for halogen uplighters, with some downlighters on the actual water. It'll give a wonderful effect of reflected water on the ceiling. We were just messing about with a couple of buckets of water and the lights, and it really is terribly effective.'

'Good,' Isobel said again.

'Made me rethink the colour scheme actually,' Philip went on. 'I was going to stay with the barn effect of brown timber and white-washed walls but I think we should go for a pale blue, it'll really show off the reflections.'

'Will it?'

'In fact we could box in the beams and put in a false ceiling so that we get a flat surface. Murray says you have to think of the water as a projector and the ceiling as a cinema screen. It's worth the fuss of building the false ceiling for the effect you get.'

'Isn't it rather expensive?'

Philip laughed. 'That's nothing to what it would cost if we put in skylights,' he said. 'I was shocked when I looked at the prices. Murray brought up the brochures to show me and said that even he thought they were a bit steep. We were looking at taking off the roof of the barn altogether and replacing it with big electric windows. On fine days you slide back the windows. We'd take out the south wall of the barn as well and replace that with windows so that we could make the pool virtually open air in summer. It makes the whole thing completely like an outdoor pool. Murray says it's a wonderful experience, to open up the whole building. Really exhilarating. And you can swim at night under the stars.'

'But you say it costs too much?' Isobel confirmed.

'I think so,' Philip said judiciously. 'But you must decide when you come home at the weekend. I won't rush into any major decisions without you. It's up to you, darling. I don't forget who's the little breadwinner.'

'Oh, no,' Isobel said quickly. 'It's your project, and you've gone into it so carefully. I'd be guided by you.'

'We'll discuss it,' he said fairly. 'I do want you to have the very best. You deserve it, working so hard.'

For a moment she felt ready to cry at his generosity when he had no idea what her work was, or how she was every day getting deeper into a complicated deception.

'I wish I was home,' she said, heartfelt.

'Why don't you come then?' he asked reasonably. 'You could always finish early, tell them you're ill or something.'

Isobel rubbed her face, and felt the slick of Zelda's foundation cream wet with her tears. 'No, no, I couldn't do that. I'll stick it out. I just felt terribly homesick hearing you talk about the pool and everything.'

'Well, it is an exciting project,' he agreed. 'And Murray really is a very talented man. He should have trained as an architect, really, he has this ability to see things. And he can describe them so that you can see them yourself. The way the sliding roof goes back and opens up the pool to the sky he just tells it so well. You'd like him, he's a wordsmith like you.'

Isobel nodded. 'I look forward to seeing the detailed plans,' she said. 'Is Mrs M. looking after you all right?'

'We had her up a ladder holding the tape measure to the beams,' he said, as gleeful as a boy. 'She was laughing and laughing because I was supposed to be holding the ladder and I couldn't keep it steady.'

Isobel tried to smile. 'It sounds such fun.'

'And then we all went down to the pub for an early lunch,' he said. 'It was too nice a day to be stuck in the house.'

'You took Mrs M. out to lunch?'

'Murray insisted. He said that she'd done a decent morning's work for once in her life.'

'Oh.' Isobel tried to imagine Philip going out to lunch with the pool man and the housekeeper. 'Are you missing me? Are you lonely?'

'Oh no!' His sincerity was unmistakable. 'I'm much too busy to miss you, darling. Looking forward to you coming home, of course.'

'Of course,' Isobel said quietly.

'Oh, look, darling. I have to go. Mrs M. and Murray want me outside again. Will you call again tonight?'

'No,' Isobel said desolately. 'This can be today's call now I've heard the news. I'll call again tomorrow, shall I?'

'Do,' he said. 'Sorry I have to dash.'

'It doesn't matter,' she said. 'Bye, darling.'
'Bye.'

That evening the darkness of Isobel's mood still had not lifted. She did not want to dine in the hotel restaurant, nor go out for dinner. Instead they ate in their room. Isobel waited in the bathroom until the waiter had brought up the big tray and laid the table, and then emerged in a towelling robe without Zelda's hair or makeup, simply as herself, defiantly unvarnished, unadorned, and looking her age.

Troy, watching the early-evening news on television, switched off the set and stood up as she came in, taking in the tiredness in her face and the sadness in her eyes.

They ate in silence. Troy poured Isobel most of the bottle of wine.

'What's the matter?' he asked, without much enthusiasm for the conversation which must ensue.

'It's Philip,' she said surprisingly.

Troy, who had expected a complaint about his going out as Zelda, hid his surprise.

'I thought this new scheme of the pool was something which might pass,' she said. 'But he's more and more keen. He's talking about electric windows for the roof and south wall now. I don't know that we can afford it.'

Troy nodded. 'How much?'

'He hasn't said. But we're basically talking about a new building if it's a new roof and a new wall, aren't we? And then digging the pool and all the equipment. He talks about filtration units and pumps and the heating unit.'

Troy nodded. 'It sounds expensive.'

'I think it will be.'

'We opened the offshore account with your £150,000, and then it's another £100,000 on hardback publication so that should be in this month. You can draw what you need out of that. But after that, it's nothing till a year from now on paperback publication,' Troy reminded her. 'But that's a quarter of a million in this year alone, and a bit less than a hundred thousand to come next year. You should be able to buy a pool or two with that.'

Isobel's strained expression lightened. 'Yes. I'm being silly. I've earned a fortune, haven't I? Enough for anything we might want.' She glanced at Troy. 'I'm very grateful, I didn't mean to complain.'

On impulse he got up from the dining table and put out his hand to her. He drew her to sit on the sofa beside him. Isobel, warmed by his tenderness, sat in the crook of his arm and rested her head companionably on his shoulder.

'Where's he getting these big ideas from?' Troy asked. 'He must know you can't afford a half of this? Unless . . . oh, Isobel, have you told him about Zelda and her advances?'

'No!' she exclaimed. 'No! Absolutely not. It's not that he thinks there is big money coming in. I told him I had done well with the last novel to explain that we had enough for a little swimming pool. He wanted it so much, and I thought it might be an interest for him, and good for his condition . . .'

'So he is thinking you've earned something like, what, £50,000?'

Isobel nodded. 'He knows I'm working on a new Isobel Latimer book. If he assumed that I get another contract for that then we'd have about £60,000 or £70,000 coming in this year.'

'Less tax,' Troy reminded her, 'and commission.'

She nodded.

'So how does he think that you can pay for the pool and all the sliding roofs and windows?'

She relaxed against his arm. 'That's it,' she said. 'He doesn't think. What happened as he became more and more ill is that he stopped thinking. I just took over that side of things. You see people do it all the time. Men who don't know how to cook, who don't even know where the tea towels are kept, because it's not their job. Women who don't know how to write a cheque. Well, that's what happened to us. We never planned it, it was never my intention. But as it happened, I took over all the control of the finances, and now he doesn't even ask about them. I give him pocket money and I pay the bills as they come in. He never even thinks about money.'

Troy nodded, privately repelled at the thought of a marriage in which a man reverted to childlike dependency. 'But he must know that you couldn't possibly afford all this as Isobel Latimer.'

She looked guilty. 'I never told him that the royalties on Isobel Latimer books were going down,' she said. 'I didn't want to worry him. He thinks we're still doing well. He thinks we're doing the sort of sales we did in the seventies. He doesn't realise we're dependent on one book at a time, he thinks all the other books are paying money too. He thinks that all the advances have earned out and I am making money on all the titles. He thinks we're really well off.'

'Well, thanks to Zelda you are now,' Troy said. 'And apparently he's not going to ask any awkward questions about how well you're doing. All you have to do when you get home for the weekend is to insist that you don't spend all your earnings on something you can't really afford. You need to keep at least a third of this back for tax.'

She nodded.

'You'll just have to be firm with him,' Troy said.

Isobel hesitated. Troy turned so that he could see her weary face. 'It's so hard,' she said in a small voice. 'I feel so sorry for him. If you had known him when he was well you'd understand why. He was so energetic and so bright, he was . . .' She broke off.

Troy looked for a moment into her face. She looked like a woman quite powerless to do anything. He thought that if her husband was beating her every night after dinner she could not look more enfeebled. He considered her for a moment and she met his gaze, her grey honest eyes looking into his dark blue ones.

'You just have to be firm,' he repeated.

Isobel shook her head. 'I can't say no to him. It just breaks my heart. He's gone from being the wittiest, most charming . . . sexiest man I ever met to an old, tired, rather grumpy invalid. I could weep every time I see him. I can't do anything that would make such a life yet more empty.' She paused. 'He is a disappointed man.'

Troy thought that it sounded like a book title: *The Disappointed Man*. 'I know what you could do,' he suggested. 'You could think about Zelda. How would she handle it? If Zelda was married to him, what would she do? By the time you get home you'll have been Zelda for a week. You can do things the way she would do them. Zelda would be able to tell someone that enough was enough. Zelda would be able to refuse someone something even if she loved him. I can see *her* saying that her love was enough, more than enough for any man. He wouldn't need a swimming pool as well.'

She brightened at the thought. 'She would, wouldn't she?'

He smiled. 'I don't see Zelda working herself to a standstill to buy something she doesn't particularly want. I can see her telling her husband very clearly that she's earning the money and he's just spending it, and it's got to stop.'

'But she's not a particularly good woman, is she?' Isobel ventured. 'We created her as someone who could revenge herself on her abusers. We didn't really give her a moral persona at all. She's not capable of that level of moral judgement. She's a fictional character, not a moral person living in a complex world.'

Troy smiled. 'It's not always an advantage to be a good woman, I should think. I'd have thought it would be great to be someone not capable of living at a level of moral judgement.'

For a moment he thought that he had gone too far, she would reject the idea of being morally reckless. But then she turned in his embrace and looked at him, her face very close to his. Troy realised that they were intimately close without the protection of Zelda's face between them. There was no layer of foundation cream and powder, there was no mask of eye-makeup and concealer. There was nothing but Isobel's scrubbed face and his, as close as if they might kiss.

They did not kiss. They gazed at each other as if they needed to know every pore, every line on the other's face. He saw how her skin darkened under her eyes into shadows which were almost sepia brown. She saw the downturned lines around his mouth which in a few years, perhaps five or ten, would mark him as a discontented man. He saw the weariness in her face, the sagging of the skin at her jawline, at her eye sockets. He saw the radiating lines from the corners of her eyes where her smiles had worn the skin into habitual folds and he realised that she rarely smiled a big, broad grin these days. At some time her joy in life had marked her face, but now the lines were like tracks of an unused road.

'You're tired,' he said, and his voice was full of tenderness as if he were speaking to a dearly loved friend who had completed a long, hard journey and was still not allowed to rest.

She was wordless for a moment, then she shook her head. 'I'm unhappy. It's different.'

He waited for her to say more.

'It feels the same to me now,' she said slowly. 'Tiredness and unhappiness feel like the same thing now. I often feel as if I am tired, and of course I do work very hard; I work and I drive myself to work harder. But this feeling of weariness, of being beaten before I'm started, of having too much to do and no ability to do it all – this isn't real tiredness at all. I know it because I feel the same when I wake up in the morning. Even if I sleep all night from ten at night till ten in the morning, I still wake up feeling tired. It's not that I am *tired* out, it is that I am *worn* out. I'm not exhausted by effort, I am exhausted at the thought of effort. I don't want the morning to come. I don't want the day to start. I want to sleep the rest of my life away. If I could go to sleep and never wake up at all – I would.'

Troy held her a little closer as if he would silence this terrible, revealing confession against his shoulder. But she would not be silenced. She wanted him to know, and she wanted to speak her own bleak confession.

'The only thing I enjoyed, *really* enjoyed, was my writing,' she said quietly. 'When Philip was ill and we thought he was going to die, it was the only thing which took me away from my fear and my grief. Then when he was sick all the time, just always always sick, my writing was the only thing which was alive and vital in the whole house. And then, for some reason, my writing grew so very hollow. I can't describe why. It seemed to me that I had written the same books about the same sort of people for all of my life. They were people like me, in houses like mine, of my sort of age, and over and over again they had to make choices: whether to confess or to conceal. Whether to trust or to doubt. Whether to stay constant or to abandon. And because they are in *my* novels, and not one of these young authors who think that nothing matters more than themselves, who think the only story worth telling is one of selfish desires and a striving to become your own individual self, because they are *my* characters, they always choose discretion, trust, constancy.' She sighed for a moment. 'My God, but they're boring.'

He would have interrupted her, but he had nothing to say as she laid bare the dry bones of her life.

'When I had my first bad review, two novels ago, d'you remember?'

Troy nodded.

'That young man, Peter Friday, he panned *The Judge and the Judging*. Part of me was hurt and offended, of course. But part of me agreed with him. He said that my writing was post-war moralising, the fiction of the fifties. He said that the time had passed when anyone wanted long complicated internal debates about morality. He said people wanted irony and action and dramatic self-development. Modern fables, he said, not how many angels could dance on a pinhead. He said I was a novelist of intellectual theology.'

'And got the sack a couple of months later,' Troy pointed out.

Isobel smiled. 'Yes, but part of me thought he was right. He said he was bored with the sort of books I write: the minutiae of family life and morality worked out in relationships. When I read his review a bit of me cried, "Hurray! at last someone with the balls to say it! At last someone to say that they are bored of this stuff, when I have bored myself with this stuff for years.''''

Troy stroked her hair.

'And the other thing,' she said, suddenly rising up out of his embrace and becoming animated. 'The other thing is that I have spent so long writing about characters like that who make thoughtful moral choices and in the end choose to do the right thing, I have boxed myself in. So when Philip became ill it was as if all my novels had been a practice for how I would behave. It never occurred to me to do anything other than support him, keep him, and submerge my own plans and my own ambitions and everything we had hoped to do into his illness. He has his disability: and I have him. I'm like a good mother, a woman so dedicated that she no longer has to make any choices, she cannot see any choices before her. She will do the right thing. She has to do the right thing. Just as I will always do the right thing, I have to do the right thing, even when I am sick with tiredness and boredom and sadness at my life.'

He waited.

'And then there was Zelda,' she said simply. She looked up at him and he saw that although her face was lined and weary her eyes, filled with tears, were a wonderful, luminous grey. He was filled with a profound, passionate pity that a woman as talented as this and as beautiful as this should be so tired that she wanted to sleep until she died, so profoundly loyal that she could not see her way out of a situation which must surely, somewhere, have some flexibility, some freedom that she could win.

'Isobel, you are so beautiful,' he exclaimed.

She did not look surprised. She looked steadily into his young face. Slowly he kissed the sad stained skin underneath her eyes. Tenderly he kissed the pale lips. She closed her eyelids and gave herself up to his gentle, charitable kisses that fell like rain, like mercy, on her face. Gently she felt him ease her dressing gown from her shoulders and the touch of his hands and his lips on her neck, on the gentle sag of her breasts, on the soft slack skin of her belly. They slid to the floor together in silence, Isobel feeling a sense of warm familiarity with Troy's touch, and at the same time a complete strangeness. They had never before been naked together. They had never before been themselves. When they had spent the two long erotic nights in bed he had been Zelda and she had been buoyed up, carried away into a fantasy of their making. Now she was a tired, sorrowful middle-aged woman and he was a man moved by a deep, passionate pity. He wanted to transform her, he wanted to see her sad, defeated face glow with a little joy, he wanted her downturned mouth to curve upwards and erase the deep grooves that framed it.

And at midnight as they moved from the floor beside the sofa to Isobel's bed he had his reward. Half asleep, lifting the covers to slide in and shivering against the sudden chill of the sheets, she glanced over to him and her sleepy smile was as joyous as any of Zelda's painted beauty.

Isobel woke early, conscious of Troy still beside her. Cautiously she turned her head on the pillow and looked into his sleeping face. His blond stubble was growing, his sleep had ironed the lines from his face. He looked young and endearing. She wanted to kiss him awake, she wanted to touch his warm, slight body, but she stayed on her side of the bed, she thought he needed his sleep and that a good lover would guard his rest.

She felt sticky and tired after lovemaking, she felt a delicious sensual ease, such as she had never known before. Always before the presence of Zelda had been an obstacle to the intimacy between Troy and Isobel, as well as their only route for contact. Now Isobel was alone with Troy and she could feel her own desire for him. For the first time she knew that he had chosen her, without a shield, without mediation. Troy wanted her now, she believed. Now they were truly lovers. She smiled and gently touched his cheek still careful not to wake him. This was her lover, she thought. This was the start of a love affair. Who knew where it might take her? It could not take her far away from her devotion to Philip, nothing could excuse her from her duty to her husband. But Troy knew that. Uniquely, wonderfully, Troy knew everything and still had chosen to love her, still had chosen to bear her down to the floor, to lift her up into bed.

Beside her, Troy stirred, and opened his eyes. He encountered Isobel's steady, loving gaze with a shock, he wondered how long she had been awake, staring into his face. He felt a powerful sense of embarrassment and a deep awareness that their relationship had become both more intimate and far more difficult.

'Wide awake?' he said brightly. 'And looking wonderful. I'll make you a cup of tea while you have your shower. It's another busy day today.'

He slipped from the bed without touching her, escaping her surprised face. As he filled the kettle and switched it on he glanced back at the bed. To his relief she was getting up, pulling the quilted dressing gown around her imperfect nakedness. He blew her a kiss. 'Another day, another dollar,' he said cheerfully. 'I'll nip across to my room and shower.'

They took the train to Birmingham after an interview with local radio and checked into yet another hotel. Troy was gentle with Isobel, considerate for her comfort. Isobel, under the helmet of Zelda's hair and behind the mask of her makeup, felt herself to be loved, felt herself to be seen for herself, understood, acknowledged, even as she wore her disguise, even as he deceived her.

At Birmingham they ate in the hotel dining room and Troy escorted Isobel to her door after dinner. She only realised that he intended to go to his own room when he hung back from the open door.

'Aren't you sleeping here?' she asked baldly.

He shook his head. He had not known how to prepare for this challenge, though he had known it would come. His answer was the inspiration of the moment. 'I'm so sorry, my love,' he said gently. 'I have such a dreadful headache tonight. I get migraines sometimes, you know.'

At once her face was suffused with tenderness. 'Oh, you should have said! I'd never have kept you at dinner.'

'I wanted to be with you,' he protested.

'No, no,' she said. 'You go straight to bed. D'you have something to take?'

'Yes. I'll be fine.'

'Shall I make you a cup of tea? Would you like a cup of tea when you're in bed?'

Troy felt the delightful temptation of hypochondria. 'I wouldn't want to trouble you.'

She was radiant. 'No trouble. You go to bed and I'll come in five minutes and bring you a cup of tea.'

Troy allowed himself to droop slightly. 'That would be lovely.'

He went down the corridor and into his own room. He stripped quickly and donned his pyjamas. He jumped lightly into bed as the door opened and Isobel came into the room, a cup of tea in her hand.

'There,' she said tenderly. She put the cup down on his bedside table and leaned over the bed to smooth his forehead. 'D'you have everything you want?'

'Everything,' he said sweetly. 'Except a goodnight kiss.'

He had expected her to bring her mouth down on his, to stir him with her touch. Now he was in his own bed, in control of their lovemaking, he would have welcomed a passionate move from her, he would have responded to an advance. But to his surprise she leaned over him and kissed him on the forehead, between the eyes, as tenderly as a mother with a sick child. 'Goodnight,' she said softly. 'Goodnight, my darling. Sleep well, I know you'll be better in the morning.'

With that she was gone, closing the door softly behind her.

Troy, sipping tea and then lying back on his pillows and drifting off to sleep, understood a little more why Isobel's marriage was such a joy for her husband and such a source of grief and weariness to her.

After that night, Troy did not want to let Isobel go home to Philip alone. He had a sense of foreboding about her return to the house which seemed so ruled by Philip, by Mrs M. and by the constant visitor: Murray the pool man. He supervised her packing her suitcase on Saturday morning in the hotel room, watching all the time for things which had come from Zelda's life and should not go back to the house in Kent.

'You have to be like a spy,' Troy reminded her, pouncing on a pair of embroidered knickers and whisking them into his suitcase. 'No connection at all between one life and another.'

'I could have bought those for myself,' Isobel complained, watching them disappear with regret.

'You could have done, but you didn't,' Troy said. 'They're Zelda's and you know it. Anyone who knows you well would pick up that you were buying different things, that you were spending more money on yourself. You can't leave clues around like that, Isobel, you've got to have two completely different lives.'

She nodded and reluctantly handed over a bottle of aroma-therapy bath oil.

'Wouldn't you buy yourself that?' he asked. It had cost little more than five pounds for a large bottle. He knew that she loved the smell and the milky colour of the bath water.

'No,' Isobel said shortly. 'I wouldn't buy something like that for myself.'

'So what do you use in your bath at home?' he asked.

She looked away from him, as if the confession somehow shamed her. 'Philip has Epsom salts for his condition,' she said. 'I never remember to buy my own. I use his.'

Troy hesitated, tempted to return the oil to her, to urge her to indulge herself a little more. But he stopped himself.

Before anything else, the deception must come first. 'Anything else to pack?' he asked coolly.

'That's it,' she replied.

They remained businesslike as they checked out of the hotel. Isobel, who had arrived as Zelda, left the hotel quickly, moving swiftly through the lobby in her dull Isobel clothes. No-one noticed the middle-aged woman in the sombre suit. No-one ever noticed Isobel Latimer. It was only when she was in Zelda's lovely clothes that she turned heads. It was only when she was acting Zelda's melodramatic character that she attracted attention. They took the taxi to the station and then boarded the train.

As they started the journey back to London, Troy returned to the question of Isobel's homecoming, and what she might find there. He was worried about the pool salesman.

'I bet he's on something like fifty per cent mark-up,' Troy said suspiciously. 'I bet he's a really slick salesman. Don't sign a thing without getting a lawyer to look at it first, Isobel, will you?'

They were travelling first class, alone in the compartment. Isobel, with her brown hair arranged neatly on the nape of her neck and wearing her plain navy suit, was watching the moving landscape outside the train window.

'No,' she said vaguely. 'I do love trains, don't you? I think they're so terribly glamorous.'

'Yes,' Troy said. 'But we were talking about the pool man.'

Isobel's grey eyes gleamed at him. 'No,' she said. 'You were talking about the pool man and I was changing the subject.'

'I'm worried about him,' Troy explained.

'I'm sure he's perfectly harmless.'

'If he's sold Philip an indoor pool with sliding roof and windows, a jacuzzi, a sauna, and a covered walkway from the house then he's not harmless. He's a sharp salesman and I'm trying to do my job and protect my client.'

She nodded. 'I know you are. But it's not just about money and contracts.'

'That's the most important thing.'

Isobel shook her head. 'Not to me. The most important thing is that Philip has found something that he is really enjoying, something that has given him a hobby and an interest and brought him alive in a way he hasn't been for years. That's worth a lot. You can't begin to understand how much.'

Troy exerted his patience. 'I'm not denying that. And it's great for him. So I'm pleased. But what I'm saying is: can't he have a hobby and an interest that does not involve you spending a huge chunk of your Zelda Vere money in one go? Can't he have a hobby and an interest that you can comfortably afford?'

'He's not greedy,' she said firmly. 'He's just got no idea of how much I am earning and how impossibly expensive the pool would be. And that's my fault. When he was ill I just took over everything, and since then I just manage everything. I haven't told him that we were in trouble financially. I just tried to manage it alone.'

Troy nodded. 'So manage this,' he said. 'You can't let him come in at the spending end of things without enough information. If he is, as you say, not greedy, but just ill-informed, then you must inform him. Tell him how much Isobel Latimer earns, add thirty thousand a year on to it if you like; but give him an idea of your budget.'

'I can't disappoint him,' she ruled. 'He mustn't be worried.'

Troy put his hand on hers across the table 'I understand,' he said warmly. 'But remember how you felt when I told you they'd only pay £20,000 for your novel and you knew you didn't have enough to live on. You don't want to be there again, with that terror of debt and nothing to show for all this work but an enormous swimming pool with a sliding roof.'

Isobel smiled. 'I know you're right.'

He saw her pleasure that he was taking responsibility for her, if only in the limited sense of advising her what to do and then leaving her to get on with the more difficult part of actually doing it.

'You must be firm,' he said.

'I'll try,' she promised.

Seventeen

Mrs M's husband, driving the Latimers' car, met Isobel at the station.

'Has the weather been nice?' Isobel asked as they left the main road and went slowly along the narrow lane. He pulled into a passing place and waited for a tractor to squeeze by before he answered.

'Very pleasant,' he said. 'Very mild for nearly February. It's like spring already. You won't have felt the benefit in London.'

'No,' Isobel said. 'And everywhere is centrally heated these days, and so hot . . .'

'It accounts for all the colds,' he said dolefully. 'And meningitis. Whoever heard of meningitis before central heating?'

Isobel nodded and watched the familiar landmarks of the road to her house. 'Is Philip well?' she asked.

'Oh yes,' Mrs M.'s husband replied. 'At least she never said any different. And she would have mentioned it if he wasn't. Very full of his pool,' she said. 'You'll've heard all about it, I suppose.'

'Yes,' Isobel said. 'I have.'

He slowed for the turn into the drive. A white hatchback car was parked in Isobel's usual place. 'That'll be the pool man,' Mr M. said, parking next door to it. 'Seems like he's up here most days.'

Isobel got out of the car and saw, with a rush of deep pleasure, that Philip had come to the front door to greet her.

'Hello,' he called from the doorstep.

'Hello,' Isobel replied, taking in his pale hair and beloved face, the shy warmth of his smile. He seemed very safe and very normal compared with the excess of the previous week. She was glad to be home, glad to be with him again. She had a momentary rise of tears at the sight of him and knew a desire to cry out and fling herself to his chest and have his arms come around her and hear him reassure her that she need never go out into the world again, never be Zelda again, never reach for Troy in the night or struggle with the complexities of the life they had made together this week.

'Oh, Philip,' she said longingly and moved towards him.

A figure appeared in the doorway behind him. Murray gave a little nod as if he were genuinely pleased to meet her. 'Welcome home.'

'Thank you,' Isobel said coldly.

'Murray's staying to lunch, we were just about to eat,' Philip said pleased. 'Lucky you got that train. You're just in time.'

Isobel nodded and entered the house. It seemed strange that the two men should welcome her into the house which until last week had been unquestionably her own, to which the very rare visitors were greeted by her. But now Murray and Philip's coats were tossed on a chair in the hall, and Murray's large blue and white umbrella, with the bright logo 'Atlantis Pools', was in the umbrella stand. Isobel paused for a moment to look at Murray's large umbrella dwarfing her stand, at his coat thrown carelessly on her chair, and then went to the kitchen.

They were not eating soup and bread and cheese for lunch. With two men to cook for, Mrs M. had transformed her usual menus. There were knives and forks at two places and as Isobel entered Mrs M. was laying a third place for her.

'Hello,' Isobel said.

Mrs M. looked up and smiled. 'Hello, Mrs Latimer. Did you have a good week?'

'Yes, thank you,' Isobel said. 'Has everything been all right here?'

Mrs M. gave her a smile which indicated the natural conspiracy of women. 'Well, we've been busy,' she said quietly so that the two men entering the room could not hear. 'We've been as busy as a bee. And happy. And well.'

'Good,' Isobel said repressively, disliking the confidential tone. 'Any post for me?'

'All on your desk, Mrs Latimer.'

Isobel nodded and turned to go to her study as Mrs M. spoke familiarly to the men. 'Philip, Murray, lunch in five minutes, so don't you go disappearing.'

Isobel checked in the doorway. Mrs M. had worked for them for seven years and had always called them Mr and Mrs Latimer, and they had known her as Mrs M.

Isobel went on through the door to her study. There was a daunting pile of post beside the keyboard of her computer. On the screen itself was something Isobel had not seen before, a new program which she had never used on her computer. It showed a plan of a garden with a large barn and a house in the centre. Isobel looked for a moment before she realised that it was a scale drawing of her house, and the barn which Philip planned to convert to a swimming pool. This was a program of Murray's to show potential buyers how their pool would look. As Isobel watched the screen changed and showed an aerial view. Now she could see the walkway from the house, which had somehow become a glazed cloister, and then the view changed again to show the aspect from the south, north, west, and east. She sat in her chair and watched the picture change, noting that the barn was matched handsomely with the look of the house, and indeed, that it was extended so that it was almost as large as the house.

'This is absolutely ridiculous,' Isobel said softly to herself.

Her door opened and Philip and Murray stood on the threshold together, looking roguish and pleased with themselves.

'What d'you think?' Philip asked. 'Murray showed me how to instal it on your computer. Shall we talk you through it?'

'I have to check my post before lunch,' Isobel said coolly. 'Can you show it to me afterwards?'

She meant to snub Murray but she caught from him a sudden gleam of a smile, as if her rejection was somehow interesting, more intriguing than an acceptance. Isobel looked away from his bright face and down at her letters.

'If you want it off your screen, just press "Quit",' Murray said. 'It's on disk, we won't lose it if you want your screen clear.'

'Thank you,' Isobel said coolly. The two men withdrew, rather like naughty boys being sent from a governess' room. Isobel returned to her post and flicked through the envelopes, half her attention still on the screen which had now dissolved to a scale drawing and cross-sections of the building. The bills in brown manila envelopes were not opened, Philip had left them to her. But any personal post with handwritten envelopes, or any interesting-looking letters with typed envelopes, Philip had opened, as he always did. If challenged he would say that he wanted to make sure that nothing urgent had been neglected. This was only partly true. With few friends and no family, Philip hardly ever received letters of his own and he envied Isobel her large pile of mail every morning.

Until this moment, Isobel had never objected to this habit of his. But now she had things that she had to conceal. She paused for a moment, looking at the torn envelopes. It would be hard to prevent Philip from opening her post. She realised now that she had never liked him doing so. It meant that all the enjoyable letters were read by him, before she could get to them. Any exciting piece of news he told her, he knew it first, even when it had been solely addressed to her. Isobel realised, and was amazed to realise, that for years Philip had been opening her personal letters and that for years she had hated him doing so, and never had the courage to tell him to respect her privacy.

Isobel leafed through the opened envelopes and glanced at a couple of invitations: one to a launch party for a small publishing house, one to speak at a literary lunch. There was a letter from Troy's office enclosing a selection of reviews for an Isobel Latimer novel which had recently been published in America. Isobel read them quickly. They were uniformly tepid. Isobel's work was known in America for being literary and needlessly complicated. Now the critics were unanimously complaining that her stories did not speak to the concerns of ordinary readers, but described a world that had long since disappeared. Isobel nodded. Her American publishers, who had taken her books for nearly twenty years, had been reluctant to buy the last novel, and had reduced their royalties. She thought it very likely that they would not want to publish anything else she might write, ever again. At the best of times English novels struggled to find a market in the United States. English novels about the scruples of the middle-aged middle-classes had become almost unsellable.

Philip put his head around the door. 'Lunch is ready.'

Isobel nodded and rose from her chair.

'I saw the reviews from the American papers,' Philip said, taking his seat at the table. Murray sat opposite him in what usually was Isobel's place. Isobel took the other side of the table, feeling excluded. 'It really proves that America is dumbing down. They simply didn't understand what they were reading.'

Mrs M. brought from the oven a substantial pie with a golden decorated crust.

'And what's this?' Murray demanded gleefully.

'Someone mentioned that they loved steak and kidney pie,' Mrs M. said. 'Someone hinted non-stop yesterday.'

Murray winked at her. 'I suppose you wouldn't consider marrying me?' he asked.

'You suppose right,' she said smartly. She went back to the Aga and returned with a bowl of peas and then, even more surprisingly, a bowl of crisp brown chips.

Isobel looked at Philip in silent amazement.

'We bought this terrific thing,' he said. 'It's a deep fat fryer. It makes chips just like a chip shop. Murray suggested it.'

'Got you a discount too,' Murray reminded him, passing

the pie to Isobel. She cut herself a small portion and handed the plate back to him.

'Yes! You should have heard him!' Philip chuckled. 'According to him, deep fat fryers are a complete drug on the market. Who's going to eat fried food these days now we're all so health conscious? Who's going to clean out a deep fat fryer, filled with dirty oil? By the time he had finished, the man was practically begging us to take it off his hands.'

'Well, fried food isn't very good for you, is it?' Isobel asked, trying to keep her voice light, her comment nothing more than a simple question.

Murray turned the brightness of his smile on her. 'My grandfather ate a fish and chip dinner every day of his life and died aged one hundred,' he said. 'I've got his telegram from the queen to prove it. I don't listen to all these health warnings. Seems to me that if you take all the advice you still die at the same age, it just feels like you've lived two hundred years!' He laughed at his own joke, and served himself chips and peas.

'Do try some,' Philip urged Isobel. 'You'll be impressed.'

Isobel put some chips on her plate and passed the bowl to Philip. Now she understood the faint, warm smell that lingered in the kitchen, it was the odour from the hot oil in the fryer. A disagreeable smell, quite unlike the hot waft from a fish and chip shop seasoned with the tang of vinegar. This was a smell which already seemed stale. Isobel imagined the stink seeping into the gingham curtains at the kitchen windows, oily, warm, volatile. She tasted a chip.

'What did I tell you?' Philip demanded triumphantly.

'They're awfully good,' she confirmed. 'Delicious.'

The two men beamed at her.

'But dreadfully fattening,' Isobel observed.

'You don't want to worry about that,' Murray said cheerfully. 'A beautiful woman like you.'

'I was thinking more about my arteries than my figure,' Isobel replied coolly.

He grinned at her. 'They talk a lot of nonsense about

health,' he said. 'What was it? You couldn't eat a boiled egg for salmonella? Next thing you can't have a steak on the bone? I tell Philip, don't worry about it. Half of the stuff is in your head. If you don't worry about it won't ever happen.'

Isobel shot a shocked look at Philip. Far from retreating into an offended shell as he usually did when the conversation even approached his illness, he was nodding and smiling.

'I tell Philip that the doctors know a lot less than they make out,' Murray said robustly. 'Who smokes the most, eh? Doctors. Which professions drink the most? Doctors and journalists. The men who say we shouldn't be drinking and the men who write up the reports! You can't help thinking it's all the more for them.'

Isobel smiled thinly but Philip laughed delightedly.

Mrs M., who had been loading dishes into the dishwasher and wiping down the worktops, glanced over at them. 'Talk the hind leg off a donkey,' she remarked.

Murray glanced over to her and winked. 'If you can make 'em laugh, you're halfway there,' he said. 'It's the selling game. It's a game, Mellie.'

Isobel registered the fact that Mrs M. had a first name that could be shortened to 'Mellie'. Amelia? Emily? She thought that she remembered Emily.

'This man could sell snow to Eskimos,' Philip said to Isobel. 'I promise you. Everywhere he's taken me to see his work the owners say that they were planning a little pool for the children, and there they are with gallons of water in an enormous pool with swim trainers and diving boards and jet masters and all the rest of it.'

'People think too small,' Murray declared. 'I just expand their parameters a little.'

'And are you expanding ours?' Isobel asked pointedly. 'While you sell us deep fat fryers on the side?'

He did not falter for a moment. 'Oh, I hope so,' he said, smiling. 'Philip had a great idea for the pool when I first came on board the project. My job was to do the detailed thinking with him, the engineering and the design work. And then the second part of my job is to make sure you get value for money. A big pool is only a little more expensive than a little one, why not have the best you can afford? And wherever you go, you'll never find anyone saying they wish they'd bought a smaller pool. Plenty saying they wish they had a bigger one – they never knew the use they'd get out of it. Nobody ever says they wish they'd settled for a paddling pool instead.'

'That's true enough,' Philip corroborated. 'They all tell me that Murray persuaded them to go for a bigger one. No-one ever says they've regretted the decision.'

'Well, presumably you don't visit the people who decided against your plans,' Isobel observed.

Nothing dented Murray's calm assurance. 'No. Why would I? If I've spent time and trouble planning the very right thing for them, the perfect scheme for their budget and for their landscape, and they decide to take my plans and get them done on the cheap by some bloke who turned up behind me – why would I go back there? I never go back. I do the best plan I can, and if they don't like it they can take a running.'

'Tell her about the people who decided against the indoor pool,' Philip prompted him. He smiled at Isobel. 'You'll like this.'

'It was a family on the other side of Chetham,' Murray started willingly. The ring of the telephone interrupted his story.

'Excuse me,' Isobel said with relief, and rose from the table.

'Oh, let the ansaphone take it,' Philip urged her.

'No, I have to go, it might be one of my students.'

'Mellie can get it,' Philip said.

'It's probably a call for Mellie,' Murray supplemented. 'The milkman again.'

Isobel closed her study door on the laughter and picked up the telephone. 'Hello?'

'Isobel?' It was Troy's voice.

'Oh,' she said. She felt a passionate rush of desire. 'Oh, Troy.'

'I just wanted to call. I'm unpacking all her lovely things

and sending some of them for cleaning. It feels awful, like sorting a house when someone has died. I needed to speak to you.'

'I'm so glad you did.'

They paused for a moment and listened to each other's breathing, as if the connection itself were enough, as if words were hardly needed.

'Everything all right?' Troy asked eventually. 'Seen the estimate for the pool?'

'Not yet,' she said. 'The pool man is here for lunch. He is telling swimming-pool anecdotes.'

She smiled at Troy's scornful laugh. 'I bet those are a wow.'

'Yes.'

'Anybody said how much the estimate is for the work, in general figures?'

'Not yet,' Isobel said. 'But he is being relentlessly charming.'

'Relentlessly?' Troy confirmed. 'Sounds about forty thousand to me.'

'More,' Isobel said. 'I cannot begin to tell you how charming he is.'

'Say no,' Troy reminded her. 'Don't forget that you've got to say no.'

'I will,' Isobel said. 'But Philip is regenerated. He's like a different man. We'll have to do something. Even if it's a much reduced scheme.'

There was a silence while Troy thought about this. 'I suppose if the worst comes to the worst you could always do another Zelda Vere novel – a sequel.'

'D'you think they'd want a sequel?'

'If it charts,' he said shortly. 'If it makes the bestseller list this week then they'll want a sequel quick enough.'

'D'you think it might be a bestseller?' Isobel asked. She felt a powerful sense of excitement. 'D'you know I've never had a book which was higher than about fifty.'

'The sales into the bookshops are good enough,' he said. 'I've got the figures in front of me now. If they sell them out the front door in the numbers that they're delivering them at the back then you'd be in with a chance.'

'I want it so much,' Isobel breathed.

There was a silence. 'When you say that, I somehow don't think of bestseller lists at all,' Troy whispered.

Isobel found that she was holding her breath for a moment. 'What do you think of?' she asked provocatively.

'I think of you, and me, and Zelda, as we were that first night, that first night in Newcastle.'

Isobel slowly exhaled. 'It was . . . extraordinary. I've never felt anything . . . I've never been . . . It's like another world. It's like another universe from here.'

They were silent again.

'I'd better go,' Isobel said unwillingly.

'Don't sign a thing without getting it checked by a lawyer. Courier it up to me and I'll have our lawyer look at it.'

'All right,' she said.

'Promise,' Troy said. 'Promise you won't sign on the dotted line or even agree until we know what the small print says.'

'I promise,' she said obediently. She had a wonderful sense that she was being powerfully, passionately protected.

'All right then,' he said reluctantly. 'Goodbye.'

'Goodbye,' she whispered. 'Goodbye.' The phone clicked as he put the receiver down at his end. 'My love,' she said into the hiss of the static.

Philip put his head around the door. 'I thought you wouldn't want pudding,' he said. 'Mrs M. made us bread and butter pudding.'

There was a burst of laughter from the kitchen, the bread and butter pudding was obviously an 'in' joke.

'No,' Isobel said. She got up quickly from her chair in case her very posture might betray that she had been talking on the telephone to her lover. 'But I'd like some coffee.'

She came back into the kitchen with a sense of being a stranger in her own house. The kitchen was now warm and sweetly scented with sugar and nutmeg. Murray was leaning back in his chair, which was pushed back from the table. He had just finished a large bowl of bread and butter pudding and the beam on his face was that of satisfied greed. Philip, taking his place beside him, had the same rosy well-being. Mrs M., clearing the plates from the table, was different too. There was an air of girlish flirtation about her. She was enjoying cooking for these two men, she was enjoying their exaggerated compliments and their teasing. The house which had been so quiet and so restrained was now far jollier, noisier. It was no longer the house of an overworked woman and an invalid husband. It was a house filled with the robust laughter of two cheerful men.

Isobel did not like the change at all.

Eighteen

When the men had finished lunch, which included coffee and indeed brandies, and which seemed to Isobel to last for longer than any lunch she had ever eaten at that table before, they insisted on taking her out to show her the barn and the swimming pool marked out on the floor before they discussed the estimate. Isobel had a slight sense that this programme had been planned between the two of them and that they thought the most successful technique to ensure her compliance would be first to capture her imagination and only later confront her with the daunting costs. She had no objection to Murray behaving in such a way, since he was clearly a determined and successful salesman; but she felt a great sense of betrayal that Philip should conspire with another man to persuade her to a course of action. Philip had always been direct with her about what he wanted; helping himself to cash from the jar of housekeeping money was a direct and simple act. She felt that this softening-up process demeaned them both.

She put a warm jacket around her shoulders as the men waited for her at the back door, and the look she bestowed on Murray was far from friendly.

'Describe it,' Philip prompted Murray. 'Like you did to me. Let's give her the full works.'

Murray opened the door and stepped back with exaggerated courtesy for Isobel to go through before him. 'Picture this,' he began. 'You're not going out into the cold garden, perhaps rainy, perhaps muddy, perhaps even snowing. You're stepping out into a conservatory.'

'A winter garden,' Philip prompted, who knew Isobel's taste in words.

'It has arched gothic windows either side, and wall space for pictures and so on, posters, or shelves for collections, a nice little Delft shelf,' Murray said persuasively. Isobel raised a sceptical eyebrow but said nothing. They started to walk across the yard to the barn.

'Now,' Murray said. 'The conservatory passageway opens up, you don't have a doorway, it opens up through an inviting archway into this glorious pool. From here you can see the lights gleaming on the blue water. You can see the vaulted roof and the reflection of the water flickering on the ceiling.'

He and Philip pulled open the big double doors of the barn. Isobel noticed that Philip managed the heavy door without difficulty.

'Ahead of you is the pool, an irregular, soft-edged rectangle,' Murray said, his voice softly seductive. 'On your right is a traditional wood-built sauna. You can smell the warm wood and the essential oils on the sauna stove. Wonderful. Next to it is the steam room, which is so particularly beneficial for chest ailments and asthma, with high temperature and clean steam. *And* you get it practically for free because it uses the heat from the sauna. That's just a little bonus that my design provides you with.'

He paused for Isobel's exclamation of delight and gratitude. She said nothing.

'Next to that, enclosed in the next archway – and remember these arches match the design of the conservatory so the whole thing ties in together design-wise – is your personal changing room. Next to that is Philip's personal changing room. Next to that a changing room for your lady guests, and next to that a changing room for your gentlemen guests.'

Isobel turned to Philip. 'We hardly ever have guests.'

Murray laughed. 'You'd be surprised how many friends you find you have when you've got a lovely swimming pool,' he said. 'I've had clients whose lives have been transformed. But Mellie will want to swim here, won't she? That's just one person. You'll find you enjoy inviting others. And, as I keep saying to Philip, it's cheaper to get it right now, to do what you want now, than to come back to me in a year's time and say what we really need is another changing area.'

Isobel pressed her lips together to contain argument, and nodded. Murray took a swift glance at her set face and gestured to the back wall.

'At the back there is a fountain, Philip has seen a Greek fountain design which when I saw it, well, it just took my breath away, it was so right for the sort of people you are and for this design. Inspired. The hot water falls from the back wall in a continual gush, like a spa, into the jacuzzi pool.' He held up his hand. 'I know, I know what you're going to say. You've seen jacuzzi pools in photographs of awful houses filled with B-list film stars. It's not like that at all. It's no more than the basin to a fountain, a simple, tasteful design. It's small, it only seats six people at a time. It's quiet, the pump only comes on when you yourself put it on. And more importantly than anything else –' Murray paused for emphasis and gently dropped his hand on Philip's shoulder '– it has *proven* beneficial effects for all sorts of conditions.' He nodded at Isobel, an intimate look indicating his concern for her husband's health.

'So. The jacuzzi pool, rather let's call it the *spa* pool, overflows into the swimming pool. That end is the deep end. So it provides warm water in the deep end and helps keep the pool temperature up, something I really recommend to encourage you to keep swimming, which is what the whole thing is here for, after all. On your left here is a small raised, carpeted area with its own special air-conditioning unit which I recommend you use as a gymnasium. You can get wonderful pieces of equipment now which work the whole body very lightly.' He nodded at Philip.

'Get some of the flab off you,' he winked. Philip laughed. Murray gestured to the south wall. 'And this wall is completely clear because it becomes a series of three picture windows, it's almost all glass. It will give you the most magnificent view down over the hill over the valley. You'll be able to watch the sun set as you swim. I really think it will be a wonderful asset. And best of all, you're not locked in. These are electric windows. On a hot summer's day, you touch the button and the windows slide back and you've got an open-air pool. Similarly, you touch a button and the roof slides back. Magic. You're never stuffy. You never get that "swimming-pool smell", you're open to the elements when you want it, and you're warm and secure when you don't.'

He beamed at Isobel.

'I see,' she said.

He nodded. 'I knew it. I knew that you would see. Of all the people in the world. Because you're an artist. I wear myself out trying to describe this sort of thing to some people and it's a waste of time because they can't see anything in their mind's eye. But a writer like you, you can visualise. You can dream. All my job here is to make sure that the dream that you and Philip had of a truly beautiful, practical asset for your home will be as wonderful as you deserve.' He looked around the lovely timbers of the old barn as if he could not wait to destroy them. 'It will be completely changed,' he promised.

'And the cost?' Isobel asked.

She had thought Murray might be thrown by her directness but he glowed as if they had come to the best part of the whole scheme. 'You're lucky,' he said. 'So lucky with this building. Well, wait, what am I saying? You had the vision to decide that this would be where you sited your pool. It's ideal, and you have the building for free. It's yours, and standing here doing nothing. So we have no building costs at all. All we have to pay for is conversion, the necessary pool equipment, the digging and lining of the pool itself, and the décor.' He smiled down at her. 'I have the figures indoors. Shall we go in?'

Isobel noted how once again she was being taken into her

own home by this stranger even as she obeyed his gesture and went back towards the house. She had a sense that Philip and he had exchanged a quick glance behind her back, but she dismissed it, certain that she was being foolishly over-sensitive. Inside the house she took off her jacket and hung it on the hook. Philip led the way into the sitting room and took his usual seat by the fireplace. Murray paused in the hall to collect his briefcase. Isobel went in and sat on the sofa and then Murray joined them, sitting opposite Philip. He snapped the clips on his briefcase, opened it and abstracted a large folder of papers.

'Now,' he said pleasantly. 'Let's break this down to ball-park figures. Building the conservatory passageway, about £20,000. We can do it a lot cheaper but that's with triple glazed windows and tiled roof. Converting the barn: knocking out the south walls and extending, rebuilding the roof, electric windows and electric roof, altogether about £25,000 for the shell. The pool itself is relatively cheap, with the sauna and the steam room and the jacuzzi feature it comes to about £30,000. Internal décor, lights and finishes, painting etcetera, I would say let's allow a generous £7000. Altogether – ball-park figure, remember – £82,000.'

Isobel blinked and glanced at Philip. He was nodding. These absurd figures were not unexpected, they were familiar.

Murray smiled at her. 'Remember, this is top of the range,' he said. 'If you can live with something a little more downmarket, we can save the money on it. So don't let the figure frighten you off.'

'I'm not afraid of it, I'm appalled by it,' Isobel said robustly. 'I thought we were talking about something for half the price of this, and even that would be too expensive.'

'You have to remember what you're getting,' Murray reminded her. 'This isn't money that is spent and gone. This is an asset which will add value to the house forever. When you come to sell the house you'll see a massive return on this. You ask anyone. Everybody likes a house with a pool, and one of this quality, and an indoor pool? I wouldn't be surprised if you didn't add 120, 150K on the value of your property with it.'

'K?' Isobel asked coldly, as if she did not understand.

'Thousand,' he replied, knowing that she did.

'And we can borrow,' Philip said. 'We can get a mortgage to build it. Anyone would lend us money to do this sort of conversion. We don't have to break into capital.'

'Capital!' Isobel exclaimed indiscreetly, and then swiftly silenced herself. 'One of the things we really congratulate ourselves on is that we don't have debts. We don't carry even a mortgage,' Isobel reminded Philip.

'You don't?' Murray queried interestedly.

Isobel flushed, she had not wanted to invite Murray any deeper into their lives. 'No,' she said shortly.

'It was paid off with my disability insurance,' Philip explained. 'I bought the house when I retired. My savings and shares and so on and Isobel's royalties only cover our day-to-day costs.'

'Well, then you're fine,' Murray said delightedly. 'You can use the whole house as security against the loan. Excellent.' He looked bright and happy as if the deal was done.

'And we're comfortable for income,' Philip reminded her. 'With the last book sold and the next one on the way. That covers us for four years easily. And my pension and savings are our security.'

'You saw the American reviews,' Isobel said, hating having to volunteer this in front of Murray. 'Foreign sales aren't good.'

Philip smiled. 'We'll manage,' he said. 'And we wouldn't borrow more than – what – £60,000? We can manage that.'

'You could get an endowment mortgage, only pay the inter-est,' Murray recommended.

Isobel looked away. 'Let's just wait a moment,' she said politely. 'What I thought we were doing was putting a small swimming pool in the already-existing barn. So we would be paying – what did you say was the cost of the pool? About

£30,000. That's fine. We can manage that and it needn't involve us in any mortgage or borrowing. I'd *like* to do that. The conservatory walkway and the sliding windows and all the rest of it is just too much. We can't afford it and we don't need it.' She looked across at Philip as if she would call out to him, summon him back to the values they had shared and the life they had lived.

'We're simple people,' she reminded him. 'We like a simple life. We're not interested in conspicuous consumption and display. We're not materialists.'

For a terrible guilty moment she thought of the golden mink coat and Zelda's luxurious wardrobe. Of course it was no longer true. She was no longer a simple woman with simple tastes. Zelda's fur coat alone had cost as much as a swimming pool. Why should she take holidays from reality into a life of extreme luxury and sensuality, and yet deny Philip the right to small pleasures at home?

'We'll have the basic pool for certain, but we can't afford much else,' she temporised. 'Perhaps the sauna.'

'If you have the sauna you can have the steam room,' Murray reminded her. 'It's a false economy to do without.'

'And the gym area is nothing,' Philip pointed out. 'Just a raised area with carpeting. We can add equipment a piece at a time. When we want it.'

'All right,' she said.

'So let's take this one at a time,' Murray said cheerfully. Isobel had thought that he might be irritated by her rejection of his scheme but he seemed delighted about it, as if it were another proposal which he could transform with his energy and enthusiasm. 'Let's get this down to the absolutely bare essentials and then price it all again.'

He pulled out a notepad and a calculator and looked at Isobel with the eager face of a good student.

'Basic pool,' he said. 'No fancy shapes to cause the tilers difficulty. Tiled? I assume?'

'Is there a cheaper way to do it?' Isobel asked.

'You can get a plastic liner but it's not very pleasing,' he said. 'And more slippery.' He nodded at Philip. 'We don't want any falls with Philip here.'

'All right,' Isobel said.

'Sauna and steam room.'

'Yes,' she said.

'Changing rooms?'

Isobel hesitated.

'If I might make a suggestion?'

She waited.

'If you're not having your conservatory walkway then you'll need changing rooms over there. You don't want to go running across the yard in your swimming costumes.'

Isobel hesitated.

'Unless you look at it the other way round,' he suggested. 'And save the money you would spend on the changing rooms by building the conservatory passage. So you can get changed in the house and stroll down to the pool in comfort.'

'I think that'd be much better,' Philip said firmly.

Isobel hesitated.

'Better value for the property as well,' Murray recommended. 'To have an attached pool house.'

'All right,' Isobel said unwillingly.

'Shall we keep the jacuz – spa pool?' Murray asked, correcting the name quickly. 'You're heating the water for the pool anyway and it does make it a bit of a feature. Without it, your pool is bound to be a bit bleak.'

'Bleak?' Isobel repeated.

'Basic rectangle pool.' Murray looked worried. 'It needs a touch of something. Something a little more personal.'

'I do think you should see the Greek fountain before you say no,' Philip said plaintively. 'I had rather set my heart on it.'

Murray smiled across at him with affection. 'That's because you've got an eye,' he said.

'Well, let's put it in the estimate for now,' Isobel said. 'We can always rethink later.'

Murray nodded and jotted it down. 'Now we scrap the sliding roof and the sliding windows,' he said firmly. 'They would have been beautiful but you can do them later if you want to. We'll build a nice false ceiling and use the cross-beams as decoration, if you like, and put in a couple of double – glazed windows in the south wall so you still have your wonderful view. Perhaps windowseats, make a little seating area.'

Isobel nodded, thinking that this trimming of the plans was surprisingly easy. She had been a nervous of challenging Murray but he seemed to be determined that she should have only what they really wanted, and what they could afford. She thought she had misjudged him.

'We should allow a couple of thou' to decorate and for lights and things,' he said. 'But that's basically it. A trimmed scheme but a neat, lean, mean scheme. Now hang on a minute while I crunch the numbers.'

They sat in silence while he tapped the figures into his calculator. Isobel glanced over at Philip and he gave her the thumbs-up sign, his face happy and hopeful.

'Eureka,' Murray exclaimed. 'I just did it twice, I couldn't believe how much we saved.'

'How much is it now?' Philip asked eagerly.

'Only £58,000!' Murray said joyfully. 'And for that you get your conservatory walkway, your pool, your jacuzzi, steam room, sauna, gymnasium in the converted barn. Lovely!'

'We'll do it!' Philip said. 'That's great!' He turned to Isobel. 'Isn't it, darling?'

'Yes,' Isobel said weakly, knowing that she could not say no to him when he was so alight with joy and expectancy. 'But I'll need to get the contract checked.'

Murray was writing rapidly on a flimsy sheaf of papers.

'I am glad,' Philip said. 'I knew you'd love the plans when you saw them. And we can convert the windows later, you know.'

'Yes,' Isobel said.

'I'll swim every day,' Philip promised. 'Think of the luxury of just running down the corridor and jumping in the pool. I'll go every day before breakfast.'

'Yes,' Isobel said with a little more conviction. 'I will too.' She thought that swimming would be good exercise for her. It would tone her muscles, help her to slim. She thought that Troy might enjoy her body a little tighter, a little more toned. She suppressed a shiver at the thought of Troy's hand on her miraculously flat belly. Determinedly, she pushed the thought of him to the back of her mind.

'Here we are then,' Murray said cheerfully. 'Sign here, Philip.' He passed the order form over to Philip and then suddenly exclaimed. 'Oh! That reminds me.' He dived into his briefcase again and brought out a copy of Isobel's new hardback book. 'Would you sign it for me?' he asked. 'It's a terrible liberty to ask you, I know. But I felt so honoured to meet you that I rushed out and bought a copy of your new book. Would you do me a very great favour and sign it for me?'

Isobel, distracted by this, did not speak out in time to prevent Philip signing the form. 'Wait a minute, Philip,' she said.

'No special dedication,' Murray said. 'Just your name. I would be so pleased.'

'Of course,' Isobel said.

Murray handed the book over to her with his pen and Isobel signed her name on the title page as she had done so often in so many hundreds of books. Smoothly he replaced the book with the clip board with the order form on it. 'And here too please,' he said. 'First time I've had an author's autograph on my order form.'

Isobel signed as he spoke, finding herself boxed in by Philip's enthusiasm, by her own tendency to comply, and by Murray's request for a signature for the book which had somehow translated itself into the authorisation for him to start work.

'Bingo,' Murray said as she put a dot after the final 'R' of her name.

Nineteen

Isobel listened to the telephone ringing in Troy's office, imagining the receptionist turning from her typing to pick up the phone. When the girl answered Isobel gave her name and imagined the girl pressing 'hold' and telling Troy that Isobel was on the line. At once, faster than ever before, Isobel was put through and Troy's hushed, intimate voice said: 'Darling?'

'Oh.'

They were silent for a moment, listening to the other's quiet breathing, aware of the other's presence.

'I miss you,' Troy said. 'I miss Zelda.'

'Me too,' Isobel said fervently.

'I keep hoping that the PR department is going to insist that she goes to the Outer Hebrides Literary Festival so we can go away together, for ages. I even rang them to see if they had anything they wanted her to do; but they've got nothing booked.'

'I could come up anyway.'

Troy sighed. 'Yes. Oh, yes. Better than nothing. Come up anyway.'

'Next Monday?'

'OK then. Can you stay overnight?'

'I'll fix it,' Isobel promised. 'Shall I come in the afternoon?'

'Come for lunch.'

They were silent again. 'I so want you, Zelda,' Troy said.

Isobel heard herself say, 'Yes,' in Zelda's entranced whisper. She cleared her throat and spoke in her own flatter tones. 'I

hope you won't be upset with me, I think I've done something
a bit stupid, but it's done.'

'Not the pool?' he asked.

'I'm afraid so.'

'You never signed? Isobel, you never signed?'

Isobel shut her eyes in a momentary grimace, dreading
Troy's anger. 'Please don't be cross.'

'Why did you?' he demanded. 'We had discussed it. We
had agreed that you should get advice, not go rushing into
it.'

'Philip wanted it so very much,' she said feebly.

Troy made an indistinguishable exclamation and said
nothing more. Isobel felt, absurdly, that she was about to
cry.

'Please don't be cross,' she said again and knew her voice
to be pitiful, beggarly.

'I'm not cross with you,' he said irritably. 'It just makes
me cross to see him costing you money. I know how hard
you work for this. And then he spends it in days.'

'I know,' she said. 'But –'

'I mean, it's not as if he makes any contribution at all. It's
easy come, easy go, for him. But this money was to pull you
out of subsistence living. This was to be your pension, Isobel.
This was to buy you some luxuries, some time off. For Christ's
sake, it was to buy you some bath oil!'

'What?' She was confused by his sudden change of tack.

'You never buy the aromatherapy oils that Zelda likes. How
much of your own money d'you spend on yourself?'

'Troy –' she pleaded.

'I mean Jesus –' Troy broke off. There was a brief silence
and then in a quite new, cold voice he said: 'I'm sorry. I forgot.
I'm just the agent. It's my job to earn it for you, not to tell
you how to spend it. It's my job to get the best deal for you
at the publishers when you're selling. Not at the shop when
you're buying.'

'Troy –' she said again.

He would not be interrupted. He was unstoppable. 'So tell

me, just as a matter of interest, as a matter of *academic* interest, how much is this pool going to cost? I wonder how much people are paying for swimming pools these days? We were saying that you could probably afford thirty thousand, weren't we? What are we talking about, thirty? Thirty-five?'

Isobel stayed silent.

'Not forty?' Troy said.

Isobel found that she was twining the curly cable of the telephone around her fingers. 'Troy . . .'

'What?' he snapped.

'Please don't be angry . . .'

'I have nothing to be angry about,' he said. 'It's not my money, you're not my wife. You must spend your advances as you see fit. It only becomes a problem for me when you want bigger advances. Then it's my job to get them for you. But, out of interest, purely academic interest, how much is the pool?'

'It's £58,000,' she whispered.

There was a dead silence from the telephone which lasted so long that she feared he had hung up on her.

'Did you sign anything?'

'I signed the order form.'

'A firm order? You are committed to it?'

'Yes, I think so.'

'Any deposit to pay?'

'I wrote a cheque,' she said, her voice very low. 'I wrote a cheque for the deposit. For a third of the total. I wrote a cheque for £20,000.'

In the silence they could both hear Isobel swallow.

'*Do* you have funds in your bank account to cover that?' Troy asked glacially.

'No,' she said quietly.

She heard him pull a filing-cabinet drawer open. 'You'll want me to make a transfer from the Zelda Vere account?'

'Yes, please,' she said humbly.

'How much?'

'I'll need to cover it. Perhaps twenty thousand?'

'Twenty thousand,' Troy repeated coldly, writing the figures down.

'Actually,' Isobel said, 'more like thirty thousand, if I may, then I'll have something in our account.'

'Thirty thousand,' he said, with icy patience. 'It'll take five days to transfer.'

'All right,' she said.

'And when are the other two lumps of £20,000 due?'

'One halfway through the work and one at the end,' she said miserably.

'You must let me know when, and I can arrange transfers,' Troy said with awful politeness. 'And then we'll have to do a final transfer to cover the tax which you will have to pay for drawing such a large sum in one year. It'll cost you something like an extra twenty thousand on top.'

'Yes,' Isobel said humbly. 'I am sorry, Troy.'

'It's your money,' he said unhelpfully. 'It's your life. You must do what you want.'

'I want you not to be angry with me,' she said with a sudden flare of spirit. 'I don't see that it's fair of you to be angry with me. You don't know what it's like here. I came home and Murray was here and everything was completely . . . and you are miles away, and it's as if none of it had ever happened. It doesn't happen to me, anyway. All that other life is Zelda's life, not mine. And then I thought that I had the week away with Zelda, and all Philip has is here. He doesn't get days away, he doesn't get a time like . . . like . . . like it was for us. I felt it was unfair not to give him something, when I had so much. And he is so much better, and Murray is so good for him, and the plans have made him so excited . . .'

Troy was silent. Isobel's explanation died away.

'Shall I not come on Monday?' Isobel asked miserably.

'No,' Troy said. 'I'm sorry. I've got no right to impose my views on you. Of course come Monday. That makes no difference to Zelda, it's only between you and Philip. I just wanted you to be better off, to be able not to worry about money. I'm disappointed that Zelda hasn't solved all your problems. And I wish . . .'

'What?' Isobel whispered. 'What?'

'I wish that it was us, planning how to spend the money together,' Troy said, his voice as low as hers. 'I wish it was me and Zelda planning things together. I suppose I'm jealous.'

It was so unexpected that Isobel closed her eyes and felt physically rocked.

'I know that it's not possible,' he said.

'It isn't,' she said firmly. 'It isn't,' even though her heart was pounding in her ears and every muscle in her body was tightening with desire.

'I know it isn't,' Troy said. 'I suppose I just think of you, trapped in that house, with a sick man, and I think of Zelda in Newcastle . . .'

She would have defended her manner of life and her husband against such a criticism but for the way he reminded her of how she had been with him. At once, unbidden, she saw Troy as Zelda, half-male, half-female, on top of her in bed with a bouffant glossy head of hair, kissing her in passion with lips that were slick and red. It was a vision as vivid as a flashback from a drug. Suddenly, Isobel was there with him again, she could feel the pressure of his hard thigh, encased in the silkiness of stocking, between her own.

'Oh, God,' she whispered.

'I'll see you Monday,' Troy replied. 'I'll transfer the money now. Phone me if you need me, won't you?'

'Yes, yes.'

'And don't, *don't* promise any more money to Philip for anything. He's had enough, right?'

'Yes,' Isobel said obediently.

'D'you promise? The £58,000 is it. You don't need to pay him any more for guilt, or for pity, or because he finds another slick salesman who persuades him he needs something.'

'No, no.'

'Promise?'

'I promise.'

'See you Monday,' Troy said tightly, and broke the connection.

'Monday,' Isobel breathed into the static.

Isobel sat alone in her study for the rest of the afternoon, staring at a screen which remained obstinately blank. She should have been working on the new Isobel Latimer book, *The Choice and the Chosen*, which was to be about free will, but she found that she had nothing very much to say about either free will or choice.

She cupped her chin in her hands and looked at the screen. 'I feel as if I have been seduced,' she whispered. 'Seduced out of intellect into a mindless sensuality.'

The cursor flickered invitingly. Isobel wrote nothing, she gazed at nothing, she thought of nothing. 'First I was Zelda,' she whispered. 'First I put on another persona like an actor. And now I find I cannot get back into the old me.'

She sat in silence as the clock ticked away the afternoon and when she emerged at four o'clock Philip was making a pot of tea and Murray's car was driving away.

'Murray didn't want to disturb you by saying goodbye,' Philip said. 'He really is extraordinarily considerate.'

'Very,' Isobel said dryly. 'I thought he'd be long gone, once he had the cheque.'

'He got Mellie to pay it in for him on her way home,' Philip said. 'And he ordered all the essentials on his mobile while he was here. It was very useful. We went through the specifications together.'

Isobel nodded. She opened the cupboard and fetched tea cups and saucers. Philip at once moved away from the worktop, leaving Isobel to take over the job of making tea.

'Chocolate biscuits?' she asked.

'Only one,' he said. 'Murray insists that I lose weight before the pool is finished. He says I am to be a poolside Adonis.' He chuckled.

Isobel smiled, putting chocolate biscuits on a plate, and then brought two cups of tea to the kitchen table.

'I'm sorry we couldn't go for the full scheme,' she said.

Philip smiled sweetly at her. 'It was a pipe dream. You can't imagine how lovely the brochures are. You see one thing and then you see another and you think – oh, I'll have that, and that, and that too – and at the end of it, it's quarter of a million or something.'

'It's still very expensive,' Isobel reminded him. She realised she wanted a response from Philip. For the first time in their life together she wanted to hear some kind of thanks, some kind of recognition that she was, in effect, indulging him with a stupendously expensive gift.

He shook his head. 'It's nothing compared to some of the pools Murray has done.'

'Murray must move in very wealthy circles then,' Isobel said acidly. 'I'm surprised he spends so much time on our modest little design.'

'He's a real enthusiast,' Philip explained. 'When he becomes attached to a project it doesn't matter to him how much it's worth. He just has to see it through to the end, and he has to see it done as well as it possibly can be done. He's a perfectionist. He reminds me very much of myself when I was a younger man. I had that same kind of drive. He said something the other day: when he wakes first thing in the morning, before it's time to get up, he lies in bed and plans swimming pools in his head. I thought – yes, I can just see me doing that, ten years ago I used to live for my work. D'you remember?'

'How long did he say it would take?' Isobel asked.

'Four to five weeks if everything goes smoothly.' Philip smiled. 'But he also said that nothing ever *does* go smoothly. He's a great realist, is Murray.'

Isobel nodded. For some reason, she felt completely exhausted. 'I only hope it's all worth it, at the end of it,' she said. 'Wouldn't we be a couple of fools if at the end of all this disruption and expense we found that we didn't fancy swimming very much? After all, we've lived here ten years and never felt the need before.'

'Not me,' Philip said certainly. 'Murray says he can tell.

There are two sorts of clients: the ones who have pools because the neighbours have them, or because they want to add value to their house. And the ones who really take to the swimming-pool life. He says he can tell straight away which is which. He says that the moment he met me he knew that I would be someone for whom swimming would become second nature. He says he just knows it.'

'Gosh,' Isobel said. 'How frightfully intuitive of him.'

They were silent for a moment.

'I'm awfully tired,' Isobel said, wearied of her own sarcasm. 'I think I'll have a bath. We'll just have a light supper, shall we?'

Philip looked slightly uncomfortable. 'You have your bath,' he recommended. 'Would you want an early night?'

'Yes,' Isobel said, surprised. 'I'm exhausted. Why?'

'It's just that while you were away we got into the habit of Murray dropping back after he'd finished work. Sometimes we go down to the village for a pint. Sometimes we eat down there, too.'

'Oh,' Isobel said, rather taken aback. 'Has Mrs M. not been cooking your supper?'

'Sometimes she does, but sometimes I skip it,' Philip admitted. 'I tell her to take it home and eat it up herself.'

Isobel nodded, thinking that in addition to paying Mrs M. a very handsome hourly sum she was now, apparently, feeding Mr and Mrs M. too, and paying for Philip to eat out.

'Rather than waste it,' Philip said.

Isobel nodded.

'You can get a good steak and chips at the pub,' Philip said. 'I don't know why we never go.'

Isobel did not remind him that they never went out to the pub in the evening because it had been understood between them for many years that his illness made him too tired to go out at night.

'So if you want an early bed you toddle off,' Philip said encouragingly. 'I'll be in later. I won't be late.'

'All right,' Isobel said. 'See you later.'

* * *

She heard Murray's car draw up as she was in her bath. Then she heard the front door slam almost straight away and the car drive off again. Philip must have been waiting for him in the hall, with his coat on, ready to go, like a little kid waiting for a special trip out.

Isobel lay back in her bath and examined the fact that her husband had a friend and a constant companion, and that this was not her. She felt little more than a sense of deep detachment. Philip had taken a liking to a man whom she would have expected him to despise. There was nothing wrong with Murray, she thought, except he was so intensely ordinary. She thought that you could meet a dozen Murrays in any lounge bar of any three-star hotel. They were middle management, they were senior salesmen. They were householders in the suburbs. They were married men with two children. They drove company cars, rather arrogantly and fast. They had a store of anecdotes and funny stories. They watched television, sometimes went to the cinema, rarely theatre. Murray was a cut above the rest because at least he had the enterprise and energy to found his own business and to live exclusively on his own abilities and wits. But, setting aside that one difference, there were hundreds of men like Murray, thousands of them. Isobel could not see why Philip should be drawn to this one. He had a charming smile and a handsome, open face. He walked like a boy and he laughed like a man whose life was filled with joy. But why Philip should have taken to him so much that they spent large parts of the day together was a mystery.

Isobel rose out of the bath and wrapped herself in a towel. Perhaps Philip needed male company, she thought. Perhaps living in an exclusively female household, with Mrs M. as housekeeper and Isobel as breadwinner, had left him hungry for a brother. Certainly he was different with Murray. He was louder, he was more robust. Lunch with Murray had been an extraordinary experience for Isobel. Mrs M. had been flirtatious and very much part of the company, Murray had been cheerful and familiar, and Philip had been entertained

249

and happy. Isobel shook her head. It had not been like her home at all.

On impulse she padded into the bedroom and picked up the bedside telephone. She knew Troy's home telephone number off by heart. She wanted to hear his voice. She had a sudden chill sense of being abandoned. Philip had gone out without her, gone without even asking her to join them. Her decision that they would have a quiet supper and an early night had not determined the course of the evening at all, as it usually did. On the contrary it had freed him to make his own choice. And he had chosen to be without her.

She heard the telephone ringing and then Troy answered the phone. There was so much noise behind his voice that she thought he must have the television on absurdly loud. He had to shout, 'Hello?'

'It's me,' Isobel said.

'Oh. Isobel. Hi.'

'Can you turn it down?'

'I'll take the call on another phone,' he said. She heard the telephone click and then in a moment he picked it up again. The noise and the music were now distant.

'That's better,' he said.

'What's going on?' She heard her voice sound inquisitorial, as if she had a right to know what he was doing and as if it were likely that she would disapprove.

'Nothing,' he said, instantly defensive. 'Just a couple of friends came round.'

Isobel wanted to ask, who? what friends? She wanted to ask, what were they doing? Were they dancing? Or else why was the music so loud? Was it a party?

'It sounds fun,' she said. Her voice did not sound light and cheerful as she had intended. It sounded horridly self-conscious and awkward.

'It's fine,' he said, to conclude the subject. 'And how about you? What are you doing?'

'I've just had a bath, I was going to have an early night.'

'Good idea,' he said warmly. 'Everything OK?'

She hesitated. She wanted to tell him how strange it felt to be in the house on her own, how disorientated she felt that Philip should have waited by the front door for Murray and that they should have driven off together.

'Philip's gone out for a drink with Murray,' she said desolately.

'So you can have a bit of peace,' Troy said as if he were pleased for her.

'Yes,' she said, her voice very flat.

There was a brief silence in which Troy waited for her to say something or to bring the telephone call to an end.

'I just wanted to hear your voice.'

'Shall I sing?' Troy suggested. 'Or recite a poem?'

She understood that he was happy, with his friends, perhaps a little drunk. She understood that she would not be able to persuade him to talk to her with tenderness or sympathy.

'No,' she said, trying to sound equally light-hearted. 'I need a lullaby, not you singing rock and roll.'

'Judy Garland,' he corrected her at once.

'Of course,' she said. 'I'll say goodnight. Have a lovely party.'

She had thought he might contradict her and say that it was not a party, just a couple of rowdy friends making too much noise. But he did not.

'Goodnight, sweetheart,' he said cheerfully, and put the telephone down.

Isobel sat for a moment with the dead receiver in her hand and then replaced it gently on the cradle.

She found that she was cold and disagreeably damp, and so she towelled herself roughly and then found a pair of warm plain pyjamas. She got into bed and consulted the pile of books on her bedside table for one which would be most likely to divert her from this sense of enfeebling depression. She realised that she felt left out, like the child who is not picked for the team, and is excluded from the playground games. She thought of Philip and Murray in chatty camaraderie at the local pub, and of Troy drinking champagne and laughing with

251

his friends. And then there was her, all on her own in a big double bed, choosing a book to read herself to sleep at half past nine at night.

She pulled up the duvet to tuck it around her more warmly. The worst thing about this feeling of being the one who was left out was her sense of aggrieved injustice. She was the breadwinner, she felt that Philip should stay at home with her, or, if he wanted to go out, go out with her. She was Troy's lover, what was he doing partying with friends when she was all alone? And she had enjoyed a taste of being Zelda the star. How could it be that there were parties and she not centre of the stage? How could it be that Philip was having a good time, and Troy was having a good time, but she was all alone in bed, retiring for the night like some sad spinster with nothing to do but read a book and pretend that this was what she preferred?

Twenty

In the morning, Isobel felt more cheerful. She woke before
Philip, and watched his handsome face for a few moments
before she slipped out of bed. When he opened his eyes he
smiled at her and said, 'Good morning, darling,' in a voice of
genuine pleasure.

'Did you have a good night?' she asked.

He chuckled. 'Excellent. Murray and I found ourselves co-
opted on to the darts team. Can you imagine it? Murray's
quite a good player but I astounded them all by getting a
bullseye.'

'Oh,' Isobel said. 'I didn't even know you could play darts.'

'I used to when I was a lad. I haven't for years. But the
bullseye was the decider, and our team won. Bill Bryce was
really –'

'Who?'

'Bill Bryce, the landlord, he was really pleased. It was a
grudge match, you see. He stood us all a round, and then
Murray and I went into the restaurant and had dinner.'

'I'd have thought you'd not have been hungry,' Isobel
remarked. 'After that enormous lunch.'

'I could have made do with a snack but Murray was starv-
ing,' Philip said. 'He runs around so much he burns it up. I
just had steak and salad. I am absolutely determined to get
some weight off.'

'Because Murray says you must be a poolside Adonis,' Isobel supplemented.

Philip smiled without embarrassment. 'Yes.'

'So what will you have for breakfast? Half a grapefruit segment?'

Philip got out of bed and stretched. 'No, toast as usual. I'm not that reformed yet. Murray has porridge.'

'Does that mean we have to have porridge?'

He glanced up, alerted by the edge in her voice. 'No, of course not. I was just saying, that's what he has. It's very good for you. He says it's very satisfying.'

Isobel nodded, pulled on her dressing gown and went downstairs.

They ate breakfast in companionable silence, reading the Sunday newspapers. Philip always started with the business section and Isobel with the books section.

'Anything interesting?' Philip asked from behind his newspaper.

'A new novel by Paul Kerry has taken a bit of a pounding,' Isobel remarked. 'They say it's facile. He does write one a year now.'

'It's like a production line,' Philip said. 'Why not take longer, why not take more care, as you do?'

Isobel said nothing but she knew very well why not. Paul Kerry, like the rest of them, had to publish regularly, had to struggle between the demands of the market as tough and unsympathetic as if he were selling baked beans, and his desire to create something profoundly satisfying to himself as an artist.

'Perhaps he needs the money,' she said.

'We all need the money,' Philip said grandly. 'But you shouldn't sacrifice artistic merit just to turn a penny. It's a balance.'

'Thus speaks the man with the £58,000 pool,' Isobel said, smiling to take the sting out of her words.

'Thus speaks the man who worked very hard in industry and bought his house outright with his invalidity pension,' Philip replied. 'So that everything earned after that is jam on the bread and butter.'

A few months ago Isobel would have remained silent. Now she replied: 'A lot of jam, £58,000 worth of jam.'

Philip smiled. 'We're lucky,' he said, as if that concluded the discussion.

He lifted his newspaper once more and Isobel saw him disappear. Something in the way that he had concluded the conversation empowered her to speak: 'I shall be away tomorrow night,' she said. 'If that's OK.'

'Of course,' he replied. 'College work again?'

'Yes,' she said. 'And I so hate the late train.'

'Coming home Tuesday?'

'I'll be home at lunchtime.'

'No hurry,' he said helpfully. 'Take as long as you like. We won't run away.'

'No, I know,' she said. 'But I'll come home in time for lunch, Tuesday.'

He nodded and was silent again. Isobel rose and made them another cup of coffee.

'Shall we go for a walk later?' she asked. 'It's a lovely day.'

'All right,' he said pleasantly. 'We could do that walk by the river and go to the pub for lunch if you like.'

'Won't that be too far for you?'

'No,' Philip said confidently. 'I did it the other day with Murray. We had a great day out.'

On Monday morning Isobel was disturbed in her study by a tap on the door. Mrs M. put her head into the room. 'Sorry to interrupt,' she said. 'But I thought you'd want to settle up.'

Isobel, who had still written nothing, turned from the blank screen. 'Housekeeping money?' she asked.

'I've got all the receipts,' Mrs M. said, diving into her purse and producing a sheaf of papers. 'For the week.'

Isobel was slightly surprised. Usually all the grocery money came out of the housekeeping jar, which she filled with notes once a week. They averaged between £100 and £150 a week and Isobel had left £200 in crisp new twenty-pound notes, before she had gone away for the week.

'I thought I had left enough,' she said.

'No, I used my own money so as not to bother Philip,' Mrs M. said.

'Oh,' Isobel replied. 'So?'

'It's £110 extra for housekeeping and £300 for my hours,' Mrs M. said.

Isobel blinked.

'I did a twelve-hour day, Monday to Friday,' Mrs M. explained. 'Except for when Philip said I could go home early.'

'And then?'

'I did ironing at home,' Mrs M. said smoothly.

Isobel opened the drawer and took out her cheque book. 'That's £410 that I owe you then,' she said, trying not to sound begrudging. 'And here's another £100 for the house-keeping jar. That should do till the end of the week, shouldn't it?'

Mrs M. hesitated. 'Well, Philip takes his drinking money out of it. When he goes out with Murray.'

'A hundred pounds drinking money?' Isobel queried.

'You know what they're like.'

Isobel said nothing. It seemed to her obvious that she did not know what they were like.

'And they often eat out.'

'When you've cooked them supper?'

'Oh, I don't mind,' Mrs M. said. 'I like to see him enjoying himself. It's no bother to me.'

'It's a bit extravagant,' Isobel said mildly. 'If you're cooking his dinner and then he goes out to eat. Perhaps you and he should decide at the start of the day whether he'll eat in or out.'

Mrs M. smiled politely but made no reply. Isobel realised that she could not make Philip and Mrs M. do anything they did not want to do, and that it suited the two of them, and Murray as well, that Mrs M. should cook lunch and dinner for Philip and then take home whatever was not wanted.

'Well, we'll soon be getting back to normal,' Isobel said,

tearing the cheque from the book. 'When the pool work is done.'

'Will you be away this week?' Mrs M. asked, accepting the cheque and tucking it into her overall pocket along with the cash.

'Just tonight,' Isobel said. 'So perhaps you could ask Philip if he wants you to cook supper for him. I'll be home in time for lunch tomorrow.'

'Okey dokey,' Mrs M. said cheerfully. 'I can do toad in the hole for them both tonight, Murray loves toad in the hole.'

Isobel raised her eyebrows but said nothing. Mrs M. went out, closing the door quietly behind her. Isobel turned back to the computer screen and found that once again she had nothing to write. But now she had nothing to write in a different way. Before she had lacked inspiration, now she was completely distracted. She was thinking, in an inconclusive, irritable sort of way, about Mrs M. cooking dinners and then taking them home to eat, about Philip taking money in handfuls of notes from the housekeeping jar, about Murray coming to the house and about Isobel paying her housekeeper to know and cook Murray's favourite meals.

It was a relief to take the train to London in the late morning and to see the familiar fields give way to the small terraced houses with the miniature gardens. Isobel loved looking into the gardens and windows of the houses which backed on to the railway line, imagining the lives of the people who owned them. Some gardens were packed with equipment for children, climbing frames, swings, see-saws, and even enormous free-standing pools, drained and empty and cold now until summer came again. Others belonged to enthusiasts and were laid out with precision, a path meandering in ordered curves down the length of the garden to the greenhouse, a pergola, an obelisk or two, a set of arches, all with plants tied in, tied down, mulched up, and organised into order. Other gardens were neglected. Isobel imagined that the occupants were problem families, housed and rehoused, a nuisance for the neighbours and a continual headache for themselves. Their gardens were tatty with collapsing outdoor furniture, dustbins abandoned at random, sometimes rubbish spilling from bin bags, rusting barbecues, rain-sodden candles left out from parties which everyone had forgotten. Isobel surveyed it all, measuring, judging, creating imaginary lives as a distraction from her own.

When she arrived at Waterloo the mess of her own house and life was quite forgotten, she felt light-hearted as she waited for a taxi, and then, as the taxi crawled through the London traffic, she felt her throat grow tight, she felt breathless. She had a sense of coming into the regions which were occupied by Troy: the bustle of the city was like his busy life, the exotic clothes and colours on the streets were his exuberant energy, the elegance and sophistication was his, all his. Isobel sat back in the seat of the taxi and credited all of the excitement and beauty of the city to one man, and knew her desire.

Troy was quick to open the door to her, and stepped back to let her go into the house. They did not touch or speak for the moment, they looked at each other as if the process of encountering each other again after an absence of a few days was something that must be experienced, even endured. They looked steadily and thoughtfully into each other's faces and Isobel thought that never in her life had anyone regarded her with such a steady, searching stare. She did not feel uncomfortable under his gaze, instead she felt his regard as a spotlight with which he truly saw her, and which identified her to them both as the star.

Troy smiled. 'Hello,' he said, and held out his arms.

Isobel slid into his arms and felt his grip around her tighten and hold her. She experienced for the first time the important moment of adulterous comfort: when the embrace of the lover is more familiar and more comfortable than the embrace of the husband. It was a switch of loyalties that she made, not at the level of moral choice, nor intellect, nor even consciousness. Isobel felt Troy's arms tighten around her, felt his hands go down to cup her buttocks and pull her pelvis closer to his, and knew at the same time a leap of desire and a sense of coming home to the man she loved best.

Troy held her close, rocked her from one foot to another. Isobel closed her eyes and gave herself up to him, let him do what he wanted. He kneaded her buttocks, squeezing and releasing the generous handfuls of flesh. Isobel felt her muscles relax and let her head droop against his shoulder, she inhaled the clean smell of his skin and the spice of his expensive aftershave. The scent of him dazzled her senses, she felt herself dizzy with desire for him, she leaned against him, letting him take her weight on his demanding hands, twining her arms around his neck so that she could drape against him.

Together they leaned back against the wall of the narrow hall, and then slid down to lie on the stairs, Troy underneath, his hands questing now, reaching up under her skirt, rubbing her urgently. Isobel gave a low moan of desire and raised herself up so that she could put her hand down to unzip his fly, to clasp him. Almost at once she recoiled. Her hurrying hand felt silk, embroidered silk. She pulled back a little and saw the pale ice blue of Zelda's French knickers behind Troy's open fly.

'Suck me,' Troy commanded.

Isobel froze, quite incapable of moving towards him. 'You're wearing her knickers,' she said.

His blue eyes opened, he was smiling. 'Yes,' he said simply.

Isobel pulled away from him so that she could see his face. 'Why are you wearing her knickers?' she demanded. 'Was it just because I was coming here, or do you wear her clothes all the time? D'you wear her things when I'm not here?'

At once he heard the fear in her voice. He put his hand over hers and pulled it back down to the contradictory sensation of silk and hard maleness. 'It was for you,' he whispered persuasively. 'It was all for you. Come on, Isobel. Do it for me . . .'

Isobel's hand felt silk and beneath his hardness and pulled away with a shudder.

'What's the matter?'

She gave a little shrug and got up from the carpeted stairs, tugged down her skirt. She was aware that she was blushing, she felt agonisingly embarrassed. Unconsciously, she rubbed the palm of her hand against her skirt.

'Nothing,' she said shortly.

'Was it what I said?'

'No, of course not.'

Troy scrambled up, adjusted his trousers, tucked away the blue silk. 'That's it then?' he asked acidly.

Isobel looked away from him to the front door, looked back. 'Troy . . .'

'Yes?'

'Nothing,' she said feebly.

In her failure to speak he grew more confident. He slid his finger around the waistband of his trousers, checking the smoothness of their fit and feeling the soft texture of the blue silk, safely hidden underneath.

'Are you sure that nothing's wrong?' he demanded, with a complete lack of any kind of solicitude in his tone.

Isobel could not find the courage to confront him. 'Nothing.'

Troy nodded and led the way up the stairs to his flat.

'Coffee?' he asked politely.

'Please.'

They went together into the kitchen and Troy busied himself with making coffee. He poured her a mug and one for himself. Isobel perched on a stool at the worktop, Troy leaned back against the sink. He was very relaxed.

'We have to do a bit of work if you don't mind,' he said, very matter of fact.

'Work?'

'We have to look at the Zelda Vere account.'

Isobel forced herself to be as businesslike as he. 'Oh yes.'

Troy pulled a sheaf of papers from a clip at the side of the worktop.

'D'you remember the figures on the contract? You got £350,000 in three lumps. Signature, hardback publication, paperback publication, yes?'

'Yes.'

'So you've been paid the first two lumps, and next year when they put *Devil* into paperback you'll get the last payment on that contract.'

'Yes.'

'So. We deducted agency fees and costs, then you repaid me the cost of your clothes and with the rest we opened the Zelda Vere account. It was £177,250.'

Isobel blinked. 'I didn't know we'd spent that much on clothes.'

He gave her a smile. 'Darling, the coat alone was £40,000.'

She nodded, trying not to look aghast. 'And all the rest?'

'It's an expensive business, being Zelda Vere. But a profitable one. Don't look so frightened. The sums work out in the end.'

Isobel laughed at being called frightened, and tried to ignore the cold sense of fear inside.

'You've just drawn £30,000 for the pool, and you will be drawing another £40,000 before the end of the year. You'll have to draw also something around £20,000 to pay as tax. Once the money enters your account you'll be liable for tax on it.'

Isobel nodded. 'I keep forgetting tax.'

'I don't,' Troy assured her. 'That leaves you with nearly £90,000 in the Zelda Vere account in Switzerland with a further £100,000 to come on paperback publication next year.'

'Still quite a lot,' Isobel said bravely.

'Not as much as we had thought, though,' Troy said, looking at her. 'Not as much as you had thought, is it?'

Isobel silently shook her head.

'Mmm. So I have some proposals to make.'

Isobel waited.

'First, we really start pushing this as a TV mini series. The main time for interest will be at the time of paperback publication but I thought we could start right away. I can get an agent in the US to take it round to Hollywood producers and see if we get some interest.'

Isobel nodded.

'We should offer Zelda as screenplay writer on the project,' he said.

'But I don't know how to write screenplays . . .' Isobel started.

Troy shook his head. 'Piece of cake.'

'No, wait a minute.' Isobel spoke with the authority that came to her when her work was involved. 'I *really* don't know how to write screenplays, and I don't watch enough television. It's not like a new form of novel writing which I could learn. It's a completely different art.'

'It's not art, it's craft,' he said simply. 'And you could learn it in half a day. But in any case, you won't have to. We'll just get a contract for you to write it and then we'll bring in a ghost writer. Or they'll sack you after they see the first draft. Either way we get double our money for the option. And this is about money, remember, Isobel. It's not about art.'

She nodded. 'I keep forgetting.'

'I don't.'

He poured more coffee in their cups. 'Now. I've been talking to the publishers about a sequel. Naturally they want another, naturally there's a bit of concern as to what Zelda could do next. So we're moving right away from the autobiography aspect of it and going for a straight novel. What they want is something very hot and new.'

Isobel waited.

'We've got to be smart here. We've got to be one jump ahead. We timed Zelda Vere just right with survivor fiction, but we've got to do it again. There'll be half a dozen big survivor books by next year, we've got to take Zelda ahead. She's got to be ahead of the crowd, not fighting in the middle. She's got to be out front.'

'Out front, headed where?' Isobel asked.

'Spirituality,' Troy said triumphantly.

'Zelda gets spiritual?' she asked incredulously.

He nodded. 'First half-dozen chapters are about wealth and

success and the richness of our heroine's life and then she has a shattering experience, a near-death experience, and then she sees a blinding light and encounters her spirit guide. He has to be handsome, he has to be aboriginal, but aboriginal from somewhere that's very fashionable, I see perhaps Africa, perhaps South America, we'll check on that. Anyway, a big holiday destination because he tells her about his previous life and we do a lot of landscape.'

Isobel nodded. 'She falls in love with him and becomes more spiritual . . .'

'And also very erotic,' Troy interpolated. 'Sex with the undead, very sexy.'

'And then she has to let him go. She has to let him go back to the spiritual world and leave their love behind her so that she can find the man she has always loved all along in the real world, the man she ignored before because he was poor. But he always faithfully loved her and now she can see his merits.'

Troy closed his eyes. 'That's fantastic,' he said. 'That'll do it. And the guy she always loved, who's he? He needs to be more than just poor.'

'He's her spirit guide's grandson,' Isobel declared. 'And very like him when he's naked. It's just that she never noticed before. They had never been lovers before. That, actually, was why he was always drawn to her. He's sort of reincarnated.'

Troy beamed at her. 'You write me a synopsis of that and the first couple of chapters and I can get you a contract for another quarter of a million,' he said. 'Philip can have his pool and you're *still* going to be a wealthy woman.'

Twenty-One

Troy took Isobel to lunch at a modish café-restaurant and pointed out to her the television stars and producers who came and went with much noise and excitement and kissing of cheeks. Isobel recognised almost no-one. Her daily work and the routine of their evenings left her no time to watch television, and since she did not have a set in her living room or bedroom, she seldom caught glimpses of programmes either. The television in the kitchen served as a companion to Philip and Mrs M. during the day and they would have known many of the people who arrived and exclaimed and ordered food and asked for specially prepared dishes. Isobel wanted to be impressed by dining with celebrities, but she could do little more than smile and nod when Troy told her a string of names that she did not recognise.

A few people came over to their table and Troy introduced Isobel to them. One man leaned down and whispered in Troy's ear and made him laugh before leaving.

'Who was that?' Isobel asked.

'Just a friend of mine.'

'Did his mother never tell him that it is rude to whisper?'

Troy smiled at her. 'D'you know I bet she did, and he was such a bad boy that he didn't listen.'

Isobel nodded and returned to the creamy dessert. 'Troy,' she asked tentatively. 'You do seem to have a lot of male friends.'

At once his face was alight with amusement. 'Yes, I do.'

'I wondered . . .' She hesitated and then took the plunge. 'I wondered if they were lovers as well as friends?'

'Did you?'

'You don't have to tell me.'

'I know I don't.'

'But I would like to know. It's part of knowing you better.'

He had to fight the temptation to lie at once, he thought that perhaps he could trust her. 'It's like this,' he said slowly. 'It's not my secret. If I tell you that someone is my lover then I'm telling his secret, right? And that's not necessarily fair. He might not want it known that he sees me. He might not be out.'

She nodded.

'So I won't tell you about individuals. But it is true to say that sometimes I have male lovers.'

'But you wouldn't call yourself a homosexual?'

Isobel's voice was little more than a whisper but still Troy flared up at her indescretion. 'I wouldn't call myself anything,' he snapped.

She withdrew a little at the flash of his temper and waited in silence. Troy ordered coffee for them and looked across at Isobel. He had never seen her like this before. She was nervous in his presence, she was anxious not to offend or annoy him. Perversely Troy realised that he rather despised her when she was cautious with him. Always before he had been her agent and she had been the talent. It had been his job to ensure that nothing irritated her, not vice versa. Equally, when she had been Zelda she had soared into arrogance and stardom and he had done nothing more than support her and encourage her. Now she was humbled by the desire to please him, and Troy had no interest in deferential women.

'Don't be like this,' he said sharply. 'You caught me on the raw. It doesn't matter.'

She looked up. 'I wanted to know your preference,' she said flatly.

'Why? You surely know my preference. We have surely experimented and demonstrated it.'

Isobel's grey eyes were shiny like polished pewter. He had a sudden, surprised sense that this was not a deferential woman but on the contrary a woman in touch with some hidden power.

'I need to know, because I want you to prefer me,' she said.

Troy recognised the pattern of their relationship: just when he took her for granted and was tending to withdraw, she plunged them into a new level of intimacy. She caught him up in the urgency and intensity of her desire and took him deeper with her.

'I do prefer you,' he said. 'We're having lunch, aren't we? And dinner tonight? We're together today, aren't we?'

'I want to be together tomorrow,' she said. 'And the next day. And the day after that.'

For a moment he could only stare at her.

'I want you,' she said.

He did not answer.

She waited for his reply.

After lunch they went to Harvey Nichols to buy clothes for Isobel herself. In Troy's terms this was an economy. 'Isobel Latimer would shop at Harvey Nichols,' he said. 'Zelda is pure Harrods.'

'At last I get clothes that we both like,' Isobel said with pleasure.

'You can't go mad,' Troy warned her. 'But you can have a smarter suit than that one.'

They bought a dark woollen suit at Betty Jackson. Troy would not let her even look at the brilliant colours of Lacroix. 'Zelda, not Isobel,' he said. They bought a deep red wool dress with a matching little jacket at Nicole Farhi.

'Good cut *and* literary connection,' Troy said with satisfaction. 'Very Isobel Latimer.'

They went to the underwear section and Troy waited happily on the chaise longue while Isobel tried on some discreet but rather sensuously silky underwear.

'Nothing too expensive or glamorous,' Troy reminded her. 'Not if you want to take it home.'

'Philip doesn't see my underwear,' Isobel said, writing the slip for the credit card.

'Doesn't he? Where d'you get undressed?'

'In the bathroom.'

'What d'you wear in bed?'

Isobel gave Troy a look that warned him to maintain a distance. 'Pyjamas.'

Troy gave a snort of laughter. Isobel took the beautifully wrapped bag from the sales girl and turned away from him.

'That is married life,' she said. 'That is what it's like.'

'Sounds like married death,' Troy said cruelly.

She stopped and turned to face him. 'Are you offering anything else?'

'No,' Troy said quickly.

'Exactly,' Isobel said.

She went down the escalator ahead of him, her back stiff with resentment. Troy laid one gentle hand on the nape of her neck and felt her relax at his touch. He leaned forward and rested his head against her cheek. 'Time to go home and make love,' he said quietly.

They spent the afternoon in bed together, in Troy's bedroom. They were both avoiding the spare bedroom with the wardrobe filled with Zelda's clothes and her two heads of hair, ghostly on the top shelf. Isobel was delighted to discover that Troy had a large double water-bed with black sheets.

'I know it's an awful cliché,' he said. 'But I love it.'

Isobel, rumpled and satisfied, lay back and smiled at him. 'It's lovely,' she said. 'You're the most glamorous man I've ever met.'

He beamed at that. 'Tea?' he asked.

'Please,' she said.

He made her Darjeeling and served it inky black with a slice of lemon in china cups as she stayed in bed.

'This is heaven,' she said.

*   *   *

In the evening Troy wanted to go to the theatre. A client of his was in a play and he had promised to see it. Isobel wore the new red dress and pinned her hair in a French roll. She telephoned Philip before they went out; but he was not there. Mrs M. answered the phone.

'I was just going out the front door,' she said. 'I'm glad you caught me.'

'Where's Philip?' Isobel asked.

'Not been in since lunchtime,' Mrs M. said cheerily. 'Murray came for lunch with him and then they left in Murray's car and I haven't seen them since.'

'Did he say where he was going?'

'No. Just that they didn't need dinner.'

'How odd. Were they going to look at swimming pools, d'you think?'

Mrs M. chuckled. 'While the cat's away the mice do play.'

Isobel restrained herself from snapping in reply. 'Would you leave him a note?' she said with careful politeness. 'Tell him that I rang and that I am going out now to the theatre, and I will call again when I come in.'

'Call again when you come in,' Mrs M. repeated. 'Okey dokey.'

Isobel put the phone down.

'Trouble at home?' Troy asked.

'No. Philip and Murray have gone out for the day together and aren't back yet. I'll ring later.'

A look of bright curiosity crossed Troy's face. 'They spend a lot of time together, don't they?' he remarked.

Isobel looked at him, her eyes slightly narrowed. 'Yes,' she said coldly. 'Why not?'

'Only wondered,' Troy grinned, knowing that she had read his thoughts and did not like them. 'Only wondered, Missus.'

Isobel rang home again on the payphone in the theatre foyer, and then again from a restaurant, after they had been back-stage and gone out to supper with Troy's client. They put him, exhausted and exuberant, into a taxi and then walked home. She telephoned again from Troy's flat and this time Philip answered.

'Are you all right?' she asked with sudden fear. His speech was slightly slurred, she thought he might have taken too many painkillers.

'A touch worse for wear,' he said, a laugh at the back of his voice. 'Don't be cross, Izzy. Murray and I went on a pub crawl and then had dinner.'

Isobel heard a muffled shout of corroboration in the background.

'Is he still there?' she asked.

'Staying the night,' Philip said. 'Too rat-arsed to drive home.'

There was another shout from somewhere in Isobel's house.

'I don't know that the spare bed's made up,' Isobel said inhospitably.

'Mrs M. did it before she left. Good woman.'

'Oh, good,' Isobel said. 'Are you sure you're all right?'

'Best I've ever been,' Philip assured her. 'Absolutely best. Blooming.'

'Blooming drunk!' came the shout.

Isobel took a little breath, held herself back from saying anything, anything at all. 'I'm going to bed now,' she said. 'I'll see you mid-morning.'

'You do that,' Philip genially advised her. 'Good programme. We're just going to have a little nightcap, a little chat about this and that, and then we'll turn in too.'

He put down the telephone without saying goodnight. Isobel waited for a moment, listening to the silence from Kent, and then she gently replaced the receiver. She turned. Troy was standing in the doorway, openly listening. One dark eyebrow was raised, his face was alight with laughter.

'Shut up,' Isobel said flatly. 'It's not like that at all.'

Troy stepped forward so that she could see his hands. He was holding a chilled bottle of Roederer by the neck and a pair of flute glasses. 'I wondered if you wanted to play?' he asked invitingly.

At once Isobel forgot Philip and Murray and her home, forgot them completely as if it were another life, an ancient life, long ago and far away. 'Play?'

'I thought we might have a little drink,' Troy said, coming into the room and uncorking the champagne with a soft pop followed by the hiss of the bubbles in the tall glasses. 'And then I thought we might invite Zelda to come out and play with us.'

Isobel shivered, there was something macabre about the way he said her name, as if she were some kind of ghost that they might raise by the ceremonial drink of champagne and the ritual of face painting. But she also knew that she and Troy had gone as far as they could go together. They had reached their limit today when she had challenged him to love her and he had sidestepped the challenge. If she wanted to make love with him tonight, if she wanted to fascinate him and entrance him, and bind him to her, then she would need to be more than Isobel Latimer, she would need to look more beautiful, to feel more sensually, to give him a greater sense of risk. Isobel Latimer would never be able to seduce and hold Troy. Isobel and Zelda together, might. Isobel stepped forward, took a glass and held it to him in a silent toast, and then drank.

At once she perceived the effect of the drink, she felt reckless, beautiful. Troy reached into his back pocket and took out his wallet. He unfolded a small envelope.

'A little coke?' he asked invitingly.

'Yes,' Isobel said. 'If you think . . .'

He looked inquiringly.

'If you know that it's not bad stuff.'

'Rat poison? Vim? Tell you what, I'll take some first and if I don't collapse foaming at the mouth then you can try some if you want. Only if you want. It's not compulsory.'

Isobel smiled and watched him fetch a book, slice the drug on the smooth laminated cover with his credit card, and then roll a twenty-pound note and sniff up a line. Finally he dabbed his finger into the remainder of the line and rubbed it on his teeth. 'Mmmm,' he said with quiet appreciation.

He handed the rolled bank note to her. 'D'you want some?'

Isobel wanted to taste what he tasted, wanted to sense what his body knew. Isobel wanted to experience the very core of Troy, she would have taken anything he offered, she would have tried anything he recommended. She took the bank note and sniffed up the line of coke and then dabbed her finger in the powder.

She waited for the drug to take effect.

'Good?' he asked her.

She shook her head. 'I don't know. All I feel is like lying down and giggling.'

He smiled. 'So lie down and giggle.'

Isobel, feeling wonderfully young and foolish, lay down on Troy's beautiful carpet and giggled. Troy's head appeared in her line of vision and he lay on his back beside her. The two of them looked up at the ceiling.

'Tell me a story,' Troy said invitingly. 'Go on, tell me all about everything. Tell me about when you were a young girl and why you married Philip and everything about everything.'

'And then we'll go to Zelda's room,' Isobel said.

'We'll do everything,' Troy promised her. 'We have time for everything.'

'I married Philip because I was in love with him,' Isobel began. 'It's as simple as that. He was working for one of the big petrochemical companies as a senior PR and I was a young academic working on the ethics of science. We met at a brains trust kind of thing. I thought he was wonderful.' She paused and sighed. 'He was blond and tall and very fit, and,' she giggled, 'he was terribly well off. I was an academic, I was paid a research grant which was next to nothing, and all my friends were the same. But here was this gorgeous man taking me out to these fabulous places and driving a sports car – did I say he had a sports car? Well, he did, a red MG – and talking to me as if what I thought really mattered. He thought I was brilliant, he kept asking me what I thought about things and listening as if I was a genius. I was awfully flattered. All the men I had known before were working at the same level as

271

me. No-one before had thought I was anything more than competent. We fell in love. We got married.'

'Did you sleep together first?' Troy asked inquisitively.

'Oh yes,' Isobel said. 'He was my first, it was terribly romantic. We got married and I carried on at work and he did too. He bought us a nice house in town, we had a good circle of friends. We used to give tremendously elaborate dinner parties, four courses all home-made. And we used to go out to friends who cooked really well too. We used to drink a bit, wine mostly, Philip became quite a wine buff.'

'And?' Troy asked.

Isobel sighed. 'I always thought I could write, but I never had any faith in it. Philip was wonderful. He bought me a word processor and taught me how to use it. He set it up for me and he insisted that I spend an hour every night writing. I wrote short stories. I used to bring them down and he would read them while I was cooking dinner. One evening he told me that he had sent one of them off to a women's magazine and it had been accepted.'

'Good moment?' Troy asked.

'Breathtaking,' she said. 'I thought it was the start of a brilliant career.'

'Well, it was, wasn't it?'

'Sort of,' she said. 'I did some more short stories and then a full-length novel. Then I became pregnant. I was so excited and happy about it. Philip insisted that I leave work at once but I thought I'd work till I was about five months. We always had plenty of money, it wasn't the money. I was rewriting my PhD thesis for publication. I wanted to finish before the baby came.'

Isobel was silent for a moment. 'I lost the baby,' she said. 'It wasn't because I was working, it was just one of those things. But I didn't conceive again. We tried. We went to a specialist. But while we were hoping that it would come right, Philip's mother died and so we left it. I started teaching, I got tenure at my university. I was young and fit, and Philip was older than me but still very fit. We thought that it would somehow happen later. It didn't.'

She brightened up. 'I had my first novel published. That was the most wonderful moment. I started work on my second. Philip was incredibly encouraging and helpful. He used to reread my work every evening and correct the grammar and the spelling. He used to take the manuscript into his office and get his secretary to retype it for me. The second novel, *Maverick Days*, won the Stephens Prize.'

'I remember reading that,' Troy said. He remembered but he did not say that he had been reading it as an eighteen-year-old student in his first year. Isobel had been in her early thirties. 'It was the book of the year, wasn't it? Everyone was talking about it.'

'Yes,' she said. 'It was extraordinary. Suddenly everybody wanted to talk to me, journalists rang up all the time asking me about things, I was on books programmes and everything. It was wonderful. Philip advised that I give up teaching and concentrate on my writing and I did. Everything started then. I had a few months of being invited everywhere, parties and literary festivals – overnight I was suddenly a star.'

She sighed. 'And in the middle of it all, when everything was going so well, Philip fell ill. At first it was like flu and he went to bed for a couple of days and we thought it was nothing. Then his temperature went up and up and he had a little fit, an epileptic fit. That was terrifying, I called the ambulance and they took him into hospital. They thought it was just a convulsion from the temperature but they kept him in for tests. The blood tests came back and they thought he had some viral infection that they couldn't treat, it just had to get better on its own.'

She sighed again. 'Well, it never did, really. He went back to work but he was so tired he couldn't get through the days. He would fall asleep in the afternoon and his secretary would try to cover up for him. Then he collapsed at work and had to come home and go into hospital again. Same thing. A flare-up of the virus. Now the immune system was probably damaged. It would get better in time, perhaps. It might recover or it might not. Nobody knew. That was the worst thing. We had the best specialists in the country and they didn't know.'

'And?' Troy prompted.

'He gave up his job, he got a very good payment from the company. We decided to move out into the country, near where he had been brought up. We bought the house, it was a bit run down, a farmhouse, we got it cheaply and we did it up. I did a lot of the decorating and on the days when he was well Philip helped me. But he was tired all the time.

'We found a new specialist who said that he thought it was probably caused by an allergy. But now it had started it was progressive, and disabling. But again, there was nothing he could do. Philip made his mind up to the fact that he wouldn't get better and wouldn't go back to work. He got a lot of pleasure from the success of my career, and it went on going well for me.' Isobel paused. 'Sometimes I used to think that there was only room for one successful person in our house. That my star rose then Philip's fell. It was as if he had nothing to do but be ill.'

She shook her head. 'I know that's silly. He's really sick. We were just unlucky.' She took a breath. 'Anyway, my career became everything to us. We don't have children, we don't have family, we don't have many friends even. The one thing we share, our hobby if you like, is the Isobel Latimer books. We always discuss them, we always look at the jackets together and the jacket copy and the publishers' schedule and the reviews. It's our main interest. It's our only interest. That's why I couldn't ever go home and tell Philip that the royalties are down, or that the publishers don't want the books any more. It would be like him falling sick all over again. The books are what we do, now that there's nothing else to do.'

'But now there's the pool,' Troy suggested. 'And Murray.'

Isobel shook her head, her hair falling on the carpet with the movement. 'That's just a passing phase,' she said. 'Murray will go when the pool is finished and when that happens, I bet you, we'll swim in it no more than once a week, if that. In three months, in six, the barn will be empty again and the reflection of the water on the ceiling will be seen by no-one.

It will all be wasted money,' she sighed. 'Down the drain. Literally. And when I have to tell him that the books are failing, we'll have nothing left to give us joy. We'll have nothing at all.'

'Except now you have Zelda,' Troy added.

Isobel turned her head at that, her eyes meeting his, her cheek against the rich colours of the carpet. 'Yes,' she said quietly. 'I thought that nothing would change, I thought that our lives were fixed. All that could happen was that Philip would get slowly worse and worse, and I would be more and more tired and more and more sad. But, as you say, now there's Zelda. And if I can keep Zelda in my life then I will never be so desperately unhappy again.'

Twenty-Two

Troy's spare bedroom, which they thought of as Zelda's room, was lit only with the glow of the orange street lights filtering through the drawn curtains. They entered it carrying the candles from the sitting room, they did not want the bright glare of the overhead light. They dressed side by side in silence, only the rustle of underwear drawn from tissue paper and the whisper of stockings marked their progress. They turned their backs to each other for help in zipping up like friendly sisters, and then they sat side by side, facing the dressing-table mirror with their identical masses of blonde hair to paint their faces.

They shared foundation cream, eyeliner, lipstick, mascara, blusher with a gentle murmur of thanks and 'after you', and when they finished they moved with one accord away from the dressing table where the transformation had been effected, and went back into the sitting room. They sat opposite each other, and took in each other in a long, erotic stare.

Troy was conscious of the silky feel of his thighs crossed over each other, of the trailing line of the shoe at his slim foot. His head felt large with the weight of the golden wig, his eyelids heavy with the eye shadow and false eyelashes. Looking at Isobel was like looking at himself in a slightly distorting mirror. She was a smaller, daintier version of him. Her hair was identical, her makeup the same. But beneath the curve of the matching blue dress he knew he would find warm, rounded breasts, a soft, dimpled belly, the slack, seductive thighs.

'More champagne?' he asked.

'I'll get it.' Isobel rose from her seat and walked across the room, conscious of his dark blue gaze on her, like a caress. She opened the bottle in the kitchen and brought fresh glasses.

'Roederer,' she announced as she came in. 'Of course we never drink anything else.'

Troy held out his glass, his gesture elegant. Isobel poured, and then took her glass and sat down again. She crossed her legs, Troy saw the side of her thigh extending into shadow under the blue dress and leaned back a little on the sofa to enjoy the stolen view. In a little while, he knew, he would undress her and she him. In a little while he would have the intense pleasure of being a woman and yet not a woman, making love to a woman.

'This is very good,' he remarked slowly.

Isobel's grey eyes appraised him, taking in the beautiful face and the poised body. 'Zelda?'

'Yes?'

'Shall we go away together? For a holiday?'

Troy thought for a moment, pushed away the objections of his work, refused to consider the appointments in his office diary. 'Do you want to?'

'I feel like this is now,' Isobel said. 'Here and now. It's never going to be like this again. I want to experience it fully now. While it's so important, while it's so passionate.'

'Because you think it won't last?'

She smiled, Zelda's beautiful, lazy, sensual smile. 'How can it?' she said simply. 'It is madness.'

'Some of it has to last,' Troy reminded her. 'If you're to write another book.'

She nodded. 'But this between us?'

'Ah. This.'

They were silent for a moment.

'Come over here,' Isobel said.

Troy raised his eyebrows in Zelda's arrogant expression. 'I?'

'Come over here, or I will come and fetch you,' Isobel

whispered, her voice full of either promise or threat; Troy could not decide which. He rose from the sofa and glided across to Isobel, took a seat beside her and leaned back, his chin raised, the line of his neck exposed.

Isobel did not move forward, she kept her seat and looked at him. 'You're so beautiful,' she whispered. 'You are such a beautiful woman.'

Troy closed his eyes and then felt the sofa move beneath him as Isobel got up. 'Keep your eyes closed,' she murmured.

He sensed her moving, heard the whisper of her falling dress.

'Now,' she said.

He opened his eyes. She was wearing Zelda's beautifully embroidered blue lace brassiere and her full breasts were brimming over the pale lace. She was wearing dark blue hold-up stockings. Nothing else. Troy found himself staring, fascinated, at the dark hair at the meeting point of rounded belly and rounded thighs, at the white, overflowing richness of the breasts, at the golden mass of hair above the painted face. She walked towards him shamelessly, she bent her head, she kissed him. Their warm lipsticked lips met, touched, pressed, licked, bit a little. Troy heard himself groan with pleasure. Then he felt her hands on his dress, pulling it up. He lifted himself slightly and she slid the dress up to his waist. Underneath he was wearing stockings like hers, and matching underwear: Zelda's blue French knickers which he had worn in secret, under his trousers, all day. His erection strained against the silk. Without taking her grey eyes from his, Isobel reached down, pushed the knickers to one side, and took him, straddled him, as if she were his unquestioned master.

In the morning they tidied the flat together like two hardworking housewives. Troy took the clothes and put them away and Isobel picked up glasses, bottles, cleared away the evidence of the cocaine, and cleaned up the kitchen. When it was all done they had a snatched cup of coffee sitting at Troy's worktop in the little kitchen.

'I have to go to work,' he said, glancing at the kitchen clock.

'I have to go home,' she said.

'I'll get you a taxi.' He got down from his stool, slipped on the jacket to his suit and went out into the hall. Isobel collected her overnight bag from his bedroom, and her bag of shopping with her new clothes, and followed him out.

It was bitterly cold and grey outside. Troy shivered at the roadside as he waited for an empty taxi. Isobel, warm in her drab winter coat, stood beside him.

'Go in, I can get my own taxi.'

'Are you sure?'

'Course I'm sure. No point you dying of pneumonia.'

He hesitated. 'If you're sure you don't mind?'

She turned and kissed him, a warm matter-of-fact kiss on the lips. 'Go!'

'I'll call you in the week,' he said. 'Write that synopsis of the new Zelda novel for me and I'll start working on it as soon as I have it.'

She nodded. 'No more than three days.'

Troy ran up the steps to the front door and raised a hand to her. 'Bye.'

Isobel waved. He opened the door and went in.

In a few moments a taxi came by and Isobel got in. 'Waterloo station please,' she said and sat back to watch the cold city going past the windows. She felt nothing. The experience of being with Troy was so intense and so enigmatic that it shocked Isobel into a state of mindlessness, the greatest release she could ever have.

But she did not forget her arrival at his flat. She knew that she had caught Troy in Zelda's clothes without the sanction of Isobel being there. She knew that was a warning, and yet she did not want to see it or hear it. Also in the back of her mind was her awareness that she had challenged him to love her and he had evaded the challenge. Troy was not asking her to leave her husband. Troy was not courting Isobel. He did not even want to go on holiday with her, they had made no plans.

Troy wanted Zelda and Isobel was nothing more than the

gatekeeper for Zelda. But when Isobel become Zelda she had the most profound and satisfying physical joy with Troy that she had ever experienced in her life. Isobel, torn between a sense of betrayal and a sense of satisfaction, gazed out of the window of the taxi, incapable of understanding what was taking place in her life. Completely and exquisitely blank, she got out at Waterloo and took the train home, her gaze on the misty countryside, seeing nothing.

Murray was there to meet her at the station, not Mr M., whom she had expected, not Philip, which would have been nice: but Murray.

'Philip overdid it last night,' he said. 'Here, I'll take that for you.'

'I can carry it, thank you,' she said, keeping tight hold of her bag and actually pulling it away from his offering hand.

They walked together to the car, Isobel's car, and Murray opened the passenger door for her. Isobel hesitated for a moment, thinking that she would rather drive her own car, but felt it would be needlessly ungracious to insist.

'Is he ill?' she demanded, her voice full of blame. 'Did he get overtired?'

'Just a bit. He looked washed out at breakfast so I sent him back to bed.' He closed the door on her and went round to the driver's side.

'Is he in pain?' Isobel asked as soon as Murray was in the driver's seat.

'Oh no, I'd have called the doctor if he had been bad. And Mellie's with him.'

Murray started the car and drove out of the car park. He drove better than Philip, with a casual confidence which irritated Isobel. He kept only one hand on the wheel, the other rested on the gear stick. His brown eyes shifted from the road ahead to the mirror in a continual, skilful flicker.

'He can't do so much,' Isobel said irritably. 'He can't go out most nights as he has been doing. And he doesn't have his rest in the afternoon any more, does he?'

'He's got an interest,' Murray said peaceably. 'He's got his teeth into the swimming pool and it's his choice to do a bit more than he used to do. I'd have thought you'd be pleased.'

'Of course I'm pleased,' Isobel snapped. 'But not when you encourage him to stay out late and do too much. He's not a well man. He can't keep up with you. If you want a friend who can go out playing darts and drinking all night you should find another friend. Philip simply can't do it.'

Murray nodded, slowed for a junction, accelerated away, judging the gap in the traffic precisely. 'He's been better these last few days than he has been for months,' he remarked. 'He told me himself how well he was feeling.'

'You weren't here months ago,' Isobel said, dangerously close to rudeness. 'So I don't think that you can really comment. But I was. I've watched him and nursed him since the beginning of this illness and I know the signs. He's been pushing himself too hard, and now he's overdone it. If I had been home I wouldn't have let him.'

Murray said nothing, watching the road.

'I should have been told,' Isobel said.

'I phoned you,' Murray said quietly. He braked for a junction and let another car go before he accelerated smoothly into the lane towards Isobel's home.

'What?'

'I did phone you. This morning, at the hotel. To tell you that he wasn't well, to check with you what should be done. Mellie said you'd want to know at once, so I rang you.'

'Oh,' Isobel said.

Murray turned a gentle, almost affectionate smile on her. 'They said you weren't there. You weren't registered as a guest. They said you weren't registered last week either, when you were supposed to be staying there to do your teaching.'

'There must be some mistake,' Isobel said quickly.

Easily Murray flicked the indicator and turned in the drive to Isobel's house. He turned his brown gaze on her, a hint of mischief beneath the smile. 'Oh, I expect so,' he said.

'Terribly disorganised these big hotels can be, can't they?'

'Yes,' Isobel said. 'They should have checked properly.'

Murray nodded. He stopped the car, put on the brake and switched off the ignition. He turned that slow, powerful smile on Isobel again. He waited for her question.

'Did you tell Philip?' she asked very casually. 'That you couldn't reach me?'

Murray opened the car door. 'Oh no,' he said. 'Why should I? I knew you were coming home. I didn't want to worry him when he was a bit down. I took a decision on my own what was best to do. I didn't call the doctor, I sent him back to bed to rest. I didn't tell him I couldn't get hold of you. I didn't tell Mellie either. I kept it to myself. I'll just keep it to myself, I think. I'll go on keeping it to myself.'

'A stupid mistake by the hotel,' Isobel insisted. She heard a ragged edge in her voice, and heaved her overnight bag out from its position at her feet. Murray strolled around to the passenger door.

'I'll take that for you,' he said. 'I don't like to see a lady struggle.'

This time she let him take it. 'Thank you very much,' she said.

Philip was up when she got home, a little pale, but clearly not very unwell.

'Murray said you had gone back to bed,' Isobel said, kissing him and stepping back to look at him.

'Nothing worse than a hangover,' Philip said. 'I took a couple of paracetamol, had half an hour's sleep and here I am, right as rain.'

'You should still have a rest this afternoon,' Isobel said.

'Don't fuss.'

'I'm not fussing, I'm just being sensible.'

The living-room door closed as Murray tactfully left them alone. They could hear him in the kitchen asking Mrs M. for coffee for the three of them.

'Murray's taking me over to his yard this afternoon, he's

got a difficult client who wants some special tiles, he asked me to help him choose.'

'Murray can choose his own tiles!' Isobel exclaimed impatiently. 'Why does he need your help?'

'He says I have an eye,' Philip said proudly. 'I can carry colours in my head. He says that's very rare. He can't do it, for one.'

'I think you should rest.'

'I have rested. I rested this morning for half an hour. That's all I need.'

'You're not well!' she cried out despairingly.

He looked at her without any affection. 'I am better than I have ever been,' he said. 'Don't you try to pull me back.'

'I? Pull you back! What d'you mean?'

Philip was about to answer when the door opened and Murray came in with the tray and three cups of coffee. 'You'll like this,' he told Isobel. 'It's called Monsooned Malabar. I saw a programme about it. They leave the beans out until the monsoon rain washes them on the drying tables. Great, isn't it?'

'I don't want any coffee,' Isobel snapped and went from the room.

Isobel opened her post and answered her letters all morning and left her study only to collect a sandwich for her lunch to eat at her desk.

'Not lunching with us?' Philip inquired pleasantly. He was using the presence of Mrs M. and Murray as a shield. He knew Isobel would not quarrel with him in front of them, and using the protection of their presence he could create the illusion of his reasonableness and Isobel's bad temper.

Isobel, knowing exactly what he was doing, and knowing that it was deliberately done, gave him a frosty look. 'I have far too much to do,' she said coldly.

The kitchen was warm with the smell of home cooking. As Isobel cut herself two slices of brown bread and slapped a thin piece of pre-packed ham between them, Mrs M. brought a casserole dish out of the oven and lifted the lid. Steam, scented with onions and gravy, wafted up.

'Good old stew,' Murray said. 'Nothing like it for a cold day.'

Philip laid the table while Murray sat, doing nothing. Isobel put a dab of mustard on the side of her plate.

'Could you bring me a cup of coffee when you've finished serving that?' she said to Mrs M. She could hear the icy tone in her voice but she was powerless to do anything about it.

'Won't you have some stew?' Mrs M. asked. 'I made enough.'

The idea that it should be a matter of comment that there was enough food for Isobel in her own house, bought with her own money, made her pale with resentment.

'I don't eat a large lunch,' she said. 'As you know, I never have done.'

'You ought to,' Murray said cheerfully. 'I find a good mid-day meal really sets me up for the afternoon.' He smiled at her. 'But of course, I'm not doing brain work like you.'

'I'll save you some for your dinner,' Mrs M. said to Isobel. 'You can warm it up.'

Isobel took her solitary little plate with the sandwich sitting bleakly in the centre and went back into her study,

She ate the sandwich looking at the blank computer screen. At the top of the screen it said *The Choice and the Chosen* and then Chapter One, and beneath it the little cursor winked, as if inviting Isobel to get on with it. Isobel regarded it without emotion, not as an enemy, not as a friend. It was a tool which no longer came easily to her hand. She felt that she had said all that she had to say about the notion of free will and individual morality. Since Zelda and Troy, everything had changed in her view. She found she was no longer interested in the minutiae of manners and morals, she was no longer interested in the discipline needed to live a good life, to be a good woman. Now she was interested only in the long, secret, silent drawing down of passion, she was interested in desire, she was interested in irresistible fascinations. She was interested in the secret workings of obsession, lust, desire.

Isobel opened a new document on the word processor and started the synopsis of her Zelda Vere book.

Twenty-Three

The Loving Ghost
This novel tells the story of a woman who is a senior
executive in a

'Um,' Isobel said to herself. 'Cosmetics? Petro-chemical? No,
perfume.'

Perfume company. Her greatest friend in her glamorous
Parisian life is her deputy

'No, not too lowly.'

is her greatest rival, a man who has a great instinctive
nose for perfume. He was her childhood friend, adopted
by friends of her parents, and they have grown up almost
as brother and sister.

Isobel, who had been an only child, paused in her writing
and thought of the deep, erotic charge which came for her
with the notion of sibling incest. To have a lover who was as
close to you as a brother would be, at the same time, the
challenging of a fundamental erotic taboo, and a great comfort.
Your lover would be the person who knew you better than
anyone else, would know your childhood, and world. Your
lover would know the things which distressed you or made
you laugh. You would never have to explain associations,
or describe past places and people. You would share
memories. And if he was a brother who looked like you,

then in loving him you would be very close to a delicious narcissism.

They even look alike.
She has lovers and friends but no-one gets very close to her. They call her *La coeur glacé*.

Isobel paused for a moment and wondered if that was correct. What was the French for frozen? Was it *gelée*? She shrugged, she could look it up later. She knew now from experience that the trick with a Zelda Vere novel was not to stop until the outline of the story had tumbled on to the page. There was plenty of time afterwards to worry about spelling and grammar. What mattered in a Zelda Vere was getting into the storytelling part of her brain and not allowing anything to interrupt. It was quite the opposite to writing an Isobel Latimer novel which depended completely on the well-considered philosophy behind the novel and then the perfectly formed paragraph.

Francine insists on buying a new and very fast sports car that has just come on the market. All her friends are excited about it and encourage her to try it and buy it with the exception of . . .

Isobel broke off. 'Pierre?' she muttered. 'Rather obvious. Jean-Pierre? Claude – too sissy. Guy? Jacques? Jean-Pierre it is.'

Jean-Pierre, who infuriates her by suggesting that she will not be able to handle such an overpowered machine.
In a rage with him, she takes the test car out on the road and drives fast, faster, insanely fast. The flickering poplar trees blur as the car speeds down the characteristic French avenue and then on a slight corner at the end of the road she loses control of the car and – there is a crash.
In a separate sequence Francine sees herself coming into a brilliant white light. She does not know where she is nor what she is doing. Out of the brilliant light comes a tall beautiful man, he is naked but for . . .

Isobel paused, shrugged her shoulders at something else she could easily look up and insert later.

> naked but for aboriginal costume. He has feathers in his long dark hair. His face is proud and dark and hawklike. 'Francine,' he says in his deep voice.
>
> He is Francine's spirit guide and as her body lies in the hospital on a life-support machine he and Francine go through her life together at every point of choice so that they can see that she has consistently denied herself the opportunity of love. We see her early childhood and schooling, in the lavender fields of the Provence region, the sexual abuse she suffered and enjoyed at the hands of an older boy

'Girl,' Isobel corrected rapidly. 'Much sexier.'

> At the hands of a most beautiful girl whom she adored. We see her adolescence and her friendship with Jean-Pierre which she never allows to grow into love. In her near-death state she sees how she hurts him, how she rejects him, how even his decision to follow her into the perfume industry is a response to her own ambition and the family's interest.

'Lavender is great,' Isobel murmured. 'Perhaps Troy and I could visit. Oh God, lavender fields in midsummer! So that I could research.'

> At the end of her spirit guide's teaching Francine understands everything, but she also knows that she is passionately in love with him. The love he has released is all directed towards him. In the spirit realm they come together, in the spirit realm they make torrid love, just once, just one doomed passionate experience, and then as she lies in his arms she slowly wakes and finds herself in her hospital bed.
>
> Stunned with disappointment, she weeps to find herself

alive and without her spirit-guide lover when she is aware that the room is filled with the scent of lavender.

'Nice,' Isobel muttered.

This is Jean-Pierre, who has brought an enormous bouquet of lavender from the fields of their home in the hopes of reviving the only woman he has ever loved. As Francine looks at him she realises for the first time both that he is the man she has always loved, and that his mystery ancestry is explained. He is the great-grandson of her spirit guide, and the extraordinary birth mark

'Must put a birth mark in earlier,' Isobel noted.

is in fact an exact copy of the spirit guide's mystical tattoo. At last she realises that she loves him and that in him she will find true happiness. The End.

Isobel sat back in her chair and beamed at the screen. There was something so delightfully facile about writing a story for plot and not for the working out of a moral theme. It was like a holiday to leap from incident to incident without ever troubling as to where the next jump might take her, secure in the knowledge that almost nothing was too far-fetched for this readership.

She glanced at the clock. Troy would not yet have left his desk. She dialled his number and was put through at once.

'Isobel?'

'Oh, Troy.'

'Everything all right?'

'I've just written the synopsis for the new Zelda Vere.'

'Isobel, you're so fast with Zelda stories, I can't think why we weren't doing this years ago.'

She giggled. 'And they're such fun. I've set it in Provence and Paris.'

'Gorgeous. When can I see it?'

'It just needs tidying up. Shall I e-mail it over to you?'

'Yes, I can't wait. Is it how you planned it?'

Isobel hesitated. 'There's kind of more to it.'

She could hear the smile in his voice. 'I knew there would be. What more is there?'

Isobel thought for a moment. Her trained, critical mind could not resist the temptation to fillet a story until she had the core of the meaning. 'I suppose it is going to be a book about a woman who has pretended that she has no desires, and then she has to go to the very brink of death to find that her desires are completely compelling. That only by knowing her desire, by looking it in the face, can she come back to life.'

There was a breath of a sigh down the earpiece. 'Yes,' Troy said simply. 'You have to look your desire in the face or else you are one of the living dead.'

'In a coma,' Isobel said. 'Breathing and eating but, in truth, not there at all.'

There was a brief silence.

'Everything all right at home?' Troy asked.

'They've gone out for the afternoon together,' Isobel said. 'Philip is helping him choose some tiles. Apparently Philip has a great eye for colour.'

'Has he?'

'I never noticed it before, but Murray seems to think he is an enormous help.' She paused for a moment. 'They had beef stew for lunch. Mrs M. cooked it for them.'

Troy did not know how he was supposed to respond to this piece of information. 'Oh.'

'They'll be late home,' Isobel said. 'Choosing tiles.'

'Oh,' Troy said again.

'I'll eat on my own,' Isobel said, her voice a little desolate. 'I shall warm up some of the stew.'

'Isobel,' Troy said cautiously. 'If Murray is coming between you and Philip then you should perhaps speak to Philip. I didn't mean anything when I said that they were spending a lot of time together, except just that. If it's bothering you, you should tell him.'

'I can't really, can I?' Isobel replied. 'Not when you think what we are doing.'

'Philip doesn't know that . . .'

'Murray knows that I wasn't staying at the hotel. He called there this morning.'

There was a sharply indrawn breath and then a long silence. 'He did, did he?' Troy said, speaking slowly to gain time. 'And what did he say to you?'

'He told me that he didn't trouble Philip with it, and I said that they must have missed me, and got in a muddle.'

'Did he believe you?'

'I think so,' Isobel said uncertainly, privately convinced that Murray had not. 'But it does make me feel as if I can't really throw him out of the house, or even complain about him. He's got something on me, you see.'

Troy was silent, thinking rapidly. 'Surely you could have a private chat with Philip and just say that you don't want Murray as a constant companion in the house all the time. Ask him to meet him out, if he wants to spend so much time with him.'

'I could try,' Isobel said without enthusiasm.

'Or just leave it, let them go and choose tiles together. It doesn't do any harm, does it? And if it leaves you free?'

Isobel did not respond to the warmth in his voice. 'It's so quiet here at night,' she said, apparently irrelevantly. 'When I'm here on my own. And when I'm not working, there's nothing to do.'

'Keep working then,' Troy advised bracingly. 'And send me that synopsis. Can you do three chapters for me as well? They'll sign a contract on three chapters and a synopsis.'

'Yes,' Isobel said. 'I'll do it over the next couple of days.'

Philip came in at nine o'clock as Isobel was sitting in the kitchen with a glass of sherry to watch the news. She switched off the television as soon as he came in.

'Hello.'

'Did you want some supper?' Isobel asked. 'I could do you some soup, and we've got some nice bread.'

'We ate out,' Philip said. 'Murray knows this excellent

Indian restaurant near the tile warehouse. We looked at tiles until we were dizzy and in the end I choose a wonderful deep purple with a kind of bronze finish. Murray says he thinks it will be perfect for the clients. I picked out the pool furniture too.'

'Furniture?'

'Handles and rails, that sort of thing. It's going to be quite a pool. It's one of the biggest contracts Murray has ever had. The profit margin is extraordinary. D'you know he stands to make a profit of about thirty thousand pounds?'

'Good heavens,' Isobel said. 'And how much profit is he making on us?'

Philip did not hear the sharpness in her voice. 'Much less than that!' he said with a smile. 'I'll be choosing the tiles for us, for a start. D'you know he paid me for today? Gave me fifty quid for consultant designer! I haven't had a wage for ten years! Made me feel quite like my old self.'

Isobel smiled. 'Good. Don't spend it all at once.'

Philip laughed. 'Too late, I spent it on dinner. But it was really good to feel that I was doing something useful, and earning a bit of pocket money. He said he might need me again some time. I'd like that. It is something I really can visualise. Most people, they can't keep the idea of shades of colours in their mind. But I can. It's a gift. I didn't even know I had it.'

'Neither did I,' Isobel said. 'I didn't even know you were that interested in interior design.'

'I don't think I'd be interested in a house, though I might go on to that,' Philip said consideringly. 'But there is something about a pool which is very attractive. You make such a special place out of nothing: a hole in the ground or an empty barn. It's a real transformation.'

Isobel let a silence fall. Then she spoke. 'I wonder if we might talk a bit about Murray. He does seem to be rather ubiquitous.'

'Ubiquitous?' Philip repeated, as if he did not understand the word.

'He's practically moved in,' Isobel said. 'Mrs M. knows all his favourite meals, he's here from breakfast to dinner, it seems to me.'

'There's been a lot of planning to do,' Philip said defensively. 'You weren't here, so you don't know. All those detailed plans, Murray and I measured up and drew them up together. We've been very busy. It's been totally time-consuming. Of course he stayed to meals. What would you want me to do? Ask him to wait outside while I ate my lunch?'

'No, of course not,' she replied. 'But now that the planning is done, he'll just be up here to supervise the builders, won't he? There's no need for him to be here every day? And with this new contract that he's got, I suppose he'll be over with them a lot.'

Philip hesitated. 'I suppose so,' he said unwillingly. 'But they're just down the road, Valley Farm, you know. I said he should drop in any time.'

'At any time?' Isobel repeated.

'It's a good thing to have him keep an eye on our pool,' Philip said. 'You know what builders can be like.'

'Yes, but . . .'

'And if he wants me to choose some colours or the décor of the other pool, I'm really happy to help him out.'

'Surely he does all that himself,' Isobel said.

'And he's good company,' Philip concluded. 'When you're writing or when you're away teaching, he's great company. I enjoy going down to the pub with him. We've been too cut off here, we've let ourselves get too isolated. We should both of us get out and about a bit more.'

He looked at her critically, in a way that he had never looked at her before. 'All you ever do is work, Isobel. You should make friends of your own. Go out for coffee and shopping trips. Lunch with the girls. We've been living here ten years and you know nobody except Mr and Mrs M. It's not good for you to be so isolated.'

'I'm not isolated,' Isobel protested. 'I have friends in London, I have friends in my work.'

'They're not real friends though, are they?' Philip insisted. 'We don't see them down here, you don't have them to lunch.'

'We live in the country,' Isobel said, irritated. 'It's hardly the Chelsea Arts Club. It's not the Groucho. Who d'you want me to have lunch with?'

'Oh, I don't know,' Philip said vaguely. 'Women of your own age. There must be a Townswomen's Guild or the WI or something that you could join.'

Isobel believed that she was hearing an analysis so crass that it could only come from Murray. 'As you know, I like to be on my own to work,' she said with careful restraint. 'As you know, writing is always a solitary sort of occupation. It's not the kind of thing you can do with constant interruptions. And I can think of nothing I would hate more than to go to an arranged lunch for middle-aged bourgeois women.'

'Absolutely,' Philip agreed. 'So you like to be on your own. But I like a bit of company. There you are then.'

Twenty-Four

Isobel continued to write *Loving Ghost* all the morning despite the noise of hearty male laughter from the kitchen. Murray had arrived shortly after breakfast with a suitcase full of tile samples and colour matches, and he and Philip were supposed to be making the final choice of colours for the pool. Isobel could hear Mrs M.'s higher voice occasionally scolding and laughing as she cleaned the kitchen and prepared lunch. It all sounded very relaxed and sociable. Isobel was naggingly aware that she was paying Mrs M. ten pounds an hour to flirt with Murray.

At midday, Isobel came out of the study and was conscious that as soon as she appeared in the kitchen an instant silence fell. Philip looked like a schoolboy caught ragging in the dormitory after lights out.

'What's for lunch?' Isobel asked pleasantly.

'Roast pork with all the trimmings,' Mrs M. said. 'But I could do you a sandwich or a salad if you'd like, Mrs Latimer.'

'Roast pork sounds lovely,' Isobel said firmly. 'I'll lay the table, shall I?'

Both Murray and Philip hurried to scoop the tile samples and the paint charts out of the way. Murray folded a set of plans.

'Is that our pool?' Isobel asked.

'No,' he said. 'It's another one I'm working on. Over in Hampshire at Fleet. I was just consulting Philip about the look of it. He's got such an eye for detail.'

'Has he?'

'We thought we'd take a run over there this afternoon and have a look at it,' Philip said. 'I need to see the building really, before I can imagine the changes.'

'Well, I thought we'd go for a walk this afternoon,' Isobel said baldly. 'I haven't been down to the village for ages. I thought we might walk down to the pub together. Mrs M. could always pick us up if you didn't want to walk back up the hill.'

'Fine,' Philip said quickly. His glance at Murray was veiled. 'I'll come over to Fleet another day then.'

'Fine by me,' Murray said. 'I envy the two of you, gentleman and lady of leisure, strolling down to the pub. And you've picked a perfect day for it.'

'You won't go to Fleet without me, this afternoon?' Philip asked. Isobel thought he sounded like a younger brother, fearful of being left out.

Murray shook his head. 'No, I'll go over to Valley Farm and show them your choice of tiles.'

Isobel watched. He seemed to be picking up his suitcase of samples, as if he was leaving.

'Be sure to tell them that the whole scheme revolves around their verdigris copper fountain mask,' Philip said. 'They must understand that's where I started from.'

'I'll tell them,' Murray said. 'Oh! Don't lay a place for me, Mrs Latimer. I'll get on. Leave you two in peace.'

'But it's your favourite –' Mrs M. protested, and then checked herself.

Murray grinned at her. 'Another time. Mrs Latimer doesn't want me under her feet all day.' He smiled openly at Isobel, charming, assured. 'I'm sorry,' he said frankly. 'It's such a happy house, this, it's a pleasure to visit.'

'Please don't go,' Isobel was driven, despite herself, into courtesy. 'There's no need to run off. Philip and I will have our walk after lunch. We can all have lunch together.'

'If you're sure you don't mind?'

Isobel shook her head and put down the knife and fork at

Murray's usual place, which used to be her place. Mrs M. brought the joint from the oven and proffered the carving knife to Murray as a matter of course. Murray stood and started to carve neat slices of crackling and meat.

'Now this is nice,' Philip said, pleased.

Isobel had to acknowledge that Philip was much better. He walked briskly down the path which he used to dawdle along to the village. They went into the saloon bar of the pub and Philip ordered drinks. He put his hand in his pocket and suddenly checked. 'I've got no money,' he said to Isobel. 'Can you do the honours?'

Isobel flushed with embarrassment. 'I didn't bring any with me,' she said. 'There are no pockets in these trousers, and I didn't bring my handbag.'

The landlord smiled indulgently at Philip. 'On the slate again?' he asked.

Philip chuckled. 'Don't you go charging me interest,' he said. 'I'll pop down tonight and clear my debts.'

The landlord nodded. 'That's sixty-two pounds.'

Isobel smiled, thinking that he was joking but Philip nodded. 'Yes.'

They took their drinks and went to sit at a table by the window, looking out on the village street.

'You owe him sixty-two pounds?' Isobel was astounded.

'I ran out of cash last week,' Philip said. 'Murray and I came down for dinner and there was no cash left in the housekeeping. I put in on the slate here.'

'But we can't do that.' Isobel was mildly scandalised. 'We hardly know the landlord.'

'But I know him,' Philip corrected her. 'Since I won the darts match I'm something of a local hero.'

'Well, I can't owe money at the pub,' Isobel ruled. 'I'll ask Mrs M. to drop off a cheque on her way home.'

'I'll come down tonight with cash, like I said,' Philip repeated. 'I'd prefer it.'

'I can write a cheque, there's no need for you to go out at

night,' Isobel said. 'You don't like driving in the dark.'

'Murray can drive me down,' he said easily. 'And besides, I don't want my bar bills settled by your cheque, Isobel. It'd look awfully odd. I'll come down with the money.'

Isobel hesitated. 'I don't see that it looks odd.'

'It does,' he said flatly. 'Let me pay my own bar bills, Isobel.'

She nodded and then cleared her throat. 'Actually, we seem to have been getting through the housekeeping money rather rapidly,' she observed in a carefully neutral voice.

'Have we?' Philip said. 'I just thought you'd not left enough when you were away last week.'

'I left £200. That's usually enough,' Isobel said.

'Things are so expensive,' Philip said vaguely. 'And I have been going out in the evenings sometimes.'

'Does Murray ever pay?' she asked.

At once he flushed and scowled at the table. 'Really, Isobel,' he said. 'What a question!'

She withdrew the challenge at once. 'I'm sorry, I didn't mean to be rude. I just wondered . . .'

'I told you he paid me for working for him the other day!'

'Yes, I know you did. Fifty pounds. And then you paid for dinner, didn't you?'

'That was my choice,' he said stiffly.

'I know. I know.'

'You do like him, don't you?'

'He's not my sort of person,' Isobel said carefully. 'I'm sure he's very good at what he does and he tells a good story and that sort of thing. But he's not the sort of person I would choose as a companion. He's not the sort of person I would have thought you would enjoy.'

'Oh,' Philip said easily, draining his glass and getting up to go to the bar. 'He's all right. Another drink?'

Philip walked back up the hill to their house with Isobel, they had no need of a lift from Mrs M.

'You are better,' Isobel observed.

'A lot better,' Philip said. 'Just wait till I get the pool and I can swim every day.'

'When do they start work?'

'First thing next week,' Philip said. 'We might be swimming by the end of March. Think of that!'

'Not really swimming weather,' Isobel observed.

'That's when we'll feel the benefit of the indoor pool,' Philip said. 'We'll get double the use out of it than we would with an outdoor one. Murray wants me to explain that to these new clients over in Fleet. They're dithering about whether to go for indoor or outdoor. I'll tell them that they must be crazy. It's no contest.'

'Are you his salesman now?' Isobel asked. She opened the little garden gate and led the way into their garden.

'I wouldn't mind it at all,' Philip said. He was only slightly out of breath despite the climb up the hill. 'It's a great business he's putting together. I wouldn't mind being his salesman at all. And it's a good product. He said to me only the other day that it's a real pleasure to sell people something that you know is going to enhance their lives, something they really want. It's not fridges to Eskimos, it's a real benefit.'

'You make him sound like a philanthropist,' Isobel said. She opened the back door and sat on the bench to take off her walking boots. Philip came in and sat beside her.

'No, he's too sharp a businessman for that,' he said. 'You don't catch him giving anything away. I should say not! He prices every job to the last bit of mosaic tile and he knows to the last pence what his profit is. But he's always fair. I've seen the figures. He's very fair.'

'Good,' Isobel suppressed a sigh. 'I think I'll go and do some work now.'

'*The Choice and the Chosen?*' Philip asked.

'Yes.'

'How's it going?'

'It's going well,' she lied easily.

'What does Troy think?'

'He thinks we'll do well with it,' Isobel said. 'We're going to sell it at an early stage. He thinks it's just the sort of thing they'll want.'

'Good,' Philip said, pleased. He put an arm around Isobel's shoulders and gave her a gentle hug. 'Clever girl. You get to work. We've got a pool to heat now, remember.' He hesitated for a moment. 'It is going all right, isn't it?'

At once Isobel heard Troy warning her that she must be like a spy, that nothing from one life could leak into another. She smiled brightly at Philip. 'Of course. What could be wrong?'

He hesitated. He was unskilled in reading her. For all of their previous years it had been she who had scrutinised his face, his movements, the set of his shoulders. She had paid loving attention to his moods. He had never learned hers.

'I was just wondering if everything was all right. You haven't talked much about the new book. Or your work in London.'

Isobel shrugged her shoulders. 'Oh, not much to tell,' she said easily. 'And the pool has been our main interest, hasn't it?'

Philip hesitated. 'Well, I think so,' he acknowledged.

She smiled. 'I think so too, then.'

Philip brought Isobel a cup of tea at four o'clock. 'I'm going down to the pub with Murray at opening time,' he said. 'I'll pay off my slate. I thought I'd pick up a takeaway for us, if you'd like?'

A takeaway curry from the village restaurant was a rare treat for Isobel and Philip, since Philip never drove at night, and Isobel could only rarely be bothered to make the trip down to the village and wait in the uncomfortable waiting area, looking at ancient copies of *You* magazine.

'Oh, what a lovely surprise,' she said.

'Chicken biryani for you?' he asked.

'Yes please. Will Murray be eating with us?'

'I think he has something to do. But I can ask him if you like?'

'Oh, let's just be the two of us,' Isobel said and was surprised when Philip kissed the top of her head and said: 'Yes, let's.'

Isobel heard Murray's car draw up outside at half past five and Philip called from the hall, 'I'll be home about seven.'

For a moment she thought that she had been unnecessarily impolite by not inviting Murray to share a takeaway with them since he was, after all, driving Philip down to the pub, waiting at the takeaway counter and then driving him home again. Then she shrugged. Murray had eaten enough meals at her house and if Philip wanted to be on his own with her then she was prepared to enjoy that intimacy. She worked till half past six. The telephone rang at six and she hesitated before picking it up, glancing at the display. It was Troy's number ringing her. Isobel sat back in her chair and clasped her hands in her lap to prevent herself from answering. She felt as if she wanted to repair the boundaries between the Zelda life and the Isobel Latimer life which had been breached on Monday when she had been Isobel and still been Troy's lover, when she had told him that she wanted him and he had not responded, when she had put her hand to his body and felt Zelda's silk underwear.

'Isobel, are you there?' Troy's voice on the ansaphone was matter of fact. It was easier for Isobel to resist the temptation to speak to him than if he had been languorous.

'Just calling to check that everything was OK. But I'm leaving the office now so you can catch me at home if you want to up to seven thirty, and then I'm going out for the evening, and I won't be home till too late. Talk to you tomorrow perhaps. I just wanted to know how the new book is coming on.'

The answering machine bleeped loudly as Troy cut the connection and Isobel felt an unreasonable sense of irritation at his brisk, businesslike tone. Of course he had no way of knowing that the message would not be heard by Philip, so it was considerate of him to make sure that there was no hint of anything more in his voice than a matter-of-fact work message. Nonetheless, Isobel felt that he had failed to acknowledge her, that she had been snubbed.

She leaned forward and erased the message. She would not keep it, she would not return the call. Tonight she wanted to be with Philip, with a clear head and a clear conscience. She was a married woman, she wanted to be a happily married woman again.

She laid the table a little before seven and put plates to warm. She opened a bottle of strong South American red wine and poured herself a glass. She was tidying the kitchen when she heard Murray's car pull up outside and Philip slam the door and call goodnight. He came into the kitchen and the rich, strong smell of curry wafted in with him.

'I'll unpack it, I know you hate to,' Philip offered.

Isobel smiled. 'I do.' She sat at the table and waited for him to bring her plate to her. 'Very good service in this restaurant,' she said, smiling.

'We try our humble best,' he replied.

They ate together in relaxed companionship. 'This is nice,' Philip said suddenly. 'I can't think of the last time that we had curry. D'you want a taste of mine?'

'Is it very hot?'

'Scorching.'

'I won't, then.'

'You miss the full sensation if you still have tonsils at the end of the meal.'

'I lack your training,' Isobel said. Philip had been in the Far East for some years with his company before they met. She got up and cleared the plates. 'Ice cream?'

'Just a scoop.'

'Still trying to lose weight?'

'I feel so much better for it. I've only lost a pound so far. But Murray says that's because I'm gaining muscle. I really do think that I might be getting fitter again.'

Isobel served the ice cream and brought two bowls to the

table. 'That would be wonderful,' she said. 'Should you go and see Mr Hammond and see what he thinks?'

'I've got an appointment in May, I thought I'd leave it till then. Murray suggested waiting and seeing on my own. Not getting involved in a load of tests and getting my hopes up.'

Isobel hesitated. She thought Murray's advice was genuinely sensible. It recognised, at the same time, Philip's genuine progress and yet avoided returning him to his cycle of hypochondria. She did not enjoy agreeing with Murray. 'I'm sure he's right,' she said.

'He's no fool,' Philip said. 'He's got a lot of common sense.'

He finished his ice cream and cleared her bowl from the table with his own. 'Shall I make us some real coffee? Murray's Monsooned Malabar is still here.'

'All right,' Isobel said. 'Thank you.'

Philip spooned coffee into the filter and switched it on. 'What about a little brandy to go with that?'

'I shall be tipsy,' Isobel protested.

'Why not?' he said. 'We don't have to be anywhere in the morning, do we? Why not? You don't have a deadline or a meeting in London?'

'No . . .'

He poured two brandy glasses and put one before her. 'Be a devil,' he urged her. 'To go with the Monsooned Malabar.'

She chuckled. 'He is funny, though.'

Philip beamed and went to pour the coffee. 'He is. He's an endearing mixture of knowledge and ignorance. He's very bright and very astute and when he learns something he really clings to it. The Monsooned Malabar is typical. He'll have seen it on a television programme somewhere and now he won't drink anything else.'

'He reminds me of some of my students,' Isobel said. 'Very bright and eager.'

'And fearfully ill-educated,' Philip finished for her. 'Yes. I should think he's very like them. He's like a boy sometimes.' He glanced at her, careful of her feelings. 'He's like the son I never had.'

Twenty-Five

Isobel got into bed beside Philip and realised that he was neither sleeping nor feigning sleep as he usually did. He gathered her to him. 'You smell nice,' he said intimately. 'New perfume?'

It was the scent of the nighttime cleanser which Isobel had been unable to resist after she and Troy had bought some for Zelda. The scent of it was erotic for her, she had smelled it on her skin and on Troy's.

'Mmm,' she said.

Philip's familiar, beloved body moved closer to her in bed. His hand pulled her closer still and she slid to rest her head on his shoulder. He bent his head down and gently kissed her face. Isobel felt awkward in a way that she rarely felt with Troy, no matter how bizarre their appearance or behaviour. She felt herself furiously blushing in the half-darkness of the bedroom. Philip stroked her hair away from her face and kissed her neck and the lobe of her ear. Isobel, trying to respond, put her hands to his shoulders, on the nape of his neck. Philip gave a small low sound in the back of his throat and kissed her lips. Isobel kissed him back, demure kisses that were completely unlike Troy's open-mouthed savaging lubricated with Zelda's scarlet lipstick. Isobel pushed the thought of Troy away from her mind, out of her marital bed, and tried to concentrate on the gentle touch of her husband, the man she had married for love and chosen to stay with for years.

Philip reached down the bed and fumbled with her pyjama

top, stroked her belly, and then moved his hand up to her breasts. Isobel lay quietly, let him touch her, waiting for the passionate response which he used to invoke. Nothing very much happened. Isobel wondered if nothing was happening for Philip too, and that was why these preambles were taking so long. Was he, perhaps, waiting for the mood to take him, and hoping that in a moment he would be filled with desire?

He tugged at her pyjama jacket. 'I think we should get rid of this,' he said and Isobel realised at the thick tone of his voice that he was aroused, that it was only she who was frozen with embarrassment. For Philip it was sexually exciting, this was what he wanted.

Obligingly she took off her jacket and slid down her pyjama trousers. Philip matched her actions so that they were naked in bed together. Isobel thought that she must remember to change and wash the sheets in the morning so that Mrs M. did not know that they had made love, then she thought that this was ridiculous – there was no reason at all that Mrs M. should not know that they had made love. They were husband and wife, they ought to be lovers. It had been Philip's illness which had interrupted the intense and enjoyable sex life they had shared together. She should be revelling in its return, not worrying about the sheets.

'This is like the old days,' Philip said delightedly.

Isobel drew closer to him and felt the sensual pleasure of warm, naked skin against her own. Philip had soft, light body hair and the tickle of the hairs against her smooth nakedness had always aroused her.

'Yes, it is,' she said, trying to convince herself.

Philip raised himself up above her and gently entered into her. To her surprise, Isobel found that he was hard, potent. They moved together companionably, pleasurably. Isobel closed her eyes and tried to think of nothing but the enjoyment of his skin against hers, of the comfort and warmth of him.

She felt herself floating away, growing more and more distant. Her body responded to his touch. Philip had been her lover for many years, he knew the caresses which pleased her. But her mind was miles away, she felt distant and cool and remote. Carefully, she did not think of Troy nor of Zelda, she thought of nothing – either erotic or repugnant. She thought of nothing, while her husband moved on her body, inside her body, and covered her neck and her breasts with his tentative kisses.

'Is it good?' he whispered.

'Very good,' she reassured him.

She could feel his urgency as his speed increased but she knew nothing more than a desire to please him, and a wish, hardly formulated, to get the whole thing over with. She arched her back and gave a few little moans of pretended pleasure. They were enough to deceive him into thinking that she had reached orgasm and wanted no more, and he jerked with sudden, greedy violence, then sighed deeply, and rested heavily on her.

Isobel waited a few moments and then moved a little. At once Philip rose up with a word of apology, and released her.

'I have to go to the bathroom,' she said, and picked up her pyjamas and went. She sat on the bidet and felt the cool water washing away the stickiness. She stood to wash her face and hands, and look at her reflection in the bathroom mirror.

Her face gave away nothing. She gazed at her dead eyes in the mirror and thought that she was as blank as the page of her new novel. There was nothing to say any more, there was nothing to think. There was simply nothing, through and through, neither in the novel nor in her heart. She dressed in her pyjamas and went back into the bedroom. Philip was lying, still naked, propped up on the pillows. He looked flushed and happy.

'I would think that was conclusive proof,' he said with a grin. 'I am a lot better. Oh, Isobel, isn't it wonderful?'

She tried to share his joy. 'Yes, it is,' she said, climbing into bed beside him. 'It is wonderful. I'm so happy that you're stronger.'

'And you've been so good,' he said, drawing her close to

him again. 'So considerate. It must have been hard for you, while I was so grouchy. And how long has it been since we made love? Months, isn't it?'

'I don't count,' Isobel said. 'I never minded. What matters most is that you feel well now.'

'I feel fantastic,' he said. 'Unbelievable.'

They lay in silence for a few moments. 'Shall I put the light out?' Isobel asked.

Philip nodded. She reached up and switched off the bedside lights and then enjoyed snuggling down to rest on his shoulder again with his arm firmly around her. 'This is the best bit,' she said. 'This closeness.'

In the darkness she felt him kissing her hair. 'You've been an angel,' he whispered. 'Just imagine how happy we will be if I get well again.'

'D'you really think you might?'

'We could travel. We always wanted to travel, didn't we?'

Isobel suddenly thought of the Zelda Vere money which could finance a new and exciting life for Philip and her together. She had thought of it as a nest egg which might protect them when his health grew worse, might pay for residential care for him. But if he was to get better, they could make a new life for themselves, a quite different life might open up for her.

'Oh yes,' she said. 'I should so love to travel. I so want to go to Japan.'

'Japan? I love the Far East. It was one of my great regrets that we never went there together.'

'Was it?'

'Yes. But now we could. And I could get back to work, earn some decent money again.'

'I doubt they'd have you back,' she said gently. 'At your age, darling.'

'I wouldn't go back to my old job.' He dismissed the idea. 'I'd run my own business, I'd do freelance work. I'd earn a fee for a job and when the job was over we could go and spend the money together. What d'you think?'

'Wonderful,' Isobel said sleepily.

Philip leaned up on one elbow and kissed her on the lips. 'Goodnight, sweetheart,' he said tenderly.

Isobel listened to his breathing deepen as he slid into sleep. She lay awake, looking at the ceiling, wondering at the future that might open before her. Zelda could be the route for her freedom, for her and Philip to find a new happiness together. Having been Zelda, Isobel might become a different sort of woman. Owning Zelda's wealth, Isobel and Philip would be free to do almost anything.

In the morning he was smiling when he woke. Isobel smiled back, tentatively, hopefully. 'You stay in bed,' he said tenderly. 'I'm going to make you breakfast in bed.'

'Mrs M. will be in in half an hour,' Isobel said.

'I don't care,' he said. 'She can think what she likes. I'm going to bring you breakfast in bed and then run you a hot bath. Would you like that?'

'Heavenly,' Isobel said, resigning herself to a morning of inaction while her deadline on *Loving Ghost* ticked away and Troy waited for her to return his call.

'You go back to sleep,' Philip commanded, putting on his dressing gown. Isobel lay against the pillows and smiled at him. Once he had left the room she looked at the bedside table. She had a couple of new books which she had been asked to read, and there was material for a lecture she had been invited to give. There were things in the bedroom for her to occupy her time usefully in the hour or so it would take Philip to get a breakfast tray organised. She knew that she should be grateful to him for his kindness. But she was used to working hard, and the interruption to her routine was no real advantage.

She heard his footstep on the stair in time to tuck the novel out of the way, sit up, and smile at him as he came in.

'Sorry I took so long. Murray gave Mrs M. a lift in and I stopped to make him a cup of coffee.' Philip opened the legs of the breakfast table and put it across her knees. Isobel smiled to indicate her delight at a pot of tea and cup, a boiled egg and cold toast.

'What's Murray doing, bringing Mrs M. here?'

'Her car wouldn't start so she called him.'

Isobel hesitated, genuinely puzzled. 'Why didn't she call us?'

'I expect she didn't want to bother us, she knows you've been working hard recently.'

'But why bother Murray?'

'Well, if he was coming up here he would drive past her door. Why not?'

'I don't want us to take advantage of him,' Isobel said, feeling that while that was true, there were other more complicated strands operating, of which she understood none.

'He's a good sort,' Philip said. 'He doesn't mind. And he likes Mellie.'

'Is he here now?'

'Yes. I'm just going down to see him. He's got detailed planning consent. The builders will start next Monday. We're just double-checking where the radiator points and the electrics are to go.'

'Excellent,' Isobel said.

'Shall I leave you in peace?'

'You run along,' Isobel said, smiling. 'I know you're longing to decide where to put radiators.'

'I want it right for you,' he said sweetly. 'I want it perfect for you.' He bent and kissed her on the top of her head. 'I know it's been hard for you the last few years,' he said tenderly. 'I've felt so ill, I'm sure I've been a misery to live with. I'm really sorry, darling, sorrier than I can tell you. Now I'm feeling so much better I understand how awful it must have been. At the time I couldn't see further than my own despair. But I've really turned a corner now. Everything will be different.'

His optimism was infectious. Isobel looked up at him. 'Oh, Philip.'

'I promise,' he said. 'Things will get back to how they were before I was ill. We'll be happy again, really happy again.

Like we were before.' He touched her cheek and on an impulse Isobel caught at his hand and kissed his finger. He smiled at her. 'You enjoy your breakfast,' he said, and went quietly from the room.

Isobel did not touch the food, instead she leaned back against the pillows and gazed sightlessly at the ceiling. 'This is where it begins,' she said softly to herself. She thought that if this was a novel it would be where the heroine has a choice to make, a major plot point. In the novels that Isobel wrote, the heroine always chose the better road, the moral decision, the path of duty and then found it a joy. 'That would be wonderful,' Isobel whispered softly to herself as she moved the tray off her knees. 'To return to Philip and find it the most wonderful thing I could do. To do the right thing and find it to be the best thing.'

Isobel returned Troy's call while Philip and Murray paced again and again the small patch of ground between barn and house. She could see the two of them from the window, the young, slim man, and the older one, just as active, just as energetic, just as able.

'It's me,' she said to Troy. 'I'm sorry I missed you yesterday.'

'Are you all right?' he asked, alerted by the coolness of her tone.

'I'm fine.'

'Everything OK at home? Pool filling up nicely?'

'It's not started yet,' she said. Philip glanced towards her window and smiled at her, a big happy beam. Isobel waved back.

'How is work?'

'I'll do a chapter a day over the next few days. You'll have to tell them it's first draft . . .'

'First draft from you is better than they get from most after the twentieth attempt,' Troy said loyally. 'They won't expect much on a first draft from Zelda. They probably think I rewrite it all, anyway.'

'You can do it then,' Isobel said smartly.

'Not me,' he replied. 'I'm the ten per cent polish, not the ninety per cent hard graft of this operation. You have the ideas and do the writing, Isobel, and I'll do the contracts.'

'Where did you go last night?' she asked idly.

'Out to the theatre and then on to a club.'

'What sort of a club?'

'A bad sort,' he said provocatively.

'Oh,' Isobel said.

'What about you?'

'We had a takeaway curry,' Isobel said, conscious of how dull her life sounded. 'It was very nice. It's rather a treat for us, because you have to get it from the village.'

'You sound as if you have to get it from a village in Madras.'

Isobel giggled. 'Not quite.'

'And did the pool man stay for dinner?'

'No. We ate on our own. We had the evening on our own.'

Troy said nothing, alerted by a lover's intuition that something had changed, but not yet knowing what.

'And was it lovely?' he asked. 'To be all on your own again with the exotic treat of a takeaway chicken kashmir?'

'Biryani, actually. Yes, it was lovely.'

'I'm so glad,' he said. 'And did he ask for an extension to the pool building to house his collection of emeralds, or was it all just simply uxorious love with no hidden agenda?'

'Simple love, I think,' Isobel replied pleasantly, hearing the irritation in Troy's voice and correctly identifying it as jealousy.

'How nice,' he said. 'How marital. Very Isobel Latimer, very *Country Life*.'

'He *is* my husband,' Isobel pointed out.

'And I am just your agent,' Troy agreed. 'I only get a cut, don't I? Not the whole cake. That's the deal.'

'Troy,' Isobel said sweetly. 'Is there something wrong?'

There was a silence.

'I rang you,' she said quietly. 'And your flat was full of people drinking and dancing and partying. Yesterday you rang me on your way out to the theatre and you made it very clear that you might not be home last night. All I have done is have a meal with my husband and go to bed with him in our bed as I have done for every night for the last thirty years. What is your problem with that?'

'Nothing,' Troy said precisely. 'Absolutely nothing. You must forgive me. I have a hangover and it has put me in a bad mood. I shall take some Alka Selzer and call you back to apologise when I am at peace with my liver. I am sorry, Isobel, I'll talk to you tomorrow.'

'That's all right,' she said. From outside the window Philip paced a distance from the house to the barn and then turned and gave her thumbs-up sign. Isobel waved and smiled at him again. In the spring sunshine he looked boyish, full of life. 'I'll talk to you later, Troy. It doesn't matter.'

Twenty-Six

Murray stayed for lunch. Isobel, in smiling accord with Philip, was not irritated by his presence at the lunch table, though Mrs M. was ostentatiously proud of the steak and kidney pudding she had made. Murray asked Isobel about her work and it was apparent that he had read the novel that she had signed for him, and he had reflected on it. The questions he asked showed him as a man of intelligence, though of limited education, and the teacher in Isobel was always drawn to people who struggled to understand for themselves.

Mrs M. cleared away the plates and made them coffee, and then left the kitchen to finish her chores in the other rooms. Murray had promised to give her a lift home and he waited until she was ready.

'Murray has made me a rather interesting proposition,' Philip said. 'I haven't said yes or no. I said I'd have to talk it over with you.'

'What's that?' Isobel asked. 'Not a waterslide park attached to our pool?'

Murray grinned. 'Funny you should say that, I was thinking myself that it would be the very thing for you.'

'He's offered me a job,' Philip said. 'I can't tell you how flattered I am.'

Isobel looked from one man to the other. 'A job?'

'I wouldn't have dreamed of it if he hadn't been so much better,' Murray said hastily. 'And if you think it would be too much for him, then forget the whole thing.'

'No, I don't,' Isobel said. 'But what job?'

'I'm rushed off my feet,' Murray said confidingly. 'It's a great thing to be, but I'm a victim of my own success. The business needs two of me. The things I offer – customer care, individual planning, after-sales reassurance – it's very intensive work. But it's what really characterises this operation. I can't handle more than two or three pools at a time, and I'm getting inquiries for five or six pools every week, seven or eight, even. Last week I had ten calls.'

'But Philip knows nothing about pools,' Isobel remarked.

'I know more than you think,' Philip said. 'I've planned ours from the ground upwards, remember.'

Murray shook his head. 'Philip has great style,' he said. 'If he tells someone that dark blue is the colour for them, then they believe him. The people over at Fleet were completely convinced. He sold them that pool, all I did was drive us there. Philip did all the work. He's got class, everyone can see that. I'm a self-made man and it shows sometimes. I've tried to knock some of the rough edges off, but sometimes I have to go into rather grand houses and I can't feel at ease there. I'm not right for them, I don't know the right things to say.' He glanced at Philip with undeniable affection. 'Not like Philip. He's got class. He's the real thing.'

Isobel found herself strangely touched by this confession. 'Surely that doesn't matter one way or another, these days,' she said, knowing that it did; but wanting to reassure Murray that it did not matter to her.

He gave her his urchin grin. 'Course it does, Isobel,' he said. 'You're a woman of the world. You know what I'm talking about. Philip can open doors for me just because of the way he walks up the steps.'

Philip gave a little deprecatory shrug. 'Well, hardly . . .'

'And the final thing is the paperwork. It's a nightmare keeping it up to date. I have to be VAT-registered and they're like bloodhounds. I'm a sole trader and I have to have apple-pie books. And it's all very confidential material. People tell you a lot when they tell you what sort of pool they want. And when I work in the – shall we say, higher echelons – there's more and more information which is more and more sensitive. There was a job I tendered for recently and I would have had to be security vetted before I could go on site. I can't hire just anybody. I want someone I can trust. Someone honest and thorough, and with proven abilities.'

Isobel hesitated, glanced at Philip. 'I don't know,' she said. Then she saw his face. He was glowing with enthusiasm and renewed energy. 'Well, what d'you think, darling?'

'I do like the work,' he said frankly. 'There's something about the whole business that I like. It's a bit of engineering and with my background that's a real pleasure, it's a lot to do with people and that's where I've always been strong, and it's out and about. I think it's ideal for me. I'm so pleased Murray thought of it. But I promised myself I wouldn't say yes or no till I'd talked it over with you.'

'I'm not the boss,' Isobel said, careful of how they appeared before Murray. 'You must do what you want, Philip.'

'He'd be a fool if he didn't listen to your opinion,' Murray interjected quickly. '*I'd* like to have your advice and I'm only one of your readers. You're a woman who knows what's what, Isobel. We'd both be fools if we went any further without asking you what you thought about it.'

Isobel recognised the warm currency of flattery. 'Oh, really! Well, I suppose my only reservation would be Philip's health. He is very much improved but I suppose I am afraid that he might slide back again.'

'I don't think I will,' Philip said. 'I certainly feel better. And I don't feel that it's a superficial improvement, like feeling a bit more cheerful. I thought at first that it was purely mental, I was having a more interesting time so I was more alert. But it's more than that. I can measure that I'm stronger. I'm walking better and my stamina on my exercises has doubled. It's a measurable improvement. And there are others . . .' He slid a smiling glance at Isobel, reminding her that they had made love for the first time in months, only last night. She turned away, but he caught the ghost of her smile.

'And eating,' Murray remarked, missing nothing. 'Your appetite's not harmed.'

'And drinking,' Philip supplemented.

'Perhaps we should go back to the specialist and see what he says,' Isobel suggested. 'Or just leave any decision until May, when you see him anyway.'

Philip shook his head. 'I want to start now,' he said simply. 'If we're going to do it I'd like to get going.'

'May is my absolutely busiest time of the year,' Murray interpolated. 'It's when everyone realises that they don't have a swimming pool and they've been promising themselves one, and if they don't order it now they won't have one for the summer. I can make more money in May than in all the rest of the year. But only if I'm set up for it. I've got to be able to get around to everyone. I have to have somebody in place for the early summer. If not Philip, then someone else. But I'd rather have Philip.'

Isobel looked from one bright face to the other. 'What can I say? It's obviously what you both want and it's obviously a good idea. What are the business arrangements to be?'

Murray paused. 'That'd be up to yourselves, really. I'd be happy with anything from a fee paid at an hourly rate to – well – some kind of profit-sharing scheme.'

'I wouldn't want to be paid by the hour,' Philip remarked.

'Oh?' Murray said. 'Whatever, really. What would you prefer, of all the options? What would your first choice be? You weren't thinking of a full partnership, presumably? Going fifty-fifty?'

'Well, why not?' Philip demanded. 'Why not?'

'You couldn't work Murray's hours,' Isobel warned. 'You couldn't be a full partner.'

'I didn't dare ask!' Murray exclaimed. 'I never thought you'd be interested. I thought you wanted a bit of a hobby job. I was just hoping to get your skills into the business at the points where I really couldn't do without you. It never occurred to me that you'd be prepared to come in with me.'

'Oh, yes,' Philip said. 'In for a penny, in for a pound. I'd much rather work for my own business than work for someone else. Even you, Murray. That's what I was telling you the other day, and I was saying only last night to Isobel. Ideally I'd look for a business I could run for myself.'

'But that would be terrific!' Murray said. 'We could draw up a partnership agreement and you could come in as a fifty-fifty partner.'

'I don't want you to commit yourself to too much,' Isobel insisted.

Murray shook his head. 'Philip can come in as a sleeping partner and just do the work that he wants,' he said. 'If it's ever too much for him then he can take a break. If you and he want to take a holiday you can just draw your share of the profits for that year and go away. You won't have any trouble from me.'

'But this is really great,' Philip said, filled with enthusiasm. 'We'll have to do it properly, mind. We'll get a proper evaluation of the business, get an audit done, and then I'll buy half of it.'

Murray nodded. 'And we'll get a partnership agreement drawn up that allows you to work minimum hours or no hours at all,' he said. 'It should be up to the two of you to decide. I don't want to push you, Philip. Your health comes first.'

'This is just what I wanted,' Philip explained. 'Like I was saying to you, if I could get back to work, I'd want to be a freelance, and work for myself.'

'Well, here you are!' Murray said, extending a hand across the table. 'Not a client but a partner! Welcome to the profitable world of swimming pools!'

They drank a bottle of champagne to celebrate. Isobel, tasting the cold, sparkling sharpness on her tongue, was inevitably reminded of Zelda and Troy but she put the thought of them away to one side. She did not want to think of them, she did not want that powerful, haunting half-life to come into her mind when her husband looked smilingly at her, his eyes glowing with warmth and happiness and his glass raised to her: 'To our renaissance, Isobel.'

She raised her glass in reply. 'To us.'

She thought it through, in her study, on her own, gazing at the screen where she should be typing out the first three chapters of the Zelda Vere novel. If Philip earned enough for them to live on she would not have to write another Zelda Vere novel. She would never have to be Zelda Vere again. Zelda Vere would fade from the consciousness of the world as rapidly as so many other brief stars of the literary circuit who wrote one novel, earned enormous success, wrote another which signally failed, and then faded completely and totally from sight. Isobel could let Zelda sink without trace.

Or at any rate, in theory, Isobel could let Zelda sink without trace.

But in practice?

Isobel thought that her life had moved rather abruptly from the scenery and matter of an Isobel Latimer novel to that of Zelda Vere. In a Latimer novel the story was always about making choices: fighting through appearance, through the false goals of ephemeral desires, to make genuine moral informed choices. In the Zelda novel everything was focused on appearance, on desires and their satisfaction. Naturally enough, the Zelda story included the possibilities of disappointment, perversion, corruption. Isobel saw, for the first time, that she could choose to live her life in either terrain. She could choose to be an Isobel Latimer heroine: a woman who eschewed glamour and sexual pleasure and chose instead duty and a higher moral life. Or she could be a Zelda Vere heroine, who said that the most important thing in the world was to recognise one's own desires and seek their fulfilment. But Isobel saw, also for the first time, that the Zelda Vere novel was the flip side of the Isobel Latimer novel: its shadow.

Isobel understood that in living her life and in writing in the way she did, there had always been a hidden, even unconscious, awareness of the contrary side. A Latimer novel was about rejecting all the things that a Vere novel emphasised, perhaps even denying their attraction. Perhaps even fleeing them in terror of being attracted. Isobel herself, in her newly discovered ability to write both sorts of novel, to live two contrasting sorts of lives, to be two completely contrasting women, had brought herself to the point of a decision. What sort of book should she write? What sort of author should she be? Which life should she live? What sort of woman was she?

On Monday morning Isobel was woken by the disagreeable noise of a man coughing and hawking outside her bedroom window. Then a radio began to play loudly, and two men started to shout at each other. Philip, drawing the bedroom curtains, exclaimed in pleasure: 'Oh, good. They're very early!' and hastened downstairs to welcome the workmen.

All day the noise went on. First they had to excavate the foundation for the walls for the passage between house and pool, they also had a digger for the pool inside the barn. The shouts of guidance and the grinding noise as the digger bit into topsoil and then into sandy rock were too much for Isobel, trying to complete chapter three of the new Zelda Vere novel in her study. She complained to Philip at lunchtime that it was impossible for her to think.

'You can't make an omelette . . .' he said unsympathetically.

Murray, who was having lunch with them, looked up from the chicken in tomato sauce which Mrs M. had cooked. 'What?'

'Well-known phrase,' Philip said briskly.

'Not known to me,' Murray said.

'It's so loud,' Isobel said. 'And it goes on and on.'

'One thing straight first,' Murray said firmly. They both stopped and waited for what he would say. 'What d'you mean: "You can't make an omelette"?'

Isobel smiled. 'It's a saying attributed to Napoleon Bonaparte. He's supposed to have said that you can't make an omelette without breaking eggs. The idea is that every good thing has some destructive elements.'

Murray nodded. 'Got it. And Napoleon Bonaparte was?'

Isobel was temporarily taken aback. 'You don't know?'

Murray gave an apologetic grimace. 'Is it a capital offence? I'm very ignorant, aren't I?'

'No,' Isobel said hastily. 'Why should you know?'

'Gave his name to the brandy,' Philip said consolingly. 'You'd know that.'

'So who was he exactly?'

'He was a French leader,' Isobel said vaguely. Confronted with the need to render a full account, she found that she herself was a little uncertain. 'He came to power during the French revolution, late eighteenth, early nineteenth century, and turned France into an empire with himself as emperor. He planned to conquer the whole of Europe and was defeated in the east by the Russians, and by England at the Battle of Trafalgar, Admiral Nelson.'

'Heard of him!' Murray said, pleased to recognise something in this story.

'He was imprisoned, escaped and raised the French again. There was a final battle at Waterloo, the English forces were commanded by General Wellington.'

'As in boot,' Philip added, frivolously. 'As in *boeuf*.'

'He died in captivity,' Isobel said. 'He was a great French hero.'

Murray nodded. 'Thank you. I like to know things.'

Isobel felt a touch of almost maternal tenderness. She smiled at him and was rewarded by a boyish grin.

'You must think I'm an awful fool,' he said.

'You can always look up things like that on the Internet,' she said. 'Or in any good encyclopedia. If you want to know things like that.'

Murray nodded his dark curly head. 'Yes, but the difficulty is that I don't know what I don't know, if you see what I mean. I knew the name of the brandy, and I knew of the battles of Trafalgar and Waterloo, and I'd heard of Nelson. But I didn't know the battles were against the French, I didn't know they were against Bonaparte. So I wouldn't think to look him up in a reference book, because I didn't even know that I should look him up.'

Isobel thought for a moment. 'What you could do would be to read a short general history and that would give you some ideas,' she suggested.

Murray nodded. 'Like what?'

'I could lend you a couple of books,' Isobel offered.

Philip glanced at her, mildly surprised. Isobel usually refused to lend anyone any of her books.

Murray beamed. 'I'd like that,' he said. 'Maybe you'll educate me.'

Mrs M. came in and cleared the plates. 'I'm ready to go when you are,' she said. Murray nodded and was about to rise.

'About the noise,' he said to Philip. 'Isobel can't work in her study with the guys crashing about outside the window, and when they come to knock the door through into the house it'll be dusty as well as noisy. How about we move her study upstairs to one of the spare bedrooms for a few days?'

'It'd still be noisy,' Isobel said.

Murray frowned and then an idea struck him. 'How about you move into my office at home?' he asked. 'Nice and quiet, nobody would disturb you there. And I'm hardly in, because I'm up here or over at Fleet most of the day.'

Isobel hesitated. 'I wouldn't like to intrude . . .'

'I'd be honoured,' he said easily. 'It's got a nice desk and chair and you could use my computer and take whatever books you need down there. Would you like that?'

Isobel hesitated. There was a resounding rumble and crash from outside as a lorry tipped out hardcore for the foundations. Murray laughed and surprisingly, intimately, tapped Isobel gently on the tip of her nose.

'Don't stand on your dignity,' he said sweetly. 'Let me help you.'

Isobel shrank back a little from his touch but knew herself to be charmed. 'All right then,' she said, smiling up at him. 'Thank you.'

Twenty-Seven

Isobel, ensconced in the unfamiliar surroundings of Murray's office, before his word processor at his heavy wooden desk, comfortable in his padded office chair, found that she could not possibly set to work until she had satisfied her curiosity. Very well aware that she was trespassing on his hospitality, she opened one of the filing cabinets which stood in a row of three along the back wall of the office. They were filled with files labelled with the names of clients, and inside, proposals of pools to be built. Isobel glanced at one at random. Some people called Birtley had ordered a swimming pool. Murray had noted that it had been completed on time. It had cost them, altogether, £25,000. Murray had noted a profit margin of eighteen per cent. He had made a profit of £4,500. Isobel raised her eyebrows and pulled out another file. Again there was the note that the work had been completed on time, again a note of the profit margin on this pool. This was an indoor pool, a more expensive venture. Murray had made a profit of £10,200 on little more than nine weeks' work. Isobel shut the filing cabinet. Murray's boast about his business was obviously true. He was doing extremely well.

She left the office and went to the kitchen. It was a small semi-detached house on a newly built estate. Murray had told Philip that he had taken the decision not to invest in big office premises but to keep his costs to the minimum. His kitchen was modern and bright with plastic lightweight units. The oven was shiny, it looked as if it had never been used. Isobel peeped in the larder unit and saw the empty shelves typical of an undomesticated bachelor. In the fridge there was milk, bread, cheese and an old box of eggs.

The sitting room was furnished from a furniture showroom. A matching sofa with two armchairs, a coffee table carrying the books Isobel had lent him, a marble-effect fireplace around a flame-effect fire. Curtains to match the armchairs, a reading light, a large television with a gadget underneath which Isobel did not recognise: a playstation.

Isobel's curiosity was aroused rather than satisfied by the bleakness of these domestic details. She hesitated at the foot of the stairs for only a moment and then she slipped off her shoes, fearful of their heels marking the carpet, and crept up the stairs.

The bathroom revealed a new side of Murray, a more sensual side. There was a separate shower cubicle with glass doors beside an extra-deep bath. It was stocked with shower gel and an after-shower oil. There were scented soaps arranged in a bowl on the sill beneath the window, which was shielded with real wood venetian blinds. There were two thick natural sponges on either side of the bath, and dark purple bath oil in a glass decanter. There was a shaving mirror which could extend to be used either at the sink or while Murray was soaking in the bath. In the rack across the bath there was a pumice stone, and a loofah. In the airing cupboard there were thick, large towels and a spare towelling dressing gown. It was a bathroom which had been carefully considered and well-planned by a man who loved scents, deep hot water, and the texture of thick towels and flannels.

Knowing that she was behaving very badly, Isobel opened the medicine cabinet which was hung on the wall beside the shower. There were cold remedies and paracetamol, muscle balm for fatigue after sports. There was a prescribed remedy for an ear infection, and an opened packet of condoms. Isobel peered at them but did not touch them. There was also an unopened packet of fun condoms – flavoured and coloured. She wondered what sort of woman welcomed lovemaking with fun condoms. For the first time she thought about Murray in bed. He would have a good body, she thought, his shoulders were broad and his belly was flat. His smile was confident, roguish, he could well be a man who liked to make a woman laugh in bed, a man who would be playful, perhaps experimental, perhaps demanding. Isobel glanced at the packet of condoms and saw that they were large size.

Very quietly in her stockinged feet, she crept into the main bedroom. He had not made his bed after getting up in the morning, the duvet was thrown back in inviting disorder. Yesterday's shirt was discarded in the corner of the room. Isobel opened the wardrobe and regarded, without touching, Murray's three sombre suits and an assortment of shirts. A tie rack held half a dozen rather handsome silk ties. The drawer underneath held his socks and underwear. Isobel saw that Murray wore silk boxer shorts and good quality socks.

Dreamily she closed the wardrobe door and looked once more at his bed. There was a dent where his head had been. His copy of her novel was laid open face down, on a little drawer unit beside the bed. Isobel opened the bottom drawer and saw the garish cover of a man's magazine with a large-breasted woman leaning forward, her white lace underwear presenting her to the camera like a bride. Isobel regarded the picture for a little while, thinking of Zelda, photographed as she came out of the limousine, showing her breasts to the unblinking eye of the lens, thinking of the male gaze to which every woman submits and which can be such a joy or such a threat. She closed the drawer without touching the magazine and stood, in silence, by Murray's bed.

Almost unbidden, her hand went out and lifted the duvet. A tiny waft of Murray's scent came to her. Isobel turned her head towards it, as if she were listening to someone call her name. The house was completely silent. Unthinking, Isobel pulled the duvet into place, and then she raised her skirt and slid between the sheets, into the soft bed. She thought she could feel a hint of his warmth still left in the mattress. She laid her head in the exact spot where Murray's head had dented the pillow. She pulled the duvet up to her face and lay in an entranced silence for a moment, breathing the light scent of his body, the erotic tang of healthy male skin: the very scent of desire. Then, oddly, she fell asleep.

Isobel was awakened by what she thought was the noise of the front door opening and she woke in shock. She leaped out of the bed as soon as she opened her eyes; but she was far, far too late. He was already there. The noise had not been the front door but the click of the latch of the bedroom door. Murray stood on the threshold of his bedroom, looking at her, jumping from his bed, her hair tousled from lying on his pillow, her skirt trailing back into the warmth of his duvet.

His face showed complete puzzlement. 'Isobel?'

'I . . .' she stammered, but she had nothing to say. Hopelessly, she twitched the duvet into place, as if she were doing nothing but making the bed for him.

He gave her a long silent look and then he turned on his heel and went quietly down the stairs. Isobel gave a little moan of distress and shame. She heard him go into the kitchen and then she heard the water running as he put the kettle on. Slowly, she continued to straighten the bed, as if that would make her intrusion any the less, as if it would ameliorate the trespass if she left his bedroom tidier than she had found it.

She went to his mirror and pinned back her hair. It had come out from the bun while she slept and she swiftly pinned it back into place. She smoothed down her skirt, it was creased. Her roll-neck cotton top was fine, but she did not look herself. She did not look calm and controlled, a little dowdy. She looked flushed and dishevelled. In despair at her failure to create a sober appearance Isobel looked around for her shoes and realised that she had left them downstairs. Murray must have seen them at the foot of the stairs when he had come in the front door. He must have seen them, heard the silence of the house, and concluded that she was upstairs. He must have followed her up the stairs, seen the empty bathroom, the empty spare bedroom and then opened his own bedroom door and seen her. He would have watched her in the vulnerable moments of deep sleep and then in the sudden start and panic of her waking.

'Oh God,' Isobel whispered in horror.

She lacked the courage to go downstairs and make a simple coherent apology; but she knew that the longer she stayed upstairs the more of an intrusion it was. And it would be a thousand times worse if he came back upstairs to ask her when she was coming down. She knew that she could not bear him to come back up the stairs again as if to see what she was doing now. Isobel hid her face in her hands for a brief moment, and then courageously straightened up, pushed back a straying lock of hair, and went, barefoot, down the stairs.

Her shoes were not where she had left them. Isobel registered that piece of information as a further notch on the ratchet of disaster, and went, in her stockinged feet, into the kitchen. Murray was pouring two mugs of tea.

'D'you take sugar?' he asked politely.

'Yes,' Isobel said. 'Just one.'

He added sugar to her mug and passed it over. 'I just popped back to make sure you had everything you need,' he said conversationally. 'Sometimes the trip switch throws, so do remember to save everything that you are writing. I'd hate you to lose it.'

'Yes,' Isobel said. She imagined that he had already glanced in his study and seen the computer screen completely blank.

'I've got to go over to Fleet this afternoon, they want to make some alterations to their final plans. Philip said he'd come with me,' Murray went on.

'Good,' she said. She hid her face in the large mug.

'Biscuit?' he asked. He passed over a packet of arrowroot biscuits.

'Thank you.'

They were silent for a moment. Isobel hesitated, trying to find the words to ask him where he had put her shoes. Just as she was about to frame a casual inquiry, Murray finished his tea, rinsed his mug under the hot tap and set it upside down on the draining board. 'I'll just get the plans from the study,' he said, as if there were nothing more to say.

He walked past her and Isobel heard him open the filing cabinet drawer. For one dreadful moment she wondered if he would know that she had been prying into his business as well as poking around his house. She sat like a statue, frozen with embarrassment, on the kitchen stool. She could not remember if she had closed the drawer of the filing cabinet properly. She heard the muted clang as he pushed the drawer shut and the noise precipitated her out into the hall to watch him, as he came from the study with the folder in his hand.

'Work going all right?' he asked cheerfully.

'Yes,' Isobel said. He knew that she had spent all the morning asleep in his bed.

'Good,' he said jovially. He went briskly to the front door, a man with business to attend to.

'Murray,' Isobel said urgently as he opened the door. He paused on the threshold and turned to her, his face warm with interest, his dark eyes very bright.

'What?' he asked.

Isobel, in her stockinged feet, tiptoed towards him and looked pleadingly up into his face.

'Where are my shoes?'

Slowly, his face came down to hers, as close as a lover's. Now she could feel his breath on the skin of her lips. His face came even closer, Isobel closed her eyes, apprehending his touch, inhaling the scent of him. He stopped just a fraction of an inch away from a kiss, his lips almost touching hers.

'I've taken them,' he whispered.

Then he shut his front door, leaving her alone in the hall; and he was gone.

Isobel went back to the study and sat before the blank screen. She gazed at the greyness and found she was incapable of any thought. The exchange with Murray had been so bizarre, so unexpected, that there was nothing she could analyse. It was like an event which had happened to someone else, or an occurrence in a dream. Isobel felt there was no handle that she could grasp to open up meaning from it.

Clearly, Murray now had a view of her and a relationship with her which was not under her control. He had already voiced suspicions about her behaviour in London, he knew she was deceiving Philip even if he did not know what she did or where she went. He had colluded with that deceit and Isobel had suffered the dangerous sense of a shared secret with him from that moment. But the incident which had just taken place, her long, dreamless sleep in the intimate comfort of his bed, his discovery of her, and the theft of her shoes – Isobel gave a little spontaneous moan at the thought of her shoes, turned from the screen and hid her face in her hands.

The telephone rang. Isobel hesitated. It rang again. The number displayed was her home number. She picked it up.

'Hello, darling,' Philip said cheerfully. 'Sorry to interrupt you. Just calling to say that they've knocked off for the day. It's safe to come home. It's all quiet here.'

'I'll come at once,' Isobel said.

'Is it not going well?'

'It's not going at all,' Isobel said.

'Oh, bad luck. Will you work there tomorrow?'

Isobel hesitated. 'Did Murray say anything about me working here tomorrow?'

'I just assumed it was an on-going arrangement. Hang on, I'll ask him.'

'Is he there?' Isobel asked in sudden alarm. 'Don't –'

But Philip had already put down the phone.

'Don't!' Isobel shouted into the receiver.

He did not even hear her. She could hear him at some distance from the phone talking to Murray: 'I'm just on the phone to Isobel. Is it OK for her to use your place tomorrow?'

Isobel heard Murray's confident reply: 'Sure. Tell her to help herself.'

Isobel flinched.

Philip came back to the telephone. 'He says you can.'

'Thank you,' Isobel said numbly. 'Do thank him. I'll come home now, then.'

She shut down the computer, pushed the chair into the desk and left the study. She glanced at the foot of the stairs in case her shoes had reappeared. They were not there. She took a quick look around the hall and the little downstairs cloakroom in case Murray had officiously tidied them away. They were missing. She did not feel she could go upstairs to look for them, and in any case, Murray could not have taken them upstairs. After he had found her in his bed he had gone to the kitchen, then to the study, and then he had left. Perhaps he would keep them in his car as he drove Philip to Fleet. Isobel put her hand to her mouth and pressed it against her lips. Why would Murray want to drive around with her shoes in his car?

Isobel opened the door and stood in her stockinged feet. Murray's drive was sharp gravel, she paused and looked at it, wondering for a moment if she could go back into the house and borrow a pair of boots. She sighed. Arriving at her home in Murray's boots would look even odder to Philip than arriving barefoot; and she did not want to be seen by Murray taking yet further liberties with his possessions.

She closed the door behind her and picked her way over the gravel. It was wet and sharp beneath her cringing insteps. Isobel reached the car and hopped in, rubbing her damp feet on the carpet. She started the engine, it was odd driving barefoot and she felt that she was hardly in control of the car. She crept home, nervously slow, certain that she would not be able to stamp on the brake in an emergency.

But even in this discomfort, even with this inconvenience, even in this confused embarrassment, she did not feel any resentment towards Murray. It was as if the taking of her shoes was some kind of enchantment, some magical penalty that he was bound to exact and she bound to suffer. Images flickered in her mind of barefoot women in mythology. Cinderella leaving a slipper which was the key for her prince to find her. Or, more ominously, of the red shoes that the vain

330

girl had insisted on buying and in which she was forced to dance to her death. Shoes were obviously some kind of archetypal symbol. Isobel gave a little whimper. Nothing seemed to help. Analysing the symbolic power of Murray's act helped her to understand it no more than puzzling over his motives. All she had done was to throw another veil of mystery over Murray's inexplicable act.

Isobel drew up at her house and stepped out reluctantly on to the wet, muddy drive. She picked her way towards the house, feeling the icy chill of the doorstep strike her bare feet. She opened the front door and felt first the prickly wiriness of the door mat, and then the smooth coolness of the parquet. Isobel, barefooted, thinking herself safe, made swiftly for the stairs just as Murray and Philip came out of the kitchen, both wearing their outdoor jackets.

'You back? We're just popping over to the people at Fleet,' Philip said. 'Where are your shoes?'

Absurdly, Isobel blushed, a deep, painful flush. She could not look at Murray, she could not meet Philip's surprised eyes.

'The heel broke,' she said hopelessly. 'I threw them away.'

'You came home barefoot?'

'Yes.'

'But they were new, weren't they? You should have taken them back to the shop.'

'I didn't think of it.'

Philip looked as if he would say more, Isobel's behaviour was clearly irrational. He glanced at Murray. Murray was looking steadily at Isobel's downturned face. He was watching the pulse of colour at the tips of her ears.

'What an odd thing to do,' Philip said gently.

'I was thinking about my writing,' Isobel said lamely.

Philip fell on the excuse with relief. 'Genius, eh?' he said, turning to Murray for corroboration. Murray did not help him at all, did not lift his solemn interrogating gaze from Isobel's discomfort.

'Well, we'll be off,' Philip said cheerily. 'I'll be back in a little while. You should change into some dry socks.'

'I will,' Isobel said quietly.

Philip led the way out of the front door and Murray tore his gaze away from Isobel's ears and went after him. The front door banged shut. Isobel stayed frozen in place, one cold stockinged foot on the bottom step, one hand on the newel post, until she heard the car reverse out of the drive, until she was quite certain that they were gone. Then, and only then, did she crumple into a heap and sit on the bottom step of the stairs and, panic-stricken, strip off her tights with the sodden feet as if they were some terrible evidence that she had to be rid of at once.

Next morning, while Philip and Isobel were eating breakfast, Troy rang. 'I haven't heard from you for a lifetime,' he said. 'I left you alone because I thought you were writing.'

'I am,' Isobel lied. 'But we have the builders in and I have moved to a temporary office, so I've been a bit distracted.'

Troy picked up at once her guarded tone. 'Are you not alone?'

'No.'

'Can you talk?'

'Not really,' Isobel said lightly.

'Shall I call back later?'

'Hang on a minute, I'll look it up,' Isobel said deceitfully. She put the call on hold, and made an apologetic face at Philip. 'Something I have to check, I'll only be a minute.'

She went quickly to the study and picked up the phone. 'I can talk now. But I can't be long.'

'D'you want to call me later?'

'Yes, that would be better.'

'Because I need to talk to you about the new Zelda Vere.' Troy paused. Isobel waited. 'And about us.'

Isobel felt a sensation which was not like desire, it felt more like anxiety. 'I'll call you later,' she said quickly. She would have said anything to escape from this telephone call until she felt more prepared. For some reason her urgency to see

Troy, to be with him, had quite dissipated and she did not know how to express this change. She did not even understand it herself.

'This morning?' he asked.

'Yes!' she said irritably. 'As I said.' She put down the telephone and went back to the kitchen.

A few weeks ago, Philip would have wanted to know who was on the telephone and what they wanted. He would have commented adversely on them telephoning so early, or telephoning Isobel at all. If they were journalists wanting an interview, or her publishers wanting her to attend a festival or some literary event, he would have complained that they never left her alone to write. If it had been a friend or colleague saying that they had been to an event, he would have complained that Isobel was never offered such opportunities. Now he merely glanced up as she came into the kitchen, took a final gulp of tea, put down his cup, and said: 'I have to love you and leave you. Murray wants me to go and see some new clients this morning, Lord and Lady Delby, no less. They're thinking about renovating their old outdoor pool, Murray is hoping he can persuade them to let him build around it and convert it to an indoor one.'

'Will you want the car?'

'Yes. Shall I drop you at Murray's on the way?'

Isobel paused. 'If you're sure that he's happy that I should be there.'

'Course he is,' Philip said simply. He rose from his seat and bent easily to tie his shoelaces. 'He invited you, didn't he?'

'Did he say anything yesterday, after I came home?'

'No. Why should he?'

'I didn't get any work done,' Isobel confessed. 'When he came home to get the file he wanted he would have seen the screen was blank. I didn't do anything yesterday morning.'

'Well, he's not your boss,' Philip said. 'I shouldn't think he even noticed.'

Isobel hesitated. Something in her reluctance to go to

Murray's house finally penetrated into Philip's awareness. He looked up at her and laughed. 'Don't be so silly,' he said bracingly. 'He's a straightforward man, and he knows absolutely nothing about how a writer works. He's offered you his office. He won't care whether you write a great novel or play Tetris Max all day. Why should he care?'

Reluctantly, Isobel went to get her coat. To go to work in Murray's house today she was wearing a long dark navy skirt, a sleek navy jumper, navy tights and a pair of navy shoes with quite high heels.

'You look nice,' Philip said as she came down the stairs. 'Quite dressed up.'

'Oh, you know,' Isobel said inconsequently.

They went out to the car together, Isobel automatically going to the driver's side.

'I can drive,' Philip said.

Isobel turned away. 'You really are miles better. Just seeing you bend so easily to do your shoelaces then made me realise.'

He opened her door for her with a pleasant gesture of courtesy. 'I know,' he said. 'It's remarkable, isn't it?'

Twenty-Eight

Once more Isobel sat on Murray's office chair and stole secretive, sidelong glances at the papers on his desk, at the pink-leaved houseplant in dry earth on the windowsill, at the anonymous biro pens in the stand beside the telephone.

Forcing herself to concentrate she opened the computer and resolutely typed the new title of the new Zelda Vere novel at the top of the page: *The Loving Ghost.* She would have to write a minimum of ten pages for a reasonable-sized chapter, and she had to write three chapters. She decided to start most simply at the beginning.

The light filtered through the simple muslin curtains – the hot summer sunlight filtered through the simple muslin curtains and the brightness woke the child sleeping in the bed – in the handcarved wooden bed. Francine Chavier opened her eyes – her cornflower blue eyes – to another beautiful day in her farmhouse home in Provence. Already she could hear the murmur of voices and the hum of the boiler in the lavender distillery. The familiar exquisite perfume of fresh pure lavender oil blew in at the open window. Francine breathed it without thinking of it, turned back her bedclothes – her crisply laundered sheets and stepped out on to the bare wooden floorboards.

Isobel nodded with satisfaction. The keys rattled comfortingly under her fingers, she liked the clicketty-click of the noise of them which signified progress in her work. She liked the quick, unwatched movements of her fingers. She had learned to touch-type at the insistence of her father, who never thought that she would make a living as an academic, and she had worked as a temporary secretary for most of her summer vacations. The confident patter of her fingers on the keys was as much a pleasure to her as an artist might take in the sensual laying down of paint. Isobel's writing occurred in her brain, in her sharp, trained intellect, and it was expressed in her dancing fingertips on the keyboard.

She wrote on, tracing the child Francine's path through the lavender fields down to the village where she went to school. At the school gate she met her friends, among them Jean-Pierre, the child whose parents owned the lavender fields on the other side of the village, the little boy who had loved her ever since they had first toddled into school side by side.

Isobel nodded. There was no need to linger over the children growing up, and besides she would need to consult a map and a guide book of the region if she were going to write much more. She left a space on the page and went on to their teenage years in the little village. The two children were leaning on a gate, gazing at the rising moon. Now was the time for Francine to express her ambitions and for Jean Pierre to say that all he wanted was for her to love him.

Isobel pushed back from the desk a little and shrugged her shoulders to release the tightness in the tendons. Her back and neck were tense from leaning towards the keyboard. She found that she was not much interested in simple declarations of love. She was a lot more drawn to the obscure, to the ambiguous.

She went through to the kitchen to make herself a cup of coffee. Murray's breakfast things were still on the kitchen table. He had eaten porridge for breakfast, and made real coffee, apparently his craze for Monsooned Malabar was still going strong. There was some coffee left in the jug. Isobel took a clean cup from the shelf and helped herself. He had run out of milk, Isobel had it black and tasted it as a strange and exotic drink.

Isobel, leaning against Murray's kitchen worktop, leisurely considered the device, so popular in literature of the Zelda Vere sort, that one could deeply, deeply desire someone and not know it. Surely no-one in real life could be powerfully beloved, or feel intense unconscious desire, and not know it? She shrugged her tight shoulders. It was just a feature of the genre; she did not need to consider it, she had only to deploy it. She took Murray's coffee back into the study and picked up the telephone to dial Troy.

'Hello,' he said neutrally.

'I'm sorry,' Isobel said quickly. 'About earlier. I didn't mean to be abrupt. It was a bit difficult.'

'What's wrong?' Troy asked. 'Is it Philip?'

'No. Philip's fine. Actually, he's never been better. It's extraordinary how well he is.'

'Is the pool man giving you trouble?'

'Oh God. I mean. No. He's –' Isobel paused. She could not think of a word to describe Murray. 'The work has started,' she said. 'It's terribly noisy. I've borrowed a room in the village so I don't have to try and work at home.'

'Whose room?' Troy asked.

'A friend of mine,' Isobel said mendaciously. 'Her children have all left home. She has a spare room. She said I could use it. She's out at work all day so I'm not in her way at all.' Isobel listened, with some horror, as the facile lies came tripping off her tongue. She was appalled at her ability to lie to Troy, which seemed somehow worse than lying to Philip. But she was appalled also that she needed to lie to him. She could not think why she was avoiding telling him that she was in Murray's house. She was quite determined not to think why she would avoid telling him that she was in Murray's house.

'So, how are you? How's the work going?'

'I was stuck for a moment, but I'm starting now. I'll do a chapter today and then another tomorrow and another by the third day. I'll send it all to you by the middle of next week.'

'Good. I had a meeting with David Quarles. He's really very keen on a new book. I gave him the general feeling of what you would be doing and he said it was just what they hoped of you.'

'Did you talk about money at all?'

'We talked around money,' Troy said precisely. 'I think he'll be up for something like another £250,000.'

'Oh,' Isobel said. Absurdly, she felt disappointed. Only a few months ago it would have been a fortune beyond her greatest hopes, but now she saw quite correctly that it was £100,000 less than her last novel.

'I didn't expect them to pay the same as the first one, remember that was at an auction, the others forced the price up. And they won't see a return on the first novel until they go into paperback next year, and even then perhaps not for five or six years.'

'Should we leave it till next year, then?'

'It's up to you,' Troy said. 'My feeling is that you're on a roll and we should go with it.'

'Yes,' Isobel said. 'And £250,000 is a lot of money.'

'It is,' Troy said.

There was a brief silence. 'I'll send you the chapters when they're ready,' Isobel said awkwardly.

'You could bring them up,' Troy said, his voice as neutral as hers. 'You could bring them up and stay overnight if you like.'

Isobel shifted slightly in Murray's padded office chair. For some reason she felt acutely uncomfortable talking to Troy like this, on Murray's phone, in Murray's office.

'I can't really say now,' Isobel said weakly.

There was a pause. 'Isobel, I think you should tell me what's wrong,' Troy said firmly. 'I get the sense that something is very badly wrong and you're doing me no favours by not telling me.'

'Nothing,' Isobel said promptly.

'You don't owe me anything, you know,' he said tightly. 'You can just say if you don't want to come and stay. You can just say if you don't want to be Zelda Vere again. You can say if you don't want to write her novel. It's no skin off my nose. I've got other clients, I'll still make a living.'

'It's not that,' she said. 'I do want to be her, I do want to do the book. I do want to see you again. But everything is so odd here at the moment.'

'Odd in what way?' he demanded.

'Philip is so much better, and Murray and he are such good friends . . .'

'You're feeling left out?'

'No! It's not that. Philip is talking about going back to work, he wants a freelance job.'

'Well, that's a good thing, isn't it?'

'Yes.'

There was another silence.

'I don't see what the problem is,' Troy said patiently. 'If Philip is better and everything is going well?'

'No,' Isobel said. 'It's just that everything is different.'

'Because Philip is no longer an invalid?'

'Yes,' she said, grasping at that explanation. 'Because he's like he used to be.'

Troy, in his office in London, thought rapidly what that might mean. 'You mean you've had sex with him again.'

Isobel suddenly realised that the renewal of her sex life with Philip had been nothing compared with Murray stealing her shoes. At the insight she gave a little gasp of horror.

'I suppose you want to get back together with him again,' Troy stated flatly.

'Yes,' Isobel said hesitantly, thinking only of how imposs-ible it was to concentrate on anything but the issue of the missing shoes. 'I think I do.'

Troy took a moment. 'Look, that's fine,' he said generously. 'I told you there was no obligation. You mustn't feel awkward about it, or anything like that. That's absolutely fine. We had a wonderful, surprising time together, and maybe we will again, maybe not. But we're both grown-ups, Isobel. There were no promises. There was never a contract.'

339

'Yes,' Isobel said weakly. 'If I gave an impression . . .'

'We both gave the impression of people behaving in a quite extraordinary way,' Troy said gently. 'You made no promises, Isobel. I have no complaints.'

Troy took a breath and changed gear to take control of the situation. 'Now. Let's deal with one thing at a time. You finish the chapters, get the work done, that's the important thing. Let's get the business fixed. Then you either send them up to me or bring them yourself, I don't mind, whatever is the most efficient. I'll take them into David and get the best deal I can for you, and then we'll see how we feel. It's all going to take about a month, all right? We can see how we feel at the end of March.'

'It's not really about Philip,' Isobel volunteered.

'What?'

Isobel thought of trying to explain to Troy about her missing shoes, of Murray's soft breath on her face, of his mouth coming so close that she thought he would kiss her.

'What's it about then?' Troy asked.

'Nothing, really. Did you say the end of March?'

'Yes.'

'The pool will nearly be finished by then,' Isobel said irrelevantly. 'I'll be back in my office. The pool men will have gone.'

Troy hesitated. 'I'll arrange for you to have the rest of the money for the pool,' he promised, thinking that was what she meant.

'Yes,' she said. 'Thank you.'

Isobel completed chapter one of the Zelda Vere novel, and started the first three paragraphs of chapter two. Then she left the desk and went into Murray's kitchen. She sat at his breakfast table with his bowl before her and his empty coffee cup at her right hand. Open on the table before his place was the book she had lent him: Trevelyan's *English Social History*. He had got as far as page ten. Marking his place was a letter headed 'Sunshine Pools USA', notifying him of a closing-down sale at a swimming-pool suppliers in Los Angeles. They were selling the entire business as a going concern, or selling showroom, offices and equipment in lots. 'Once-in-a-lifetime opportunity for the right go-getter,' it said.

The phone rang. Isobel jumped as if she had been caught doing something wrong. She hurried into the study and answered it uncertainly, reading the strange number from the base of the telephone. It was not a caller for Murray, but Murray himself.

'Excuse me troubling you, Isobel, but Philip asked me to call you and see if you want me to take you home for lunch? He's staying on with the Delbys but I'm coming past my house in about ten minutes.'

'Thank you,' Isobel said unsteadily. 'Yes, I should like to go home. I'm finished writing for today.'

'I thought it best that I should warn you I was coming,' he said.

'Thank you,' Isobel said with affected coolness.

'You are welcome. Ten minutes then,' he said politely, and rang off.

Isobel saved her work, and copied the chapters on to her disk to take away so that Murray could not spy on her as she had spied on him. She sat for a few moments in Murray's office chair. Then she thought she should wait for him on the doorstep, so that they were not alone in the house together, which would be awkward after the experience of yesterday. She put on her coat and went out of the house, closing the front door behind her. In a few moments his car came up the drive and stopped beside her. Isobel walked towards the car, feeling her high-heeled shoes shift on the gravel, opened the passenger door and got in. Murray gave her a pleasant neutral smile.

'How is it going with the Delbys?' Isobel asked quickly, to preclude any more intimate conversation.

'Like a house on fire,' he said, turning the car. 'I left Philip and them discussing colour schemes. They're going to go for a conservatory building over the pool, and a complete reno-vation of the pool. Can you believe it? It's a huge project.'

'Oh, well done,' Isobel exclaimed.

'A lot of it is thanks to Philip,' Murray said. 'They have a really old pool and they wanted to reline it with a modern one and buy some modern features. But Philip did this complete riff –'

'Complete what?'

'Riff.' Murray saw her uncomprehending face. 'Um. Riff. Talk. He got really excited about it and said it was a treasure and that it would be an act of vandalism to convert it and that it should be lovingly modernised and renovated.'

'Why, how old is it?'

'Built in 1930 and completely hideous,' he said briskly. 'But they started off by looking for the cheapest offer they could find, we were the third company to quote, and now they think they're the National Trust. Philip is promising them a photo spread in the pages of *Country Living*. He says it's a spectacular example of Art Deco.'

'And is it?' Isobel asked, amused.

'Nah,' Murray said comfortably. He reached into his pocket and drew out a packet of cigarettes, lifted it to his mouth and pulled out a cigarette with his lips. He put the car's glowing lighter to the end of the cigarette and then suddenly said: 'Sorry, you don't mind, do you?'

'I don't mind,' Isobel lied. 'I didn't know Philip knew about Art Deco and pools.'

Murray gave her a grin. 'He doesn't,' he said. 'Well, he didn't. But he does now. I briefed him as we went up the drive.'

'So if you're the one that knows about it, why didn't you do the talking?'

Murray slowed a little to turn into the narrow lane to Isobel's house. 'I told you,' he reminded her. 'Because he's got class. When I talk about Art Deco pools and sympathetic restoration I sound like a wide boy. When Philip does it he sounds like a gentleman. They loved him. They'll probably ask him to stay to lunch.'

Isobel was seized with a sense of complete panic that she

might have to have lunch with Murray on their own. 'Oh, they wouldn't do that, would they? Ask the pool man to lunch?'

Murray shot an amused sideways smile at her. 'You did,' he pointed out.

'I didn't mean . . .' Isobel, flustered, broke off. 'I meant, people like that . . . I didn't mean that pool men aren't . . .'

'I know exactly what you meant,' Murray said happily.

They drew up outside Isobel's house. Isobel got out of the car but hesitated with the door still open as Murray kept the engine running.

'Aren't you coming in?' she invited, dreading his acceptance.

He gave her a grin as if he had caught her out. 'Asking the pool man for lunch?' And then when Isobel said nothing, he shook his head. 'I can't, I've got to go and catch up on some paperwork. D'you want to use the office tomorrow?'

'If I may,' Isobel said.

'Fine,' he replied. He waited for her to slam the door. She hesitated for a moment. The moment stretched. Murray looked at her in her navy skirt and top and her navy high-heeled shoes. Isobel looked back at him. Then she slammed the passenger door as he raised a hand to her and drove away.

Twenty-Nine

Isobel completed the third sample chapter of *The Loving Ghost*, now renamed *Kiss of Death*, and e-mailed it to Troy as she had promised. She had worked for most of the week in Murray's office and had held herself to a strict regime of three hours work and then returning home for the rest of the day. She did not go upstairs in Murray's house again. She had a superstitious sense that something would have been left for her, some sort of present, invitation, reward or trap. Something would have been set up to trace her, if she put so much as one foot on the stairs up to Murray's bedroom. And she did not want to be rewarded, invited, or entrapped by Murray.

She heard nothing from Troy except a brief note acknowledging the arrival of her e-mail. But in the middle of the second week when she and Philip were at dinner he said:

'Murray put his halfway bill in today, Isobel. Can you write him a cheque?'

'How much for?' she asked.

'We owe him £19,000,' he said.

'I'll have to get some money transferred from the savings account,' she said. 'It'll take a couple of days.'

'How much money do we have at the moment?'

It was such an unusual question for Philip to ask that Isobel had no answer prepared. 'I don't know, I'd have to look at the bank statement.'

'Have you got it? Could I see it?'

'It's with the accountant,' Isobel said hurriedly. 'I sent everything off to him the other day.'

'And you don't know how much you've got in the savings account?' he asked critically.

Isobel managed a smile. 'I'm sure it's enough. Why did you want to know?'

'Because of the business evaluation. I've got a man doing the audit and we'll have the figures by the end of the week. I want to be able to buy into the business as soon as we can. As it is, the picture changes almost every day. His business is really doing very well. We want to get in on it as soon as we can, before he lands a really huge contract and the value of the business goes way beyond our means.'

'Yes,' Isobel said hesitantly. 'D'you have any idea how much it is worth?'

'We'll get an exact figure at the end of the week. But I would guess the business must be worth about £500,000 to £600,000.'

Isobel gasped. 'Murray?'

Philip laughed at her stunned face. 'The Delby contract alone is worth £200,000,' he said. 'And his house is owned by the business, counts as one of the assets. The pool at Fleet I know is worth £60,000 and there's that other one at Valley Farm. He's got another couple of possibles that I haven't seen yet and two definite orders on the coast. It adds up very fast.'

'But how much would we have to find to buy into the business?' Isobel asked.

'I'd like us to go for half,' Philip said. 'I'd feel secure with a complete fifty-fifty split and then if we ever disagree about anything, like where we want the business to go, then we know that I can't be overruled. I don't want to work for him in his business – much as I like the man. I want this to be at least half my business.'

'But you and he agreed that you wouldn't have to work full time,' Isobel reminded him.

'We're going to pay ourselves an hourly rate,' Philip said. 'We'll share the profits and draw them out of the company as and when we agree to do so. But for the day-to-day work we'll pay ourselves a rate. So that's fair.'

Isobel nodded.

'So how much have we got in savings and investments?' Philip asked. 'I think we should cash it in.'

'I'd have to look,' Isobel repeated feebly.

'Well counting the house, which must be worth about £500,000, we must have assets, bonds and Peps and saving schemes of something like another £100,000, mustn't we?'

'Yes. Something like that,' Isobel said, keeping her voice as light as possible. 'But we wouldn't mortgage the house, would we?'

Philip shrugged. 'It's just exchanging one asset for another. I'd be perfectly happy to take out a loan against this house to buy into Murray's business which is making a turnover, a *turnover*, mind, of something like £300,000 a year.'

Isobel nodded. 'When will we know how much we should pay?'

'The end of the week,' Philip said. 'Can you ask the accountant how much we've got in shares and bonds? Get a general figure? And ask him to have a look at which ones we should sell to raise something around £300,000.'

'I'll ask him,' Isobel said. 'He's going to ask me if we're sure.'

Philip grinned. 'You've seen the work that Murray's getting. I want a slice of that business, Isobel. We're going to make a fortune.'

Isobel made no pretence of telephoning the accountant. She knew there was little more than three thousand pounds in their savings account, and no shares and no bonds left at all. There was a small insurance policy on her life, but no-one would insure Philip after his illness had been diagnosed. Instead, she telephoned Troy.

'Hello, it's me.'

'Hi,' he said. 'I got the chapters printed and biked them

over to David Quarles this morning. They really are very good, Isobel.'

'Thank you,' she said.

'Is something wrong?'

'I was just calling to ask you to arrange a transfer of funds to me,' she said with careful politeness.

'Swimming-pool money?' he asked.

'Yes. They're halfway through. You might as well transfer the whole payment to me. They're finishing ahead of time.'

'That's worth paying for, I should think,' Troy said politely.

'They've been very good.'

Isobel heard the click of his pen cap. 'How much would you want this time?'

'I think £40,000, say £50,000.'

'I'll get it done today. It'll be five days, remember.'

'Yes, that's fine,' she said.

'And how are you?' Troy asked pleasantly.

'I'm very well.'

'And Philip?'

'He's very well.'

'Good.' Troy paused in case anything more was forthcoming. 'Would you like to come up for lunch when I have an offer from the publishers that we can discuss?'

'Yes,' Isobel said. 'That would be lovely.'

'I'll call you as soon as I hear. Next week some time, I should think.'

'Thank you,' said Isobel. 'Actually, there is something else.'

'What's that?'

'Philip wants to make an investment.'

'An investment?' Troy said guardedly.

'Yes. He wants to buy into a partnership, he wants to buy into a business. He feels so well he wants to get back to work.'

'Yes, you said he was so much better.'

'I have to find the capital to buy him in,' Isobel said. 'He wants to buy into the pool business.'

'The pool?' Troy said, thinking for a moment that he had misheard.

347

'The swimming-pool business.'

'Well, it's a pity he didn't think of it before, you could have got it at cost price,' Troy said facetiously. 'But at least you know that the profit rates are tremendous.'

'We do know that actually,' Isobel said a little stiffly. 'We're getting the business properly audited and Philip wants to buy in as a full partner. He wants fifty-fifty.'

There was a little silence while Troy absorbed this.

'Hello?' Isobel said.

'You're buying half of the pool man's business?'

'Yes. Why not?

'I'm just wondering if this is such a good idea?'

'I think it is,' Isobel said. 'He really does get on extraordinarily well with Murray, and the business is clearly doing well. And Philip does have a great talent for selling, he always did. And if he could make some money it'd take the pressure off me.'

'The pressure is off you,' Troy pointed out sharply. 'With the second Zelda Vere novel earning something around £250,000 and her first novel earning £350,000, you don't have any pressure any more. It's properly invested, it's earning you a reasonable income. You're out of the woods. Can't Philip just work for the man, if he likes the business so much?'

'He wants to be a partner, not an employee,' Isobel said with dignity.

'Well, so do I,' Troy said impatiently. 'But alas for me, I have to earn a living. Can't you tell Philip that he can earn his way into the business? Start at the bottom and work up?'

'He's sixty-one!' Isobel glared up. 'He's not worked for ten years! He's hardly going to walk into a job tomorrow! He can't start at the bottom and work up, he'll be retired before he's got anywhere. This is an opportunity he can buy into where he can use his skills and enjoy himself and make some reasonable money. I'm not going to tell him "no", just when he's starting to feel well again.'

'Of course,' Troy said, retreating from Isobel's anger. 'And it's your choice completely. But I would be failing in my duty as your agent if I didn't advise you to get proper independent advice.'

'Oh, don't!' Isobel said impatiently. 'Don't get all dignified. We're getting proper advice. I told you, we're having the whole thing valued. We're doing it right, of course. But if Philip wants it, then it's only fair that the Zelda Vere money should buy it for him.'

'What sort of money are you talking about?' Troy asked cautiously.

'About £300,000,' Isobel said very quietly.

There was a silence.

'Isobel, that is *all* the money from the second book,' Troy pointed out, aghast.

'I know,' she said tightly.

'That is everything you will earn on Book Two and more.'

'It's the proper price for the business.'

'What if it goes wrong? What if people suddenly stop buying pools?'

'I've seen the orders,' Isobel said. 'It really is doing well.'

'Say the pool man drops dead. Say Philip gets sick. What then?'

'Then we're no worse off than we were before I was Zelda,' she said. 'But this time Philip will know where the money has gone. He'll understand about it, and I won't have to lie and lie to him and pretend that we're OK when we're not.'

'But it's your money this time,' Troy pointed out. 'And you've got to earn it yet, remember. You've got a whole new novel to write to earn the money and you have to do this work in secret, and at the same time as your other writing. Then you have to promote the novel, in secret again. This isn't his pension and his insurance money put by over the years, this is hard-earned money that *you* have to make and make it quick. You can't throw it all down in a gamble that Philip is well enough to run a tough business in a competitive market?'

'Yes I can,' Isobel said staunchly.

Troy, in his London office, thought for a moment how very

much he disliked the way she stood on principle. A mere second, a breath later, and he knew that the stubbornness was a part of Isobel that he admired, a characteristic of hers unlike anyone else's that he knew. And she might sound like a predictable, middle-class housewife sometimes, but he had seen her naked, he had seen her with her head thrown back, quite given way to passion. She had whispered things to him that no woman had ever said before, she had led him on to behaviour which he would never have dared without her.

'I don't want to quarrel with you,' he said gently. 'You must do what you want to do. I just don't want to see you give something up that has cost you, and is going to cost you, a great deal of time and effort. You're earning this money all on your own, Isobel. I don't see why you should hand it over to Philip and the pool man to play with.'

'Because Philip supported me when I started my writing,' Isobel said passionately. 'Because he's so hopeful and excited at starting his life again. Because I told him that the money was there when it wasn't, and I can't tell him the truth now, not now when he really needs it. Because I *want* to give it to him.'

'You won't have the lump sum until you've signed the contract for the second book,' Troy reminded her. 'And even then you'll have to deliver the complete manuscript to get £125,000.'

'I know,' she said. 'I thought I'd mortgage the house and pay off the mortgage when the money comes in from the new Vere novel.'

'Mortgage your house?' He was astounded.

'Why not?'

'I thought you said you'd never mortgage it, I thought you always said that it was your only security.'

'I can always write another book,' Isobel said. 'I can always earn more.'

Troy thought for a moment that she sounded more like Zelda Vere than Isobel Latimer. 'I suppose you can. But you're behind the game instead of in front of it. And that's a danger-ous place to be.'

'I'll catch up,' she said, and this time he knew without doubt that it was Zelda's voice. 'Of course I can catch up.'

Thirty

Work on Isobel and Philip's swimming pool continued rapidly, through days of heavy rain. The builders joked about it being a good thing that it was an indoor job as they sloshed about in greyish mud. Almost nothing remained of the barn but the structural beams and the roof. The wall had been knocked out of one side for the picture window which would look down the hill to the valley below. They had taken out the back wall to allow the digger to drive in. The beautiful old wooden front doors of the barn had been taken away so that the connecting conservatory could come in from the house.

The builders worked under the shelter of the old roof and the driver manoeuvered the little digger in and out of the shell of the building with scoops full of soil, followed by big oblong-shaped rocks. Next the men went into the vast gulf which would be the swimming pool to cut it into precise shape, then they started the work of laying the floor and the walls of the pool.

Isobel and Philip went out every evening, when the men had gone home and the site was silent, to look at the transformation of their barn into something new and very strange. Isobel mourned the loss of the shadowy walls, the half-floor of the granary above, the lovely old wooden shute polished over hundreds of years by sacks sliding down to the floor below; but Philip envisaged the project as it would be, when finished. Where Isobel saw a great cave dug out of the floor of the barn and the walls torn away, he saw a place of light and warmth, lively with the reflection of water on the white ceiling, filled with the plash of water from the fountainhead into the spa pool.

'I do see why you and Murray find it so fascinating,' Isobel said. 'There is something very mystical about making a lake.'

'There is,' Philip agreed. 'And I like the nuts and bolts of it too. The plumbing and the heating. They're interesting technical problems: how to do it, where to site the gear.'

'And what about Murray? What does he like?'

Philip laughed, amused. 'He likes making the money. He's a very astute businessman. But he knows a lot about pools as well. He learns all the time. When he goes to renovate a pool he spends half the day in the local library looking up the history of the house so that he knows what he's going to see. When he builds a new pool he has half a dozen plans in his head before he's even met the owner. He's a huge enthusiast.'

'But why swimming pools?' Isobel asked. 'Why isn't he selling computers, or cars, or anything else?'

Philip shrugged. 'Never asked him.'

'I suppose real men don't talk about motivation,' Isobel teased him.

Philip laughed. 'We just grunt about pipes.'

Every day the pool progressed. Once the digger went away the work was quieter, and Isobel returned to her study and watched the changes through her study window. The low brick wall for the conservatory from house to pool was built and ready for the windows, which were on order. They were delivered and erected like a gigantic kit, which at first looked impossibly large and ugly and then somehow assembled into a pleasing passage from house to barn which Isobel could imagine carpeted and decorated with indoor plants.

Philip came to her with the bill in his hand. 'COD for these guys, I'm afraid.'

'How much?' she asked, opening the drawer where she kept her cheque book.

'There's £4,000 to pay,' he said. 'You've already paid the deposit.'

She wrote the cheque, looking at the several noughts after the four.

'Don't forget we owe Murray his halfway payment.'

'I have it,' she replied. The transfer had come through from Troy as he had promised.

Philip gave her a grin like an indulged boy. 'It looks like an awful lot now,' he said. 'But it *is* adding value to the house. We are going to be awfully pleased with it.'

'I know we are,' Isobel said, smiling in reply. She waited till he had left the room with the cheque and then turned back to the screen and switched on the Zelda novel. She had started chapter four and was working as fast as she could. With money flowing out of the Swiss bank account at the rate that it was going she thought it very important that she should be ready to deliver the new novel as soon as the contract was signed.

Troy rang her to tell her that the contract would be ready within the week on a sunny March day when the daffodils were bobbing around the silver birch trees that lined the lawn. From her study window Isobel could see the open entrance to the barn and, inside, the tops of the heads of the men bobbing around as they were tiling the pool. One of the walls was back in place and the skeletal structure of what would be the sauna and steam room were in place against it. The back wall was finished, built, plastered and mounted with the fountainhead, the circular spa pool below it. Only the third wall was still open. There had been a delay with the windows which still had not arrived, and they were leaving the yawning gaps open until they had finished everything else, so as to have a wide entrance for bringing machinery and equipment in and out.

'I have good news,' Troy said cheerfully. 'The publishers have agreed to pay in two parts. You get about two thirds as soon as we sign, they know that the novel is on the way, and then a third on hardback publication next year. It's unusual but I persuaded them that Zelda needs to buy a house at the Cap d'Antibes for her writing.'

'Oh, does she?' Isobel said, at once diverted. 'How lovely for her.'

'Yes she does,' Troy said. 'I had a weekend over there a couple of weeks ago. It's a most exquisite place, on an outcrop, looking out over the sea. They have this gorgeous house built out over the sea on stilts. You sail your yacht in underneath to tie up and go up the stairs to the living room. It's the perfect writer's retreat. I mentally bought it for Zelda.'

'Oh, she'd love it,' Isobel said. She paused for a moment. 'Who did you go with?' she asked, her voice carefully indifferent.

'Just a couple of guys,' Troy said, equally light.

'Oh?'

'It was the house of a friend of one of them. An artist. He's selling up. If you weren't spending all your money on swimming pools . . .'

'Yes,' Isobel said to silence him.

'You could have bought it,' Troy persevered. 'You could have had a completely different life.'

Isobel said nothing. She looked out her study window and thought of the house built on stilts over the sea, of the Mediterranean sunsets, of being with Troy.

'I find I can't settle,' Troy suddenly exclaimed. 'Since Zelda, and all the rest of it, I can't feel comfortable as I used to. It's as if something has been . . .'

'What?'

'Opened up. Let out. And I can't pretend that it isn't there.'

'It's the same for me in a way,' Isobel acknowledged. 'I discovered a side of me that I didn't know I had. Flamboyant and acquisitive – vulgar, I would have called it before.'

'And now that you know you have this side?' Troy asked. 'What happens now?'

'Oh, now I know, I know what to do,' Isobel said with certainty. 'I have to guard against that side of me. I know that I am capable of immense desire and greed and hunger for all sorts of experiences that simply aren't allowed to me, if I want to continue living here, if I want to lead my life as a wife, as a respected writer, as a member of a rural community. For a few brief weeks I had both. But I'd have got caught.'

She thought of Murray's sideways gleam and his inscrutable silence. She thought for a brief, uncomfortable moment about her missing shoes. 'I did get caught actually,' she said. 'But I think it doesn't matter.'

'You had a look at that side of yourself and put it back in the box again,' Troy suggested.

'Yes.'

'Well, I can't do that,' he said passionately. 'I can't cut myself up into convenient chunks and say I'll only live like this, I'll only acknowledge that bit. I have to experience it. I know it now. I can't leave Zelda in a suitcase and say, that's it, I'll never see her again, I'll never be her again.'

'But you can't have her without me there,' Isobel said simply.

'Why not?' Troy asked. 'You don't want that part of your life, you just said so. If you don't want her, why can't I have her?'

'How could you?' Isobel asked. 'Without me to be her?'

'I could be her,' he said. 'I could be her as well as you.'

'No you can't!' Isobel insisted. 'You can't just take her off and be her on your own.'

'Well, you can't put her away and decide that she's finished with,' Troy argued. 'She's not a character in one of your books. You can't suddenly decide to kill her off. Her clothes are here in my flat, her shoes are here, her hair is here. She's waiting here. I can choose to bring her alive on my own if I want.'

'But she's part of *our* life together,' Isobel protested. 'She's ours. You wouldn't let me bring her home on my own. You said she had to be kept in a box. You said it had to be watertight.'

Troy hesitated. 'I did,' he said unwillingly. 'But I never said to put her away forever. I can't bear the thought of her being put away forever.'

Isobel checked at the desolation in his voice. 'Perhaps we just have to let her go,' she said, as if they were discussing the death of a beloved friend.

'I can't bear it,' Troy said. 'I can't see how I can live my life without her.'

Murray was staying for supper that evening and he and Philip were going down to the pub later to play darts. Isobel sat through dinner with the two of them wondering what Troy was doing in London, how she could convince him that the loss of Zelda was a grief which would have to be borne. The two men invited Isobel to come with them to watch the darts match; but she shook her head. 'I'll have an early night. I've done a lot of work today.'

'Every time I look through the window and see you typing I wonder how you can concentrate,' Murray said. 'So much work! Have you finished the book yet?'

'Oh no,' Isobel said. 'It takes much longer than a few weeks. It takes years.'

Philip put his hand over hers. 'And then she rewrites it four or five times,' he said. 'You think you work hard, Murray, you should see Isobel here. She'll spend all day sometimes worrying about exactly the right word for the right sentence.'

The two men looked at her admiringly. Isobel smiled at Philip, avoiding Murray's gaze.

'It's taken me all this time just to read one book,' Murray said. He reached into his briefcase and put Trevelyan's *English Social History* on the table. 'Could you lend me another one? I really enjoyed that.'

Isobel picked it up. 'I'll look something out for you,' she said vaguely, her mind still on Troy. 'English history again, or shall we go elsewhere?'

'American history?' he asked. 'I don't know anything about America and I'd like to. West Coast, especially.'

She nodded. 'I'll find something.' She took a sudden decision and turned to Philip, keeping her voice deliberately light. 'I had a call from Penshurst Press this morning, about a jacket for a novel. They're reprinting it in a new edition and they want me to see the new version.'

'Oh, yes?' he asked. 'Paying an extra royalty, are they?'

'A little,' she said. 'You know you never make much. I thought I'd go up and have a look at it tomorrow. I might stay overnight.' Carefully, she did not look towards Murray at all.

'Why not?' Philip said. 'And I don't need Mrs M. to sleep in, I'm really well these days.'

'I'll keep an eye on him,' Murray promised her. 'I'll ring you if anything goes wrong. Where will you be?'

'At the Frobisher Hotel, where I always stay,' Isobel said smoothly. She looked up and met his eyes for one moment and saw a gleam of amusement, the recognition from one cheat to another. So might a professional poker player acknowledge the presence of another hustler, someone else who could take a cut. Isobel looked away, breaking the unspoken confederacy. 'I'll call here at six o'clock to make sure that everything is OK.'

'Yes, do that,' Philip said. 'Or I can call you.'

'I don't know what time I'll get in,' she said quickly. 'It's easier if I call you.'

'Let her call you,' Murray advised Philip confidentially. 'Set her mind at rest that you're OK in the evening, and then she can go out on the town with the girls.'

Isobel smiled thinly. 'Hardly.'

'Oh, all right,' Philip said. 'If that's what you want.'

Philip had said he would take her to the station in the morning but a call came for him from Lord and Lady Delby, who had found some kind of painted fresco underneath the wallpaper of their pool room. Philip wanted to see it.

'I'll run you down to the station,' Murray offered.

'Thank you,' Isobel said coolly.

Together they went out to his car and he held open the passenger door. Isobel got in and they drove in unbroken silence to the station.

'Have a lovely time, won't you?' Murray said provocatively, as she got out.

Isobel hesitated and looked back into the car. Murray's face was in shadow, he looked as if he were smiling.

'It's not exactly a lovely time going to the publishers to look at book jackets,' she remarked.

He leaned forward, the gleam of his smile was very apparent. 'I had forgotten that was what you were doing,' he said. 'Of course. The publishers.'

Isobel held his gaze and nodded.

He gave her a quick wink. 'I'll meet the train tomorrow if you tell Philip what time when you ring this evening.'

Isobel straightened up. 'Thank you, but I expect Philip will want to meet me himself.'

'Sure,' he said. 'Whatever you want, Isobel. You know that.'

Thirty-One

Isobel rang Troy from Waterloo station. She had to half-shout to be heard over the noise of the station announcements.

'I had to come,' she said. 'I'm sorry. I just had to see you.'

Even in the noisy concourse she could hear the sharp intake of his breath. 'You had to see me?'

She realised the potency of what she had said. 'Yes,' she said helplessly. 'I had to.'

'Oh well, come,' he said, recovering. 'Come over straight away. I can take the rest of the day off.'

Isobel joined the queue for the taxis, thinking how only a few weeks ago she would have been in a haze of delight at the prospect of spending the day, and the night as well, with Troy. Now she felt nothing but anxiety as to what they would say to each other and how he would be, and a dread that he might try to seduce her to return to the erotic delirium of the days on tour, tempt her into being Zelda again.

She paid the taxi outside Troy's house and pressed the doorbell for the office. The intercom buzzed her in and Isobel smiled tentatively at the beautiful girl at the reception desk. 'He said go straight in,' the girl said with blank unfriendliness. Isobel went past the desk into Troy's office.

Troy was seated behind his desk, talking on the telephone, he gave her a big smile and waved her to a chair as he finished the call. He said, 'Yes. Absolutely. Love you,' brightly into the receiver and then hung up. Isobel wondered who he had been talking to with such warmth as he leaped up from the chair, took both her hands in his and kissed her: one cheek and then the other. 'You look fabulous,' he said. 'Very country and fresh and clean.'

Isobel recoiled slightly from the bright insincerity of his touch. 'You make me sound like a detergent.'

'Spring fresh,' he said. 'Ready to hang out to dry.'

Isobel sank down into Troy's low chair again.

'Coffee?' he asked.

'Could we go upstairs to your flat?' she asked, glancing at the open door to the reception desk.

'Good idea,' he said cheerfully, and led the way out of the office into the small hall and up the stairs to his flat above.

Isobel had half-hoped and half-dreaded that he would take her in his arms as soon as the door was shut behind them, but he merely led the way to the kitchen and poured coffee into the filter.

'I've got this new coffee,' he remarked. 'Monsooned Malabar. It seems that they leave the beans on the drying tables . . .'

'I know,' Isobel said rudely. 'I know all about it.'

'Oh.' He got out his French coffee cups in silence.

'Can I go and look at her things?' Isobel asked.

He glanced up, surprised. 'Of course you can.'

Isobel went down the short corridor to the spare bedroom. She opened the door. At once she could smell the evocative scent of Zelda: expensive, discreet, haunting. It summoned up the handful of nights that Isobel had been Zelda or had been with Zelda when this scent had been lingering on Troy's smooth skin.

The curtains were drawn, the room was in mysterious, shadowy daylight. Isobel opened the drawers of the dressing table and there in the top one was Zelda's collection of cosmetics, with the little brushes and wands laid neatly side by side. Next drawer down was her underwear, the embroidered blue set of which Troy had his version, and also a set in palest yellow, and one in cream. Troy had wrapped them in lightly scented tissue paper, they were like waiting Christmas presents, hidden away. The next drawer held unopened boxes of expensive unused tights and stockings.

Isobel closed the drawers and went over to the wardrobe. She could not see the beautiful clothes, they were shrouded in their covers and clearly labelled in Troy's neat handwriting: yellow day suit, pink day suit, blue dress size 12, and then the dress he had worn: blue dress size 16. Beneath the rack of clothes were Zelda's shoes with red velvet trees inserted in some, and others packed neatly with tissue paper to keep their perfect shape. The large pair that Troy used was arranged as prettily as the others.

Isobel regarded Zelda's shoes as if they were somehow enchanted. If she stepped into them she would become a different person, live a different life, have a different future. She thought of the red dancing shoes that the girl was tempted to wear in the fairy story and how they forced her to dance and dance away, out of her life, away from the people who loved her, away from the village where she belonged – to her death when she died from an excess of dancing in pretty shoes.

Isobel closed the wardrobe door and leaned back against it as if she were holding it shut against someone pushing to come out. She had a brief vision of herself in one of Zelda's lovely suits, perhaps the yellow one. She saw herself walking down a staircase, a man below looking up admiringly at her long legs in the silky stockings, at the sway of her hips, Zelda's signature sway, as she glided down. The staircase in her mind was rather small for such a film-star descent and then she realised that, incongruously, the imaginary staircase was the one in Murray's house, and the man looking up was –

Troy stood in the doorway, the coffee cups and saucers in his hands, watching her holding the wardrobe doors shut. 'Do you want to try something on?' he offered.

Isobel shook her head, stepped away from the wardrobe. 'I don't know what to do with the clothes,' she said. 'I suppose we'll have to do a second tour for the second book?'

He nodded. 'Yes. If you want to. You don't have to. A

second book takes less of a push. They might not mind if you didn't want to do it.'

'I'd have to see. It'd be next year, wouldn't it?'

He nodded. 'Early next summer. In time to catch the holiday reading trade.'

Isobel sipped her coffee, consciously resisting the temptation to sit on the little stool before the dressing table and open the makeup drawer. 'It depends,' she said vaguely.

'On what?'

'On how Philip is, on how his new business is doing, on how my other writing is going. I mustn't neglect that, and I am finding it very hard to write in both styles.'

'You want to go back to the life you had before Zelda,' he observed.

She shot a swift, guilty look at him. 'Yes, I suppose so. Yes, I do.'

Troy was not in the least disturbed. 'Well, that was the plan. You were being Zelda so that you could lead your life as Isobel Latimer with a bit more comfort and a bit more financial security. You've achieved what you wanted. You're where you wanted to be.'

'But the experience en route . . .'

He waited.

'. . . was very surprising,' Isobel finished weakly.

He smiled. 'For me too.'

There was a brief silence.

'You're not tempted?' he asked. 'Being here, with her things?' He opened the wardrobe door, took out a hanger at random and pulled off the cover. It was the delicious dark navy cocktail dress. The dark navy beading gleamed in the dim light, the lining of the skirt rustled softly. Troy draped it over the double bed with a seductive whisper of sound. Isobel regarded it solemnly as if it were more than a dress, as if it were a doorway to another life altogether.

'Of course I'm tempted,' she said slowly. 'But I don't know where it would take me.'

'That's exactly what temptation means to me,' he said. 'Not

knowing where it would take me. It's not the thing in itself, though that's always very pleasant. But it's not putting on the dress, or watching you put it on. It's not me being Zelda nor you being her. It's where it takes us next that intrigues me.'

Isobel took a small, involuntary step backwards and felt the dressing-table top press against the back of her thighs, halting her retreat. 'I don't want to go anywhere next,' she said. 'I have to stop where I am.'

Troy smiled a wistful smile. 'Ah. That was my impression over the last few weeks.'

He picked up the hanger and gave the dress a little shake, as if to blow away the dust of rejection, of disappointment. He slid the cover over the top and zipped it up. He returned it to the wardrobe and shut the door. The gentle clunk was a very final sound.

With unspoken accord they left the room together and went through to Troy's living room. Two empty bottles of Roederer champagne stood on the table, and a couple of glasses, one with a trace of crimson lipstick on the rim. 'Sorry about the mess,' Troy said, picking up the glasses and dropping the bottle in the wastepaper bin.

'What will you do?' Isobel asked, going at once to the centre of her anxiety.

'In what sense?'

'What will you do without her?'

Troy hesitated. 'I shall continue as I was before her, I suppose,' he said. 'I shall miss her. I shall miss knowing you in that way too. I shall miss our time together, it was exceptional.'

Isobel nodded.

'But I'm quite happy,' Troy said. 'I shall do as you have done, I suppose. Put the whole experience away in some part of my imagination and get on with my life. Now and then I may pause and have a look at it, remember what it was like, and then put it away again. I don't expect to find another Zelda, a new one.'

'No,' Isobel said quickly. 'You couldn't reproduce it, could you? You couldn't do it again.'

Troy's expression was veiled. 'It was unique.'

'And you wouldn't try,' Isobel pressed him. 'You wouldn't revive Zelda without me? She was something we completely shared, we'd have to be together if she was there. You wouldn't be her on your own?'

Troy hesitated. 'I don't see why I shouldn't, if I wanted to,' he said carefully. 'It's not as if she were your copyright, Isobel.'

'I'm not claiming ownership!' Isobel cried. 'I just can't bear the thought of you being her without me here. I dread it, I've been thinking and thinking about it and it is quite horrendous!'

Unconsciously she gestured towards the dirty glasses. Troy did not shift his gaze from her face.

'Why?' he asked tightly.

'I think of you in dreadful clubs, and with awful men, female impressionists and what-d'you-call-them, cross-dressers, and a whole muddle about who is what exactly. And it seems so dreadfully . . .'

'Dreadfully what?'

'Dreadfully vulgar,' she whispered, her eyes on his set face.

He smiled but there was no warmth. 'Don't you think you're being a tad judgmental?' he asked. 'What seems vulgar to you might be just fine to me. I think I have to be free to live my own life,' Troy observed, an edge of hardness at the back of his calm voice. 'As you live yours. You have made your choices and I will make mine. You don't want to be with me and taste some experiences – that's fine, that's your choice. But equally, your decision not to participate can hardly preclude my choice. You can decide to cut yourself off, to cut yourself out, but you cannot also cut me out too.'

Isobel looked quite dashed by the formality of his language. 'Why are we talking like this?' she whispered. 'I just really want you not to be Zelda any more. Won't you promise me that you won't be her ever again?'

'To protect me?' Troy asked.

She nodded.

'To protect her?'

She nodded again. 'I just want the whole thing to stop,' she said. 'We started it together and we took it further than we meant. I was really a part of that. Looking back now I know that it was because I was so desperately unhappy with Philip. But now Philip's so much better . . .' She broke off, seeing the sudden flare of suppressed anger in Troy's face.

'Now Philip's so much better you don't need this outlet any more,' he said sharply. 'And so you want to stop. That is of course your right. As you say, it was a relief for you then, one you don't need any more. So you are right to stop. But in addition, you want me to stop too.'

Guiltily, Isobel nodded.

The angry look suddenly left Troy's face. 'Oh, Isobel,' he said affectionately. 'You're very disarming when you're so honest. But really, I can't live my life on the basis of whether you're getting on well with your husband or not.'

She put down her cup and saucer on the low table next to the empty champagne glasses. The cherry lipstick stain was like a scarlet crescent moon. 'I see that,' she said unwillingly. 'But it is also true that we created her together and I want us to agree to stop together. You can go on and do something else, anything else you like, with someone else. I don't expect to control your life. But I do feel that I have a right to a say in her. When I am writing in my study on my own, I am her then. I write as her. She is still inside my head. I don't think you can just run off with her. She is me then, and I am her.'

'She is our shared ghost,' he suggested.

She nodded. 'I want her to finish this novel and earn the money and then go away and never be heard of again.'

'But part of me is now her, just as part of you is her while you are writing. You may not need her any more except for her writing. But I do. I still need what she gives me,' Troy said.

Isobel looked at him pleadingly. 'Can't you do without?'

'Why should I?'

'Because I'm asking. Because we did make her together. She's half mine, after all.'

Troy shook his head. 'You are making a claim to ownership again.'

'Oh, so what if I am?' Isobel demanded, suddenly driven beyond the language of courtesy.

Troy's look was hard, unflinching. 'If you are going to claim that you own her, that she's something that can be owned, you *are* speaking of her as a commodity, as a cake which we can cut up and share: a slice for you, a slice for the publishers, a slice for me. You have made her into a thing, not a person, not a ghost. And to me, that is *far* more vulgar than anything that might ever go on in a nightclub.'

Isobel looked guilty. 'Yes, I see.'

'Is she an object that we made that we can box up or cut up or shut up, or is she an identity that we created, as valid as Isobel Latimer and Troy Cartwright?' Troy challenged her.

'If I say she's a person?' Isobel queried.

'Then she has her life to lead.'

'If I say she's a thing?'

'Then you're no better than all the rest who take a woman like you and cut her up into shares: her writing talent for the publishers, ten per cent to me, ninety per cent to Philip; her caring ability, one hundred per cent for Philip. Her sexuality and her love of life? We don't want it at all; one hundred per cent put in a box. No-one wants the whole woman, nobody even wants to see her. And it was that very thing, being sliced into pieces and half of you being unwanted, that made you so unhappy before we even came up with Zelda. I thought that the whole point of her was that she restored to you the parts of you that you had denied to be a good wife to a sick husband?'

'And for you?' Isobel returned the challenge. 'What did she bring to you?'

Troy turned away so that she could not see his face. 'Oh,

what does it matter now?' he said sulkily. 'Since you say that she has to go?'

Isobel had an uncomfortable lunch with Troy at the neighbouring bistro but did not stay for the afternoon or the night. When they went back to his flat for coffee she told him that there were things she had to do at home and he politely ignored the overnight bag which she had left in the hall by the front door. He rang through to his office and asked the receptionist to order Isobel a taxi and he carried her bag down to the car when it arrived.

'Let me have everything you're writing as soon you can,' he said. 'Just first draft. I want to see where you're going. You don't have to dot all the i's and cross the t's, I just want a general idea of the arc of the story from beginning to end.'

'I've never sent you anything half-baked,' Isobel protested.

'It's different with this,' he said shortly. 'I have good reasons to see it at once.'

'Well, it's nearly written now,' Isobel said. 'I could send you the first draft within a couple of weeks. But you couldn't show it to anybody, it's not ready for publication. It needs another draft, possibly two.'

'I just want to see it,' Troy said. 'A couple of weeks would be great.'

He kissed her, a polite London kiss, one cheek and then the other, with no warmth, no caress hidden behind the slight brushing of lip against skin. Isobel put her hands on his forearms and held him for a moment. 'I am sorry that it was like this in the end,' she said. 'I did really . . .'

He smiled, not letting her finish the statement, whatever it was that 'she did really'. 'See you soon,' he said lightly, held the door open as she got into the back of the cab and then slammed it gently shut.

Thirty-Two

Isobel rang Philip from Waterloo station, as soon as she saw the time of her train displayed on the departures board. Mrs M. answered the phone. 'I was just calling to say that I'm coming home early,' Isobel said. 'I'm not staying up overnight. I'll be home in time for dinner.'

'The boys were going out for dinner,' Mrs M said indulgently. 'Something to celebrate, apparently.'

Isobel curbed her irritation, and did not allow herself to ask Mrs M. what they were celebrating. 'Is Philip there?' she asked.

'He went down to Murray's house. They went down together. Doing some paperwork, they said.'

'I'll need to be picked up from the station,' Isobel said. 'Could you phone Philip for me and ask him to meet the train. I'll be on the three o'clock.'

'Of course,' Mrs M. said. 'Shall I leave a salad for you? Or will you be eating out with the boys?'

Isobel reflected for the moment on the complete absurdity of her sixty-one-year-old husband and his forty-five-year-old friend being referred to as 'the boys' by a woman who was herself in her thirties. In the eighteenth century these would have been elderly men, in the mediaeval period they would have been patriarchs. In any time before the nineteenth century, given that she was working class and fertile, Mrs M. herself would probably have been dead. Isobel found that she was speculating on the death of her housekeeper with questionable relish. 'Do you know where "the boys" are going for dinner?' she asked.

'Maison Rouge,' Mrs M. said. 'They asked me to book a table at eight.'

The Maison Rouge was an expensive restaurant in the nearby town of Fielding. Isobel raised her eyebrows. 'They must have something to celebrate,' she remarked. 'I'll decide when I see Philip. You needn't leave anything for me, I can fend for myself.'

'All right then,' Mrs M. said agreeably. 'I'll tell him to meet you off the three o'clock.'

Isobel half-expected Murray's car when she came out of the station into the drab March afternoon, but it was only their car parked opposite the entrance with Philip at the wheel.

'Didn't stay overnight then?' he remarked.

'It hardly took a moment to look at the jacket of the book after all,' she said lightly. 'Then I had a quick lunch with Edward and it was so early I wanted to come home.'

'You could have shopped,' he suggested. 'Or gone to the library, or seen someone for tea.'

'I wanted to come home,' she said, and was rewarded by him reaching out to touch her hand as it lay in her lap.

'That's nice,' he said. 'And it means you can come out with us tonight. We've had the partnership deeds drawn up. We're all ready to go as soon as you write the cheque.'

'The valuer has set a price?' she asked.

'Yes. It's hardly fair actually, because only today Murray got an inquiry from a school. They want a price for a full-size Olympic pool for competitions and galas. It'd be hundreds of thousands of pounds. But Murray said he wouldn't count it into the deal because we have to have a cut-off point somewhere. But it made me see what a bargain we're getting.'

'How much?' Isobel asked.

'Breathe in,' Philip said. 'It's £350,000.'

Isobel was aghast. 'That's £100,000 more than we thought!' she exclaimed.

'I know,' he said. 'But there's no arguing with the figures,

370

Isobel. They speak for themselves. Murray has contracts and assets worth £700,000. If I want half of the share of the business then I have to buy in at half the commercial price. Fair's fair.'

Isobel thought rapidly. There was not enough money in the Swiss bank account to cover such an expense, and no more coming in this year until the delivery of the full manuscript of the second novel.

'It's all our savings,' she said. 'And then some. It really is a big amount.'

'I know,' Philip said. 'But you've seen how he works. We want to be in on this business, Isobel. And I don't want less than fair shares and equal say in it.'

'We'd have to take out a mortgage on the house,' she said. 'We can't cover it all from our savings. We'd have to take out a big mortgage.'

He nodded. 'It's absolutely OK. We'll be turning a profit, a big profit, within the year.'

Isobel smiled despite herself at Philip's enthusiasm and determination. 'I haven't seen you like this in years,' she said.

He beamed at her. 'I haven't felt like this in years,' he agreed.

'I'll ring the bank when I get home,' Isobel said. 'How soon d'you want the money?'

'At once!' he exclaimed. 'I did say we'd need it as soon as the valuer put in his report. I did warn you. I don't want to hang about. It's not fair on Murray if he sees us hanging back.'

'I think Murray is doing well enough out of this,' Isobel observed acidly. 'There aren't that many people in the world who would want to buy into his business with your abilities and this sort of capital behind them.'

'Anyway,' Philip said stubbornly.

'I'll get a cheque as soon as I can,' Isobel said. 'Within a week.'

*　　*　　*

Reluctantly she dialed Troy's number.

'Hello,' he said pleasantly. 'Get home all right?'

'Yes,' she said. 'I'm sorry to bother you but I need the money from the Swiss account, for Philip's business. And I need the advance on the second novel as soon as possible.'

'I can't get you that until you deliver it,' Troy said. 'You said you could do a rough draft very soon?'

'Yes.'

'I can get the money if I show them that, I can tell them you need it at once for your Cap d'Antibes house.'

'I wish,' Isobel said ruefully. 'In fact I am about to become the swimming pool impresario of Kent.'

'You're sure it's a good deal?'

'Positive.'

'Say a fortnight then, a month to give you time to deliver and them time to pay?'

'All right,' Isobel said unwillingly. She said goodbye and put down the phone, and then called the bank. She caught them just before they were closing. She had a sense of shaking dread as she was put through to the mortgage advisor.

She explained that she wanted to mortgage her house for about two-thirds of its market value, and that she would pay the loan off within a couple of months. The mortgage advisor, accustomed to dealing with large sums of money in this prosperous part of the country, did not balk at the figure of £350,000 and promised to call back at once.

Isobel put down the receiver and put her face in her hands. Never before had they carried a mortgage on their house. It had been a great comfort for Isobel that Philip's disability insurance had bought the house outright and so that whatever financial difficulties they had experienced afterwards, with falling royalties and continuing expenses, Isobel had always known that her house was secure.

'It's only for a couple of months,' she reassured herself. 'And then the Zelda Vere money arrives.'

Determinedly she turned to the computer screen and started up the computer. She was now at chapter twenty-four, she would need at least fifty chapters to make the heavy paper-back book that the publishers and readers demanded. Her heroine had experienced her near-fatal crash and was lying in hospital. Her spirit guide had arrived through the swirling mists of anaesthesia. Isobel turned with a wry smile to the pleasurable task of writing a scene of erotic lovemaking with the undead.

She was deep in the writing when the telephone rang at her elbow and she emerged from the embraces of the spirit world to take the call from the bank's mortgage arranger. The man confirmed that they were prepared to take out a mortgage on the house and grounds which would yield a sum of £350,000. Isobel heard the frightened quaver in her voice as she asked him to put the forms in the post at once.

'It's only for two months,' she tried to comfort herself.

Murray had not expected Isobel at dinner. He was waiting for Philip in the bar, he had not seen that the table inside the restaurant had been laid with three places. He looked surprised when he saw her, he looked at her with sudden attentiveness.

Isobel thought it might be the way she had done her hair, which was pinned on top of her head instead of at the nape of her neck and gave her an unmistakable touch of Zelda's glamour. She had used eyeliner and mascara and knew that she was looking well in a cocktail dress which was modest by Zelda's standards – a pale grey with a high collar and short sleeves – but rather stylish for Isobel.

'Isobel, how lovely to see you!' Murray exclaimed, rising to his feet. 'You didn't stay in London, then?'

'No,' she said shortly.

'I thought you were coming home tomorrow,' he said.

'I decided against it.'

'Was everything all right?'

Isobel turned to the waiter who was hesitating for their drinks order. 'A dry sherry please,' she said.

'Was everything all right in London?' Murray asked again as Philip was ordering his drink.

Isobel looked at him, uncertain whether or not she was imagining a spark of malice at the back of his concerned voice.

'Everything was fine, thank you,' she said coolly. 'I just finished earlier than I had thought I would and there was no reason for me to stay.'

'Oh, no reason,' he said as if that explained everything. 'Well, I'm so pleased that you could make it to dinner here. It makes it a real party.'

Isobel smiled and turned her attention to the menu.

To her surprise they had a pleasant evening, there was a genuine sense of celebration. Isobel banned the men from getting out their business plan at the table but they had most of the figures in their heads anyway, so for much of the dinner they were calculating figures and estimating profits.

'The fact of the matter is simply that we are all going to be millionaires by next Tuesday,' Isobel said gaily.

'Oh, at least,' Philip replied. 'Here's to us!' He raised his glass and they drank a toast to the business.

'Signing tomorrow?' Murray confirmed.

'Next Monday,' Isobel corrected him. 'As soon as I get the cheque from the bank.'

'Monday then,' Murray said. 'Damn. It's early closing. I was going to buy myself a new Ferrari.'

Isobel and Philip went to the bank together to collect the cheque. The years of illness and passivity had left their mark on Philip, he did not ask how the money had been raised, he was content still to leave it all in Isobel's hands. She told him that it had taken all their savings and investments and she had been forced to take a loan from the bank as well, secured on the house, but Philip's only reply had been to assure her that they would see a better return on this investment than on anything else, he would be paid a wage from day one, and they would pay themselves a slice of the profits within the quarter.

Together they took the cheque around to Murray. Philip

drove, Isobel sat with her handbag on her lap, the cheque inside, made out to Murray's business account. He greeted them at the door. 'I was just making coffee,' he said. 'I should have put champagne on ice, I suppose.'

'Not at half past ten in the morning,' Isobel said. She handed the cheque to Philip, who proffered it to Murray.

'Here you are. Don't spend it all at once.'

'You'll be drawing it back again in profits at the end of the quarter,' Murray promised.

'I know it,' Philip said. 'Have you heard from the school? Are they pleased with our figures?'

'They want to meet with us this afternoon,' Murray said, leading the way to the kitchen.

Isobel glanced at the foot of the stairs, where she had left her shoes. The carpeted space of the first step was still empty.

'I took the liberty of saying that we'd both be at the meeting,' Murray said. 'I hoped you'd be able to come?'

'Of course,' Philip said. 'We'll have to get our diaries together and plan out what we're doing for the rest of the week. But of course I'll come this afternoon.'

'You mustn't overdo things,' Murray warned him. 'We're so busy that we could both work a forty-eight-hour day.'

'No, he mustn't,' Isobel supplemented.

'I've never felt better,' Philip said. 'Don't fuss.'

Murray exchanged a smiling glance with Isobel. 'Coffee for everyone? And then I'd better get back to work. I want to have some designs ready to show the school this afternoon.'

'Anything I can do?' Philip asked eagerly.

'Could you do the costings while I run the drawings through the computer?'

'Absolutely,' Philip said. 'Are we going to give them a couple of options?'

'I thought we'd do three basic designs and assume they go for the middle one. People almost always do.'

'I tell you what,' Isobel interrupted. 'If I can have the car, I'll go home and leave you two to get on with it.'

'Yes, of course,' Philip said. He handed her the car keys

and gave her an absent-minded kiss on the cheek. 'Murray can drop me home after we've been to the school.'

'Should be around four,' Murray said to Isobel.

Isobel nodded and went out of the kitchen, as she let herself out of the front door she heard Philip say eagerly: 'But we should give them a breakdown of separate units so that they can have extras, if they want a more basic pool with add ons.'

Thirty-Three

In the weeks that followed Isobel had the house to herself in a way that had not happened since before the long years of Philip's illness. Most mornings she and Philip ate breakfast together and then he took the car and went down to the village to Murray's house to start work. Some days he would drive out to talk to clients of the business, some days he would stay at the office and do the paperwork while Murray went out. Either way he was out of Isobel's house from nine in the morning till about five or six o'clock at night.

Isobel had thought that she would miss him but she found that she loved the silence of the empty house. She worked far better, alone in the house without a sense of Philip wandering around, without the cackle of the distant television, without Philip continually putting his head round the door to ask helpfully if she would like a cup of tea or if they would have lunch early. Philip in his illness had not been a true companion, though Isobel, conscious of her love for him, had persuaded herself that she enjoyed having him in the house all day. She realised, now that she was free of him, that the floorboard creaking on the stairs under his tread, the click of him opening the front door to look for the postman, had been naggingly distracting. Philip's loneliness and Philip's boredom had seeped under the door of her study like a lingering sour smell.

Now that Philip was busy and happy and diverted and enjoying the company of a friend, Isobel found that it was she who was prowling around the house. But she did it with a delightful sense of having the freedom of her own domain. When she worked in the study she enjoyed her privacy and solitude. When she wanted a cup of tea she went out to the kitchen and revelled in the tidiness, in the luxury of being able to make one cup, her own cup, and not be delayed by Philip complaining about the poor quality of daytime television or wanting to tell her something he had just seen on a chat-show.

Isobel cut back Mrs M.'s hours partly because she did not need her but, secretly, also because she wanted the house wholly to herself. She found even Mrs M's presence an irritant. The bang of the door in the morning, her constant observation of their married life, her exploitation – so it seemed to Isobel – of the friendliness of Murray's nature, had made Mrs M. less of a help to Isobel and more of a rival woman in the very heart of the home.

'If I don't have a full-time job here I shall have to look somewhere else,' Mrs M. warned her. 'I want to be flexible, Mrs Latimer, but I have to have a full-time job.'

'I quite understand,' Isobel said. 'But as you see, since Mr Latimer is well and working away from home I really don't need someone in the house all day.'

'There's still all the cleaning and the shopping and the laundry,' Mrs M. pointed out.

'Yes,' Isobel said, thinking that the shopping at least would be substantially improved if she took it under her own control. The housekeeping money in the jar on the kitchen worktop was still in a constant state of flux. Mrs M. said that she was spending as little as she always had, and Philip said that he took nothing more than a couple of pounds for a sandwich at lunchtime. Clearly the system had broken down some months ago; only now did Isobel feel strong enough to face Mrs M.'s sulking.

'You'll need somebody to do your chores,' Mrs M. pointed out. There was an unspoken sense that Isobel was too lazy to do her own housework, and that she might try to manage for a few days but her efforts would soon fail.

'I certainly need somebody,' Isobel agreed. 'I am very busy at the moment. I am finishing a new novel. But I don't need someone for seven, eight hours a day. I should think four hours, three times a week would be plenty. But perhaps you don't want to work that? At six pounds an hour?'

Isobel extracted small, malicious satisfaction at the prolonged silence as Mrs M. tried to calculate four times three times six, and then finally said indignantly: 'That's only seventy-two pounds a week!'

'It's all I need.'

'I doubt very much you'll get someone to come all the way out here for that sort of money,' Mrs M. said stoutly. 'It's hardly worthwhile.'

'I shall have to see then, won't I?' Isobel said. 'I shall have to advertise. If you don't want to do it?'

'I'll do it,' Mrs M. said crossly. 'But I'll have to look around for something else, Mrs Latimer. I can't manage on seventy-two pounds a week.'

'I'm quite sure you can't,' Isobel said waspishly, thinking of the extravagance of Mrs M.'s housekeeping. 'And as soon as you get something that would suit you better you can tell me, and of course I'll let you go.'

'I only hope Philip doesn't tire himself out, get ill again, and have to come home for nursing and looking after,' Mrs M. said piously.

'I hope so too,' Isobel concurred. 'And if the situation changed I would tell you at once.'

'Wouldn't do any good if I was in another post,' Mrs M. said. 'It would be awful if I got another job and then you needed me back. When he's ill he's very particular. He likes having people around who know his little ways. He'd miss me if I wasn't here.'

'Yes, possibly,' Isobel agreed. 'But he's well now.'

'For the time being,' Mrs M. said ominously.

'So for the time being you can come in Monday, Wednesday and Friday for four hours a day,' Isobel said briskly. 'And I shall do the shopping.'

'I can't do Friday,' Mrs M. said, in order to have the last word. 'It'll have to be Monday, Wednesday and Thursday.'

'*Just* what would suit me,' Isobel said irritatingly. 'Monday, Wednesday and Thursday, nine till one.'

When Mrs M.'s hours were reduced the house was even more peaceful. Isobel had a sense of reclaiming her home, ironic since now for the first time it was owned by the bank. She wandered from room to room, straightening cushions and pushing the tables back into place. She bought flowers and arranged them so there was always a fresh vase in the hall. The tulips were in bloom and Isobel bought white, golden and red tulips to put on her desk.

Oddly enough, the only thing she missed was not Philip – it was the presence of Murray.

Work at the swimming pool was ending, the plaster and grouting were drying. They had finally joined the conservatory passage to the house, the boiler was ready to fire, the decorators were whitewashing the walls, the floor specialists would lay the carpet tiles and the extension would be finished. Murray still came up most mornings, to check that the work was going on steadily, but he never came into the house any more. Sometimes if Isobel was at her desk she would see him from the window and he would wave at her, but he never came to the door and tapped on it to speak to her.

One day she waved to him, thinking that perhaps she had been impolite, she really should invite him to come in for a coffee, but he simply tipped his broad-peaked baseball cap to her and carried on talking to the workmen. The next morning Isobel swung open her window and called out to him, and he strolled over and leaned against the wall, smiling down at her.

'Is everything going all right?' she asked.

Murray shot her a quick, measuring look. She had never before inquired after the progress of the pool. He looked at her as if he thought that she was opening the batting for some game of her own devising, as if he were fascinated to know what she was secretly thinking.

'It's going fine,' he said briefly. 'Surely you had no doubts?'

'Oh no,' Isobel said quickly. 'I just saw you, and thought that I'd ask.'

'Fine,' he said again.

There was a brief silence. 'Would you like a cup of coffee?' Isobel asked.

Again he interrogated her face as if to read her. 'I wouldn't want to interrupt you when you're working,' he said politely.

'It's all right,' she said, but she did not repeat the invitation and he did not move from his post, leaning at her window, looking down at her.

'Is Philip coming home for lunch?' she asked at random.

'I don't think so,' he said. 'You could always call and ask him. He's in the office today.'

'Yes, I know.'

There was a silence. Isobel could think of nothing to say, nor could she think how to end this conversation which she had initiated. Murray, leaning against the wall, patiently waited for her to tell him what she wanted, why she had summoned him.

'So you are all on your own in the house today,' he observed. 'And every day.'

'Yes,' Isobel said shortly.

He nodded and waited, as if she might say something more.

'Goodbye then,' Isobel said abruptly.

Murray gave her one of his long, veiled smiles. 'Goodbye,' he said and levered himself up from the wall and strolled away from her. Isobel watched him go, the slope of his shoulders where his hands were tucked into the pockets of his baggy jeans, the stride of his big boots, the slight swagger of his walk. Then she slammed the window shut as if to keep out a sudden, disturbing vernal breeze.

Without Philip, in the silence and peace of the house Isobel worked intensely, putting in hard, long hours. She knew that in the new Zelda Vere she was not writing an important book, she was not even aiming at a mediocre book. She was undertaking the exercise of writing quite a bad book:

stereotype characters, careless dialogue, clichéd imagery, but with a gripping and developing storyline. Isobel found that by only obeying the demands of the story and caring nothing for the telling of it, and certainly nothing for realism, probability, or moral or ethical issues, she could write extraordinarily fast. Writing a Zelda Vere novel was a question of dreaming a powerful and exciting story and then simply typing as fast as she could all the developments and changes which occurred to her in the process of getting the original story down on paper.

She finished when she had promised she would finish, and printed the seven hundred pages with a note to Troy.

> *Here it is. I warned you that it is a first draft and there are many things I will rework on the second draft, but you were anxious to see it straight away.*
>
> *We had to go ahead with buying into the pool business without waiting for the payment from the publishers so I would be really pleased if you could get them to pay promptly now, I do hate having a mortgage on this house. As soon as they pay can you draw me a cheque for £350,000? It can come to my account. Philip thinks it is his old shares and pensions that I have cashed in.*
>
> *I hope you are well. I think of you . . .*

Isobel wrapped the whole manuscript in stout brown paper, taped up the ends and the corners, tied the whole package with string, and put on some walking boots and walked down the hill to the village post office.

The woman accepted the parcel without comment. Isobel paid, and then paused by the sweet counter, remembering her joy on the day that she posted the first Zelda Vere novel, remembering the sharp, sweet taste of the black chocolate around the brazils, and then the wholesome nutty flavour of the crunch of the nuts inside their chocolate shell.

'Anything else?' the woman asked.

'No,' Isobel said with an odd sense of disappointment. She hardly ever ate chocolates anyway, she told herself. And a large box of chocolate brazils was a bit of an extravagance. Also, Isobel did not feel celebratory. She felt only that she had completed a task which earned her money that she needed. There was nothing luxurious about writing a not-very-good overlong novel. It had been a slog. Now she must turn to the beginning again and write the second draft. Undeniably she was richly paid for it, but also, undeniably, there was no joy in this work, as there had once been for Isobel when she had been a fine writer, struggling to improve her art, and proud of it.

Isobel was surprised when she did not hear from Troy the next day, nor the day after. He normally telephoned her as soon as he had read a new novel to give her an immediate response. She waited for him to call all weekend. On Monday morning, while Mrs M. noisily hoovered upstairs, Isobel shut the door of her study and called Troy's number.

'He's not here today, can I help you?' the receptionist asked brightly.

'Not there?'

'No.'

'This is Isobel Latimer, I wanted to talk to him. Can you tell me when he'll be back in the office?'

'He's gone on holiday,' the girl said indifferently. 'Was it urgent?'

'On holiday?'

'Yes.'

Troy had never taken a holiday in all the time that Isobel had known him. Sometimes he went away for a long weekend, but he had always been a constant presence in his office and his flat as Isobel always had been in her house.

'How long has he gone for?' she asked.

'A month,' the girl said.

'I had no idea, he never mentioned it to me,' Isobel protested. There was an unhelpful silence.

'I have just sent a package to him, a manuscript,' Isobel said. 'Can you tell me, did he receive it?'

'I don't know,' the girl said.

Isobel thought rapidly. If Troy had not received the parcel and it was opened by someone else it would be very apparent that the author of the Zelda Vere novels was Isobel Latimer and the carefully constructed facade of deception would rapidly collapse.

'It's very important that I know,' she insisted. 'I sent it recorded delivery. Someone must have signed for it.'

'A big, heavy brown-paper parcel?' the girl asked. 'Wrapped up old-fashioned with string and everything? I signed for it. And I gave it to him, but he took it upstairs. He had it before he went away. It's not in the office now.'

Isobel felt intensely reassured. Whatever else was happening, Troy had not forgotten their commitment to absolute discretion about Zelda.

'Do you have a telephone number for him?' she asked.

'No,' the girl said. 'Just his mobile.'

Isobel experienced a flood of relief. 'Oh, of course. I'll call him on that.'

'D'you have the number?'

'Of course I have the number,' Isobel snapped. 'Thank you, anyway. Goodbye.'

As she replaced the telephone on the set she realised that she was trembling. She paused for a moment and sat silently, with her hands in her lap.

She turned to her address book and looked up his mobile telephone number. At least she could speak to him and make sure that he was safe and that whatever he was doing for these long four weeks away from his office, he was not completely out of touch.

She dialled the number. To her immense relief it was answered at once, on the first ring; but then a terrible disembodied voice said in robotic tones: 'The number you are calling is unobtainable. You may record your message after the tone. If you wish to re-record your message at any time you can press hatch 1 on your telephone.' There was a sharp bleep of sound.

'Troy,' Isobel said in an anguished whisper. 'I'm so upset that you should go away like this without warning. I feel . . .' She broke off. Impossible to dictate to an ansaphone the churning muddle of her emotions. 'Please call me,' she said. 'Call me at once.'

He did not call. Isobel ran to pick up the phone on the first ring for the whole of the day, and when Philip came home in the evening she found she was straining to listen for the telephone all through dinner while he talked enthusiastically about his day's work.

They were to start filling the Latimers' pool the next day. 'And two days after that we'll have our first swim,' he said. 'How about we ask Murray over for dinner and we have a little party? A pool-opening party. Is there anyone you'd like to ask down from London? What about that Troy?'

'He's away,' Isobel said, trying to keep the desolation from her voice. 'I don't know where he is.'

Next morning, as soon as Philip left the house she ran to her study and tried again.

'The number you are calling is unobtainable. You may record your message after the tone. If you wish to re-record your message at any time you can press hatch 1 on your telephone.'

'Troy,' Isobel said. 'It's me, Isobel. I am very concerned that you should go away without warning. Please call me today without fail.'

She put down the telephone and opened up the computer. She had planned to start rewriting the Zelda Vere novel today but although she opened chapter one and she could see a glaring inconsistency about the description of the house, she felt she had no energy to even type a correction.

The telephone rang. Isobel jumped, snatched it up.

'Hello?' she said urgently

'It's me, darling,' Philip said. 'Guess how I'm calling you?'

Isobel could have wept with disappointment. 'I don't know.'

'A mobile phone. Murray just bought me one. Now you know I'm a proper young executive.'

'Oh, lovely,' Isobel said.

'I'd better give you the number so you can ring me when I'm out of the office.'

'Can you tell me when you come home? I'm expecting a rather important call.'

'It'll only take a minute.' Philip sounded slightly aggrieved. 'If you've got a pen there.'

'Yes, yes, all right.'

Slowly he dictated the number and then made her read it back to him.

'So who's so important?' he asked.

'What d'you mean?'

'That you're waiting for their call?'

'Oh, nothing.' Isobel improvised at random. 'I mean, Troy's office have an American publisher interested. He said he would ring me.'

'Surely not now,' Philip said. 'It's five in the morning over there. He must have meant ten o'clock tonight.'

'I don't know,' Isobel said. 'Perhaps he meant tonight.'

'They must have done,' Philip persisted. 'They're not going to do business at five in the morning, are they?'

Isobel gritted her teeth. 'I'll call back straight away and check,' she said. 'I probably misunderstood.'

Philip chuckled affectionately. 'Not your strong point is it?' he asked lovingly. 'Time zones.'

'I'll call them back,' Isobel said. 'I'll do it now.'

'All right,' Philip said. 'I'll get on. Lots to do. We're going to the school again today. Murray was right, they went for the middle-price version.'

'There's the doorbell,' Isobel said desperately. 'I really must go.' She put the phone down as Philip remarked that it was early for the postman, and dropped her face into her hands. 'Oh, Troy,' she whispered. 'Where are you?'

Thirty-Four

Isobel, incapable of work, incapable of sitting still, went for a long walk in the afternoon, taking the steep path which ran from the back of the house to the top of the Weald. The cold wind blew in her face and brought colour to her cheeks as she strode briskly along the wide path, trying to walk away from her thoughts and from the terrors that grew as she sat in her study and stared at the silent telephone.

'Well, if the worst comes to the worst he's only away for less than a month,' she reasoned aloud, the wind whipping her words away. 'I have to carry the bank loan for a month and he won't have delivered my novel to the publishers so that makes the money a little late. I lose some money because I'm late repaying the loan but only a month's repayments. Two months at the most.'

She nodded, she was starting to feel more cheerful. 'I must keep things in perspective,' she said. 'He's a grown man, he can go away on holiday if he wants to.'

Isobel paused and looked southward. In the distance she could see the grey gleam of the sea like a slab of pewter. She could see the dark green of the land and the speckle of grey and white houses, and the occasional high chimney. Closer to the foot of the hills was the patchwork of fields, small farms as dainty as toys, a little red tractor ploughing a green field, laying a stripe of brown earth across it with a plume of seagulls following behind the plough.

'It was my decision to stop our affair,' Isobel said. 'I can't control his life now.'

She thought about the lipstick on the champagne flute on the table in his living-room. It was Zelda's colour. She had been hiding that fact from herself until this moment but now, as she strode out she nodded her head at the recognition. It was the bright lipstick that they had chosen for Zelda in Harrods that day for 'presence'. Either Troy was seeing a woman who drank Roederer and wore Zelda's favourite lipstick, or else he had been Zelda with another person, he had been Zelda Vere without Isobel in attendance, without Isobel to help him dress, without Isobel's consent.

'Well, and so what?' Isobel said miserably. 'I can't run his life. He's a free man. I can't stop him.'

She walked all afternoon and came home tired as it grew dark. She had taken one decision: that she would not telephone Troy more than once a day. But that she would telephone him, without fail, every single day. Isobel had no faith in technology, she was not sure that the robotic voice really did record messages, or could be trusted to pass them on. Isobel decided that she would telephone his mobile telephone every day and phone his office every other day to see if he had called in to collect any messages or transact any business. She would not call him more frequently than that. She would try to write the second draft of the Zelda novel. The quicker it was finished, the sooner she could move back to writing the new Isobel Latimer novel, and only thoughtful, worthwhile Isobel Latimer novels would be her work from now on. Only Isobel Latimer's confined secure life would be her life from now on.

And whatever games Troy might play in the privacy of his flat would not impinge at any point on Isobel Latimer, living quietly in the country, with no traceable connection to Zelda Vere at all.

She was making a cup of tea when she heard Philip's car draw up, followed by Murray's. They first went to the pool house and then came into the kitchen together by the back door.

'Hello,' Isobel said. 'Would you like some tea? I'm just making a pot.'

'Love one,' Philip said. 'You?'

'Yes, please,' Murray said.

'It's turning the water on day,' Philip announced. 'We just checked. The paint's dry on the walls, we're ready to go. Do you want to do the honours, Isobel? Ladies first.'

'Oh yes,' she said trying to sound enthusiastic.

Philip was too pleased with the pool to hear the strain in her voice but Murray gave her a quick, searching glance. Isobel led the way down the new conservatory passage to the barn. Everything smelled of new paint, the place was echoey and cold. There was a hard, new, modern feel to it, very unlike the softness of the old beams and the floor of worn cobbles.

'It'll look much better with water in the pool,' Murray said, sensing her disappointment. 'That'll put some life in the place. And the pool will keep the whole building warm.'

Philip was uncoiling the hosepipe. 'Ready?' he said.

Isobel went to the tap. 'I declare this pool ready to fill,' she said, and turned on the water.

The water gushed from the hosepipe into the pool. The two men stood at the edge and stared down into the deep end six feet beneath them.

'Take a while to fill,' Philip said.

'Best part of two days,' Murray replied. 'You can run a couple of hosepipes in from the taps in the yard if you're feeling impatient. But it's only an extra day or so.'

'I can't wait,' Philip said.

Isobel turned away and went back towards the house. The passageway was painted white until they could decide on a colour scheme. The floor was grey carpet tiles. They had not bought curtains yet and the hard light poured in on the grey and white. Isobel thought that the passageway looked and smelled like some dreary institution. She had an uneasy feeling that she had colluded in knocking the domestic comfort out of her own home, she had been the destroyer of her own contentment.

Soberly, she made the pot of tea and put biscuits on the kitchen table with the two mugs of tea for the men.

'Was it ten tonight?' Philip asked as he came in the kitchen.

'Ten?'

'The time they're going to ring you?'

For a moment Isobel was completely blank. She was conscious of Murray's acute gaze watching her struggle to remember the lies. 'Oh. From New York. Yes.'

Philip turned to Murray. 'She wanted me off the phone this morning because she was waiting for a call from New York. I had to point out that they'd have got up in the middle of the night to make the call. Of course they're going to ring at ten tonight.'

Murray nodded and drank his tea. 'Are you published in America?' he asked politely.

'I used to be,' Isobel said. 'But they didn't take the last book. I am hoping to find a new American publisher.'

'She's too English and literary,' Philip said loyally. 'Too clever for them by half.'

Isobel smiled. 'It's just changing fashions,' she said sadly. 'I was very in at one time, now I'm out. I'll probably be in again in a couple of years.'

Murray looked at her with a curious sympathy. 'But it must be very hard,' he said. 'You must wonder what you're doing wrong. You must want to write a different sort of book, to change with the market.'

Isobel shot him a quick, apprehensive look and said nothing.

'Oh, she'd never do that,' Philip interrupted. 'She doesn't write for the market. She's an artist, not a hack. She writes literature, not bestselling trash.'

Murray said nothing but continued to look steadily at Isobel.

'I just write the sort of book that comes to me,' she said awkwardly.

'Did you get much done this afternoon?' Philip asked.

'I got a bit stuck so I went for a walk,' Isobel confessed.

'What it is to be a lady of leisure!' Philip exclaimed. 'We were in the most boring meeting in the school. I don't think they're going to take a decision without at least three months of calling us in and asking us the same questions over and over again.'

'Taxpayers' money,' Murray said. 'Our accounting and billing is going to have to be spot-on all the way through if they're this fussy at this stage.'

'It will be,' Philip said. He finished his tea and put down his mug. 'You can depend on it. I think I'll just take another look at that pool. See how it's filling up.'

He went out of the room, Isobel got up from the table and went to the sink, busying herself with emptying the tea pot and rinsing it out. She was conscious of Murray sitting in his usual place in the corner.

'It seems odd without Mellie,' he said.

'I like it better,' Isobel said tightly.

He nodded. 'D'you miss Philip during the day?'

'Not when I'm working.'

'And when you're stuck you go for a walk,' he said. 'Or you could take a rest, have a little sleep.'

Isobel flushed scarlet at the mention of an afternoon sleep. She flicked a tea towel from the Aga and wiped some glasses.

'I must go,' Murray said. He waited for a moment in case Isobel should ask him to stay for supper. She said nothing.

'Hope your call comes through,' he said.

'My call?'

'Your ten o'clock call from New York,' he reminded her. 'Don't forget you are supposed to be waiting for a call from New York at ten o'clock. That's twice you've forgotten that it's a really important call, and that you're waiting for it.'

'It's probably just an inquiry,' Isobel said calmly. 'I'm not really hoping for much from it, that's why I forgot it.'

He nodded. 'I thought it was a big deal, that you had to keep the line clear.'

'Not particularly,' Isobel said.

'I'll see myself out,' he said, and went.

Isobel nodded. She did not say goodbye.

That night she dreamed of Zelda. She was dancing in a beautiful ballroom, she was wearing a ball gown of white, she looked like a bride. The chandelier above her head sparkled with great crystals of glass, there was an orchestra playing and long white lilies in vases. Dancing alone, in a ballroom lined with people, Zelda waltzed round and round. Isobel found she was standing watching, enclosed in a passageway lined with glass, like the bleak corridor between her house and the pool. She was calling out to Zelda but she could not be heard. Nobody could hear her. She was trapped in the passageway, neither in one place nor another, and nobody could hear her when she cried out a warning to the beautiful dancing woman who was Zelda, who was Troy, who was herself.

She woke. It was only five o'clock in the morning, still dark. She crept out of bed and went quietly downstairs. The kitchen was warm from the Aga though the rest of the house was chilly. Isobel made herself a cup of tea and drank it leaning against the comforting heat of the stove. She took the cordless telephone and dialled Troy's mobile number, which she now knew off by heart. The robot woman invited her to leave a message for Troy. Isobel did not trust her, did not think she was recording the messages, did not think she was passing them on, did not believe that Troy had any idea that she was faithfully calling him every day. She put the telephone and slid down to sit on the kitchen floor with her back to the warm oven. She felt that it was a question of endurance.

Philip was not surprised to wake and find the bed empty. Isobel often woke early and started work if a book was going well. But he was surprised to come downstairs and find her making breakfast, and not before her word processor.

'I thought you were working,' he said. 'I was going to make you some tea.'

'I did some, and then I got tired,' she replied.

'You do look pale,' he said. He looked more closely. 'Are you coming down with something? You do look awfully pale.'

'Yes.' Isobel seized on the easiest explanation. 'I think I am a bit off colour.'

'Better go back to bed. Should you go and see the doctor?'

'Just tired, I think. I'll have a rest later on.'

'You can call me if you need me to come home. I'll have my new mobile switched on.'

Isobel's eyes suddenly filled with tears and she moved into her husband's arms. 'I'm so glad I've got you,' she said weakly. 'At least I've got you.'

'Why?' Philip hugged her gently. 'Of course you've got me. You've always got me. What d'you mean?'

'Nothing.' She dried her eyes on the sleeve of her dressing gown. 'I'm in a funny mood. Hormones, I expect.'

'Would it be the change of life?' Philip asked.

Isobel recoiled at what she heard as an insult, a deeply intimate insult to the very heart of her womanhood from the man she loved.

'Oh yes,' she said fiercely, hating him for not understanding, hating him for snatching up a cliché which blamed her body, instead of struggling to understand her. Instead of asking why she was awake at five in the morning, and crying at eight, he chose to treat her as a sick woman.

'Oh yes. The menopause. That'd probably be it. The end of my life as a fertile woman. The death of my fertile cycle. That'd be it, all right. That's all I need.'

Isobel telephoned Troy's office. The receptionist was bright. Yes, Troy had called in and picked up his messages. He said he was travelling around and so he would not leave a telephone number, nor could they forward parcels to him. He was collecting e-mail messages now and then. If there was anything urgent, Isobel could write an e-mail to him.

Isobel started a letter.

My dearest Troy,

Please telephone me, I need to hear your voice. I feel very anxious about what you are doing and why you are so long away from the office. Also, I would have thought you would have delivered the new ZV book. I need the money, as you know. Please tell me what is going on. I feel very lost without you.

Isobel.

She pressed 'send'. There was a reassuring telephone noise of bleeping and dialling and the hiss of static, and then an icon on her computer flashed a little telegraph pole. Isobel sat before the screen and watched all this activity as if it might help, as if it might somehow draw Troy from wherever he was, out from his limbo and back to her. She sat watching until the little telegraph pole stopped flashing and a message came up on the screen to tell her that the letter had been sent and that she was now disconnected.

Isobel nodded. Indeed, she felt disconnected. She realised that it was not Troy floating in limbo, not Troy lonely and without communication. On the contrary, Troy was travelling, Troy was checking in, Troy was being bombarded with communication, with telephone messages and e-mails. The person who was lonely was Isobel: as lonely as she had ever been, her husband at work with his friend, the only lover she had ever had gone away for twenty-eight days, and not replying to her calls. Her Zelda Vere persona taken from her and her Zelda Vere book stranded between author and publisher in her agent's empty flat. Her new Isobel Latimer book unwritten, and at the moment unwritable.

Isobel went out into the hall and pulled on her walking boots. She set off up the track to the height of the Weald. She did not know what else she could do.

The level of water in the swimming pool invisibly rose. Despite her lack of interest in anything but Troy, Isobel found that she was drawn to the pool house. She spent long minutes watching the trickle of water from the hosepipe into the pool, incapable of seeing any rise in the level of the water. But when she went away and came back an hour later it was clearly higher.

Philip wanted a party, a proper party with champagne and caterers and pretty girls in swimming costumes. 'You must know hundreds of people,' he urged Isobel. 'Invite them down.'

'Terrific showcase for our work,' Murray pointed out. 'We could have brochures printed.'

'Do 'em as napkins,' Philip said.

'That is a brilliant idea,' Murray said. 'That is absolutely inspired. Let's get it costed.'

'I don't know hundreds of people who would come to a swimming-pool party,' Isobel said coldly. 'All the people I know are middle-aged academics and writers. They have neither the vanity nor the inclination to take their clothes off and fling themselves into the water all together. And we can't afford a big party.'

Murray and Philip exchanged a brief, inscrutable glance of men jointly encountering female irritability. Isobel had a terrible thought that Philip would have told Murray that she was suffering from mood swings because of the menopause. She gave him a blistering look. 'We're very stretched buying into the business,' she said shortly. 'We can't afford to give a party as well.'

'Fair enough, perhaps sometime in the summer,' Philip said, placating her. 'And when the pool heater has been on for a day and got the temperature up we'll have our own little party. Fancy a dip, Murray?'

'Absolutely.'

'You can come up and swim every morning,' Philip said. 'I shall be swimming before breakfast. What about you, Isobel?'

She managed a grudging smile. 'Perhaps later in the day,' she said.

*   *   *

They turned on the pool heater that evening and the next morning Isobel woke alone in bed. She went downstairs to the hall in her dressing gown and peered through the glazed corridor to the pool room. A scatter of Philip's pyjamas and Murray's clothes down the corridor indicated that they had shed their clothes as they had run down towards the swimming pool and plunged in naked. Even with the double glass doors shut at the end of the corridor she could hear them shouting and whooping with joy and then an explosive shriek and gurgle as one of them was soundly ducked.

Isobel turned from the sounds of carefree boyish play and went wearily back up the stairs to her bedroom.

Every morning she wrote an e-mail to Troy. Every afternoon at about two o'clock she called his mobile telephone and left a message. Every third day she called his receptionist who airily reported whether or not he had telephoned in. Generally he had not done so. The messages became more and more of a ritual, a sacrifice to an unresponsive god, as Isobel surrendered any hope that he might reply. Towards the end of the month she was writing nothing more than a line, recording nothing more than a desolate sentence.

'It is Isobel again. Please phone me.'

She knew that there was nothing in her voice that would encourage him to call her, nothing in her voice that would compel him to call her. She had lost that bright arrogance that she had learned as Zelda. She had lost that peculiar ability to take him to the very brink of his secret desires. All she could do now was to beg him to remember her, wherever he was, whatever he was doing, whoever he was with, whoever he was.

'It is Isobel again. Please phone me.'

The month passed extraordinarily slowly. Philip maintained his pattern of swimming every morning and most mornings he and Murray swam together like two joyful boys and then invaded the kitchen to make bacon sandwiches and drink coffee. Isobel stayed in bed later and later in order to avoid Murray at the breakfast table, where he glowed with health and joy.

Philip banked two thousand pounds in wages from the pool company, which barely covered their living costs and the loan payments. The final sum was now due on the pool and Isobel did not know how they would find the money. She thought that she should telephone some newspaper editors and do some reviewing work to earn a few hundred pounds, she thought she should write some short stories for the small amount of money they would bring in which might tide them over. But she found that she could not write. All she could type, and she typed it every morning, was:

'It is Isobel again. Please phone me.'

She knew that nothing would break her from this deadlock of imagination, of desire, of debt, but the return of Troy, the return of Zelda. Isobel alone could not tolerate her life. She had thought that she would return to Philip, she had thought that Philip would take them into prosperity and comfort. She had thought that the problem had been Philip's illness, and once Philip's illness was miraculously cured then there would be nothing in her future but joy.

Now she knew better. It was Troy that she wanted. Troy and Zelda. And Troy – and perhaps Zelda – were gone for a long, long month.

On the last day of April Isobel telephoned the receptionist. The girl was brusque now, knowing. She was clearly convinced that Isobel had an obsessional crush on Troy and perhaps even that Troy had gone away to escape Isobel. The girl was never rude, but her voice rang with contempt, the powerful contempt of the young and beautiful for the middle-aged and ordinary.

'Is he coming back tomorrow?' Isobel demanded.

'He hasn't said,' the girl said. 'He's got no meetings booked.'

'Has he called in?'

'No, Mrs Latimer.'

'If he calls in will you please tell him that I want to speak to him, that it is a matter of extreme urgency for me?'

'I'll tell him if he calls.'

'He did say that he'd be away a month?'

'I told you he did.'

'Then he should come home tomorrow?'

'Perhaps he will,' the girl said. 'He hasn't told me. I just work here, you know. It's not my job to . . .'

'To what?' Isobel said sharply.

'To manage . . . clients.'

'I just need to discuss a novel with him,' Isobel said, grasping at her dignity.

'He knows,' the girl said. 'I've told him and I've left a message on his ansaphone and on his e-mail. He knows you want to talk to him, and that it's about a novel, and that it's extremely urgent.'

Isobel bit her lip, she was afraid that she might cry out down the phone to the bright, indifferent voice. 'I'll call tomorrow to see if he is back,' she said.

'There's no need,' the girl said. 'I'll call you the moment he gets in.'

'All right,' Isobel said, knowing that she could not wait for the call. 'You'll call me the moment he gets in.'

'I just said so.'

'Yes. Thank you.' Dully, Isobel put down the telephone. She went out to the kitchen. The plates from breakfast were still on the table, the dishes from last night's dinner were in the dishwasher unwashed. Mrs M's prediction that Isobel would not manage the housework was coming true. There was nothing in the fridge for supper that night and they had eaten takeaway meals twice this week already. It was working out more expensive than when Mrs M. had been doing her extravagant shopping trips.

The telephone rang. Isobel flew back into the study and snatched it off the hook. 'Troy?'

'Is Mr Latimer available, please?'

'No,' said Isobel. She could hear her voice shaking.

'And is this the number for Mr Murray Blake?'

'No,' she said. 'I can give you his number.'

'But this is Atlantis pools?'

'This is our home telephone number,' Isobel said irritably. 'I don't take trade inquiries on this number.'

'This isn't a trade inquiry,' the man's voice said firmly. 'And we need to speak to Mr Latimer and Mr Blake as a matter of urgency. Could you give me a number where they can be reached?'

Isobel dictated Murray's home telephone number. 'Yes, that is the number we have tried. Mr Blake does not return our calls.'

'I don't know anything about that,' Isobel said.

'What is his address?'

'Look, who is this?' Isobel asked crossly.

'It is a personal matter,' the man said smoothly. 'Do you have Mr Blake's address? Then I need trouble you for nothing more.'

Isobel dictated the address of Murray's home.

'Thank you,' the man said, and disconnected the telephone.

Isobel sat beside it, waiting for it to ring, all morning.

It did not.

Thirty-Five

Philip came home in irritable silence that evening. Isobel, frying two pieces of steak that she had found grey and icy at the back of the freezer to accompany frozen peas and baked potatoes, was reminded that he was still carrying the illness which had made him sick for years, and that they would be foolish to forget that he might at any time be sick again.

'Are you all right?' she asked.

He glanced at her from his seat at the kitchen table. Isobel noticed that he did not lay the table, he did not do so much as fetch his own knife and fork. The disappearance of Mrs M had meant that Isobel moved smoothly into all her work. Philip, now considering himself the breadwinner and the working man, would not come home from a working day to do housework at night.

'What d'you mean – am I all right?'

'You seem very quiet.'

'I'm thoughtful.'

Isobel did not ask what he was thinking about. She knew it would be something to do with the business, it would be something about swimming pools. She did not refrain from asking out of consideration for his need for silence but because she had no interest in the answer. In the days before Philip's illness she had been genuinely interested in his work, interested in the anecdotes he would tell about his day: the people he had met, the things they had said. When he had started work with Murray Isobel had first thought that people ordering and choosing swimming pools were a poorer vein of anecdotal material than his first employers. Then she realised that it was she who had changed. She simply was not interested in Philip's daily experiences any more. She had fallen into the habit of being interested only in his health. For ten years she had never asked him what he was thinking, only what he was feeling. Now that he was feeling nothing abnormal they had no topic of conversation that was mutually engaging. Philip was still proud of her work and opinionated about it, he would have been ready to discuss her writing; but Isobel had nothing to say about it, and she had not written for days. With Troy away there were few developments to report, and there was nothing she could say of the pain she was suffering. She was quite incapable of writing at all. She evaded Philip's inquiries about the progress of the book by saying it was at the thinking stage.

Other than her work, they had nothing to talk about. Philip might speak about the pool business and Isobel might nod and interject mild noises of encouragement but she did not mean it. She had given up pretending that she thought it was interesting. She was interested in nothing but the return of Troy.

'An odd thing happened today,' Philip remarked. 'Couple of chaps turned up at the house, Murray's house, wanting to see Murray. They had my name too.'

Isobel turned the steak, which sizzled wetly, and put the peas on to boil.

'Murray hustled them outside. I got the definite impression that he didn't want me to meet them.'

Isobel reached into the Aga and brought out the baked potatoes, split them and buttered them on the plates.

'I think they were some kind of debt collection agency.'

'Oh?' she said without interest.

The peas came to the boil. Isobel lifted the steaks from the pan, put them on the plates, drained the peas and tipped them on one side of the plate. She collected knives and forks on her way to the table and put everything down in one inelegant scramble.

'Debt collection agency,' Philip said. 'I mean official. Like bailiffs.'

'Murray in debt?' she asked, suddenly attending.

'It's not the company, so we're OK,' Philip said. 'If there had been any thing odd there, the audit would have found it. The investment's OK. But you don't send two blokes out in a brand new Ford executive-range car to pick someone up for a parking fine.'

'What d'you mean, pick him up?' she asked. 'They didn't arrest him?'

'No, what I'm saying is he got them out of the house and did whatever business it was on the doorstep. That's odd for a start. Usually we do everything together. The other thing is that when I asked him what they wanted, he said that they had got the wrong papers, there had been a mix-up. But they had his name and they had my name.'

'I think they may have telephoned here,' Isobel said. 'Someone rang, a man, for the pool company and they had your name and Murray's but not Murray's address.'

'And you just gave it to them?' he demanded, as if she had done something wrong.

'Why shouldn't I?' she asked irritably. 'Why on earth not? How am I to know that they don't want to order a swimming pool? And more to the point, how come they have our telephone number and not Murray's?'

'No, that's not the point,' Philip said, cutting into the tough steak and chewing it without complaint. 'The point is: what do they want and how much? I'm not having him drawing money from our company to pay off old debts.' He nodded at her. 'Now you see why I wanted an equal partnership. I can put my foot down now. What I say goes.'

Isobel rang Troy's office every few minutes from nine o'clock though she knew that the receptionist did not start until ten. At ten past ten the girl answered the telephone.

'We've not seen him yet, Mrs Latimer,' she said. 'He sent me some e-mail instructions.'

'Did you tell him that I wanted to speak to him?'

'He knows.'

'Did he send any instructions about me?'

'No.'

Isobel sat in silence for a few minutes then her sense of hopelessness and misery overwhelmed her. 'Oh, what shall I do?' she cried out.

The girl heard the despair in her voice and responded with embarrassed silence. 'Not much you can do,' she said quietly. 'I said I'll call you as soon as he gets in.'

'Will you?' Isobel demanded.

'I said I would.'

The girl disconnected the phone. Isobel realised that she had made a fool of herself without any concealment. Soon it would be known in the small circle of literary London that Isobel Latimer was hopelessly in love with her homosexual agent; a relationship deliciously, scandalously doomed from the start. People who had been irritated by the high moral tone of Isobel's books and by her success in previous years would relish the gossip. There would be speculation about the failure of her marriage, there would be much clawing over her private life disguised as sympathetic discussion. Rivals and acquaintances would find reasons to telephone her and ask her how she was, in tones of false sympathy. Isobel would have to brace herself for a wave of empathy.

At lunchtime Isobel went down the bleak unwelcoming corridor to the pool house. The water from Philip's Grecian fountainhead trickled into the spa pool, which steamed a little. The pool itself was a deep blue, perfectly crystal clear. Isobel, still wearing her skirt, stepped out of her court shoes, stripped off her tights and sat at the brink of the deep end to paddle her feet in the water. It was pleasantly cool on her bare legs, and from her seated position the pool looked long and welcoming. She thought how easy it would be to slide into it, still wearing her clothes, and to let herself drown. She was a weak swimmer, in her heavy skirt, shirt and jumper she would be quickly waterlogged and would sink. Anyone finding her would assume that she had fallen in. The finances of the house would collapse, Philip would lose his home and his new pool. He would never understand what had happened to the stocks and shares they had once owned, but he would still have his pool company, he would still have his friendship with Murray. There would be the lump sum of her life insurance to keep him going. And he would never know about Zelda Vere, about Troy, about the massive deception, about the unforgivable adultery, about the intense pain that Isobel was suffering now.

'Don't do it,' a loud voice said cheerfully.

Isobel swung round, nearly overbalanced and grabbed on to the aluminium steps of the pool to keep her balance.

It was Murray, smiling, bright, over-confident as ever. 'You look like you were about to plunge in and drown yourself.'

'I was enjoying the quiet,' Isobel said pointedly. She wondered if he would notice her pallor and the fatigue in her face.

'You probably have enough quiet,' he said. 'Don't get out now much, do you? What happened to the London trips? I thought they were going to be a regular thing?'

Isobel tried to keep the pain from her face. 'I was doing a course of lectures to stand in for someone,' she said. 'She came back early.'

'I thought she was on maternity leave? How did she get back early?'

Isobel looked at Murray's innocent, inquiring face. She could not be bothered to think of a lie which would convince him. She looked at him almost as if she were about to ask him to pity her, to let her escape this verbal fencing. 'Why would you want to know?' she asked simply. 'Why does it matter now?'

'I just remember things,' Murray said. 'I have a retentive memory for detail.'

Isobel nodded and started to get to her feet. Murray reached behind her and picked up her shoes as if to pass them to her. In a sudden, instinctive movement Isobel grabbed at them. For a moment he held the toes and she held the heels and their gazes locked. His grip on them was firm, Isobel pulled them ineffectually but he did not let go. They tugged in silence for a few moments and then she gasped out a question:

'Who were the men who came to your door?'

'Debt collectors,' he said in the same tight, determined tone as hers. 'A business I had before. It went bust. I still owe a bit on it.'

'We didn't know about that,' she accused. 'Did we?'

'No, I don't think you did.'

'How much will you have to pay them?'

'They'll deal,' he said. His voice was lazily confident, but he did not slacken his grip on the toes of her shoes. 'They always come to some sort of deal.'

'Where will you get the money from?' she pursued. 'From the company?'

'I can't take money out of the company without Philip's consent, you know that. I'll get some from somewhere. Where does anyone get money from? Where d'you get yours from?'

The turning of the attack was so sudden that Isobel loosened her grip on the shoes and at once he snatched them from her and held them away, out to the side, at the full stretch of his arm. She would have to reach across him, close to his body to get hold of them. She hesitated. 'Where do you get your money from?' he taunted.

'From my royalties,' she said. 'And we had Philip's invalidity pension, and some savings.'

He smiled at her as if he knew as well as she did that the money had run out.

'Amazing royalties for a literary novel,' he remarked.

'I didn't know you knew anything about publishing,' Isobel said sharply.

Murray gave her a small, sly smile. 'I can count. I can add up.'

He put the shoes carefully down on the floor, side by side, and he held out his hand to her. As if they were dancing some strange formal dance, Isobel put her wet, cold hand into his and let him hold her hand as she stepped into her shoes. When she had them on her feet and was half an inch higher she realised that her eyes were level with his mouth. He was smiling. He turned and went quietly from the pool house, without another word. Isobel watched him go and found that she was shaking with rage.

It was only an hour later that she calmed down, and then she found that she had gone an hour without thinking of Troy. She had escaped from grief for a whole hour. For a moment she almost felt grateful to Murray and wished he would come back and irritate her again.

Three days passed and Troy did not return to his office.

'This is getting ridiculous,' Isobel said angrily to the girl. 'I shall consider moving to another agent. I must see him.'

'Perhaps you should write an e-mail to him,' the girl said. 'He is doing his business by e-mail, I am sure he is representing you perfectly well.'

'I need to see him!' Isobel exclaimed.

'You are the only client of his who seems to mind,' the girl said rather sharply. 'Everyone else seems OK about it.'

Isobel checked for a moment. 'I am waiting for a royalty payment,' she said.

'I don't think you are, Mrs Latimer,' the girl said carefully. She was afraid of provoking an hysterical outburst. 'We have all the advances logged on the computer, I check them and pay them out. I've been doing it since he went away. I made sure that your payments are up to date. You're not due anything until you sell your next novel.'

Isobel said nothing. She could not claim Zelda Vere's royalties as her own. 'Does he say when he is coming back?' she asked.

'No,' the girl said. 'He sounded very happy. He said he was having a good time.'

'Does he say where he is?'

'No.'

'Can't you trace him, can't you trace the e-mail address to see where it's coming from?'

The girl was offended. 'Well, for one thing you can't do that with an e-mail,' she said. 'And for another thing I wouldn't do it. He can have a holiday wherever he wants, I think. And if he wants to come back a bit late then he can, I think.'

Isobel held the phone away from her ear so the self-righteous little voice deteriorated into the chirrup of an unimportant bird. She put the phone down while the girl was still speaking.

Isobel woke in the night and wrote an e-mail to Troy which went on for twenty pages. She did not send it. In the morning she came down and reread it in growing horror. It was the ranting of a deeply disturbed woman. If someone else had shown it to her she would have said it was a tirade from a madwoman. It was filled with accusations of theft of identity, of transformations, of raising ghosts and being haunted, accusations of sexual addiction, of obsession.

'This is crazy,' Isobel said, looking at the screen. 'If I go on like this I shall be insane.'

Mrs M. found another full-time job as she had threatened to do and no longer came in even for the twelve hours a week. Isobel went into the kitchen and found that last night's supper dishes were still on the table. Murray had obviously been in for breakfast with Philip after their swim, there were two coffee cups and two cereal bowls among the debris on the table. The remains of Murray's porridge was setting rock solid in the saucepan in the sink.

Isobel switched on the kettle to make tea and set to clearing up the kitchen. She turned on the television to drown out the tirade to Troy which was still running in her head. She knew that she would be hearing her own voice: begging, pleading, threatening, for all the rest of the long day.

Suddenly she jerked her head up and stared at the screen. A familiar name had penetrated her consciousness, she reached out a soapy hand and turned up the volume.

There was a blonde woman sitting beside the sea, the sunset behind her, a small table beside her with a couple of books artfully arranged and a vase with an orchid. She was wearing a beautifully cut suit and her hair was a great helmet of spun gold. Her face was thoroughly made-up, her eyes brilliant blue, her mouth the familiar shade of cerise. The name Zelda Vere appeared on the bottom of the screen just as Isobel whispered: 'Zelda.'

It was an interview with Zelda Vere, who was publishing a second novel which had once again been sold for historic sums. The interviewer was making much of the 'Midas touch' of the novelist. Zelda said what she always said: she prided herself on being a storyteller who told the stories that people wanted to read. That what was important was to give people their dreams.

'And you yourself lead a dream life,' the interviewer suggested. 'Your first book was a story about rags to riches and you have lived that life, haven't you?'

Isobel found that unconsciously, as she watched, she was mirroring the gestures that Zelda made on screen. The slow downward nod indicating emotional vulnerability about the past, then the raising of the chin and the slight toss of the head indicating her courage and determination to leave it all behind her.

'Oh, yes,' Zelda said in her beautiful throaty voice. 'I know what it is to be poor and to struggle. I know what it is to make your own fortune, to make your own luck. I know what it is to be ruthless and I know what it is to be filled with regret.'

'And this recent book is based on your own experience.'

Zelda's eyes were shadowed with mystery. 'I had a very serious accident,' she said. 'A car accident. I had to undergo extensive surgery. I am still recovering.'

Isobel gasped as the meaning of this sunk in.

'Plastic surgery?' the interviewer asked.

'I was cut to ribbons,' Zelda whispered. 'But during the dark nights of pain I had an extraordinary experience. I encountered a spirit guide, a man who came to me and took me through the pain, through the fear and through the agony to the other side – to bliss.'

'This was a spirit guide?' the interviewer confirmed.

'An angel,' Zelda said firmly. 'I swore that if I lived through this experience I would base my next novel on the wisdom he taught me and on the deep, deep pleasure he showed me. So that everyone could benefit. I've called my new novel *The Angel's Kiss* and it also comes with an instructional book to tell you how to achieve peace of mind and how to experience deep sexual joy from finding your own angel, the angel that is within you.'

The interviewer turned back to the camera. 'Thank you, Zelda Vere, from her hideaway in the south of France. And now, back to the studio.'

Isobel felt her knees buckle beneath her. She staggered forward and gripped the worktop while a wave of nausea went through her. 'My God, my God,' she whispered over and over again.

It was too much for her to absorb. Troy's confident transformation, the totality of the appearance of Zelda, the masterly handling of the interview, the reworking that he had already done on the book and the brilliant double production of a spiritual guide book linked with the novel which would make him a fortune, which would double his royalties, treble his success.

But it was not the theft of the novel, or even the theft of Zelda herself that had Isobel retching into the washing-up water. It was the terrible certainty that Troy had spent this month changing himself to Zelda forever. Isobel had heard at once the reference to extensive surgery and had known at that moment that this was not a fictional biography solely to introduce the story of Francine, the heroine of the novel. Isobel had a dreadful sense of conviction that Troy had indeed undergone surgery, he had cut aside Troy, he had created Zelda out of his own skin.

Isobel found that she was clutching herself, her hands gripping her breasts, and moaning at the thought of him mutilating his own desirable body in order to pass as a woman. She groaned at the thought that Zelda's breasts under that well-fitting suit were no longer a padded bra strapped on Troy's hard chest, but that he had poisoned himself with hormones to force his slim, hard body to sprout them like some strange unnatural swellings. He had allowed a surgeon to slice into his adorable penis, to invert it, to turn it inside out, to stitch it back into his own body as some dreadful fake vagina which he could use for dreadful fake sexual pleasure. He had murdered his own maleness to become Zelda. He had killed Isobel's wonderful boy lover to become the false woman they had created together.

Isobel felt vomit rising in her throat and she bent over the sink and retched again until her body heaved and there was nothing left to expel. 'God, my God,' she whispered over and over again.

She staggered to the kitchen table and collapsed into a chair. She laid her face down on the solid wood and inhaled the reassuring homely smell of Murray's porridge, as if only that simple odour of domestic normality could keep her sane.

She sat in silence for hours, knowing nothing but her horror and her bewilderment. When she finally raised her head her cheek was printed with the grain of the wood of the table like a new set of wrinkles, like the very tattoo of grief.

It was half past two in the afternoon, the morning had gone by as Isobel had held her horror to her, had learned the full enormity of what Troy had done.

She rose to her feet and walked unsteadily to her study. The rewrite of the Zelda Vere novel was hidden in a file on the illuminated screen before her. Isobel clicked on the file coldly, and deleted it without rereading another word. Her novel, Zelda's novel, had been stolen from her and sold, it was gone. She no longer need think about the second draft. And Troy was gone too, she thought. He might continue to manage his other clients from long distance or he might simply announce his retirement. For her, there could be nothing but silence. He must have known she would see this interview or, if not this one, then others. He would be doing a series of interviews, he would have known it was inevitable that sooner or later Isobel would see one, and next year she would see a Zelda Vere book published with a title she had not chosen and with material that she had not written. He must have known, in his beautiful house in France, that she would see his betrayal, his theft of her work, of Zelda, of her happiness.

Isobel knew that Troy was secure as Zelda. She had given him enough material for him to work on when she handed over that rough first draft. A Zelda Vere novel was all story, there was nothing else. It was a simple enough matter to add the dialogue, to spice up the characters, once the strong structural bones of the story were laid down. Troy would have done it well.

If there were ever to be a third Zelda Vere book he might find himself in some difficulties, but he could hire ghost writers easily enough. Once the name of Zelda Vere had a following of fans, then subsequent books would probably continue to sell. Even if the sales diminished he would still have made enough money to live whatever life he chose.

The money. Isobel pressed her cold hands against the throbbing muscles of her neck and realised that she had lost her alternative life as a beautiful and glamorous woman with a young and handsome lover, she had lost her immensely successful nom de plume, and she had lost all her money as well. Troy was the sole signatory on the Swiss bank account, Isobel did not even know the account number. She could show evidence that Zelda Vere had once paid a huge amount of money to Isobel Latimer, but she had no evidence to show that the remaining money was also hers. If she wanted to destroy them all then she could reveal the fraud, show that Troy the agent and Zelda Vere were the same bizarre person. But then everyone would know that she too had been Zelda, would know that she and Troy had gone away together, would conclude quite rightly that they had been wildly perverse, wildly delightful lovers, but that Troy had found the courage to go on, while Isobel had stopped.

Thirty-Six

Isobel subsided and lay with her head on her desk. She ceased to think, she had no way of grasping the enormity of what had happened. When she closed her eyes all she could see was the golden hair and blue eyes and voluptuous figure of Zelda Vere with the Mediterranean skyline behind her. When she opened them she saw the silently waiting computer. Isobel lay with her head on the desk alternately opening and closing her eyes, and thinking nothing.

The closing of the front door warned her that Philip was coming into the house, she hurriedly sat up, blinking as if she were dazed by the daylight. She got to her feet and stumbled into the kitchen, and found him staring at her.

'Are you ill?' he asked, seeing her dressing gown and the kitchen as he had left it at breakfast time.

'What time is it?'

'Five o'clock.'

'Yes. I have, er, I've been sick. I think I have some kind of tummy bug.'

Philip looked helplessly round the kitchen. 'Can't we get Mrs M. to come over?' he asked. 'This is really getting a bit out of control.'

Isobel looked at him blankly. She thought that she should tell him that the washing up hardly mattered, since the house would be repossessed.

'You phone her,' she said flatly. 'She won't come for me.'

He paused at that. 'Why won't she . . . ?' Then he saw her

face. 'I'll phone her,' he said. 'All right, Izzy. I'll phone her, we'll get this sorted. You go to bed. Shall I bring you up a cup of tea?'

Isobel shook her head. 'I don't want anything,' she said. 'I just want to sleep and . . .'

She did not finish the sentence. She wanted to sleep and never wake up. She went slowly, wearily, up the stairs and got back into bed still wearing last night's pyjamas. She had a brief, poignant moment when she thought of Zelda's lounging pyjamas and her silk negligees, and the nights when she and Troy had slept together naked. She heard herself give a soft moan of pain and then she lay back on the pillows and stared at the ceiling. When she closed her eyes she could see Zelda's perfect profile against a Mediterranean evening sky. When she opened them she could see the cobwebs on the ceiling. She opened and closed her eyes while the ceiling grew dark and then the room grew dark and it was night at last.

Philip got up in the morning and went for his usual swim. Murray did not join him. Mrs M. let herself in with her key at nine o'clock. Isobel, wakeful but unmoving, heard Philip laugh at Mrs M. bringing her swimming costume and promising himself the pleasure of seeing her in her bikini. He warned her that Isobel was ill and that she should be offered some breakfast. Isobel heard him lower his voice so that he could whisper something about women's troubles, and then he shouted up the stairs:

'I'm off now, see you tonight!'

The front door slammed, he was gone.

Mrs M. came up the stairs and tapped on the bedroom door. She pushed it open and stood on the threshold, looking around the untidy room with ill-concealed satisfaction. 'Is there anything I can get you, Mrs Latimer?' she asked. 'Philip said you were ill. A funny turn, is it? Hot flush? Start of the change?'

'Nothing,' Isobel said. She knew that the dizzy feeling in her head was partly from hunger but she did not want any food. She wanted nothing but to rid herself of the picture of a beautiful face and an exquisitely cut suit and the knowledge that she was completely and utterly ruined.

She lay in her room and heard Mrs M. moving around downstairs and then the familiar crash and thump as she got the hoover out and started vacuuming. Isobel started to drift off to sleep and then she heard the crunch of car tyres on gravel. She lay still, indifferent. Then she heard the front door open and Philip's tread as he came up the stairs. Even in her haze of misery she heard something was different. He was walking as if he was ill again: the slow, dragging pace and the heaviness of step. Isobel struggled up in the bed and was sitting when he opened the bedroom door and came in.

His face was sallow, all colour drained from it, his shoulders bowed, his body exhausted.

'What is it?' Isobel asked, half-knowing already.

'Murray's gone,' he said, his voice thin, like a disappointed child who cannot believe that everything has gone wrong. 'He's done a flit. He's skipped.'

Isobel gathered the duvet up to her chin as if it would shield her from her husband's defeated face. 'Gone?'

'Last night. His house is like a tip. He stripped it of everything worth having. He's taken the money, all the money that was in the bank.'

'Our money?'

'Yes.'

There was a long silence. Philip sat heavily in the little bedroom chair. It creaked under his weight. 'Don't lean on the arms like that,' Isobel said irritably.

They were both silent.

'Why did he go? Was it those men?'

'Those men were just the tip of the iceberg,' Philip said. 'It was VAT. He's never paid any VAT, he's been filling in false returns. He owes hundreds of thousands of pounds. Once they saw what he was doing they came round to arrest him. It was criminal fraud. It isn't just owing a bit of back tax, he was doing this in a big way.'

'He can't have thought he'd get away with it?'

'I think he was putting a nest egg together to run away with,' Philip said. 'He may have planned this from the beginning. We were just the cherry on the top.'

Isobel heard her snort of laughter. Then she dropped the duvet and flung herself back on the pillows, laughing hysterically, laughing unstoppably. Philip's grave face was turned to her, waiting for her to stop the wild noise, but she could not stop until her laughter suddenly turned to choking big sobs at the thought that Troy had been right, that Troy had tried to warn her, but she had not listened. She had thought Troy did not understand about business. Now she found that Murray had taken their money and Troy had taken her life.

'What can we do?' she asked soberly at last.

Philip shook his head. 'Nothing,' he said. 'We won't see the money again unless they arrest him before he's spent it all. We might get some back if they get Interpol on to him, but nobody knows where he is or where he might have gone. Spain's my guess. But nobody knows for sure. They're starting to do searches of the airports but if he's gone by boat or by the train it'll take ages to trace him.' He shook his head. 'It was a good business,' he said stubbornly. 'That's the stupid thing. We've got a full order book. I might plug away at it. No reason that I shouldn't make a go of it in a small way.'

'You know nothing about swimming pools,' Isobel said cruelly, feeling her face grow cold and tight from the tears drying on her cheeks. 'It was his business. You never knew anything about it. You were just fronting it.'

'I've learned a bit,' he said defensively. 'We could run it from here. We could run it together.'

Isobel was about to protest when she realised that protest was meaningless. There was no danger of Philip making her run a little swimming-pool company from her home; there would not be a home.

'Not from here,' she said sadly. 'We won't be able to keep the house. I had to mortgage it to raise the money for the pool business.'

'But what about my shares?' he demanded. 'And my pension?'

She looked at him as if he were an overgrown child that she was tired of shielding from the adult world. 'They went long ago,' she said. 'I've been struggling to make ends meet for years. My book advances didn't ever come to much and then they were less every time I did a new book. I never told you because I didn't want to worry you. When you wanted the money for the pool business and said you were prepared to mortgage the house and you were so sure . . .' She broke off. 'I mortgaged the house for two-thirds of the value,' she said simply. 'If we can't keep up the repayments, we'll lose it.'

Philip did not even recoil. 'We'll buy Murray's house,' he said, thinking rapidly. 'We'll own half of it outright anyway as our half of the company. We can go and live there.'

She thought of the little housing estate, of the cold living room furnished like a showroom, of the office where it would be her responsibility to do the paperwork for the pool business and answer the telephone to inquiries, send out brochures. She thought of the neighbours they would have, of walking to the shops, of gardening in the little patchwork of back garden, and Philip coming home in the evening to talk about a swimming pool he might be able to build if he was lucky enough to get the contract.

'I don't feel very well,' she said. 'I want to rest now.'

At once he was all concern. Isobel saw that if she could not bear to face her life in the future then she still had another option. She could be ill, just as Philip had once been ill. She could have some mysterious illness which was undiagnosable but which was disabling enough to prevent her from doing anything she did not want to do. She might become allergic to dishwashing detergent, or to fabric conditioner, and then Philip would have to wash the dishes and do the laundry. She might become allergic to carpet mites and Philip would have to do the vacuuming. She might simply have a terrible time with the menopause which he had so suddenly invented and

she could spend the next ten years going to hormone specialists and gynaecologists and trying all the different versions
of HRT. She leaned back against the pillows and felt sick to
her innermost core at the thought of her future. There would
be nothing for her but a choice between despair and invalidism.

'Can I get you anything?' he asked.

'I'd like a cup of tea and a boiled egg with some toast,' she
said. 'I haven't eaten since yesterday. I feel so ill, Philip. Three
minutes boiled.'

Isobel remained in bed for a week, nursed with a sadistic joy
by Mrs M. who brought her cold tea and soft toast in the
morning and said, every day: 'Seems like everything always
goes wrong at once, doesn't it?' and sometimes: 'It never rains
but it pours.' And once, most revealingly: 'I used to envy you,
you know. It seems funny, looking at you now.'

Isobel was not stung by the gradual revelation of spite, she
almost welcomed it. She felt that her whole life had been
maintained by her ability to fictionalise it. She had pretended
that she was a woman so good, so noble, that she could love
and support her husband even while he was lazy and ill and
bad-tempered. She had pretended that she could hold and
entrance a much younger lover, and that when he wanted
more, she could be the one to forbid him to go further. And
finally, she had pretended that she was a woman who could
give up her sexuality, give up her power, and give up her life.
For the week while she lay in bed Isobel thought that this
might be the ultimate role that she played in the fiction which
was of her own creating. She might be a woman, in the end,
who was capable of giving up everything, even her health,
rather than take her energy and her power and challenge the
world.

She thought about Murray more than she thought about
Troy. She thought that Murray was a man who would never
take to his bed as she was doing, never hide in illness as
Philip had done, never mutilate himself to become something
different, as Troy had done. Murray would sicken, confuse or

417

cut up the rest of the world before he would let it destroy him. Isobel felt a languid sense of admiration for the man who had wrecked the pretence that had been her life. At least Murray's role in it all had been very clear to him. Sometimes she thought that he had deliberately, oddly, tried to make it clear to her too. She wondered what would have happened if she had ever risen to the challenges he laid down for her. What would have happened if, instead of being frosty and reserved, she had met his bright inquiring gaze and told him about Zelda, about Troy, about her secrets. Would he then have told her about his own?

Philip uncovered the extent of Murray's debts during the week that Isobel lay in her bed, and argued passionately and often successfully that profits from the swimming-pool company of which he was part owner could not be claimed by debtors from Murray's past failed companies. Philip and Isobel would indeed lose their beautiful home and she would never wake again to the view from the window that she knew so well under so many different skies. But they would be able to buy into Murray's house. Philip rose to the challenge as if it were a thing of joy. He labelled all the furniture of their old home that they could fit into Murray's little house, he planned how they should manage. He commissioned estate agents, and a sale board went up in the lane outside their gate.

Isobel dragged herself from bed to bathroom and was given an appointment to see a specialist who worked on total allergy syndrome. She never called Troy's office, she never called him on the telephone. She never e-mailed him. She knew that part of her life was over as surely as if she had drowned herself in the swimming pool that day. Most days she wished that she had drowned herself in the pool and the greatest grudge she bore Murray was that he had come barging in with his bright command, 'Don't do it!', and stopped her.

But, most of the time she walked and talked as if she were indeed drowned. She felt as if she was seeing Philip through six feet of chlorinated water, as if his words were coming to her strangely muffled as she drifted in the middle of the pool.

Philip had no time to drive her to see the specialist. He was meeting with advisors on liquidating the business. Mr M. drove her to the discreet large Victorian house in Tunbridge Wells, and waited outside while Isobel walked wearily up the steps.

The waiting room had the hushed, respectful silence of a top-class beauty salon. There were glossy magazines and a large aquarium with tropical fish. Isobel looked at the sheen of the light on the water and thought of Murray selling them downlighters and uplighters and a new false ceiling to catch the benefit of the light on the water.

The receptionist whispered her name and Isobel went slowly, dragging her heavy feet, down the hall to the large bow-windowed front room where Mr Proctor waited for her at the door and solicitously guided her into a chair. He took her medical history in a low, soft voice, Isobel whispered her replies as if she were too exhausted to speak. Yes, indeed she had enjoyed almost perfect health for all her life. She had never been allergic to anything. She had never suffered a major accident or a major illness. She was clearly a healthy woman.

Mr Proctor gestured to the nurse who helped her to a bed behind the screens. They wrapped her in a soft cashmere blanket, as light as swan's-down and as soft. They put head-phones on her head and played her classical music. Mr Proctor came in and palpated her belly, touched her feet, gazed into the iris of her eyes. He had a set of tiny test-tubes which tinkled in their velvet case. He put one, and then another, in her hand and gently took her other hand and pressed against it, seeking an allergic reaction. Isobel let him handle her as if she were a corpse.

When he had completed all the little tubes in the box, he drew up a chair and told her to close her eyes. Isobel, lulled by the music and comforted by the warmth and the gentle touching, felt herself drifting off to sleep while he placed one printed card, and then another, gently on the blanket covering her heart.

'I think you are suffering a sense of deep sadness,' he whispered to her.

Isobel felt, warm fat tears swelling up under her eyelids. 'Yes,' she said simply, thinking of Troy, of the money, and of a life which now felt so completely wasted.

'I have a sense that you have been bereaved,' he suggested.

'Yes.'

'This could be a new loss or an old one,' he hinted.

Isobel shook her head and felt the warm tears spill out and roll down her cheeks. 'A new one,' she said.

He nodded. 'A love affair?' he asked. 'This is all confidential, Mrs Latimer. Was it a love affair?'

Isobel felt her face convulse and the tears start to fall. 'No,' she said desolately. 'Not really. I lost it before it even started.'

Mr Proctor charged her £134 for the consultation and another £100 for an elixir which she had to take four times a day in water. Isobel learned at last the pleasure which Philip had known of spending large sums of money on hope.

'Will I feel better soon?' she asked him.

He nodded. There was no doubt at all. 'You'll have a little allergic reaction,' he warned her. 'Stay in bed, rest, and call me if you are at all worried, call me if you are concerned about anything. And come back next week at the same time.'

Isobel liked the sense of being able to call him, of having a safe point in the week, of knowing that she would come back and be wrapped in the blanket once more, and allowed to weep for her deep, dreadful loss.

She walked slowly to the car and sat back in the seat with a sigh.

'Better?' Mr M. asked.

Isobel shook her head. 'I think it's going to take a long time,' she said. 'I think we'll have to make up our minds to the fact that it's going to take a long time. I may never fully recover.'

*   *   *

Philip wanted to box up her books and sell them. There would be no room for all of them in the new house but Isobel could choose a hundred of her favourites and they could be shelved in the room that used to be Murray's office.

'I'm really not well enough to do it,' Isobel said. 'Mr Proctor says I have to rest.'

'Could Mrs M. do it for you?' Philip asked.

'How could she?' Isobel asked. 'I doubt she reads more than a magazine.'

'Shall we just keep the classics then?' Philip asked. 'What? The Dickens and the Austens. But what history books d'you want to keep?'

'Oh, I'll do it,' Isobel said irritably. She got up from her bed and put her feet in her slippers. Already Philip was gone, she heard him run down the stairs and his brisk steps in the hall. The front door slammed, the car engine roared. Isobel wrapped her dressing gown around her and drifted slowly down the stairs to sit in her familiar chair and turn round to gaze idly at the full shelves. She sighed, the task of sorting the books into those she could not bear to lose and those that could be sold was much too much for her. The book Murray had borrowed, *English Social History*, was still on the desk where he had left it. Idly, she picked it up. His bookmark, the leaflet announcing the closing-down sale for the pool company in Los Angeles, fluttered out from between the pages and fell on the floor. 'The chance of a lifetime,' it said boldly.

Isobel bent and picked it up, she held the brightly coloured leaflet between her fingers and she gazed out of the window where Murray had once leaned and waited for her to speak, to the pool house where he had once held her hand as she stepped into her shoes when he asked her where she got her money from.

Thirty-Seven

Isobel, her hair cropped short into a boyish bob, wearing tight blue jeans and white sweater, shoved her own small suitcase on the luggage belt and asked the check-in girl for a window seat.

'And shall I check you in for your return journey, madam?'

'I'm not coming back,' Isobel said tightly.

Murray, in the brilliant sun of California, eating peaches by the pool in his back garden, looking at the proofs of his mail shot for his new pool business, heard the street door slam and heard a floorboard creak as someone entered his new house. He thought for a moment that it was careless of him not to lock the door properly. He must remember that he was not in England now, that he would never be in England again. He rose from his chair without fear, to deal with whatever might have walked in from the bright streets outside his home and was only half-surprised to see Isobel standing there in the shade of the back doorway, looking out at him. She was holding a suitcase in her hand. He noted with one glance that she now had bobbed hair, light clothes; and that she was both furious, and sexy.

With a charge of incomprehensible desire which hit him delightfully in the belly, he saw that she was barefoot.

'I've come for my shoes,' she said.

Murray nodded. 'At last.'

The Little House

Philippa Gregory

'This is Gregory at her most chillingly convincing. Sunday lunch with the in-laws will never be the same'

Cosmopolitan

It was easy for Elizabeth. She married the man she loved, bore him two children and made a home for him which was the envy of all their friends.

It was harder for Ruth. She married Elizabeth's son and then found out that, somehow, she could never quite measure up.

Isolation, deceit and betrayal fill the gaps between the two individual women and between their two worlds. In this complex psychological thriller, the disturbing depths of what women want and what women fear become all too apparent as Ruth confronts the shifting borders of her own sanity. Laying bare the truth behind the comfortable conventions of rural England, this spine-tingling novel pulses with suspense until the whiplash of the denouement.

'Insidiously gripping'   *Independent*

ISBN 0 00 649643 1

A Respectable Trade

Philippa Gregory

'The great roar and sweep of history is successfully braided into the intimate daily detail of this compelling and intelligent book' PENNY PERRICK, *The Times*

Bristol in 1787 is booming, a city where power beckons those who dare to take risks. Josiah Cole, a small dockside trader, is prepared to gamble everything to join the big players of the city. But he needs capital and a well-connected wife.

Marriage to Frances Scott is a mutually convenient solution. Trading her social contacts for Josiah's protection, Frances finds her life and fortune dependent upon the respectable trade of sugar, rum and slaves.

Into her new world comes Mehuru, once a priest in the ancient African kingdom of Yoruba. From opposite ends of the earth, despite the enmity of slavery, Mehuru and Frances confront each other and their need for love and liberty.

'Filled with authenticity.' *Today*

ISBN 0 00 647337 7

fireandwater

The book lover's website

www.fireandwater.com

The latest news from the book world

Interviews with leading authors

Win great prizes every week

Join in lively discussions

Read exclusive sample chapters

Catalogue & ordering service

www.fireandwater.com
Brought to you by HarperCollins*Publishers*